His Kind of Woman

Suzy and Jill have worked hard for their independence and they're not about to give it up now. If that means being on their own—then so be it.

Except sexy Gil and handsome Colin have other plans for them and are very hard to resist...

Dear Reader,

Welcome to Desire.

We have some really exciting, intense stories this month. None more so than our **Up Close and Passionate** volume, which includes Maureen Child's BACHELOR BATTALION book, *Last Virgin in California*, and Alexandra Sellers's latest THE SULTANS novel, *Undercover Sultan*. Look out for the last instalment of THE SULTANS next month in **Seduced by the Sheikh**.

Fayrene Preston's THE BARONS OF TEXAS trilogy continues with the love-life of the next sister in line for her inheritance, Jill. This wonderful book has been paired with Peggy Moreland's winner, *The Texan's Tiny Secret* in **His Kind of Woman**.

And Baby Makes Three rounds off the month and includes *Having His Child* by Amy J Fetzer and *Mixing Business…with Baby* by Diana Whitney. These two heroes have to decide whether they want bachelorhood or fatherhood…

Enjoy!

The Editors

His Kind of Woman

**PEGGY MORELAND
FAYRENE PRESTON**

™SILHOUETTE®
DESIRE™

DID YOU PURCHASE THIS BOOK WITHOUT A COVER?
If you did, you should be aware it is **stolen property** as it was reported *unsold and destroyed* by a retailer. Neither the author nor the publisher has received any payment for this book.

All the characters in this book have no existence outside the imagination of the author, and have no relation whatsoever to anyone bearing the same name or names. They are not even distantly inspired by any individual known or unknown to the author, and all the incidents are pure invention.

All Rights Reserved including the right of reproduction in whole or in part in any form. This edition is published by arrangement with Harlequin Enterprises II B.V. The text of this publication or any part thereof may not be reproduced or transmitted in any form or by any means, electronic or mechanical, including photocopying, recording, storage in an information retrieval system, or otherwise, without the written permission of the publisher.

This book is sold subject to the condition that it shall not, by way of trade or otherwise, be lent, resold, hired out or otherwise circulated without the prior consent of the publisher in any form of binding or cover other than that in which it is published and without a similar condition including this condition being imposed on the subsequent purchaser.

Silhouette, Silhouette Desire and Colophon are registered trademarks of Harlequin Books S.A., used under licence.

*First published in Great Britain 2002
Silhouette Books, Eton House, 18-24 Paradise Road,
Richmond, Surrey TW9 1SR*

HIS KIND OF WOMAN © Harlequin Books S.A. 2002

The publisher acknowledges the copyright holders of the individual works as follows:

The Texan's Tiny Secret © Peggy Bozeman Morse 2001
The Barons of Texas: Jill © Fayrene Preston 2000

ISBN 0 373 04754 1

51-0702

*Printed and bound in Spain
by Litografia Rosés S.A., Barcelona*

THE TEXAN'S TINY SECRET

**by
Peggy Moreland**

PEGGY MORELAND

published her first romance with Silhouette in 1989 and continues to delight readers with stories set in her home state of Texas. Winner of the National Readers' Choice Award, a nominee for *Romantic Times* Reviewer's Choice Award and a finalist for the prestigious RITA Award, Peggy has appeared on the *USA Today* and Waldenbooks bestseller lists. When not writing, she enjoys spending time at the farm riding her quarter horse, Lo-Jump. She, her husband and three children make their home in Round Rock, Texas. You may write to Peggy at PO Box 2453, Round Rock, TX 78680-2453, USA, or e-mail her care of eHarlequin.com.

For Helen Heilmann, Janelle Shields and
Vickie Monroe, Kentuckians who took this
displaced Texan under their wings, offering
friendship and moral support.
Thanks, ladies!

One

Gil Riley considered himself a simple man with simple tastes. He liked his jeans worn, his beer cold and his horses—as well as his women—gentle, but with enough spirit in 'em to make the ride exciting. Though his age placed him in a generation that shunned family values, considered work a four-letter word and embraced the theory "if it feels good, do it," Gil didn't quite fit the mold. He honored family second only to God, considered his mother an angel straight from heaven and his father one of the wisest men he'd ever known. He believed a hard day's work strengthened a man's character, treated women with the respect he was taught they were due, and never did anything without first weighing the consequences upside down, sideways and backward.

All of which made him wonder how in the hell he'd ended up in an airless room filled with blowhards, suck-ups and women whose mothers had obviously never taught them that a man's privates were just that. Private.

Duty, he reminded himself as he clasped a hand thrust his way and responded with a "good to see you, too."

Though the handshake he offered was firm and the sentiment sincere, Gil delivered both without slowing down. He feared if he did, and he was waylaid by one more person wanting a favor or had to dodge another female's straying hands, he would...

Well, he wasn't sure what he would do, but, whatever it was, he was sure it would be shocking enough to make the headlines in the morning paper.

With his smile feeling as if it were set in concrete and his tie like a noose around his neck, he set his sights on a possible escape route in the distance. He hadn't taken more than two steps in that direction when a beefy hand closed around his arm from behind and dragged him to a stop. Struggling to keep his frustration from showing, he turned to find a balding man, shaped like a whisky barrel and about as tall, beaming up at him, a horse-faced young woman hugged up against his side.

"Have you met my niece, Melanie, Governor? My brother Earl's oldest girl. Visiting here from California."

Yet another first-lady-of-Texas hopeful, Gil thought wearily. It was all he could do not to cry.

Thanks to his bachelor status and his exalted position as governor of the state of Texas, he'd received more propositions in the past year than a prostitute would in a lifetime on the streets.

Though he was tempted to tell Melanie that the rumors flying that he was gay were true, thus stanching any hopes she might have of becoming his first lady, manners and protocol—along with an ingrained sense of honesty—demanded that he extend a hand in greeting instead. "Pleased to meet you, Miss Melanie."

"Graduated magna cum laude from Stanton last spring," her uncle added proudly. "Brains and beauty in the same package. A rare find in a woman these days." The man gave his chin a jerk, setting the loose skin beneath it to flapping and Gil to wondering if he ought to duck. "Yessiree, a rare find."

Gil eased his hand from the I'm-not-letting-go-until-the-ring's-on-the-finger grip Melanie had on him. "Yes, it is, isn't it?" he replied vaguely.

Someone shouted his name from across the room, and Gil pushed his smile a notch higher and lifted a hand in greeting. "If you'll excuse me," he said, softening his smile to one of apology for Melanie. "I hope your stay in Texas is a pleasant one." With a nod to the woman's uncle, he turned and began to weave his way through the crowd again.

He reached the swinging door he'd spotted earlier and glanced quickly around to make sure no one was looking. Seeing his bodyguard approaching, he slashed a finger across his neck—his signal that he was taking a breather—and pushed his way through the door. Once on the other side he stopped, heaving a sigh of relief, and the door swung back and smacked him on the backside, knocking him a step further into the room. But Gil didn't mind the whack on his rear, considering it small payment to escape the pressing crowd.

From somewhere he heard a woman's voice. "The caviar's on the tray. Get it out there quick. And add more champagne to the fountain. These pigs are swilling it down faster than a drunk would a bottle of rotgut after a week on the wagon."

Frowning, Gil leaned to peer through a gap between the pots hanging above the long kitchen island. The woman stood before a commercial range on the opposite side, stirring a large pot, her back to him. Balanced on three-inch platform sneakers dyed an iridescent pink and with her white-blond hair anchored on top of her head by a rhinestone clip shaped like a star, she looked to Gil more like a refugee from a punk rock festival than a member of any catering staff.

Before he could make his identity known, she dragged her forearm wearily across her forehead and added, "Better check the supply of champagne glasses while you're at it. It wouldn't occur to these morons to simply ask for a refill. Oh-h-h, no-o-o," she said, sounding more than a little resentful. "They've got to grab a fresh glass every time a waiter passes by."

Finding the woman's sour disposition a refreshing

change from all the saccharine smiles and bogus compliments he'd suffered in the other room, Gil rounded the island. "You could've just tapped a keg, set out some plastic cups and saved yourself the hassle."

She whipped her head around, her gaze slamming into his. He saw the recognition flash in her eyes and prepared himself to graciously accept the apology he was sure she'd offer for mistaking him for one of the caterer's crew.

To his surprise, instead she turned her back to him and resumed her stirring. "If you're lost, the party's on the other side of the door."

"I'm not lost. I'm hiding."

She whacked the spoon against the side of the pot, set it aside, then crossed to the refrigerator, wiping her hands on a bib-style apron two sizes too big for her petite frame. "Well, hide someplace else. This kitchen's small enough without you in here cluttering things up."

Though her tone was anything but friendly, Gil decided he preferred her porcupine-disposition to the phony graciousness he'd experienced from the political elite gathered in the other room. Crossing to the range, he watched as she opened the refrigerator and stretched to retrieve something from its depths. As she moved, the back of her apron parted, exposing a cute little tush and well-shaped legs covered in leopard-print spandex capris. At the sight, he puckered his lips in a silent, admiring whistle.

When she turned from the refrigerator, he quickly dipped his head over the pot she'd been stirring, pretending interest. His mouth watered at the decadent scent of melted chocolate that rose to tease his taste buds. "Need some help?"

"Yeah, right," she said dryly, and shouldered him out of her way to add milk to the mixture. "Like the governor of Texas would actually stoop to scullery work."

Clucking his tongue, Gil shrugged out of his suit jacket and tossed it over a stool. "Just proves you can't judge a book by its cover...*or* its title," he added pointedly, as he loosened his tie. He tucked a dish towel into the waist of his slacks, then plucked the spoon from her hand and tipped his head toward the island. "Why don't you take that tray of caviar out to the guests before they come in here looking for it and discover my hiding place?"

She snatched the spoon right back. "My staff takes care of the serving," she informed him coldly, "and *I* do the cooking."

Gil lifted his hands and stepped aside, hiding a smile. "Just trying to be helpful."

"If you want to be helpful, you can get out of my—"

The swinging door banged open behind them and a young woman staggered into the kitchen, weighted down by a large tray of dirty dishes. She angled the tray onto the stainless steel island and blew a weary breath up at her bangs. Bracing a hand against the counter, she lifted a foot to slip her shoe off her heel.

"I swear, Suzy," she complained, "if you hadn't promised that I'd get to see the governor up close and personal, I never would've agreed to work this gig.'' The shoe hit the floor and she moaned pitifully, squeezing her fingers around her aching toes. ''No man's worth this much pain. Not even the governor.''

Another insult hurled his way. Gil couldn't remember the last time he'd had this much fun. ''Are you sure about that?''

The young woman snapped to attention, her gaze meeting his, then quickly ducked behind the island, but not before he saw her cheeks flame. Gil heard her muttered curses and fumbling as she struggled to squeeze her swollen foot back into her shoe. Seconds later she popped back into view.

''S-sorry, Governor,'' she stammered, as she smoothed her skirt back over her hips. ''I didn't know you were in here.''

Smiling, he pressed a finger to his lips. ''Shh. Don't tell anyone. I'm hiding.''

''Hiding?'' Peering at him curiously, she rounded the island. ''From who?''

Gil nodded toward the door. ''Them.''

She squinched her nose. ''I don't blame you,'' she whispered. ''Nothing but a bunch of browners out there.'' She wiped her hand on her skirt, then offered it to him along with a wide grin. ''Hi. I'm Renee.''

Taking her hand, Gil bowed slightly over it. ''Gil Riley, Renee. It's a pleasure to meet you, ma'am.''

''Oh, for pity's sake,'' Suzy muttered, and pushed her way through their joined hands, breaking the contact. She crossed to the island, grabbed the tray of caviar-topped crackers and shoved it at her assistant.

"If you're done with the formal introductions, you can serve these to the *browners*."

Renee turned for the door with a long-suffering sigh.

"Remember," Gil called after her. "Mum's the word."

Bracing a hip against the door, Renee tossed him a smile and a wink over her shoulder. "Don't worry, Governor. Your secret's safe with me."

Chuckling, Gil picked up the spoon Suzy had abandoned and began to stir as the door swung shut behind Renee. "Cute girl."

"Hands off. She's jail bait."

Gil shrugged as a timer sounded, and Suzy headed for the oven. "Cute jail bait."

She shoved a tray of miniature pastry shells onto the countertop next to the range, then snatched the spoon from his hand. "Men," she grumbled.

Fascinated by this woman, but unsure why, Gil propped a hip against the counter and folded his arms across his chest. "You have something against men?"

"Nothing a mass castration wouldn't solve."

He flinched. "Ouch."

She tipped her head toward a plastic tub filled with utensils. "If you're staying, make yourself useful and hand me that ladle."

He retrieved the requested item and passed it to her. "Anything else, boss?"

"Yeah," she snapped. "Don't call me boss."

"What should I call you?"

"Suzy."

"Suzy...?" he prodded helpfully, hoping she would reveal her last name.

She slanted him a quelling look. "Just Suzy."

"Okay, Just Suzy. I'm Gil."

She rolled her eyes as she ladled thick chocolate into the shells. "Like I don't know who you are."

"Which obviously doesn't impress you overly much."

"Why should it?"

He could've hugged her for that response alone. "Why, indeed," he replied, smiling.

The timer sounded again, and before Suzy could stop him, Gil removed another tray of pastry shells from the oven, placed it on a rack to cool, then resumed his position at the counter, watching as she continued to fill the shells.

He had always thought a person's work habits revealed a lot about their personality and mood, and saw that this little lady was no exception to the rule. She tackled her duties with a confidence and an economy of motion that indicated she was no stranger to a kitchen. Yet he noticed a jerkiness in her movements and a tenseness around her mouth that told him his presence annoyed the hell out of her. She was also independent, he noted, zeroing in on the determined set of her jaw, the stubborn thrust of her chin, which told him that she was a woman who wouldn't need or want anyone's assistance...especially, it seemed, his.

But, dang, if she wasn't a pretty little thing, he

thought—if a person took the time to look past the garish makeup and the wild hairdo. Intrigued, he watched her hunch a shoulder to her heat-flushed cheek to brush away a wayward strand of hair and was tempted to help her out by tucking the lock behind her ear. But he refrained from doing so, mindful of her comment about castration and the number of knives within easy reach.

Wondering what had given her such a low opinion of men, he let his gaze drift to her mouth, pursed at the moment in an irresistible blend of annoyance and concentration...and found his thoughts shifting to wonder what she would taste like, what kind of response he could arouse from her if he were to give in to the sudden impulse to kiss her. If all her passions ran as deep and volatile as her temper, he suspected he'd be in for one hell of a ride.

"Do you work for the catering company?" he asked, hoping to discover her identity.

"I *am* the catering company."

"Should I be impressed?"

She glanced his way. "Most men are," she replied, then arched a brow and added, "though it's seldom my cooking that impresses them."

"Must be that winning personality of yours."

"That, too."

He tossed back his head and laughed, enjoying the verbal sparring. "So what do you do when you're not catering, Just Suzy?"

"Governor?"

Gil turned to find his bodyguard standing in the doorway. "Yes, Dave?"

"People are starting to notice you're missing."

Gil dragged the dish towel from around his waist with a weary sigh, feeling the full weight of his responsibilities settling back on his shoulders. "I'll be right there."

Dave touched a finger to his temple, then slipped back through the door as quietly as he'd appeared.

Gil picked up his jacket and shrugged it on. "It was nice meeting you, Just Suzy."

"Yeah, yeah," she muttered, busily plunking fresh raspberries on top of each filled tart.

Unable to resist teasing her a little more, he stepped up behind her and leaned to press his lips close to her ear. "If there's ever anything I can do for you…"

She jerked away, narrowing her eyes at him. "Like what? Washing my dirty dishes? Or did you have something a little more intimate in mind?"

Chuckling, he snugged the knot of his tie between the points of his collar. "Whatever your needs are," he informed her as he headed for the door, "just give me a shout, and I'm all yours."

With only a security light to illuminate the dark alleyway where the catering van was parked, Renee hovered at Suzy's elbow, worrying her thumbnail. "You don't think the rumors that he's gay are really true, do you?"

Remembering the governor's suggestive parting

comment, Suzy scowled as she shoved the last crate of glasses into the rear of the van. "Probably."

Renee's frown deepened, then she huffed a breath. "Well, I don't think he is. He just doesn't look gay, you know?" She sighed dreamily. "Oh, man, did you see his eyes? Paul Newman blue. And that drawl of his. I bet he could turn sex into a three-syllable word."

Suzy caught the door and stepped back, forcing Renee back, as well. "I thought your relationship with Rusty was exclusive?"

Renee gave her chin a defensive lift. "It is, but there's no harm in looking."

Suzy slammed the rear doors with a little more force than necessary. "Yeah, I've heard that line before," she muttered. "But usually delivered by a male caught with lipstick on his collar." Seeing Renee's wounded look, she immediately regretted the sharp words and slung an arm around her young employee. "Don't mind me. I'm just tired."

Renee's shoulders drooped wearily beneath Suzy's arm. "Me, too. Need me to follow you home and help you unload?"

"Nope. I'm leaving everything in the van until morning."

"You sure?"

Suzy hugged Renee to her side before giving her a push toward the parking lot. "Yeah, I'm sure. Now scoot. And give Rusty a kiss for me," she called after her.

Renee lifted a hand in farewell. "I will. Good night, Suzy."

"'Night."

Suzy watched until Renee was safely inside her car and pulling out onto the street, then headed for the driver's side of the van, anxious to get to her own home and bed. Catering an event of this size and importance was a physical and mental drain that took her days to recover from. Unfortunately, she didn't have days. She had a luncheon for the local garden club scheduled for noon the next day. Or rather today, she thought, stifling a groan as she stuck her key into the door lock.

Gravel crunched on the drive behind her, and she froze as a shadow fell over her, blocking the glow from the security light behind her. Silently cursing herself for not asking one of the security guards hired for the party to escort her to her van, she shifted her keys between her fingers and whirled, thrusting out her hand as if she held a weapon

The dark figure—a man she realized, gulping back the scream that rose—skidded to a stop with the blunt end of the key just inches from his chest and shot up his hands.

"Is that thing loaded?"

Though the man's face remained in shadows, Suzy recognized the voice. The governor. Furious with him for slipping up on her and frightening her, she dropped her arm. "Are you crazy?" she snapped, fisting the keys within her palm. "You could get yourself killed, sneaking up on a person like that."

He lowered his hands and teased her with a smile. "Would you miss me?"

Scowling, she wrenched open the door. "Get real."

He caught her elbow, stopping her before she could climb inside. "I'd miss you."

His voice was low, husky and sounded sincere enough to have her pausing...but only for the length of time it took for her to draw in an angry breath. Jerking free of his grasp, she spun to face him. "You don't even know me."

He hooked a hand over the top of the door and smiled down at her, his casual stance irritating her even more. "No, but I'd like to. How about dinner?"

"I've already eaten."

"A drink then."

"I'm not thirsty."

He shifted in front of her and pushed his palm against the side of the van, neatly pinning her between himself and the vehicle. He leaned closer and she drew back, wary of the seductive gleam in his eyes.

"Then we'll skip the preliminaries," he said in a voice that would melt the lock off a chastity belt, "and go straight to bed. Your place or mine?"

Suzy planted a hand against his chest, stopping his forward movement. "Neither." She gave him an angry shove. "Now beat it, Romeo, before I start screaming and have every cop in Austin swarming all over the place."

To her surprise, instead of becoming indignant, as she might have suspected, or using his greater strength to overpower her, he dropped his head back and laughed. Then, before she could duck, he surprised her again by dropping a kiss on her cheek. "I like you, Suzy."

Grimacing, she dragged the back of her hand across her face. "Yeah. Most men do."

He took a step back and slipped his hands into his pockets. "I'd like to see you again."

With room to move now, she climbed into the van and slammed the door. "Not if I see you first," she muttered as she rammed the key into the ignition. She gunned the engine, ripped the gearshift into drive and sped off, setting the glasses in the rear of the van rattling.

She rolled down her window as she turned onto the street...and would have sworn later that was the governor's laughter she heard chasing her down the street.

Gil stood before the windows in his office in the Governor's Mansion, his arms folded across his chest, staring out at the grounds below. Though late-afternoon sunshine spotlighted a neatly tended rose garden, he saw nothing but the scowling face of a flashily dressed, sharp-tongued blonde.

Thoughts and images of the caterer he'd met at the party the weekend before had filled his head all week, making it difficult for him to complete the simplest task and impeding his ability to concentrate on a particular topic for any length of time. Both of which were an oddity for Gil, as he couldn't remember a single woman in his past who had dominated his thoughts so completely.

Not that he hadn't had his fair share of female relationships, he reminded himself. He just hadn't met one like Suzy before.

Just Suzy.

A smile tugged at his lips as he envisioned her again, standing at the side of her van, dressed in those ridiculous-looking pink platform sneakers and leopardprint pants, brandishing her keys at him as if they were a weapon. She probably would have used them, too, if he hadn't spoken, thus revealing his identity. A hellcat, he thought, silently admiring her spunk.

"Gil? Are you listening to me?"

Startled, he glanced over at his secretary, then offered her a rueful smile. "Sorry, Mary. I guess my mind wandered."

She closed her day planner with a snap and rose, her lips pursed in disapproval. "And no wonder. You've been burning the candle at both ends since the day you took office. You need a vacation. Why don't you go to the ranch for a couple of days and relax?"

Though a trip to his ranch was appealing, he shook his head. "No rest for the weary. Not right now, at any rate."

"Well, there's nothing here that won't keep until tomorrow." She headed for the door. "At least go upstairs and put your feet up before you have to go to that meeting tonight."

"Mary?"

Her hand on the knob, she paused, a brow arched in question. "Yes?"

"Do you know who catered that party last weekend?"

She frowned slightly. "No. Why?"

He lifted a shoulder. "No particular reason." He dropped a hand to his desktop and shuffled a few papers. "Do you think you could find out for me?"

"Well, yes," she replied hesitantly, clearly puzzled by the request. "I'm sure I could."

He lifted his head and gave her a grateful smile. "Do that for me, would you? And give me a call if you're successful."

Suzy hadn't read a newspaper in years, avoided television newscasts like the plague and turned the dial if a news bulletin happened to interrupt the music playing on her favorite radio station. She despised the news, no matter what the format, and considered those who reported it lower than scum.

But her aversion to news and the news media hadn't prevented her from recognizing the governor of Texas when he'd slipped into the kitchen at the party she'd catered over the weekend. From the moment Gil Riley had tossed his cowboy hat into the ring and announced his intent to run for governor, he had become the most-talked-about man in the state of Texas. Within days of his announcement, his name and picture had appeared on billboards scattered along Texas roadways and on the rear bumpers of every make and model of vehicle, from the beat-up farm truck to the luxury sports car.

A nonpolitician—and a rancher, at that—running for governor was enough of an oddity to grab the attention of the entire populace. He quickly won the hearts of his fellow Texans by promising to represent the common man, especially those in rural areas, and put an end to big business and government taking over the Lone Star State and forcing families from their homes and off the land their ancestors had fought for and labored on for years.

But his platform wasn't all that caught the voters' attention. His youth, his Marlboro Man rugged looks and his bachelor status appealed to the masses as much as did his stand on the issues.

Especially to the women.

Throughout the months preceding the election, he was gossiped about and fantasized about in beauty salons, during coffee breaks and at the checkout lines in grocery stores. By the time November rolled around and his landslide victory announced, there wasn't a single woman in Texas who hadn't woven a secret dream or two of becoming his first lady.

Even Suzy.

And why not? Suzy asked herself with a defensive sniff. With his slow Texas drawl, his hard, lean body and that you-can-trust-me killer smile of his, the man was a natural woman-magnet. And if the stories told about him were true—which she seriously doubted, since he was, after all, a politician—he had more going for him than just a handsome face and a to-die-for body. He was intelligent and possessed an almost uncanny business sense, with a degree from Texas A&M and a successful cattle operation to substantiate both. And he was a philanthropist, to boot, she remembered hearing somewhere, donating both his time and his money to causes that focused on abused children and troubled teens.

Handsome and with a tender and generous heart. What more could a woman ask for in a man? she asked herself.

Scowling, she rammed her wide-brimmed hat farther down on her head. "One who doesn't live in a fishbowl," she reminded herself.

With her knees buried in rich brown dirt, she kept her head down and her gaze focused on the weeds sprouting in her garden, telling herself that she wouldn't think about Gil Riley anymore. He was a walking, talking nightmare she didn't need in her life or her head right now or at any time in the future, no matter how attractive she found him.

But in spite of her determination to do otherwise, thoughts and images of the governor continued to drift through her mind as she worked in her garden, just as they had from the moment he'd waltzed into the kitchen at the party she'd catered, catching her unawares with his suggestion that she should've tapped a keg, instead of serving flutes of champagne.

Tapped a keg.

A smile twitched at her lips at the memory. But the smile slowly melted when a pair of cowboy boots moved into her line of vision only inches from her hand.

It can't be, she told herself, staring in horror at the tips of the custom-made boots.

"You're hard as hell to track down, you know it?"

It not only *could* be, she realized, recognizing the governor's distinctive drawl, it *was*. She forced a swallow, then was careful to fix a frown on her face before looking up. "What are you doing here? Hiding out again?"

"No. I came to see you."

His smile was as warm and guileless as the sunshine that beamed down on her face. But it was wasted on Suzy. She'd learned long ago not to trust a man's smile or be fooled by one's charm. She sank back on her heels and narrowed her eyes at him. "Why?"

He lifted a shoulder. "No reason. Was just in the neighborhood and thought I'd drop by and say hello."

She rocked forward, planted a gloved hand against the ground and started pulling weeds again. "Okay. You've said it. Now beat it, before I call the cops and have you arrested for trespassing."

Instead of leaving, as she'd hoped, he hunkered down opposite her, braced an arm on his thigh and dipped his head down to look at her. "Have I done something to offend you?"

She crawled to the next plant, refusing to look at him. "You're still breathing, aren't you?"

"Yeah, and obviously that doesn't please you." He

duck-walked to keep pace with her. "But what I want to know is why?"

With a frustrated huff, she fell back on her heels. "Is there a law that says every woman in the state has to drop at your feet and pant when you say heel?"

A slow grin spread across his face. "No. But if that's what it takes to get you to agree to go out with me, I'll see what I can do to push a bill through Congress to that effect."

She rolled her eyes and leaned to snatch at a weed. "Don't waste your time." He closed a hand over hers, stilling her movements, and she jerked up her head to glare at him.

"Look," he said patiently. "All I'm asking for is a little of your time. A chance to get to know you, and for you to get to know me. Now, that's not too much to ask, is it?"

"Suzy? Is that you, dear?"

She groaned at the sound of her neighbor's warbling voice coming from the other side of the privacy fence. "Yes, it's me, Mrs. Woodley!"

"Are you all right, dear? I thought I heard a man's voice."

She snatched her hand from beneath Gil's. "Nosy busybody," she muttered, then raised her voice, "Yes, I'm fine, Mrs. Woodley. Just visiting with a—" she glanced at Gil and curled her lip in a snarl "—*friend.*"

"Who, dear?"

Hissing a breath through her teeth, she scrambled to her feet and grabbed Gil's hand, tugging him to his feet, as well. "No one you know, Mrs. Woodley!" Dragging Gil behind her, she ran for the house. "I'm going inside now, Mrs. Woodley," she yelled. "Talk to you later."

Before the woman could respond, Suzy yanked Gil inside the house and slammed and locked the door behind them. Ripping off her hat and gloves, she tossed them onto the table as she raced to the window that faced her neighbor's house.

Gil chuckled as he watched her jerk down the shade. "I take it Mrs. Woodley is a bit like Gladys Kravitz."

She snorted as she darted past him to pull down the shade over the window above the kitchen sink. "Worse. And if she finds out the governor's at my house, she'll be on the phone telling all her friends. Wouldn't surprise me if she herded them all over to ask for your autograph."

He lifted a shoulder. "I'd be happy to give all your neighbors my autograph."

She sent him a withering look as she headed down a hall.

Shaking his head, Gil followed. "Are you going to pull every shade in the house?"

"You're darn right I am." In the living room she dropped a knee onto the sofa and stretched to grab the shade that partially covered the window behind it. She froze, then leaned over the back of the sofa to peer outside. "Oh, no," she moaned.

Gil crossed to stand behind her, stooping to see what had disturbed her. "What is it?"

She grabbed the string and jerked down the shade. "Not *what*. Who!"

Not having seen anything out of the ordinary, he straightened. "Who, then?"

She pushed from the sofa and stood, wringing her hands as she stared at the front door, as if she expected it to burst open at any moment. "Reporters."

"Reporters?" Gil moved to the end of the sofa and lifted the shade a fraction to peer outside. He glanced over his shoulder. "You mean those guys in that black sedan across the street?"

She gulped, then nodded.

He laughed and dropped the shade. "They aren't reporters. They're my bodyguards. Although Dave acts like an overprotective father at times."

"Are you sure?"

"Sure I'm sure." He opened the door and shouted. "Hey, Dave! Show this lady your ID."

The man behind the wheel lifted a hip, pulled out his wallet and flipped it open. Sunshine glinted off a silver badge he held out the open window. Gil glanced over at Suzy who had joined him at the door. "Satisfied?"

"They go everywhere you go?"

"Yeah," he said as he closed the door. "Well, not *everywhere*," he amended. "I *am* allowed to go to the rest room alone."

Suzy glanced up in surprise, then sputtered a laugh when she saw the teasing in his eyes. "Well, it's good to know that at least some things in life are still sacred."

"Do that again."

Her laughter dried up in her throat as she watched the amusement in his eyes soften to wonder. She took a nervous step back. "Do what?"

"Laugh." He caught her arm and turned her around to face him, holding her in place by her elbows. "I like the sound of it."

Heat from his hands radiated up her arms, setting off warning bells in her head. Though she knew she should send him packing, she found she couldn't move. But it wasn't his strength that held her in place, though she could feel the power in the hands that gripped her. It was something in his eyes. A warmth. A gentleness. And something in his voice. Warmth again. And a huskiness that made her toes curl inside her tennis shoes.

He touched a finger to the corner of her eye, and a slight smile curved his mouth. "And I like what it does to your face. It softens your features. Makes you seem friendlier, more approachable."

He drew the tips of his fingers along her cheek, and a shiver chased down her spine. "What...are you doing?"

"Touching you. Is that okay?"

Before she could reply, he placed a thumb against her lips and smoothed it along the crease. Another shiver chased down her spine as he slipped his hand around to cup the back of her neck. Her eyes riveted on his, her pulse thrumming, she watched the blue in his eyes darken, turn molten.

"I'm going to kiss you, Suzy," he said quietly.

Even as he offered the warning, he was lowering his face to hers.

And Suzy, God help her, was pushing to her toes to meet him halfway.

Two

Suzy knew one thing for sure.

Gil Riley sure as heck wasn't gay.

No man could kiss a woman like *this* and be anything but totally heterosexual. She couldn't think. Couldn't breathe. Couldn't move.

Well, maybe she could move, she decided belatedly and lifted her arms to loop them around his neck. The change in position brought him a step closer, his chest chafing against her breasts, his arms winding around her waist. With a skill that sent her blood racing, he teased her lips apart with gentle flicks of his tongue.

And forced her to add a new item to the governor's already lengthy résumé: master seducer.

He's good, she thought, giving herself up to the sensual rock of his mouth over hers, the erotic play of his tongue. Maybe too good, she thought with a shiver. Mesmerized by the pillowed softness of his lips, the commanding pressure of his mouth, she was only distantly aware of him sliding his hands from her waist to splay them across her buttocks. But when he tugged her up against him, she forgot about his mouth and the seductive lure of his lips, her attention snagged by the hard column of the erection nudging her abdomen. Alarm bells clanged in her head.

What are you doing! What is he doing! You don't need this kind of trouble. Get rid of him. Tell him to get lost. Toss him out the door on his ear!

She intended to heed the warnings. She really did! And would have, if he hadn't, at that moment, dug his fingers into her buttocks and lifted her, dragging her body up the length of his, until their groins were flush, their mouths perfectly aligned. With her held tightly against him, he deepened the kiss, softened it, then deepened it again, sending her pulse tripping, her mind reeling…and her good intentions skipping straight down the proverbial road to hell.

As he spun the kiss out, his tongue tangling with hers in an erotic dance for dominance, she lost all sense of time, all sense of place, all sense of self. She felt as if she were caught in the eye of one of Texas's famous twisters, her body battered by a constant barrage of sensations and emotions, her mind stripped bare of all thought and reason.

She wanted this man, she realized with a suddenness that made her heart stumble a beat. More than she'd ever wanted any man before, she wanted Gil

Riley. But even as her mind registered this need, he tightened his arms around her, all but squeezing what was left of the breath from her lungs. A groan rose from deep in his throat, and she sensed the regret in the sound, felt it as he eased his hold on her and let her slide back down his body, tasted it as he slowly dragged his mouth from hers.

Weakened, she braced her hands against his chest and drew in a shaky breath, telling herself that it was her imagination, that his kiss hadn't held the power, the perfection that her mind insisted on attributing to it. But when she opened her eyes and met his gaze, saw the heat there, the same surprise and passion that clouded her own, she knew she was in trouble.

He touched a finger to the moisture he'd left on her lips, and a smile curved one side of his mouth. "You're one hell of a kisser, Just Suzy."

And so was he, she thought, gulping. Before she gave in to the temptation to throw herself back into his arms for a second go at him, she inhaled deeply, drawing in the oxygen she needed to clear her head, steady her pulse and ease from his embrace. "You're not too shabby a kisser, yourself, guv."

He laughed and the masculine sound filled the room and vibrated through her, filling her with an unexpected sense of longing and regret she couldn't even begin to explain.

"I like you, Suzy."

Because she was afraid that she was beginning to like him, too, she turned away. "So you've said."

"My life isn't my own right now, but I'd like to spend what free time I can manage with you."

She closed her eyes, digging deep for the strength, the flippancy she needed to send him on his way. Plucking a pillow from the sofa, she slapped a hand against it, fluffing it. "Sorry, guv, but my dance card is pretty full."

"There's a private reception Friday night to dedicate a new children's wing at one of the local hospitals. Will you go with me?"

She dropped the pillow back to the sofa and turned, a brow arched in question. "This Friday?" At his nod, she lifted her hands. "Sorry. I've already got plans."

He stared at her a moment, as if weighing the truth in her refusal, then slipped his fingers into his shirt pocket and pulled out a small envelope. "If your plans should change, this will get you in the door." He dropped the invitation onto the coffee table, then touched a finger to his temple, his smile returning. "See you around, Suzy."

"What's this?"

Suzy glanced over her shoulder and swallowed a groan when she saw the card Renee was holding. Wishing she'd tossed the invitation into the garbage, as she'd intended, she turned back to the sink and continued to wash strawberries. "Some stupid reception for a new wing at a hospital."

"Are you going?"

"No."

"Why not? Everybody who is anybody is going. I read about it in Paul Skinner's gossip column. Even the governor will be there."

"So?"

"So go! Rub elbows with the rich and famous. Play Cinderella for a night."

Suzy snorted a laugh. "Yeah, right. Like I have any aspirations of being Cinderella."

Renee picked up the colander filled with freshly washed strawberries. "Oh, come on, Suz. Every girl dreams of being Cinderella at least once in her life."

Suzy followed Renee to the island, drying her hands on her apron's skirt. She picked up a knife and selected a strawberry from the colander as she settled onto a stool beside her assistant. "Not me. I quit believing in fairy tales a long time ago."

"Bull hockey."

Lifting a brow, Suzy turned to level a look on Renee. "I beg your pardon?"

Renee ignored her and continued to slice strawberries. "*Every* girl dreams of being Cinderella and meeting her own Prince Charming. Even *you*," she said, and stubbornly met Suzy's gaze.

Huffing a breath, Suzy resumed her coring. "Even if what you said were true, and it's not," she added, slanting Renee a warning look, "I certainly wouldn't find my Prince Charming at a hospital wing dedication." She sputtered a laugh. "Imagine *me* attending a reception with a bunch of snooty old do-gooders."

"Everyone there isn't going to be old and snooty. Remember? The governor's going and he's definitely not old. And he's not snooty, either. In fact, I think he's about as down-to-earth and friendly as any person could possibly be. And if there *is* such a man as Prince Charming,'' she added, ''Gil Riley certainly fits the bill.''

Before Suzy could argue the point, the doorbell sounded and the telephone rang at the same time. Renee laid down her knife and rose. ''I'll get the door.''

Hoping that by the time her assistant returned to the kitchen, she would have forgotten all about the stupid invitation, Suzy picked up the phone. ''Suzy's Succulent Sensations,'' she said into the receiver.

''Suzy?''

She squeezed her eyes shut at the quaver she heard in the familiar voice, recognizing it as a sign her mother was having a bad day. Determined to be cheerful, she tucked the phone between shoulder and ear, reached for the knife again and began to core strawberries. ''Hello, Mother. How're you doing today?''

''Okay...I guess.''

Suzy heard the self-pity in the response, but refused to fall prey to it. ''That's good. Are you planning to work in your garden today?''

''No,'' her mother replied in a lifeless voice that threatened to suck Suzy down into an equally despairing mood. ''I just don't have the heart for it today.''

''But it's a such a beautiful day,'' Suzy insisted, knowing from experience that staying inside with the curtains drawn would only darken her mother's depression more.

"Is it?" her mother replied vaguely. "I hadn't noticed. Suzy?"

Suzy heard the tears building and tensed. "What is it, Mother? Has something happened?"

"No. No." She sniffed noisily. "It's just that last night I dreamed your father—"

Suzy stiffened, curling her fingers around the knife's handle. "Don't call him that."

"I'm sorry, dear. The reverend, then. I dreamed the reverend called and wanted to see us. It seemed so real," her mother continued, her voice quavering with a mixture of fear and hope.

"You know what the doctor said," Suzy reminded her sternly. "You're not to focus on your dreams or to even think about them. You're supposed to occupy your mind on something else. Do you have any new books to read?"

"No." Her mother sniffed delicately. "I haven't felt much like getting out and going to the library."

"How about a jigsaw puzzle? I'll bet the new ones I brought you are still in the top of the hall closet."

There was a slight pause, and Suzy could almost see her mother turning to gaze vacantly at the closet door.

"You brought me puzzles?" Suzy heard her mother ask, as if she'd totally forgotten about Suzy's visit and her placing the boxes there.

"Would you like for me to come and visit you?" Suzy asked, her concern growing. "I have desserts to make for a party tonight, but I could come later this afternoon, after I've delivered them."

"No, dear. I'll be all right. I'll just take down one of the puzzles you brought and work on it today."

"Good idea, Mother. And go outside for a while," Suzy begged. "Being out in the sun and fresh air will do you a world of good."

"Oh, my gosh! Look, Suzy! Roses! Dozens of them!"

Suzy glanced up, her eyes rounding as Renee returned to the kitchen, carrying a huge vase of yellow roses. Dumbfounded, she angled the receiver back in front of her mouth. "Mother, I need to go. I'll call later this afternoon and check on you, all right?"

"Yes, dear. That would be nice."

At the click, indicating her mother had hung up, Suzy returned the phone to its base, staring as Renee set the vase of roses opposite her on the island.

"Aren't they gorgeous?" Renee cried, laughing gaily. "And look! There's one sunflower tucked right in the middle." She quickly unpinned the small envelope from the ribbon wrapped around the sunflower's stem and thrust it at Suzy. "Open it and see who they're from."

Fearing she already knew who had sent the roses, Suzy plucked a strawberry from the colander, pretending disinterest. "Probably some grateful hostess we catered a party for."

"Then you won't mind if I look." Without waiting for permission, Renee ripped open the envelope and pulled out the card. She gasped, slapping a hand over her heart. "Oh, my God, Suzy! They're from the governor!" She lifted her head, her eyes wide, then dropped her gaze to the card again, and read, "'The roses are standard trying-to-impress-a-woman fare, but the sunflower is simply because it reminded me of your sunny smile. Hope to see you tonight.'"

Her cheeks burning, Suzy snatched the card from Renee's hand and stuffed it into her apron pocket.

Renee rounded the island, her mouth sagged open. "The governor sent you the invitation to the dedication?"

Suzy lifted a shoulder. "So what if he did? I'm not going."

"But you have to go!" Renee slid onto a stool, her knees bumping Suzy's as she spun to face her. "This is the opportunity of a lifetime! A date with the governor, for cripe's sake! The hunkiest and most lusted-after bachelor in the entire state. You'd be a fool not to go."

Suzy slipped off her stool, gathering the pile of cut stems into her hands. "Then I'm a fool." She crossed to the sink and poked the cuttings down the disposal. "Because I'm sure as heck not going *anywhere* as the governor's date."

And she *wasn't* going to the dedication as the governor's date, Suzy assured herself as she stopped inside the hospital's lobby to tug the strap of a high-heeled sling back over her heel. She was going to the dedication to prove a point...both to herself and Gil Riley.

They were totally unsuitable for each other.

She had known he wasn't the man for her from the moment she'd seen his picture on a billboard and felt the first flutter of attraction. That realization was confirmed the evening he'd slipped into the kitchen at the party she'd catered and she'd experienced firsthand his particular brand of heart-fluttering charm. And she'd had her nose all but rubbed in their unsuitability when he'd stood in her living room and kissed her senseless.

Yet, in spite of the obviousness of their unsuitability, Gil remained clueless...and persistent. But Suzy was willing to take whatever steps necessary to prove to him what she'd already ascertained, even if it meant possibly exposing herself to the public eye. Prior to going to the dedication, she'd carefully weighed all the dangers and convinced herself that she could conceal her identity from the unsuspecting guests. It was a private party, after all, thus the press wouldn't be present. Besides, she had chosen a disguise so outlandish, her own mother would have trouble recognizing her!

Straightening, she wiggled her hips to ease the body-hugging spandex fabric of her black micro-mini skirt back into place. She spotted the entrance to the new wing just ahead of her, and a smug smile curved her lips as strains of Mozart's ''Moonlight Sonata'' played by a violinist drifted out to her. She could just see the expressions on the faces of the stodgy, stiff-necked guests when she made her entrance. *She* knew she and Gil Riley were unsuitable...and, before the night was over, so would he.

Tossing over her shoulder the long tresses of the red wig she'd chosen to wear for the evening, she headed for the entrance.

"Excuse me, miss."

Suzy stopped and glanced to her right. A prune-faced woman stood at the entry, dressed in a pink slap-me-if-it-isn't-a-grandmother-of-the-bride silk shantung suit. Suzy arched a brow—the one she'd adhered a rhinestone to its end. "Yes?"

The woman lifted her chin, looking down her nose at Suzy in disapproval. "This is a private party, by invitation only."

"Yeah, I know." Hiding a smile, Suzy glanced over the roomful of guests. "I'm supposed to meet my date here." She caught a glimpse of Gil standing with a group of distinguished-looking men and looking positively mouth watering himself in a black tux and silk crewneck, off-white sweater. "There he is now." She lifted a hand. "Hey, Governor!" she shouted, waving her hand over her head. "Over here! I forgot my invitation, and this chick won't let me in."

Gil glanced her way—as did nearly everyone else in the room. Seeing this as the perfect opportunity to prove her point, Suzy gave the deep vee of her sequined halter top a tug closer to her naval—silently thanked God for double-sided tape—then cocked a hip and crooked her finger.

A hush fell over the room. Even the violinist

stopped playing. Though embarrassment burned through her as the crowd openly stared, Suzy kept her expression sulky and her posture slutty, holding her breath while she waited for Gil to turn his back on her, refusing to acknowledge her as an acquaintance, much less as his date. Once he did, she promised herself, she was out of there, point proven.

She watched him murmur something to the men he was standing with, then, to her amazement, he headed her way. Was that a smile twitching at his lips? she thought in dismay. By the time he reached her, he was laughing fully.

The prune-faced woman hovered nearby, wringing her hands. "I'm so sorry, Governor. I tried to tell her the party was by invitation only."

Gil looked down at Suzy, his eyes filled with amusement. "It's all right," he said, and offered her his arm. "She's my date."

Suzy slipped her arm through his and, unable to resist, tossed the wide-eyed woman an I-told-you-so smirk as Gil escorted her into the room and toward the buffet table.

"You really know how to make an entrance."

She looked up at him, all innocence. "An entrance? Me?"

He seared her with a look from the top of her trailer-trash hairdo to the tips of her scarlet-woman painted toenails. His lips quirked in a smile as he returned his gaze to hers. "Yeah, you." He unwound his arm from hers, picked up a plate from the buffet table and handed it to her, then selected one for himself. "But what I'm wondering is," he said, as he levered thin slices of smoked salmon onto first her plate, then his, "who you're trying to fool with that getup." He glanced her way and arched a brow. "Want to tell me about it?"

This wasn't going at all as she'd planned, Suzy reflected miserably as she fixed a smile on her face and shook the hand of yet another guest Gil introduced her to. Although she had succeeded in shocking nearly every person at the dedication with her trailer-trash hairdo and slutty outfit, her appearance hadn't seemed to faze or embarrass Gil at all. In fact, he'd treated her as if she were visiting royalty, insisting upon escorting her around the room and introducing her to what seemed an endless stream of people.

And if she'd had any clue she was going to have to march a country mile at the stupid dedication, she sure as heck wouldn't have worn these four-inch spiked heels!

Wincing, she braced a hand against his arm and lifted a foot to readjust the high-heeled sandal's strap, in hopes of easing the ache in her arch.

"Shoes hurting your feet?"

She glanced up, saw the amusement in his eyes and quickly dropped her hand from his arm and her foot to the floor. "No."

He bit back a smile. "Liar." He caught her elbow and guided her toward the entrance. "Let's get out of here."

"Suzy?"

At the sound of her name, Suzy stopped and turned, dragging Gil to a stop, as well. Her eyes widened when she saw her friend, Penny Thompson, hurrying toward her. "Penny!" she cried in surprise. "What are you doing here?"

Laughing, Penny grabbed her hands. "Me? What are *you* doing here?"

"I asked first." Suzy shifted her gaze higher, as a tall, handsome man stepped up beside her friend. "Don't tell me," she said dryly. "Let me guess. The Cyber Cowboy is a major contributor."

Grinning, Erik Thompson, Penny's new husband and the owner of Cyber Cowboy International, looped an around his wife's waist. "Okay, I won't tell you." He bent to drop a kiss on Suzy's cheek, then straightened, choking on a laugh as he got a good look at her attire. "I thought girls like you hung out on street corners."

Batting her eyelashes, Suzy sidled up to him and dragged a finger down the front of his tuxedo shirt. "Why, when all the johns with money are right in here?"

Penny slapped her hand away. "Watch it, sister. He's taken."

Laughing, Suzy fluffed her hair. "That's the kind of man I like best."

"I'll have to remember that."

Having forgotten all about Gil, Suzy shot him a frown as he joined them. "Trust me. It wouldn't help your case any."

Chuckling, Erik stuck out a hand. "Hello, Governor. It's a pleasure to see you again."

"Good to see you, too," Gil returned, then smiled at Penny as he caught her hand between his. "And you must be the woman who knocked Erik off the Most Eligible Bachelor List." He winked at Erik in approval. "An easy fall to take, when a man has a woman as pretty as this one to come home to."

Rolling her eyes, Suzy grabbed Gil by the sleeve. "Come on, Governor Smooth, before I'm forced to put on boots to wade through all this BS. Call me, Penny!" she tossed over her shoulder as she dragged Gil away.

When they reached the entrance, a man stepped forward, obviously one of the hosts for the evening.

"You're not leaving so soon, are you, Governor?"

"Not just yet. I thought I'd show my friend here some of the rooms in the new wing."

The man spread an arm in welcome. "Please, be our guests."

With a nod of thanks, Gil led Suzy to a bank of elevators. Once inside and the doors had closed, he dropped to a knee, and reached for her foot.

Startled, she tried to pull away. "What are you doing!"

He managed to slip off the left shoe, then glanced up at her. "Taking off your shoes."

He shifted to reach for the other, and she shoved at his head, tottering as she tried in vain to angle her foot out of his reach. "If I wanted my shoes off, I'd have taken them off myself."

He stood, dangling both shoes by their heel straps in front of her face. "No you wouldn't. You'd rather suffer the pain than take them off and destroy the image you're trying to project."

Pursing her lips, she snatched her shoes from his hand. "I'm not trying to project any kind of image."

"Yeah, you are." He pushed a finger against the crease between her brows. "Every time you take a step, you wince, a dead giveaway that you aren't accustomed to prancing around in four-inch spiked heels."

Though it was all she could do to keep from weeping with joy at the relief her arches were currently experiencing, Suzy refused to admit he was right. She folded her arms across her chest and stubbornly turned her gaze to the indicator marking their ascent. "It just so happens I *like* wearing high heels."

He moved to stand beside her, mimicking her posture. "Mmm-hmm."

She shot him a frown as the doors slid open. "I do. And as far as the personal tour goes, you can forget it. I'm going home."

She reached to punch the button for the first floor, but Gil caught her hand before she could press it.

"Later," he said, and gave her hand a tug. "There's someone I want you to meet first."

Suzy grabbed the edge of the door and held on. "I don't want to meet anyone else," she wailed miserably. "I've met enough old geezers tonight to last me a lifetime."

"This person isn't old." One by one he plucked

her fingers from around the door. "In fact, she's younger than you. And nicer, too," he added, as he dragged her down the hallway behind him.

Suzy's brows shot up at the slight. "I'm nice!"

"Mmm-hmm."

"I *am* nice."

He stopped before a door. "Did I say you weren't?"

"No. But you made that sound as if you didn't believe me."

He braced a hand against the door and pushed it open. "Mmm-hmm is a sound of acknowledgment."

Jerking up her chin, she pushed past him. "*Not* when you say it—" She skidded to a stop, her heart lurching when she saw a young girl perched up in the hospital bed. "Sarcastically," she finished weakly, unable to tear her gaze from the girl's shaved head.

Gil strode past her. "Hi, Celia." He sat down on the side of the bed. "How are you feeling today?"

The smile the girl offered him was weak, but filled with obvious affection. "Okay. What are you doing here so late?"

He took her hand and clasped it between his own. "I was at the dedication downstairs and decided to sneak out and visit my favorite girl."

She ducked her head, blushing. "I'm not your favorite girl."

"Yes, you are." He leaned close to whisper in her ear. "But don't tell Suzy. She thinks I'm crazy about her."

The girl glanced Suzy's way and smiled shyly. "Hi. I'm Celia."

It took Suzy a moment to find her voice. "Hey, Celia. I'm Suzy."

"Cool hair. Is it a wig?"

Hearing the wistfulness in the girl's voice, Suzy ran a self-conscious hand over her wild mane of hair. "Yeah." She took a step closer to the bed and wrinkled her nose. "Blew the minds of a few of those blue-haired old ladies downstairs."

Celia laughed softly. "I'll bet you did."

Suzy felt Gil's hand close around hers and glanced at him. He winked and tugged her to his side, sliding his arm around her waist as he turned his attention to Celia again.

"Have your parents been by today?"

The girl's smile faded and her eyes filled with tears. "No. But I didn't really expect them," she added quickly. "They both work, you know. Besides, they've got my brother and sister to take care of."

Gil squeezed her hand. "They'd come if they could."

"I know. Oh," she said, her face brightening. "I forgot to tell you thanks for the present."

She pulled her hand from his and twisted around to retrieve something from beneath her pillow. Turning back, she held a portable CD player out for him to see. "It's really cool. Thanks."

Chuckling, Gil drew his arm from around Suzy and picked up the headphones. He placed them over his ears and punched the play button. Wincing, he ripped them right back off. "What the heck kind of music is that?" he cried.

Laughing, Celia placed the headphones over her own ears. "Alanis Morissette's new CD. Cool, huh?"

Gil stuck a finger in his ear and wiggled it around, as if trying to restore his hearing. "It's obvious you have no taste in music. Next time I come for a visit, I'm bringing you one of my Dixie Chicks CDs. Now *that* is music."

"Excuse me, but visiting hours are over."

All three turned to find a nurse standing in the doorway.

Reluctantly Gil stood, then bent to place a kiss on Celia's cheek. "Hang in there, champ," he murmured. He gave her hand an encouraging squeeze as he straightened.

Gulping back the sudden flood of emotion that crowded her throat, Suzy backed toward the door. She forced her lips into a smile and waggled three fingers. "Nice to meet you, Celia."

Celia dragged off the earphones. "You can come to visit again, if you want."

The hopefulness in the girl's voice tore at Suzy's heart. She swallowed hard and nodded. "Yeah. Sure thing."

"I'll drive you home."

Still reeling from the emotional scene she'd witnessed, Suzy stepped away from the pressure of Gil's hand at the small of her back, anxious to get away from him before the tears that threatened burst out into a torrential flood. "I have my car."

He caught her elbow, stopping her. "Then you can give me a ride."

Over his shoulder she spotted his bodyguard standing at a discreet distance. "Dave can take you." She started to turn away, but he tightened his grip on her elbow, restraining her.

"Dave has other plans. Don't you, Dave?" he said, raising his voice loud enough for his bodyguard to hear him.

"Yessir, I do."

Gil shrugged. "See? What'd I tell you?"

Rolling her eyes, Suzy jerked free of his grasp and headed for the parking lot. "Is lying for his boss part of Dave's job description?"

Gil matched his stride to hers. "That wasn't a lie."

She kept walking. "Uh-huh."

"It's true," he insisted. When they reached her car, he took the keys from her hand, unlocked the door, then handed them back to her and grinned. "But he would've lied, if I'd asked him to. He's that loyal."

Rolling her eyes again, Suzy slipped behind the wheel and started the engine. "Men," she muttered under her breath.

Chuckling, Gil climbed in on the opposite side and closed the door. "Need directions to my place?"

She jerked down the gearshift. "Unless they've moved the governor's mansion in the last couple of days, I think I can find my way."

She made the drive across town to the mansion in

tight-lipped silence, while Gil kept up a steady monologue at her side. If asked later, she couldn't have repeated a word he said. All she could think about was seeing him holding the hand of that poor young girl with all her hair shaved off.

She started to make the turn onto the street in front of the mansion, but Gil placed a hand on the wheel, preventing her from doing so. He gestured to the rear of the property and a private entrance. "We'll use the back way."

She drew in a shuddery breath, silently praying she could continue to hold the tears at bay. "Okay."

She turned onto the drive, pulled beneath the portico and stopped. Forcing a smile, she turned to him. "Home sweet home. See ya, guv."

"Come in and I'll make us something to drink."

"Sorry. I don't drink and drive."

"Not even coffee?"

"Hate the stuff."

"Come in, anyway."

"It's late."

He leaned over and shut off the engine, palming the keys. "Not that late."

With her mouth hanging open, Suzy watched him round the hood. Wrenching open her door, she leaped from the car. "Give me my keys."

Ignoring her, he strode for the mansion's back door. "If you want 'em, come and get 'em."

Suzy stormed after him. "Give me my keys!"

He stepped inside, leaving the door open behind him. "Like I said, come and get 'em."

Fuming, Suzy balled her hands into fists at her sides, counted slowly to five, then marched inside, slamming the door behind her. She thrust out her hand. "The keys."

Gil merely lifted a brow.

She jabbed a finger against his chest. "The *keys*," she repeated and turned her palm up expectantly.

Frowning, he braced his hands low on his hips. "What is it with you, anyway?"

"I don't like you."

"Oh, really? So I guess you always kiss men you don't like the way you kissed me the other day."

Heat rushed to her face and she quickly turned away before he saw it. "Yeah. I'm sadistic, so shoot me."

"You're not sadistic. You're a softy. And you put on one hell of a tough-girl show to hide it."

Furious that he'd hit so closely to the truth, she whirled. "Dammit! Give me my keys!"

"Nope." He took a step toward her.

Fearing if he touched her, she'd tumble, sobbing, into his arms, she took a step back. "Just give me my damn keys."

"I will...once you explain the tough-girl act."

He took another step, and she took one in reverse. Her back hit the door, and she pushed out a hand, flattening it against his chest. With her gaze on his, the tears that she'd kept banked since leaving the hospital surged to her eyes. "She's dying, isn't she?"

He hesitated a moment before answering. When he

did, his voice was low, heavy with regret. "Yes, she is."

She squeezed her eyes shut. "Oh, God," she moaned.

"Suzy..."

Hearing the empathy in his voice, she stiffened her arm, fending off any attempt he might make to comfort her. She opened her eyes and gulped as she met the sadness and compassion in his gaze. "Who is she? A relative?"

He shook his head. "No. Just a patient I met while visiting at the hospital."

A tear slipped over her lower lash and streaked down her cheek. "You don't even know her, yet you bought her a CD player?"

He lifted a shoulder. "She likes music."

She sniffed and dragged a hand beneath her nose. "She likes music," she repeated, "so you bought her a CD." She choked on a watery laugh, then buried her face in her hands. "Oh, God," she sobbed miserably. "Then it's true."

"What's true?"

When she didn't answer, he caught her hands and forced them from her face. "What's true?" he asked again.

Unable to stop the tears, they streamed unchecked down her face. "You're a nice guy." Her breath hitched, and she slid down the door, sitting down hard on the floor, her hands still gripped in his, her gaze riveted on his face. "You really are a nice guy."

Three

Gil stared down at Suzy, baffled by the tears and how they related to what she'd just said. "Being a nice guy is a bad thing?"

Sniffing, she dragged her hands from his and dropped her chin to her chest. "Yeah. *Real* bad."

"I'm nice, and that's bad." He scratched his head, trying to find the logic in that association. Unable to do so, he dropped down on the floor beside her with a sigh and stretched out his legs. "I'm afraid you're going to have to explain that one."

She sniffed again, swiping a hand beneath her nose. "Good-lookin' and nice, too. Deadly combination."

Chuckling, he shook his head as he pulled a handkerchief from his back pocket. He dipped down to look up at her as he pressed it into her hand. "How 'bout if I start kicking puppies and stealing candy from little kids?''

She blew her nose, a halfhearted smile trembling on her lips. ''You'd still be good-lookin'.''

''I'll get a scar, then. A really ugly one. Would that help?''

She glanced over at his finely honed cheekbones, strong square jaw and blue, blue eyes. Even with a scar, the man would be drop-dead gorgeous. ''Maybe,'' she said cautiously, not wanting him to know how physically appealing she found him. ''Depends on where you put it.''

He tapped a finger against his lower jaw. ''How about here?''

She shook her head, the bump of his elbow against her arm making her even more aware of how close they were sitting. A stretch of the neck and a pucker, and their lips would meet.

''No. Here,'' she said, and reached to touch the high ridge of cheekbone. Unable to resist, she dragged her finger slowly to the corner of his mouth, following its path with her gaze, mesmerized by the warmth and textures she encountered. She bumped her finger over the fullness of his lower lip and she wet her own, remembering the feel of his mouth on hers, the weakness, the need his kiss had left her with.

A shiver took her and she glanced up…and saw that the teasing was gone from his eyes. He caught her finger, and she held her breath as he drew it away from his mouth. Almost wept when he leaned to touch his mouth to hers. Emotions, already exposed, were laid open, leaving her vulnerable, susceptible to his every move. Her chest ached with them, her throat swelled with them, her eyes filled with them. And when he framed her face between his palms...she was hopelessly lost.

She'd never experienced tenderness in a man. Never such deliberate gentleness. She hadn't thought she needed either of those things or even wanted them. But his kiss, his touch, produced a thirst she feared she could never slake, not now that she'd had a taste of it. If he'd asked, at that moment she knew she would have done anything he asked of her, surrendered her very soul to him without a moment's hesitation.

With his hands cupped tenderly around her face, he drew back and slowly pulled his mouth from hers. At the loss, she gulped back the tightness that burned her throat and forced open her eyes to meet his gaze. Heat simmered in the blue depths she stared into. The same heat she felt steeping behind her own eyes. But beneath the heat lay a veil of quiet compassion, promising so many things. Safety. Security. Understanding. Love? Were those the things she needed in her life? Were those the missing elements that kept her from feeling whole? Free? That kept her hobbled to an unsavory past and a family association she'd struggled for years to escape?

Too weak to move, too *moved* to speak, she closed her eyes and dropped her forehead against his. He's wrong for you, she told herself. Perfect, yet wrong. She drew in a shuddering breath, held it a moment, then released it slowly, trying to find her balance, her center, the strength she needed to move away.

But before she could make that move, he slipped a hand beneath her hair and cupped the back of her neck, squeezing as if he understood her confusion, her conflicting emotions, perhaps even shared them. The quiet strength in his hand, the comforting warmth in it, lulled her, and she let her mind drift, allowing herself to imagine her life differently. With a man in it. This man. Sharing moments like this. Laughing with him. Cuddling with him. Letting him love her. Permitting herself the freedom to fall in love with him. Such wistful thoughts, she scolded silently. Yet, sitting with him, his body a wall of strength and comfort against hers, it seemed almost possible.

The gentle squeeze of his fingers on her nape finally drew her back to the present, their place on the floor. Had seconds passed? Hours? She didn't know. Didn't care. She knew only that she wanted to hang on to this moment, remain this way with him forever.

But she couldn't. Not with Gil Riley. Not if she wanted to maintain her privacy, protect her identity. Not if she wanted to keep her past tucked safely away.

Digging deep for the willpower she needed to separate herself from him, she lifted her head.

And he smiled.

He didn't say anything, do anything, demand anything of her. He simply smiled that soft, heart-melting smile of his.

"I like you, Suzy."

Though she tried, she couldn't tear her gaze from his. "So you've said."

He tightened his fingers at her neck and drew her face toward his, the smile tugging the curve of his lips higher. "Have I?"

"Ye-es."

He touched his mouth to hers, and she squeezed her eyes shut against the need that swelled inside her.

He withdrew to nip at her lower lip. "I hate it when I'm redundant."

Though everything within her cried out for her to throw her arms around this man and hold on tight, she pressed a hand firmly against his chest, forcing him back even further. Her mouth went dry at the handsomeness of his features, the heat she found in his eyes. Knowing she had to do something to end this before he managed to seduce her completely, she wet her lips. "M-maybe I'll take that drink, after all."

Thirty minutes later they were sitting on the floor again, this time in the upstairs den of Gil's private quarters. They sat side by side, their shoulders touching, their backs braced against the sofa, both staring at the empty fireplace, lost for the moment in their own private thoughts.

Suzy didn't know what thoughts filled Gil's mind, but hers were focused on him, trying to decide how much of him was hype and how much was real. She knew all too well that an image could be created and projected totally opposite of—or at least masking—a person's true self. Hadn't she created one for herself?

Hadn't she learned the method from the master of mask wearers himself, her own father, who had used his mask to selfishly garner money and power?

Troubled by that thought, the possible similarities in personalities between her father and Gil, she slid a sideways glance at him. "Did you always want to be governor?"

He snorted and shook his head. "Hardly."

"Then why did you run?"

He moved his shoulder against hers in a shrug. "Duty more than anything, I guess."

"Duty?"

He drew up a leg and rested his arm on it, dangling his wineglass over his knee, his gaze still on the empty fireplace. "Someone had to stand up for the common man. Why not me?"

"Do you have higher aspirations?"

He glanced her way. "Like what?"

"Senator. President."

"Hell, no," he said with a shudder.

She continued to study him while sipping her wine, looking for a crack in the mask, any indication that he was lying. When she found none, she shook her head and turned her gaze back to the fireplace. "Weird."

"What's weird?"

"You."

"What makes you say that?"

"You're a politician. All politicians aspire to a greater office, more power."

He pulled his index finger away from his glass and aimed it at her. "I'm *not* a politician."

"Sure you are. You're the governor, aren't you?"

"For the next three years. But then it's over. When my term ends, I'm hightailing it back to my ranch."

Surprised by the fervor of his response, she scooted around to face him. "You sound as if you don't really enjoy being governor."

"I don't."

"Then why did you run?"

"Duty."

"You said that already. Duty to *whom?*"

"The common man. The rancher, the farmer, the small businessman. It was way past time someone stood up for them, pushed for legislation in their favor for a change."

"And you felt it was your responsibility to take that stand for them?"

"Not just for them. For me, too. I'm one of 'em. What affects them, affects me."

She clasped her hands dramatically over her heart. "The white knight, charging in to save the damsel in distress. The town marshal, dedicated to bringing law and order to the Wild West." Chuckling, she shook her head at the grand and selfless images his explanation had drawn. "Surely you must have a few vices?"

Smiling, he rolled to his side and stretched out an arm along the sofa behind her. "One." He nipped at her bare shoulder. "I have a weakness for smart-mouthed blondes with an attitude. Especially ones who wear red wigs."

Laughing, she pushed at his head. "Get outta here."

He drew back, holding up a hand. "Scout's honor. My heart goes pitter-patter every time I think about you."

"Pitter-patter?" she repeated, then laughed again.

He touched a finger to her lips…and her laughter dried up in her throat. He looked so serious, so awed…by her?

"What?" she asked, uncomfortable with the intensity of his gaze.

"Your laugh. I like hearing it." He leaned to brush his lips across hers. "Makes my heart smile."

And he made her heart all but *stop*. With his kisses, with all his sweet-talk. And that scared the holy hell out of her. "Maybe I should take my act on the road."

He withdrew slightly, drawing his brows together. "Why do you do that?"

"Do what?"

"When things begin to get intimate, you always make some sarcastic remark."

"Do I?" She knew damn good and well she did. She'd worked for years perfecting the technique.

"Yeah, you do."

She batted her eyelashes at him. "I guess it's just part of my irresistible charm."

He laughed, then leaned to kiss her. "I don't know why I find you so irresistible, but for some damn reason I do." He opened his mouth more fully over hers and stole her breath. "And you know what else?" he murmured, dragging a hand down her arm.

"What?"

"I want to make love with you."

She placed a restraining a hand on his chest. "Gil—"

Before she could say more, he captured her mouth completely, silencing her. Slowly he drew back to press a finger across the moisture he'd left on her lips. "I've wanted to make love to you since the first night we met." He lifted his gaze to hers, and she found the earnestness of his expression as debilitating and arousing as his lips, his voice. "You're all I think about. All I *want* to think about. And that really chaps me, because no woman has ever had that effect on me before."

"Gil—"

"There's something right about us," he continued, refusing to let her speak. "Something clicks when we're together. When I hold you or kiss you—" Groaning, he caught her hand and dragged it down his chest, pressing it against the column of flesh that tented his slacks, showing her the effect she had on him.

"I want to make love to you, Suzy," he said again, his voice huskier now, more insistent. "I need to know if this is just lust...or something more."

With her hand held against the length and growing hardness of his erection, she could only stare, her body trembling, moved beyond words by his confession, by his obvious arousal, yet at the same time terrified by it all. She wanted to believe that he was lying, that he was simply delivering a polished line he used to lure women into his bed.

But something in his eyes told her that he wasn't lying. There was a sincerity beneath the heat that told her he spoke only the truth. Something, too, that warned her he wasn't the kind of man who considered sex a sport. This wouldn't be a casual falling in and out of bed for Gil Riley. He would give himself totally to an affair, as he did to everything he undertook, and would expect nothing less in return.

And that's what frightened Suzy, twisted her stomach into knots. She'd never given herself totally to anything or anyone before. And most certainly never a man.

She wet her lips and forced a swallow. "And if it's not just lust?"

He drew her hand back to his chest and fisted it against his heart. "What if it is?"

But what if it's not! she cried inwardly. She couldn't allow herself to fall in love with Gil Riley. Any kind of relationship with him would be insane, self-destructive, potentially suicidal. She hated the media, avoided it at all costs, and he lived out his life on the front page every day. He was a cowboy, and she was…well, she was just Suzy, a free spirit, a woman who changed her hair color and style to suit her mood, a woman who chose her wardrobe for its shock value, rather than for its suitability or practicality.

But as she continued to stare into his eyes, her palm recording every thunderous beat of his heart, she could only come up with one reason why she *shouldn't* refuse him.

She wanted to make love with him. And nothing, no matter how great the risk, could stop her from doing so, if only just this one time.

Knowing that, she leaned into him, found his mouth with hers and gave him the answer she didn't have the courage to voice.

At her surrender, he slipped a hand beneath her hips and hauled her across his lap. He quickly took the kiss deeper, the pace faster, the heat higher until she was all but blinded by it. The gentleness and tenderness she'd discovered and appreciated in him earlier was gone, but she decided she preferred the urgency, the desperation she tasted in him now, and matched it with an impatience of her own.

She felt his hands roaming her hips, smoothing down her legs, then back up, pushing her skirt higher on her thighs and her breath from her lungs. She felt him slip a finger beneath the elastic of her panties and gasped as he found her center. She groaned low in her throat, the sound echoing in her mind, as he slid a finger into her honeyed opening. The heat became unbearable, the need to have him inside her an obsession that took control of her mind and hands, her very soul.

Her movements frenetic, she shoved his jacket from his shoulders, then tugged his sweater from his slacks, whimpering her frustration at the awkwardness of their positions until he joined in her struggle to free him of his clothes. With his chest at last bare beneath her hands, she tore her mouth from his and pushed back on his lap. "I want you," she said, gulping for air as she reached for his belt buckle. "Now."

He worked with her to shove his slacks and underwear to his knees. "Do I need protection?"

She ripped off her panties and sent them flying across the room. "No. I'm on the pill." She jacked her skirt to her waist as she shifted to straddle him, then lifted her gaze to his and pressed a finger against his lips. "Lust," she told him, as she lowered herself down. "Lust," she repeated more determinedly, then tensed, gasping, when he lifted his hips to meet her.

With one smooth thrust, he buried himself inside her. She dropped her head back on a sob and dug her nails deeply into his shoulders as her body convulsed violently around him. He pushed deeper and, on a strangled cry, she clamped her thighs at his hips, his name a silent scream through her mind as pleasure ripped through her body like jagged bolts of lightning across a dark, summer sky.

Desperate to share with him the pleasure, she inhaled deeply, then raised her hips, drawing him out, until only the tip of his sex joined them. "Lust," she said again, as she lowered herself and began to ride him. "Lust," she all but sobbed, as he thrust harder and faster, pushing her over the edge again and again, until her climax seemed a continuous spasm of blinding pleasure.

Breathless and trembling, she clung to him, fearing

she would shatter if she lost her grip. And when he reached his own climax, his hands gripped tightly at her hips, holding her against him, his seed filling her, she could only cling more desperately, stunned by the sensations and emotions that rocked her, tears of both joy and regret pushing at her throat and stinging her eyes.

Still numbed by what she'd experienced, Suzy watched Gil reach for his slacks.

"Lust," she said, as if by voicing the word aloud she could convince herself that what they'd just shared was a temporary emotion, one they'd satisfied once and for all with their frenzied, if fantastic, lovemaking.

"I don't know," he replied doubtfully.

Her eyes rounded. "You don't know," she repeated, feeling the panic rising to squeeze at her chest.

"If it were just lust, I don't think I'd already be plotting ways to throw you down on the sofa and make love with you again, do you?"

Suzy glanced at the sofa, gulping as she imagined them there, their bodies tangled and slick with perspiration, their hips melded, their bodies joined intimately. "I don't know. You might."

"Well, since we're both unsure, I think we should give this a little more time before we make a final determination. Let's go to my ranch."

It took a moment for the unexpected invitation to sink in. She snapped her head around to stare at him in surprise. "Go to your ranch?"

Seeming to warm to the idea, he pulled up his zipper. "Yeah. I was planning on asking you to go with me tomorrow, anyway, but if we leave tonight, it'll give us two full days there together."

"I don't know," she replied hesitantly.

Smiling, he slipped his arms around her waist and tugged her hips up against his. "Come on, Suzy," he coaxed as he bent his head to nuzzle her neck. "It'll be fun. A relaxing weekend at the ranch, with nothing to do and no one to bother us." He lifted his head, his expression and his voice both filled with boyish pleading. "Please? It'll give us a chance to work on our lust theory some more."

Two full days alone with Gil Riley with unlimited sex? Still flushed from their last lovemaking session, she wanted to scream *yes* at the top of her lungs, but visions of a wagon train of news media trailing their every step made her continue to hesitate.

"If you're worried about the media knowing we're there," he added, as if reading her mind, "they won't. My ranch is remote, and night offers us the perfect cover to get there undetected."

"How can you be sure?" she asked, feeling herself weakening.

He gave her a confident smile. "Trust me. I just know."

She caught her lower lip between her teeth, knowing she should refuse him, but knowing, too, that she wanted to go. A weekend, she told herself. Really only two days, when she considered that it was presently the middle of the night. "I'll need to go home and pack a bag."

"Why?"

Exasperated, she held out her arms. "I can't very well run around all weekend dressed like *this*."

He rubbed his groin suggestively against her. "To be honest, I was hoping you wouldn't be wearing anything at all."

Heat poured through her bloodstream at his suggestion, at the feel of his arousal rubbing against her groin. "But I'll need my toothbrush," she insisted stubbornly, struggling to remain sensible, rational.

"No, you won't." He dipped his head over hers, his lips curving against hers in a smile. "I keep an extra set of toiletries on hand, in case of emergencies such as this."

It occurred to Suzy to ask if those emergencies were always of a female nature, but then he opened his mouth completely over hers, stealing her breath and emptying her mind, and she couldn't think at all.

He released her with a reluctant groan, then tucked a shoulder into her midsection and lifted her off her feet.

She grabbed for his belt. "Gil!" she squealed. "What are you doing!"

"Carrying you."

"Put me down, you ignoramus, before you drop me!"

He locked an arm over the back of her knees and headed for the door. "Uh-uh-uh," he scolded. "No name calling."

She grabbed for the door frame as he passed through the opening, but her fingers slipped from the jamb.

"Gil!" she screamed, her head bumping wildly against his back as he loped down the stairs. "You're going to crack my skull!"

"Governor?"

Gil skidded to a stop on the landing and looked over the banister to the hallway below. "What is it, Dave?"

Suzy moaned pitifully, just imagining the view of her backside Dave was receiving. "Put me down!" she hissed at Gil.

"Is everything okay up there?" Dave called.

Gil bent over and planted Suzy on her feet. "Everything's fine. We were just horsing around."

Glaring at Gil, Suzy jerked her skirt back over her hips, then turned and forced a pleasant smile to her face. "Hello, Dave."

He grinned up at her. "Hi. Having fun?"

"Oh, tons," she said dryly.

Gil slung an arm around her shoulders and started her down the stairs. "We were just leaving for the ranch."

Dave glanced at Suzy, his surprise obvious, then quickly turned away. "It'll only take me a minute to get my things."

Reaching the doorway to the kitchen, Gil ushered Suzy through it. "Take the weekend off, Dave," he called to his bodyguard, stopping him. Winking, he lifted a hand in a wave. "See you Monday."

* * *

Suzy awakened to darkness and a strange—and empty—bed. Blinking sleepily, she pushed up to her elbows and glanced around, looking for Gil. Across the room the patio door stood ajar. Wondering if he'd gone outside, she scooted off the bed and padded across the room. With her arms hugged across her bare breasts, she paused in the doorway and found him sitting in a willow chair, his back to her, naked as the day he was born.

As if sensing her presence, he held out a hand. "Come watch the sunrise with me. It's a sight to behold from this spot."

Her heart melting at the sweetness of the invitation, the ease he obviously felt with her, she crossed to him and placed her hand in his. He glanced up, smiled, then drew her down across his lap.

Content, she snuggled against his chest and looked around. The stone patio spread fan-like twelve feet or more from the bedroom door. Scattered about the smooth flagstones were clay pots filled with plants unidentifiable in the darkness and a matching willow chair next to the one which they shared. In the distance, oak trees stood like towering sentinels at the perimeter of the yard. Beyond them she could just make out the shape of pipe fencing, and beyond that, a dark sea of grass, the dew on the gently swaying blades gleaming like diamonds in the fading moonlight.

And cloaking it all was a peacefulness, a quiet serenity so pure it brought tears to her eyes.

"It's beautiful out here," she whispered, in deference to the stillness.

He tightened his arms around her and drew her closer to his chest. "Yeah, it is."

"Have you lived here long?"

"All my life."

She glanced up, hearing the pride in the simple answer, the satisfaction, then looked over his shoulder. "But the house looks almost new," she said in confusion.

"I meant on the ranch, not in this particular house."

"Oh."

Chuckling softly, he hugged her to him, and the sound rumbled against her ribs, drawing a smile to her lips and to her heart. She settled back against him.

"But you're right," he said. "The house is fairly new. I had it built about five years ago."

She turned her head to peer over his shoulder again, curious about his home. She hadn't been able to tell much about the house the night before. They'd arrived late and gone straight to his room and to bed...though not necessarily to sleep, she remembered.

Warmed by the memory of their lovemaking, she turned to look at him again and reached to lay a hand against his cheek. A night's growth of beard scraped her palm, the line of jaw she traced her fingers along straight and strong. A man's man, she thought, admiring the strength in his shadowed profile. A man who would never run from danger, one who would fight for justice and fairness for all. One who would find satisfaction in working with the land and who was more than capable of meeting whatever challenges it presented.

Sighing, she let her hand drop to cover his at her waist and tucked her head beneath his chin, her thoughts dreamy as she joined her gaze with his to stare at the gray-pink sky. A tiny sliver of gold appeared at the crest of the farthest hill, heralding the arrival of the morning sun. The sight was glorious, breathtaking in its beauty.

"Do you miss not living here, now that you're governor?" she asked curiously

"Every day."

Hearing the wistfulness in his voice, she hugged his arms to her waist. "Then you should make it a point to come more often," she told him.

He turned his lips against her hair. "Would you come with me?"

She tipped her head back to look up at him and smiled. "Maybe."

Returning her smile, he slid his hands up her middle and covered her breasts. "Just maybe?" He stroked his thumbs across her nipples, making them stiffen and her breath catch in her throat. "That doesn't sound very promising," he murmured. He bent his head over hers. "What if I promise to make the trip worthwhile?" he whispered, before brushing his lips across hers.

Heat crawled from the tips of her toes to curl in ribbons of warmth in her belly. "Mmm," she hummed silkily, and reached to loop an arm around his neck. "How?" she asked as she drew his face closer, the kiss deeper.

He didn't reply, but showed her, shaping his fingers over her breasts and squeezing as he slipped his tongue inside her mouth. He teased her with his hands, his lips, gentle bumps of his nose against hers, followed by deep thrusts of his tongue, until her body trembled with need.

She felt the prod of his sex as it grew, lengthening and hardening against her buttocks, and suddenly wanted more than anything to have him inside her, filling her. Twisting around on his lap, she locked her arms behind his neck as she straddled him, bracing her knees on the willow chair seat and hugging his thighs with hers.

"Let me love you," she whispered as she rained kisses over his face and down his chest. Slowly unwinding her arms from around his neck, she slid her hands over his shoulders and down to his abdomen.

He sucked in a breath, tensing, as her fingers encircled his sex. She lifted her head to press a soft smile against his lips. "Let me," she said again and guided him to her. She swept her tongue across his teeth as she sank down, taking him in. A groan rose in his throat and she swallowed the sound, glorying in the power she felt as she began to slowly ride him.

Pleasure poured through her in waves at the feel of him moving inside her, and she flowed with it, danced with it, wanting to share the sensations with him. Everything about him excited her, aroused her: the muscled chest her hands roamed; the short, sleep-mussed hair she ran her fingers through; the taste of him on her tongue; the varying textures of his skin beneath her hands. His sex sliding lazily in and out of her.

Then, suddenly, he dug his fingers into her hips and drew her hard against him, thrusting faster and faster with an urgency that demanded a greater speed, a more desperate race toward satisfaction. The pressure built inside her, ballooning until she was sure she'd explode.

As quickly as he'd increased the pace, he stopped and held her against him. "Wait," he murmured against her lips.

Desperate for the satisfaction that taunted just out of her reach, she tore her mouth from his. "No," she cried, pumping her hips wildly against his in a frantic bid for him to resume the pace.

Instead, he banded his arms around her and pushed to his feet, frustrating her even more. Crazed by the desire that clawed at her, she fought against his arms and pushed at his chest as he guided her legs around his waist.

"No. Please," she sobbed, burying her face in the curve of his neck. She tasted the salt of her own tears, the fever of the passion that heated his skin.

"Shh," he soothed. "Look."

When she stubbornly kept her face tucked in the curve of his neck, he caught her chin and forced her face to the side. She blinked at the haze of passion that clouded her eyes, slowly focusing on the sun as it crowned, spilling an ever widening pool of golden light over the dark hillside. Her eyes widened in awe, and she clung to Gil, entranced by the sight.

On a distant level she felt the nudge of his nose against her jaw, the spread of his smile against her cheek...the slight bow of his body as he pushed inside her. She turned to look at him, her eyes questioning.

With his gaze on hers, he thrust deeper, and pleasure arced through her, forcing the breath from her lungs and his name past her lips on a shocked gasp. He tensed, his eyes darkening, his jaw clenching. She felt his body jerk once...then again and again as he climaxed.

The golden glow of the sunrise seemed to blend with the warmth of his seed and spread slowly to her limbs, setting her body aglow from within. Then, like an explosion, she reached her own climax, the sensation a pulsing stream of light and color that swept through her body, swirling behind her eyes and illuminating her soul. Wanting to hold on to the glorious sensation as long as possible, she arched back, clinging to Gil, her hips melded to his.

Groaning, he began to turn, spinning faster and faster with each revolution, until she was dizzy and laughing. She dropped her head back and flung out her arms, trusting the hands that held her to keep her safe, while she embraced the sunrise, the radiant light that washed over their bodies like a blessing of golds, pinks and lavenders that seemed to come straight from heaven itself.

Four

"Wow," Suzy murmured, awed by the spacious kitchen she followed Gil into.

"Like it?"

"Like it," she said incredulously as she turned a slow circle, trying to take it all in. "This is unbelievable!" Running her palm over a counter topped with squares of tumbled stone, she leaned to look out a window that took advantage of the gorgeous view of green pastures and cedar and oak-covered hills in the distance. She glanced his way. "Did you design this yourself?"

He crossed to a beverage center and pulled out the makings for coffee. "Most of it, though I did ask my mother for help with the final layout." He measured grounds into the filter. "I built the house to live in, and since I plan to someday share it with my wife, I figured Mom knew more than I did about what things a woman would want in a kitchen.''

Amazed that he would consider his wife's preferences when he didn't even have one, she could only stare. "That's really sweet," was all she could think of to say.

He shot her a wink. "No. That's prior planning." Chuckling, he switched on the coffeemaker. Then he turned, bracing his hips against the counter and folding his arms across his chest. "There are those who accuse me of thinking everything to death before I make a decision, my mother included."

At the second mention of his mother, Suzy couldn't help wondering about their relationship. "Are you and your mother close?"

He shrugged. "I suppose. Though no closer than my father and I are. Why do you ask?"

Thinking of the dysfunctional relationship she shared with her own mother, she wandered the kitchen, dragging her hand over the tumbled stone counter and avoiding his gaze. "No particular reason. Just curious."

"They live about a mile from here in the old home place. That's where I grew up. What about you? Are you close to your parents?"

She stiffened at the question, then forced her shoulders to relax, pretending interest in the microwave's complicated control panel. "There's just my mother. My parents divorced when I was young."

"Your father didn't maintain contact with you?"

She shook her head. "No. But no great loss. From what I remember of him, he was a jerk."

"That's a shame," Gil murmured sympathetically, then smiled. "I'd like for you to meet my parents. I think you'd like them."

And Suzy prayed he'd *never* meet her parents. Especially her father. "Yeah," she replied vaguely. "Whatever." She opened the sack of items they'd purchased at a convenience store on the drive to the ranch the night before. "Hungry?"

Gil watched her pull out the package of sweet rolls, knowing she was trying to change the subject and wondering about it. But he'd let her, he decided. For the time being, anyway. They had the rest of the weekend to get to know each other.

He pushed away from the counter. "Hungrier than a bear." He poured two cups of coffee, then joined her at the breakfast table. Lifting his cup, he blew on his coffee, studying her through the steam that rose above the rim. What a paradox, he thought, suppressing a smile as he let his gaze drift over her freshly scrubbed cheeks, the sleep-mussed blond hair and the delicate curve of one shoulder not quite covered by the shirt he'd loaned her. Or, if not a paradox, she was, at the very least, a talented actress.

From the moment he'd met her, he'd suspected she used the exotic makeup and outrageous clothing as a disguise of sorts to conceal a different personality, a different woman entirely. And when he'd gotten a look at her home, with its cheerful yellow siding, gardens spilling with flowers of every color and description, and the eclectic, yet cozy, collection of furnishings with which she'd filled the interior, he was even more convinced that she wasn't at all like the image she chose to project to the world. All the makeup and clothing was nothing but a facade she hid behind. But from what was she hiding? he asked himself, the question drawing a frown. Or from whom?

She took a bite of her roll, then glanced up, as if sensing his gaze. "What?" she asked, dabbing self-consciously at her mouth.

"Do you realize you've never told me your name?"

If he hadn't been studying her so intently, he would've missed the flash of panic in her eyes before she dropped her gaze and picked up her napkin.

"I told you my name," she said as she wiped the sugary icing from her fingers. "It's Suzy."

"Your *full* name," he persisted.

She looked up and met his gaze squarely, almost defiantly. "Suzy," she repeated, then masked the defiance behind a dazzling smile, meant to disarm him. "I figure if one name is good enough for Madonna and Cher, why not me?"

Though his gut told him to pursue the issue, Gil decided to let it drop, not wanting to chance ruining what remained of their weekend together. He'd already discovered that Suzy was like a young colt unused to human handling, one who spooked easily and unexpectedly. One who required a gentle and patient hand. "So you plan to pursue an acting and musical career?"

At his teasing, she cocked a saucy brow. "Maybe. Think I could?"

Chuckling, he shook his head. "I don't know. Do you sing?"

"In the shower."

He lifted his cup in a salute. "That's a start." He took a sip, winking at her over the cup's rim. "But you could probably get by on your beauty alone."

She rolled her eyes. "Yeah, I'm sure I look really beautiful right now without a smidgen of makeup on and wearing one of your old shirts."

He set down his cup and selected a sweet roll. "You don't need makeup. In fact, you're even more beautiful without it." He took a bite of the pastry, his eyes filling with amusement. "And as far as the shirt goes, the only way you could possibly look better is without it."

"You politicians," she said, dismissing the compliment with a flap of her hand. "You're full of nothing but a lot of hot air."

He leveled a finger at her nose. "I've already told you once. I'm no politician. And I don't lie, either. When I tell you something, you can bank on it being the truth."

Relieved that the conversation had taken a different direction, Suzy folded her hands beneath her chin. "Okay," she said, accepting his warning as a challenge. "If you speak only the truth, then tell me what it is about me that you find so attractive?"

Hooking his thumbs in the waist of his jeans, he

rocked his chair back on two legs. "Where do you want me to start?"

"The list is that long?"

"Long enough." Chuckling, he dropped his chair back down and leaned to rest his forearms on the table. "But I'll give you the *Reader's Digest* condensed version. From the first, you intrigued me. Most people, once they find out I'm the governor, treat me differently. Like I'm somebody special or something. You don't and didn't from the beginning. In fact, you were downright rude."

"I wasn't rude! I was busy and you were in my way."

"You were rude."

"Okay," she said, conceding the point only because she was anxious to hear more. "So I was rude."

"And that's what intrigued me. Most folks would've stopped what they were doing and tripped all over themselves in an effort to please me or impress me. But not you." He laughed and shook his head. "I liked that."

"You were attracted to me because I was rude," she summarized sourly. "That's certainly gratifying."

"That was only the first thing that attracted me." He picked up his cup and took a sip. "Then there was the sex."

She held up a hand. "Uh-uh. There wasn't any sex. At least not initially."

"No, but the idea was there. The question of

whether or not it would be good between us. You were wondering about it, too."

"I certainly was not!"

He reached across the table and caught her chin in his hand. "You were, too. At the party you catered, and again the afternoon I came to your house. Come on," he prodded, stroking a thumb persuasively across her lower lip. "Admit it."

Scowling, she pushed his hand away. "Okay," she said grudgingly. "So maybe I was. But only briefly," she added stubbornly. "I assure you I didn't lose any sleep over whether or not we would be sexually compatible."

"I did."

Surprised that he would confess his infatuation with her so freely, she was tempted to ask him to elaborate, but feared if she did he'd expect the same of her in turn. "Why haven't you ever married?" she asked instead.

"Never found the right woman."

"In thirty-six years you've never met *one* woman you would consider marrying?"

His eyes twinkled mischievously. "Nope."

She pressed her lips together and eyed him dubiously. "It's rumored that you haven't married because you're gay."

He lifted a brow. "Do you think I'm gay?"

She choked on a laugh. "Hardly. But doesn't it bother you that they print lies about you?"

"Why should it? *I* know it's not true."

"Yeah, but don't you think some people accept what they read as the gospel?"

"I suppose they might."

"And that doesn't bother you?" she asked in disbelief.

"No. Should it?"

"Well, yes!" she cried and pushed to her feet. "The media shouldn't be allowed to print lies about you or anybody else for that matter." She marched to the sink and dumped out her coffee. "It's an invasion of a person's privacy, a direct infringement of an individual's personal right to life, liberty and the pursuit of happiness, as guaranteed by the constitution of the United States."

Surprised by her fervor, Gil rose, too, and followed her to the sink. He stuck his cup under the faucet, glancing her way as he rinsed it out. "The constitution also promises freedom of speech and press."

"To speak and print lies?" she returned. "I think not." She turned and paced away. "The media should report only the truth and leave it at that. They shouldn't be allowed to sensationalize the news just to increase their readership and up their ratings."

"No, they shouldn't," he agreed. "So how do you think we should go about putting a stop to it?"

Suzy whirled. "We? As in you and me?"

"Yeah. Obviously you feel strongly about this topic. Why not take your anger and put it to good use?"

She took a step in retreat, horrified at the thought of placing herself in direct contact—and possibly conflict—with the media. "I...I couldn't. I don't know anything about the law or politics."

"You don't have to. All you have to have is a desire to change things and the courage to take a stand for what you believe is right."

She took another step back, shaking her head. "I couldn't," she said again. "I wouldn't know the first thing about how to begin. I'm a caterer, not a politician."

"And I'm a rancher," he reminded her pointedly, then softened the scolding with a smile. "You've already taken the first step, whether you realize it or not. You've recognized a wrong that needs to be righted."

Fearing that if she didn't do something and quickly, he would appoint her chairman of a committee to investigate media practices or something equally frightening, Suzy did what she always did when she found herself in an uncomfortable situation. She fell back on sarcasm. "Yeah," she scoffed, "and after I whip the media back into shape, I think I'll start on health care reform. Now that's a topic that really stirs my blood."

"There's need for change there, as well, both on a state and national level."

"Yeah. Whatever." She faked a yawn and stretched lazily. "All this talk about changing the world is making me tired," she said wearily. "Want to take a nap?"

He shook his head. "As tempting as I find that

proposition, I need to check on my cattle. You can ride along with me, if you like."

"On horses?"

"Horseback is the only way to reach some of the land we'd be traveling."

She shuddered. "If it's all the same to you, I think I'll stay right here and nap. I didn't get very much sleep last night," she reminded him drolly.

Gil collected his cowboy hat from the counter and settled it over his head as he opened the back door. "And if I have anything to say about it, you won't be getting any tonight, either."

Suzy did try to nap, but sleep evaded her; her mind churned with memories and fears stirred by her conversation with Gil about the media. Every time she closed her eyes, she saw the headlines that screamed her father's misdeeds to the world, heard the incessant ringing of the phone and the heartbreaking sound of her mother's hysterical sobbing. But most of all, she saw *him*. Her father. The infamous Reverend Bobby Swain. With his perfectly coifed hair, his custom-made suit, standing with his arms uplifted, eyes closed, wearing a beatific smile...the same smile he had used to win unsuspecting women into his fold and eventually into his bed.

And the media had reported it all.

When the rumor of his misdeeds had first surfaced, like hounds on a hunt, reporters had chased and dug until they'd uncovered all the reverend's dark secrets and exposed him for the fornicator he was. But in their glee of tearing down the temple of sin the reverend had created for himself, they'd destroyed Suzy's mother, as well. When the first story had broken, Suzy remembered watching her mother on television, the beautiful and regal Sarah Swain, standing stoically at her husband's side, her loyal and loving gaze fixed on him as he denied the stories printed about him, contending that they were the work of the devil in an effort to destroy his ministry.

But with each new woman the media dragged before the camera with her claim that she, too, had had an affair with the famous TV evangelist, Sarah Swain's faith in her husband, as well as her emotional stability, had slowly dwindled away, until she was merely a shadow of the confident and loving mother Suzy had once known.

The media had destroyed their entire family structure, dragged her mother's name onto the front page right along with the reverend's, heaping shame and humiliation upon the family, until Sarah had finally collapsed beneath it. At Sarah's parents' insistence and under their direction, she had divorced Bobby Swain, changed her name and secretly relocated in Elgin, a small rural town east of Austin, Texas, in hopes of protecting herself and her daughter from any further humiliation.

Though the scandal had destroyed their family, it hadn't harmed Bobby Swain...at least, not for long. He'd weathered the storm seemingly unscathed and continued to preach his message from the pulpit, gathering more and more followers, while lining his pockets with their donations. But all that had ended when a disgruntled contributor had sued the reverend for misappropriation of church funds. The lawsuit that followed was what had finally destroyed him, and he wound up locked behind a set of gates that were anything but pearly.

During that second scandal Suzy realized that her mother's attempt to escape her association and relation to the reverend by changing her name and moving were in vain. The media had scoured court records until they had tracked down Sarah and Suzy in Elgin. They began to print allegations that the reverend had secretly funneled funds to his former wife and daughter that rightfully belonged to the church. Mother and daughter took another beating by the press that lasted for months after the reverend was locked away in prison.

It was then that Suzy had decided to quit using her last name entirely and had pumped up her efforts to look and act nothing like a preacher's daughter.

She had good reason to hate and avoid the media, she reminded herself. And that's why she didn't want to go head-to-head in a battle with them, as Gil had suggested. For her mother's sake, as much as her own, she wanted, *needed* to maintain her privacy, guard her identity, keep her relationship to the reverend in the past where it belonged.

But how she could do that and continue to see Gil?

With a groan, she rolled from the bed and scraped back her hair, digging her palms against her temples. She couldn't possibly have a relationship with Gil without the media finding out and dragging out all her family's dirty laundry to air again. And her mother would never survive another battering by the press. Her health and her emotional stability were much too fragile for her to suffer through all that again.

Suzy dropped her arms and forced herself to calm down, telling herself she was only borrowing trouble. So far no one knew that she was seeing Gil. And after this weekend there would be nothing to know. When they returned to Austin, they'd go their separate ways, Gil to the governor's mansion and she to her home, and it would be over.

Oddly she found that reassurance more depressing than comforting.

Knowing she needed to focus her mind on something else, she wandered to the kitchen and dug around until she'd found enough ingredients to throw together a meal, taking solace in the familiar activity of cooking. As she worked, she rid herself of the melancholy that stubbornly lingered by experimenting with all the fancy gadgets and state-of-the-art equipment Gil's mother had selected for her son's future wife.

It was while stooping to check on the roast she'd placed in the oven that she recalled Gil's earlier comment. *A wife to share my home with someday,* she remembered him saying.

A yearning spread through her as his words echoed in her mind, and she moved to stand before the window above the sink, hugging her arms around her waist as she stared outside. Even though she knew it was impossible—stupid even to entertain such fanciful thoughts when she knew their relationship would have to end with the weekend—she couldn't help wishing that she could be the woman with whom Gil would someday share his home.

As she stared, her mind clouded with if-only dreams, Gil rode into her line of vision and dragged her from her thoughts. She leaned closer to the window, watching as he loped his horse toward the corral. He looked so natural in the saddle, so at ease, so...masculine. And when he reined the horse to a stop and swung down from the saddle, she pressed her hand against her heart, experiencing for the first time that "pitter-patter" she remembered him claiming he felt each time he thought about her.

Could she be falling in love with him? she asked herself, her blood chilling at the mere thought.

Lust, she reminded herself and turned from the window and ran outside, suddenly impatient to see him, to touch him.

"Gil!" she shouted, waving her hand over her head as she ran toward the corral.

In the act of slipping the bridle from the horse's head, he glanced up, and a smile slowly spread across his face. He hooked the bridle over a post, closed the corral gate behind him, then turned and opened his arms. Suzy ran into them, laughing when he scooped her off her feet and up against his chest.

Pressing back in his arms, she looked down at him,

her laughter giving way to a lusty sigh. Unable to resist, she plucked off his hat, tossed it aside, then planted a kiss full on his mouth.

"Hey," he said. "What's this all about?"

Her gaze on his, she combed her fingers through the damp crease his hat had left on his hair. "I missed you."

"Damn," he murmured, grinning. "Maybe I ought to leave you alone more often."

She fixed a mean look on her face. "Try it, cowboy," she warned, "and you might find yourself tied to my bed."

"Mmm-mmm." He hitched her higher on his chest. "This is sounding better and better all the time."

Laughing, she dropped a kiss on his mouth. "Hungry?"

"For you? Always."

She pushed at his shoulders to put her down. "I was talking about food."

He deposited her on her feet. "You cooked something for us to eat?"

"No," she replied dryly. "I ordered takeout."

Draping an arm along her shoulders, he headed her toward the house. "I hope it's Chinese. I've had a yearning for chow-mein all day."

"Very funny."

He bumped his hip playfully against hers. "You started it. So what did you cook?"

"Beef with a mushroom cream sauce, green beans and roasted onions. It was all I could find to make a meal." She slanted him a disapproving look. "Your pantry is pitifully bare."

He shrugged. "I'm not here often enough to warrant stocking in a large supply of groceries."

With her gaze going to the wide expanse of green pastures and the hills in the distance, she slipped an arm around his waist. "I don't know how you manage to stay away," she said with a sigh. "If this was my home—"

Gil jerked to a stop, pulling Suzy to a stop, as well.

"What?" she asked, glancing up at him, then turned her head to follow his gaze.

"Somebody's coming."

He'd no sooner voiced the warning, than she saw a car top the ridge. She dropped her arm from his waist and stepped away, putting distance between them. "Who is it?"

He squinted his eyes, trying to identify the vehicle, then swore. "Skinner."

Suzy whipped her head around to stare at Gil, her eyes wide with alarm. "Paul Skinner? The reporter?"

Frowning, Gil braced his hands on his hips. "Yeah."

Suzy spun for the house, but Gil caught her arm, stopping her. "Too late now," he said with a jerk of his chin toward the rapidly approaching car. "He's already spotted us."

Eyes blazing, she wrenched free and ran.

Gil started after her, then stopped and, with a frustrated sigh, turned back to wait for the reporter.

Skinner braked to a stop and climbed out, lifting a hand in greeting. "Afternoon, Governor."

"Paul," Gil replied, acknowledging the greeting, but not returning the man's smile. "What brings you out this way?"

"Dropped by the mansion earlier today and was told you were out of town for the weekend. Put two and two together and figured you were here at your ranch."

"This is usually where I come when I want to get away for some downtime. I make no secret of that."

Gil's subtle reminder that Paul was invading his private time went right over the reporter's head. Or at least the man pretended it did as he stuck his hands in his pockets and rocked back on his heels, looking around. "Nice place you've got here," he commented.

Gil set his jaw, struggling to remain civil, knowing nothing would be gained by antagonizing the reporter. "I think so. Was there something specific you needed?" he asked, hoping to hurry the reporter on his way.

"Nope. Just wanted to get a gander at where the governor of Texas spends his free time. I'm thinking about doing a series of articles along that line." Paul's gaze reached the house and lingered there a moment, then he glanced at Gil, a brow arched expectantly. "Seems I scared off your guest. I hope I didn't interrupt anything."

Knowing that the reporter had indeed spotted Suzy and was fishing for an explanation of her hasty departure, Gil shook his head. "No. Not at all." He slung a companionable arm along the man's shoulder and turned him around, strolling along with him as he headed him back to his car. "That article you mentioned sounds mighty interesting. I'll have to plan a barbecue and invite all the media out for a tour of the ranch."

They reached the car and Gil leaned around Paul to open the door and added with a wink, "I'll personally see that you receive an invitation." He waited until Paul climbed inside, then slammed the door behind him and stuck his head in the window. "By the way, Paul," he said, "a closed gate around these parts means the same as a locked door to you city boys. Pass through one uninvited, and you're liable to find your butt shot full of lead."

Scowling, Paul reached for the key. "Yeah. I'll remember that."

Gil straightened and slapped a hand against the top of the car. "Mind that you do." He took a step back. "Watch out for armadillos on the drive back to town. Those dang critters think roads were built for their personal crossing."

Paul jerked the gearshift down. "Yeah, I will," he muttered.

Gil watched the reporter wheel his car around and head back the way he'd come. When the car topped the ridge and disappeared on the other side, he turned for the house.

When he entered the kitchen, he found Suzy standing at the sink, her arms buried to the elbows in dishwater. He could tell by the stiffness in her shoulders, in the jerkiness of her movements that the reporter's visit had upset her.

Hoping to reassure her, he crossed to stand behind her and slipped his arms around her waist. "No need to fret. He's gone now."

She whirled, and he was stunned to see that her face was flushed with anger and her eyes gleamed with tears. "You promised," she accused and twisted from his embrace. She stalked away, then swung back, dragging a hand beneath her nose. "You said that the media would never know we were here. Trust me, you said!" She tossed up her hands, sending soap bubbles flying. "And fool that I am, I did!"

"Suzy—"

When he started toward her, she pushed out a hand. "No. Don't. I don't want you to touch me. Not ever again. I just want to go home."

Gil stopped, reining in his own anger, his need to hold her, knowing that any movement at all from him would only upset her more. Like a colt when cornered, she would kick and fight against anything or anyone who drew too close. So he waited, watching until the rapid rise and fall of her breasts slowed, the trembling in her hands stilled. He waited until she sank to the floor in a heap and buried her face in her hands, sobbing.

Then he went to her. He eased down on the floor beside her and gathered her into his arms. She turned into his chest willingly and buried her face against his neck, clinging to him with a desperation that closed his throat and made any attempt to comfort her with words impossible.

So he soothed her with his hands, with his lips, with whispered murmurs that had no meaning, made no sense, just comforting sounds that vibrated against her hair, her cheeks, her lips. He held her until the sobs stopped, until the trembling in her body ceased. Then he held her tighter, holding her close to his chest, to his heart.

"I'm sorry, Suzy," he murmured, pressing his lips against her hair. "I'm so, so sorry."

She inhaled a shuddery breath and slowly eased from his embrace, dragging her hands beneath her eyes. "No. I am. It wasn't your fault. I shouldn't have blamed you. I was just so...so mad."

He tucked a knuckle beneath her chin and tipped her face up to his. "You forgive me, then?"

She smiled a watery smile, unable to do any less than he asked. Laying a palm along his cheek, she said, "Yes, I forgive you. But I still want to go home. I should never have come here in the first place."

He covered her hand with his. "Why, Suzy? Tell me why?"

She stared into his eyes, seeing the confusion that swirled in the blue depths, the need for understanding. She wanted to tell him everything. Bare her soul and put an end to the charade. Expose the identity she'd struggled for years to hide. The words were there on the tip of her tongue, in her heart. But she couldn't voice them. Not when she stood to lose so much. The loss of her privacy. The loss of the identity she'd worked so hard to assume.

But as she continued to meet his gaze, held by the warmth that had first drawn her to him, the comfort and tenderness that she knew lay beneath, she realized her biggest fear was Gil's reaction. That was what kept her silent, the words locked inside. Would he be shocked if she were to tell him who her father was? Would disgust and revulsion replace the confusion that now swirled in his eyes? Would he turn away from her in loathing? Would he take her home as she'd requested and never want to see her again? Worse, would his association with her ruin his effectiveness as governor? Taint the record of a man who wanted only to serve?

He'd given her nothing but honesty from the first, she told herself, feeling the tears choke her. And what had she given him in return? Nothing but artful evasion and glib replies to all his questions. Knowing he deserved so much more, more than she'd ever given any man, she slowly drew her hand from beneath his.

"All right," she said, then firmed her lips to control their trembling. "But it's not pretty," she warned.

He caught her hand in his and squeezed. "What we fear usually isn't. But sometimes when we hoard our fears, keep them to ourselves, they seem bigger, more insurmountable than they really are."

She would've laughed at that if she weren't so choked by tears at his kindness, at his offer of understanding. Unable to meet his gaze any longer, she dropped her chin and rubbed her thumb across his knuckles, searching for the courage she needed to share her secrets. "It's my father," she began hesitantly. She lifted her gaze, needing to see his reaction when she told him. "My father is Reverend Bobby Swain."

A frown furrowed his brow, as if the name meant nothing to him, then slowly smoothed as recognition dawned.

"Bobby Swain?" he repeated, as if unsure he'd heard her correctly.

She nodded, shame heating her cheeks. "Y-yes." She watched his face, waiting for the revulsion to come, knowing she had to tell him all. "I haven't seen him since I was six years old. Mother changed our names and moved us to Elgin after she divorced him."

Though his gaze remained on hers, his expression free of any emotion, she sensed the shock her announcement drew.

Sighing, she eased her hand from his and started to rise. "So now you know why I hate the media, why it's impossible for me to see you again."

He caught her hand and tugged her back down to his lap. "No, I don't." When she tried to stand, he vised his arms around her waist, forcing her to remain on his lap. "I know only that your father was a less-than-honorable man and that you don't want to be associated with him."

She shoved at his chest. "Don't you understand?" she cried. "If the media finds out who I am, it'll start all over again. They'll dig out all the old stories and print them again."

"You have nothing to be ashamed of. You did nothing wrong."

"But he did!" she screamed. "And I'm his daughter!"

When he remained silent, his gaze steady and unflinching on hers, Suzy groaned, fisting her hands against his chest. "Think, Gil. Think how having your name associated with mine will affect your popularity with the public, your hopes of accomplishing anything during your term as governor."

"And it may have no effect whatsoever."

She pushed against his arms, managing this time to break free and rise. "Are you nuts?" she shouted down at him. "Of course it will have an effect! They'll drag your name through the dirt right along with mine, and you'll lose all your credibility, all your support."

He pushed to his feet, never once moving his gaze from hers. "I'm willing to take that chance."

"Well, I'm not! And I won't let you!"

He caught her by her elbows and drew her to him, a smile curving the corners of his mouth. "I love a woman with gumption."

She flattened her hands against his chest, desperate to make him understand. "Gil, please. Listen to me. You don't know what you're saying, what all you stand to lose. I've been there. I've seen what the press can do to a person. I—"

He closed his mouth over hers, silencing her warnings. She struggled against him, trying to twist free, but he only tightened his arms around her. Tears stung her eyes at his stubbornness…and the tenderness with which he kissed her.

Unfurling her fingers from the fists she'd curled against his chest, she lifted her hands and wrapped them around his neck. She felt his smile against her lips, the increased pressure on her mouth when he stooped to catch her beneath the knees. Knowing it was useless to fight him, she let him carry her to his room and to his bed, determined to make him listen once he released her.

But when he laid her down, then stood looking at her, his eyes filled with a desire that set her skin on fire, all argument melted from her tongue. And when he ripped open her shirt—his shirt—and dropped down to capture the budded peak of a breast between his teeth, her mind went blank. She could only think of the cleverness of the mouth that suckled her, the heat that raced through her veins, the arrows of sensation his suckling shot to her belly.

And having him inside her.

Five

"**S**uzy?"

Sprawled across Gil, she could only manage a weak, "Hmm."

"I don't think this is just lust."

She flipped her eyes wide, but in the darkness she couldn't see his expression, only his shadowed profile. "You don't?"

"Uh-uh." He rolled to his side and gathered her into his arms. He bumped his nose against hers, the stretch of his smile spreading along her jaw. "I don't think I'll ever get enough of you."

She tensed, the fears he'd distracted her from by carrying her off to bed returning with a vengeance. "Gil..."

"What?"

She sat up, scraping her hair back and holding it away from her face, trying to find the right words to convince him that this was a mistake. She quickly discovered there weren't any. "We can't do this."

He pushed himself to an elbow. "I know it'll be tough. But we can find a way to keep the media out of our relationship."

She bolted from the bed. "I'd think that Paul Skinner's appearance today would have proved to you how impossible that is."

His eyebrows drew together as he watched her snatch up his shirt and push her arms into the sleeves. "No. It just proved to me that I need to take better advantage of all the security that's provided for me."

She stopped with her back to him and squeezed her eyes shut, knowing that all the security in the world wasn't enough to keep out the press. Not when they smelled a story.

Slowly she turned to face him. "Gil," she said carefully. "It would never work. You know that. When your term is over—"

He rocketed from the bed and to his feet. "When my term is over?" he repeated. "Hell, that's *three* years from now!"

"I know it is. But that's the best option I have to offer."

"Well, it's not good enough." His anger faded as quickly as it had appeared. He crossed to her and caught her hands, squeezing them within his own. "Suzy, I don't want this to end here. I *won't* let it end here."

Tears threatened at the desperation she saw in his eyes. "It has to."

He gripped her hands tighter. "Dammit, it doesn't!"

"We can't see each other as long as you're governor."

He dropped her hands and turned away, rubbing at the sudden tension in his neck. "I won't walk away from my duties as governor. I can't."

Tears flooded her eyes that he'd even consider that as an option. "I'd never ask you to."

He swung back around to face her. "Then give me a chance. *Us* a chance. There's a way we can pull this off. I know there is. There are things I can do to protect you from the press. I can—"

She dropped her chin to her chest and shook her head. "You couldn't. You saw the proof of that as well as I did today."

He grabbed her by the arms. "I won't give you up. And I sure as hell won't wait until my term is over to see you again."

"Gil—"

"No," he said fiercely. Then, groaning, he dragged her against his chest and crushed her to him. "We can make this work, Suzy." Rocking her back and forth, he pressed his lips against her hair. "I know we can."

She knew better than to believe him. She'd already seen how easily the press could scale the walls of his privacy, invade what should rightfully be his private life. But she desperately wanted what he wanted.

Time together. The chance to play this out. The opportunity for a normal life. A life that perhaps included him.

Lifting her face, she met his gaze and did what she'd sworn she would never do again. She placed her trust in a man. This man. And she did so for the second time.

Surprisingly cheerful for such an ungodly hour and after such an emotionally draining weekend with so little sleep, Suzy kneaded dough while swaying her hips to the beat of the Platters' song currently playing on the oldies station she had tuned her radio to.

In spite of her apprehensions and arguments to the contrary, Gil had finally convinced her to see him on the sly until he could come up with a way to make his involvement with her public without harming either of them. Though she found the whole idea of sneaking around distasteful, the idea of waiting three years to be with him was even more so. But as Gil had said, if they were careful—

A knock sounded at her back door and she glanced at the oven clock in surprise, wondering who would be dropping by this early in the morning.

Wiping her hands across the front of her apron, she crossed to the back door and opened it. A smile of delight spread across her face when she saw that it was Penny on her stoop. "Hey, girlfriend. What are you doing out so early?"

Pushing past her, Penny stormed into the kitchen.

"Where have you been all weekend? I've called you a thousand times."

Surprised by her friend's anger, Suzy closed the door. "Sorry. I was out of town."

Penny flopped down on a chair at the table and snatched her purse to her lap. "You might've called and told me."

Hearing the tears in her friend's voice, Suzy started across the room. "What is it?" she asked in concern. "Has something happened to Erik? Have you left him?"

Penny sniffled, waving away Suzy's fears. "No. He's fine. We're fine." Her eyes full of tears, she caught Suzy's hand and pulled her down onto the chair next to hers. "Have you seen the Sunday paper?"

Dread hit Suzy like a bucket of cold water on the face. "No. Why?"

Penny let go of her hand to pull a newspaper from her purse. "Prepare yourself," she warned, dabbing at her eyes as she offered the folded paper to Suzy. "It's in Paul Skinner's column."

Suzy tore her gaze from Penny's to stare at the newspaper, then unfolded it and began to read. She'd read only three lines before she leaped to her feet. "It was a private party," she cried, wadding the paper in her fist. "The press wasn't even invited. How did he get in?"

"I doubt he did."

Suzy spun, holding the fisted paper above her head. "Then how do you explain *this*?" She dropped her arm and snapped open the paper, her voice filled with bitterness as she read, "'More than a few guests were shocked at Friday night's gala celebrating the opening of the hospital's new wing, when a young woman, decked out in an outfit better suited for one of the girls at LaGrange's infamous Chicken Ranch, attempted to crash the party, insisting she was the governor's date. Guests were even more shocked when the governor acknowledged the woman's claim by offering her his arm and remaining by her side throughout the evening's festivities.'"

Suzy slapped the paper against her leg, her face flushed with rage. "Now you tell me how Paul Skinner could possibly know what I was wearing if he wasn't there?"

"You know as well as I do that gossip columnists have sources who provide them with information. Someone probably saw you at the party and called him, anxious to be the first to share the juicy tidbit."

Suzy's lip curled in a snarl. "The slimeball."

Sniffing, Penny gestured at the paper. "What about that part at the end? The part where he mentions seeing a woman with the governor at his ranch. Was that where you were all weekend?"

Not having read that far, Suzy paled. Her fingers trembling, she opened the paper and scanned to the paragraph Penny had mentioned. "'Since the governor was seen in the company of at least one, perhaps two women this weekend,'" she read aloud, "'one can only assume that the previous rumors concerning his sexual preferences were nothing but malicious mudslinging, planted by those opposed to his unorthodox manner of conducting government business. Oh, and by the way, Governor, was that one of your shirts the young woman seen with you at your ranch was wearing?''

Ripping the paper in two, she flung the pieces away from her. "That slimeball!" she cried. "That vicious, sneaky slimeball!"

Penny caught her lower lip between her teeth and rose. "He didn't mention you by name. Maybe he doesn't know who you are."

Suzy slammed her fists to her hips. "And how long do you think it will take him to track down the mysterious woman the governor escorted around the dedication, considering Gil introduced me as Suzy to nearly everyone there?" Knowing only too well the answer, she buried her face in her hands. "Oh, I knew this would happen," she wailed. "I just knew it!"

The telephone rang and she snatched her hands down to stare at it in horror.

Penny took a hesitant step forward. "Do you want me to answer it?"

Suzy flung out an arm to stop her. "No...I will." She drew in a deep breath, then picked up the receiver. "Hello?" She listened a moment, then banged down the receiver.

"Who was it?" Penny asked as Suzy stormed past her to the island. "A reporter?"

Suzy snatched up her rolling pin. "No. The governor."

"And you hung up on him?" Penny asked in dismay.

Suzy whacked the rolling pin against the last remaining mound of dough and began to roll it furiously back and forth. "You dang right I did. I don't need this nightmare." She dashed a hand beneath her nose, angered even more by the tears. "I should've just told him to go to hell in the first place and been done with it."

"Oh, Suzy," Penny murmured, crossing to place a comforting hand on her friend's shoulder. "You can't hide from the world forever."

Suzy stopped rolling and turned to fix Penny with a steely-eyed look. "Wanna bet?"

"Get me some backing on the drought aid for farmers in West Texas and we'll talk." Gil glanced up as his secretary slipped into his office and quickly covered the phone's mouthpiece with his hand. "Were you able to reach her?"

She shook her head. "Sorry. Still no answer."

Pressing his lips together, Gil moved his hand from the mouthpiece. "Fine," he snapped into the receiver. "We'll talk then." He dropped the phone back onto its base, then slumped back in his chair and turned his head to stare out the window on his left, wishing he could get his hands on Paul Skinner's scrawny neck. What he'd give for five minutes alone in a dark alley with the bastard.

"Governor?" his secretary said hesitantly. "If

there's nothing else pressing, the lieutenant governor is waiting to see you. He said it's important.''

Sighing, Gil sat up and pulled his chair back up to his desk. "Tell him to come on in."

He pulled out his itinerary for the day, looking for a break in his schedule that would allow him the time to drop by Suzy's house. She was there, he told himself. She was simply hiding from the press...and obviously from him.

A newspaper landed on his desk, and he glanced up, frowning at Richard Marvin, his lieutenant governor, the man who had tossed it there. "I see you've seen the paper, too."

Richard dropped down on the chair opposite the desk and reared back, rolling the ever-present toothpick to the corner of his mouth. "Yeah, I saw it. The question is, is it true?"

"Which part? That the dress she wore to the dedication was better suited for one of the girls at the Chicken Ranch in LaGrange? Or that she was wearing one of my shirts at my ranch?"

Sighing, Richard pulled the toothpick from his mouth. "I take it both are true."

Gil leaned back in his chair, folding his hands behind his head. "Essentially. Though I would argue Skinner's description of the outfit she wore to the dedication. I've seen teenage girls at the mall dressed in getups a lot more risqué than what Suzy had on."

Richard scowled. "This is serious, Gil."

Gil dropped his arms. "I know it is."

"I guess my next question, then, should be what are you going to do about it?"

"Nothing."

"Nothing?" Richard repeated, rising. "Do you realize the damage this kind of piece can do to your credibility? Your ability to successfully push through the legislation you've campaigned so hard for?"

Hearing his lieutenant governor repeat almost the same warnings Suzy had voiced drew a wan smile from Gil. "Yeah. I'm aware."

"And you're going to take this lying down?"

"I didn't say that."

"No, but you *did* say that you weren't going to do anything about it. What you *should* do is request a retraction, hold a news conference and offer some kind of explanation, denying your involvement with this woman."

"I won't do that. It would be a lie."

Richard dropped down to the chair and let his head fall back. "Please tell me she can be bought. That we can pay her off to keep her quiet."

"I'd never do that."

Richard lowered his chin to glower at Gil. "You don't have to. *I'll* see that it's done."

Gil rose and crossed to the window that faced the capitol in the distance, needing the reminder of his responsibilities, the reasons he had sought this office in the first place. He knew things like this went on. From the beginning of time, public figures had erred, sinned, then made deals behind closed doors and passed money under tables to keep their misdeeds from becoming public knowledge.

But the men who had done those things weren't Gil Riley. In his opinion their way was the cowardly way. And Gil Riley was no coward. And, in his mind at least, he hadn't committed any sins. Not when the woman he was involved with was the first one he had ever seriously considered spending the rest of his life with.

"No," he said and turned to face Richard. "I won't let you do that. I'm entitled to a life separate from this office. And what I do on my own time should have no effect on my work here."

Richard snorted. "You're kidding, right?"

"No. I'm dead serious."

Richard pushed slowly to his feet. "Listen, Gil. You aren't John Wayne and this isn't some movie you're starring in, so don't think the audience is going to stand up and cheer because you defended a woman's virtue. This is the real world. People fight dirty here. Things don't operate the way you think they do."

"Maybe not. But they should. I never claimed to be perfect, Richard. No man is. To pretend otherwise would just be building on a lie that's existed too damn long."

"And there's nothing I can do to change your mind?"

"Not on this."

Clamping the toothpick between his teeth again, Richard shook his head as he headed for the door.

"God be with you, then, son, because the press is going to rip your guts out and feed it to the public and laugh like banshees while they're doing it."

Over a week had passed since the weekend Gil had spent with Suzy at his ranch...and the ugly article had appeared in the paper. But a previously scheduled trip to Washington to meet with other state governors had prevented him from attempting any further contact with Suzy. But now the time for a showdown had come.

He knew he was taking a chance on making a fool of himself and possibly making an already bad situation worse, but he was willing to take the gamble, if it meant seeing her again and talking to her.

Dressed all in black and feeling like a cat burglar, he parked two blocks from her house and crept through the dark neighborhood, keeping to the shadows. When he reached her house, he darted across the lawn and through the gate that opened to her backyard. Breathing a sigh of relief that he'd made it that far without detection, he tipped his head back and looked up at the dark windows, trying to decide which marked her bedroom.

With only three to choose from, he picked up a rock and threw it against the glass closest to him. It hit with a *thunk,* then rolled back down the roof and to the ground. He waited, praying that he'd chosen the right one and Suzy would appear at the window. When a minute or more passed without a sign of her, he picked up another rock and threw it at the second window.

Another *thunk,* the rattle of stone striking against the shingles as the rock rolled down the roof sounding like a symphony of bass drums in the silence. A dog barked somewhere down the street, and Gil grabbed another rock, desperate to rouse Suzy before the dog woke the whole neighborhood.

Just as he wound up for another throw, a light went on in the room, and a shadow appeared behind the sheer drapes.

"Suzy?" he called, trying to keep his voice as low as possible, yet be heard.

Snatching back the drapes, she shoved up the window and stuck her head outside. "What are you doing here?" she whispered angrily. "Go away!" She ducked back inside and started to lower the window.

"Suzy!" he shouted. "Please," he begged. "We need to talk."

She pushed her head out the window. "No! Now get out of here before someone sees you."

A light went on in the house next door. Gladys Kravitz's house, Gil remembered...and began to smile. He waited a moment, listening, and choked back a laugh when he heard Suzy's phone ring.

Spying a tree growing close to the corner of the house, he jogged over to it, grabbed a limb and swung himself up. He climbed higher, until he found a limb that fanned out over the second story, then tightrope walked along it, leaping onto the roof when the branch began to bend beneath his weight.

He made his way carefully to the window and lifted it, relieved when he found she hadn't taken the time to lock it. Sitting down on the sill, he threw first one leg over, then the other.

She whirled to glare at him as he dropped down into her room, the phone pressed to her ear. "No, Mrs. Woodley," she said into the receiver. "You don't need to call the police. I'm fine. And I don't see anything out of the ordinary in my backyard."

She rolled her eyes. "Yes, I'm sure. In fact I'm looking out my window right now. It was probably that old tomcat of Mrs. Pruett's on the prowl." She pursed her lips, listening. "Yes, ma'am, I know her cat does his business in the flower pots on your porch. And yes, I really do think that Mrs. Pruett should be forced to control her pets."

Sending up a silent thanks for nosy neighbors, Gil crossed to Suzy and lifted her hair from her neck to nibble there.

She swatted at his head. "Listen, Mrs. Woodley," she said, her breath growing short as he skimmed his lips lower, "I'm going back to bed now. Why don't you do the same? Thanks for calling."

Gil took the receiver from her hand and replaced it on the base.

"Are you crazy?" she whispered angrily. "She might have called the police instead of me!"

Shifting in front of her, Gil slipped his hands beneath her hair, lifted it off her shoulders, then dropped it behind her back. "But she didn't." He bent his head to nibble on her neck again.

"She was going to," Suzy insisted, struggling to escape the pleasure of the feel of his lips against her skin. But she quickly discovered that he'd managed to trap her between himself and the bed and there was no escape left to her. "Gil! Stop it!"

He slid his hands down her arms and linked his hands behind her waist. Rubbing his groin against her middle, he smiled down at her. "Why? Mrs. Kravitz has gone back to bed. I heard you tell her to go there myself."

She pressed her hands against his chest and leaned back as far as she could, desperate to put distance between them. "Her name isn't Kravitz. It's Woodley."

"Okay. Then, Mrs. Woodley has gone back to bed." He bent his knees to peer out the window. "Yep," he said, smiling smugly as he straightened. "Her light's already out. We're all alone."

"We're *not* alone. And as long as you're governor, we'll *never* be alone." She gave his chest an angry shove. "Now get out of here."

Her push didn't budge him, but it did manage to wipe the smile off his face. Narrowing his eyes, he forced a knee between her thighs. "I'm not going anywhere until we talk this through."

Before he'd voiced the warning completely, Suzy found herself flat on her back on her bed and him stretched along her length, his face only inches from her own. "Now," he said, obviously pleased with himself. "As I said, we're going to have a little chat."

She turned her face away, as much to hide her tears

as to rebuke him. "I don't have anything to say to you."

"Fine. Then I'll do all the talking." He shifted to a more comfortable position. "I know you're upset about Skinner's article."

"Upset!" she cried. "I'm—"

He pressed a finger against her lips, silencing her. "Okay, maybe *upset* is too mild a word. You're mad. Furious. Outraged." He drew his finger away to catch a tear that had escaped and brought it to his tongue. The action made fresh tears surge to her eyes.

"And I don't blame you," he said softly, stroking her cheek. "Skinner was wrong to print what he did. Morally wrong, if not legally. But don't you see?" he said, his voice as well as his expression growing earnest. "Knuckling under to his pressure, and refusing to see me or talk to me, only gives him more power. He comes out the winner in this deal, not us. Ah, Suzy," he murmured, catching another tear that slipped from the corner of her eye. "I'd do anything to make this less painful. To spare you any embarrassment or humiliation. But I won't give you up. That's the one thing I can't do."

She gulped, trying to swallow back the emotion, the tears. "He'll win anyway. If I agree to see you, then he'll make the connection and he'll ruin you politically." Unable to hold back the tears any longer, she let them fall. "I don't want to cause you problems, Gil. I'd do anything to keep you from being hurt because of me."

He swept a hand across her cheek and leaned to

press his lips to hers. "Then stand beside me. We'll face them together and offer them the truth. If we rob them of the ammunition they might use against us by revealing it first, then we leave them powerless and with nothing left with which to hurt us." With a hand framed at her cheek, he slipped off her, then gathered her close to his side. "We can beat them at their own game, Suzy. Together we can beat them."

Suzy believed him. God help her, but she believed him and wanted to take that stand with him. But she couldn't. Not when this involved her mother, too. Not without first talking to her mother and preparing her for what might come.

"I need to talk to my mother first." She lifted her head to meet his gaze. "They'll drag her name into this along with ours. I won't do that to her. Not without discussing it with her first."

He drew her head back to his shoulder and pressed his lips against her hair. "Then talk to her. First thing in the morning. I'll go with you, if you want."

She closed her eyes and shook her head, already dreading the confrontation. "No. I need to do this alone."

Six

Suzy slept curled against Gil's side, not waking until he stirred just before dawn. Knowing that he had to leave before her neighbors started awakening, she rose with him, holding the front door open just wide enough for him to slip outside.

On the porch he turned back and touched a finger to his lips then to hers. The thoughtfulness in the gesture, the tenderness with which he then cupped his hand at her cheek and stroked a thumb beneath her eye, touched a place in her heart that had never been penetrated before.

"Call me," he whispered.

Then he was gone, leaping off her porch and jogging across the lawn to disappear into the darkness. She closed the door against the loss and turned her back to it, tears filling her eyes. She loved him, she realized, the pain like a fist twisting in her chest.

And, oh, God, how she hated to ask her mother to suffer the indignities that her loving him would surely demand.

Anxious to get the meeting with her mother behind her, she showered and dressed quickly, leaving her house just as her neighbors began to depart for work. Without any traffic to slow her, she made the trip to Elgin in less than twenty minutes. She parked her van in her mother's driveway and sank back in the seat, staring at the house they'd shared for thirteen years, before Suzy had left to strike out on her own.

Though early-morning sunlight washed over the small frame structure, staining the weathered wood a soft, warm gold, the house still managed to look shabby, abandoned, as lifeless as the woman who inhabited it.

As Suzy stared, her vision blurred by tears, she realized all that her mother had sacrificed when she'd divorced the reverend. Not only a husband and the love of her life, but a lifestyle that had provided her with a grand and elegantly decorated home in Dallas, designer clothes enough to fill a dozen closets and friends who dropped by at all hours of the day, competing for her attention.

And now she had this, Suzy reflected sadly. A rundown house in a rundown neighborhood. Clothes ordered from a discount catalogue, because she refused to go out shopping, fearing someone might recognize her if she dared. And no one to relieve the unrelenting passage of time, the loneliness that clung to the house like a shroud.

The reverend's infidelities and greed had stripped Sarah Swain of all she'd once held dear, including her emotional well-being.

And now Suzy was here to ask her to suffer it all again.

Suzy carefully timed telling her mother about Gil, knowing that anything unexpected or shocking might send her mother into an almost catatonic state. She greeted her mother in much the same way as she did at every visit. Pressing a kiss to her pale cheek with its paper-thin skin, asking about her health, her activities since their last visit. She waited until they were seated at the kitchen table, sharing a cup of tea before first broaching the subject of Gil.

"I've met someone, Mother."

"That's nice, dear."

Though her mother had responded, Suzy could tell by the way she continued to mindlessly move her spoon through her tea that she hadn't really heard what Suzy had said.

She laid her hand over her mother's, stopping her idle stirring. "Mother," she repeated, "I've met someone."

Sarah glanced up. "A man?"

Suzy nodded, her lips trembling in a smile. "Yes. A very nice man."

"You've never mentioned meeting anyone before. Is this serious?"

Suzy hesitated, unused to sharing her feelings, even with her own mother. "Yes. I think it is."

"Then you must bring him here. I'd like to meet the young man who's won my daughter's heart."

Tears filled Suzy's throat at the request, shamed by her earlier reluctance for Gil to meet her mother. She squeezed her mother's hand, saddened as always by the delicacy of the bone structure, the weakness in the fingers that had once held hers so tightly, so confidently, as together they'd skipped down the winding staircase in their home in Dallas. "I will, Mother. Soon. I promise."

They sat a moment in silence, Suzy watching her mother's face, while her mother stared at her tea, her mind already drifting to only God knew where.

"Mother?"

Sarah glanced up and blinked. "I'm sorry, dear. Were you saying something?"

"That I would bring the man I've met for a visit."

"Oh, yes. Do. I'll bake a cake."

Suzy wondered if tomorrow her mother would even remember that her daughter had been there for a visit, much less recall that she'd promised to bake a cake when Suzy returned with Gil. "Mother, there's something I need to ask you."

"All right, dear."

Suzy peered at her mother intently, as if in doing so she could will her mind to clear, to remain focused. "The man I've met is the governor of Texas."

Her mother stared at her a moment, then her jaw

slowly went slack. "The governor of Texas? Oh, my, Suzy, that's quite...impressive."

"Yes, it is," she said carefully. "But, Mother, you must understand that my seeing him will surely draw attention. Because of his position, people will want to know who I am. My background."

If possible her mother's face paled even more. "Oh, Suzy," she murmured, her voice quavering. "Must you tell them everything?"

Suzy tightened her grip on her mother's hand. "That's why I'm here. If left up to me, I'd tell them nothing. But there are those who won't accept me at face value. They'll dig into my past, and eventually they will find the connection. Right now, no one knows of my association with Gil. But for us to continue to see each other, I have to know that you're prepared for whatever might follow, because what affects me will affect you, as well."

Her mother stared at her, her face drawn, her lips trembling, looking years older and much more feeble than a woman of her age should. But when she spoke, it was with a clarity, a strength that Suzy hadn't witnessed in a long, long time.

"Do you love him?"

Tears filled Suzy's eyes. "Yes, I think I do."

"And does he love you?"

"I think so, though it's really too soon to say. We've known each other such a short time."

"Then we must do whatever is necessary for you to be with him." Smiling softly, she laid her hand over their joined hands and squeezed. "There is no greater gift we have to offer another than our love, and no greater responsibility than accepting love in return. Cherish it, honor it, but most importantly never dishonor the gift that is given to you. If you remember these things and practice them every day, happiness will be yours, no matter what trials may come your way."

Suzy reached for the receiver, then jerked back her hand, frowning at the phone as she wiped her damp palm down her thigh. He'd said to call him, she told herself for the third time. But making the call meant stepping out of the safe world she'd created for herself and into his, exposing herself to those who surrounded him and to the press. It meant swimming with him in the fishbowl in which he lived.

She snatched up the phone. "So you'll grow fins," she muttered as she quickly punched in the number he'd left a zillion times on her answering machine. A female voice answered on the first ring.

"Governor Riley's office."

She gulped, her fingers growing slick on the receiver. "May...may I speak with Governor Riley, please."

"I'm sorry. The governor is in a meeting. Would you like to leave a message?"

Suzy hesitated a moment, wondering what type of message to leave and how much information she dared reveal. All systems are go? Mother gave us her blessings?

In the end, she simply blurted, "Tell him Suzy called," and hung up.

Clutching a hand at her knotted stomach, she turned from the phone, then spun back to stare at it in surprise when it rang. Cautiously she picked up the receiver. "Hello?"

"Hi."

She pressed a hand over her heart, sagging as the warmth in the familiar drawl spilled through her.

"Suzy? Are you there?"

She snapped to attention. "Yes. I'm here." Then she sagged again, laughing. "I was just surprised to hear your voice. I called less than a minute ago, and your secretary said you were in a meeting."

"That's the standard line she delivers. A way to screen my calls. Have you talked to your mother?"

She heard the anxiousness in his voice and smiled at it. Hugging the phone to her ear, she sank down on the sofa and stretched out, pillowing her head on a cushion. "Yes."

"And?"

She laughed, delighted by the impatience she heard in his reply. "We have her blessings." The sigh of relief that passed through the phone wires made her wish she were close enough to hug him. "So what do we do now?"

"Besides making wild passionate love?"

She laughed again. "Yes, besides that."

"We begin."

Begin? Shivers chased down her spine at all the simple word represented. A beginning with Gil. The possibility of a future together. "When can I see you?" she asked, suddenly anxious to see him, to touch him.

"What are you doing right now?"

Startled, she glanced around. "Nothing. Just lying on the sofa."

"Are you dressed?"

"Well, yes," she said, then frowned. "Why?"

"Get undressed. I'm on my way."

She sat up, scraping back her hair. "But, Gil—" There was a click, then a dial tone. Pulling the phone from her ear, she stared at it, then sank back against the cushions, the receiver hugged between her breasts. And laughed.

Suzy sat in the middle of her bed with the covers gathered to her waist, watching as Gil dressed. "A press conference?" she repeated, suddenly feeling nauseous. "Today?"

"Yep." He buckled his belt, then sank down on the edge of the bed and reached for his boots. "I figure the longer we wait to make some kind of announcement, the more time we're giving Skinner to dig the information out on his own." He tugged on one boot and glanced over his shoulder to wink at her. "But don't worry. You don't have to be there."

She slumped forward, dropping her forehead against her knees. "Thank God."

He laughed and reached to ruffle her hair. "Chicken."

She lifted her head. "Cluck. Cluck."

Chuckling, he pulled on his other boot, then stood, stomping his feet to shake his pants down over the heels. "Okay, Chicken Little, I'll call you and let you know what time I'll be on." He braced a hand on the mattress and leaned across it to kiss her. He drew back and pressed a fingertip against her lips, his smile growing tender. "It's going to be okay, Suzy. I promise you. Everything's going to be okay."

"Six o'clock news."
Suzy clutched the phone tighter to her ear. "Tonight?"
"Yeah, tonight. I've got to go and get ready. Wish me luck."
"You know I do. And, Gil," she added before he could hang up.
"Yes?"
She hesitated a moment, wanting desperately to tell him that she loved him. Instead she whispered, "Thank you," and replaced the receiver.
After hanging up, she looked at the clock, then around her kitchen, knowing that she'd go crazy if she had to stay in her house all afternoon, waiting for the press conference to air. On sudden inspiration she raced for the stairs and to her room, then out of her house, slinging a tote bag over her shoulder.
Two hours later she stepped back and critically eyed her work. "Well, what do you think?"
Her gaze on the hand mirror Suzy had given her, Celia stared at her reflection, "Is that really me?" was all she could manage.

Suzy laughed. "Well, of course it's you, silly. With a few enhancements, of course."

Celia touched a tentative hand to the shoulder-length wig Suzy had brought her, then ran a fingertip across her eyebrow, admiring the gold sparkles that glittered on the lid beneath it. She turned to look at Suzy, her smile radiant. "Wow. I look really cool."

Suzy rolled the cart out of the way and sat down on the edge of the bed. "Better than cool. You look positively outrageous."

"Think Gil will like my new look?"

Suzy wrinkled her nose and shook her head. "Probably not. He claims to like his women natural."

Celia glanced back at her reflection in the mirror, the excitement melting from her face. "Not when natural looks like a creature from a sci-fi movie."

Unable to bear the sadness in the girl's voice, Suzy scooted to sit beside her and slipped an arm around her shoulders. "There's nothing wrong with the way you look."

"Yeah," Celia replied miserably. "All the guys go for bald-headed girls."

"I don't know," Suzy replied. "A shaved head sure didn't hurt Demi Moore's looks *or* her popularity with the men."

Celia gave herself a closer inspection, then set aside the mirror and sank back against the pillow beside Suzy with a smile. "You're right. Bald *is* beautiful." She dug an elbow into Suzy's ribs. "Who knows? I might even make the cover of *Vogue*."

Laughing, Suzy hugged Celia to her side, then

glanced at the television where the news played on the screen, minus the accompanying sound. She quickly reached for the controls and turned up the volume. "It's time," she said, and reached for Celia's hand. "The news conference is about to start."

Celia squeezed her fingers around Suzy's, watching with her as Gil walked out the front door of the governor's mansion and crossed the porch, stopping before a podium lined with microphones.

"God, he's gorgeous," Suzy whispered. "And would you look at him? He's so calm!"

"Shh," Celia shushed. "I can't hear what he's saying."

Catching her lower lip between her teeth, Suzy forced herself to concentrate on Gil's voice and not on his face and her own stretched nerves.

"...elected by the people of this great state to fulfill the duties of governor. That is, and will continue to be, my focus until my term of office has ended.

"While campaigning for this position, I had the opportunity to meet many of you in person. Others I've spoken with on the phone or communicated with by letter. The man you met and conversed with, the man you elected as your governor, is just that. A man. A man with the same hopes and dreams shared by many of you. A man with the same rights guaranteed to each of you by the constitution of the United States. Among those is the right to life, liberty and the pursuit of happiness."

Firming his lips, he closed his hands around the sides of the podium. "Well, last week my rights were challenged. An article appeared in the newspaper, which I felt was inflammatory, unnecessary and certainly unkind to the parties involved." He lifted a hand as if to stave off an argument. "Now I know that our constitution also guarantees freedom of speech and press. But was that freedom written and fought for to hurt people? To allow one person to raise doubts about another person's character? To skew the facts for the sole purpose of entertainment?"

Shaking his head, he dropped his hands from the sides of the podium. "I don't think they were. I believe they were established to protect *all* people, not as a shield for a few to hide behind while they hurl accusations at the innocent. The constitution protects everyone. Elected officials, movie stars, singers, professional athletes. Everyone," he repeated, and brought his fist down on the podium for emphasis.

"I do not believe that these rights give public figures permission to behave improperly. But they do entitle them to a life separate from their chosen career. A normal life that allows them to make a few mistakes, to do things without having to worry about the rest of the world seeing it reported on television or reading about it in the newspaper the next day."

He paused, and a smile tugged at one corner of his mouth, as if he were amused by some private joke. When he spoke again, his voice was softer, a little sheepish. "I think most of you are aware that I'm single. And not for the reasons you might have heard or read," he added, arching a brow. "I'm single because I've never met a woman I'd consider spending the rest of my life with.'' He inhaled deeply, then shook his head as he released the breath. "At least, I hadn't until recently."

Suzy gasped, her fingers gripping Celia's.

"But I've met someone," he continued, unaware that Suzy's heart was threatening to pound right out of her chest. "Someone whom I truly enjoy being with. Someone with whom I'd like to spend *more* time. She owns a local catering business here in Austin. Her name is Suzy Crane. Or at least that's the name she's gone by since she was about six. Prior to that time, her last name was Swain. Her father is the Reverend Bobby Swain."

He paused again, as if to give the listeners a chance to absorb the importance of that name.

"For those of you who might not be familiar with Reverend Swain, he was a television evangelist who was involved in a scandal about twenty years ago that was widely reported by the media. Before it was over, the reverend's wife divorced him, changed her name and moved with their daughter to another town, in hopes of protecting her child from any more unsavory press. After a while the public forgot about the scandal...or they did until the reverend was indicted nine years later for misappropriating his ministry's funds. Then it started all over again. But the media wasn't satisfied with reporting the reverend's current misdeeds. No, they had to dig up the old scandal, as well. And although Suzy and her mother were no longer involved with the reverend, hadn't had any contact with him since the divorce, their names were dragged through the mud a second time, right along with the reverend's."

He gripped his hands on the podium and looked directly into the camera, and seemingly into the eyes and hearts of every viewer. "Now I ask you. Was that necessary? Was it even fair? Was it respecting those two ladies' right to life, liberty and the pursuit of happiness?" He lifted his hands from the podium and into the air. "Well, of course it wasn't. Simply by association, they were tried and convicted right along with him, their lives torn apart a second time. Wounds that had taken years to heal were ripped open and exposed for the world to gawk at and whisper about. Memories best forgotten were splashed across the front page of every newspaper in the country and headlined every television news program to haunt them again."

He firmed his lips. "I don't want that to happen a third time. I don't want to see Suzy's and her mother's names dragged through the dirt. But because of my position and my involvement with her, I'm afraid that's exactly what will happen. And that's why I'm here this evening, telling you all this, bearing my soul as well as Suzy's. I want you to hear it from me, from us, before you read about it in the newspaper or hear it on the news. Before the truth becomes so twisted you can't distinguish fact from speculation."

He began to slowly gather his notes. "From the cradle my parents taught me never to judge a person unless I'd first walked in their shoes. They taught me, too, that a person's appearance can be deceiving, that

I needed to look beyond the clothes they wore or the color of their skin and judge them by their actions, the size of their heart."

He slipped his notes into his breast pocket, then braced his hands onto the lectern and looked directly into the camera again. "And that's what I hope each of you will do. I hope you'll weigh carefully what you read or hear on television. Take the time to weigh the evidence and make decisions for yourself and not let others make them for you. And I hope, too, that from this point forward you'll demand honesty from the media, a return to integrity in reporting the news. Perhaps even compassion. There's a lot of good that goes on this world of ours, much of it unreported. Please don't allow anyone to force feed you only the bad. Demand the good and watch it grow." He stepped back from the podium and lifted a hand in farewell. "Thank you for your time. Good night."

The program cut to a commercial, but Suzy continued to stare at the screen, transfixed. "Oh, my gosh," she murmured, drawing a hand to her heart. "He was wonderful. Absolutely wonderful." She twisted her head around to look at Celia. "Didn't you think he was great?"

The makeup Suzy had applied to Celia's face was running in rivulets down the young girl's cheeks. "The best. Oh, Suzy," she said, and flung her arms around Suzy's neck. "You're so lucky to have a man like Gil to love you."

Suzy wrapped her arms around Celia and turned her gaze to the screen where the news program had resumed, blinking back tears. "Yeah, I know."

Seven

After she returned home from the hospital, Suzy's phone rang off the wall. It seemed everyone she knew—and some she didn't—had seen Gil's press conference and called to offer their support and congratulations. Between calls, she managed to place one to her mother

"Mother? It's Suzy. Did you watch the press conference?"

"Yes, dear. David and I watched it together."

"David?" Suzy repeated, tensing. "David who?"

"Well, I don't recall his last name. Just a minute and I'll ask."

"Mother, wait!" Suzy cried, wondering if her mother was hallucinating or if she did in fact have a total stranger in her house. But it was too late. She could already hear her mother calling to someone in the other room.

"Langerhan," her mother replied, returning to the phone. "David Langerhan. It was so nice of Gil to send him over to watch the program with me."

"Gil sent him?" Suzy repeated, her concerns in no way appeased.

"Yes. He was afraid that after the news conference aired the press might attempt to contact me, so he sent one of his men over. It really wasn't necessary," her mother added, lowering her voice, "though I have enjoyed his company."

Suzy couldn't decide whether she should jump into her van and race to her mother's house or call the police. Trying to think rationally, she asked, "Could I speak with David, please?"

"Certainly, dear." She heard her mother cover the mouthpiece with her hand, then her muffled voice as she called the mysterious David to the phone.

There was a rustle of movement as the phone changed hands, then a male voice. "Hi, Suzy."

She all but wilted onto the sofa. "Dave," she said in relief, recognizing the voice of Gil's bodyguard. "I'm sorry. I didn't realize it was you with Mother. When she said she'd watched the press conference with David, I thought—" She laughed weakly. "Never mind what I thought. Is Mother all right?"

"Best I can tell. No one has called or come by, which is a good sign, I'd think."

"Yes. That is a good sign. How long do you plan to stay?"

"As long as she wants me. Those were Gil's instructions."

"If you need to leave, I can come and stay with her."

"No need. I've got things covered here. In fact, I really need to go. It's my turn at Scrabble."

Suzy's eyebrows shot up. "You're playing Scrabble with my mother?"

"Yeah," he replied, and sighed heavily. "And she's beating my socks off. Is there such a word as mbira?"

Suzy laughed. "I haven't the faintest idea. Why don't you challenge her and see for yourself?"

"Already missed two turns doing that. Listen, I gotta go. The longer I take for my turn, the more time I'm giving her to come up with another word to stump me."

"Go on and play then," she said, laughing. "Tell mother I'll talk to her later."

As she replaced the phone, there was a knock at her door. Praying it wasn't the press, she tiptoed to the door and peered through the peephole. Seeing Gil on her front porch, she threw the door wide. She was in his arms before he had time to brace himself.

Knocked off balance, he staggered back a step, wrapping his arms around her to steady them both. "Hey. What's this all about?"

With her arms linked behind his neck, she smiled at him. "You are undoubtedly the sweetest, most thoughtful man I've ever known."

Chuckling, he lifted her higher on his chest and

walked them both inside the house, kicking the door closed behind them. "And how did you come to that conclusion?"

"I just talked to Mother. And Dave," she added. "I was so wrapped up in myself, I didn't even think about her watching the program alone. But you did," she said and drew his face down to hers. "And that was so, so sweet," she whispered against his lips.

Moaning, he tightened his arms around her and backed toward the sofa. When his legs bumped the cushions, he dropped down and shifted her across his lap. He slowly withdrew his mouth from hers and wound a stray lock of hair behind her ear. "I have a confession," he admitted reluctantly. "It wasn't my idea."

Puzzled, Suzy sat back. "Whose was it?"

"Dave's. He asked me if your mother lived alone, and when I told him she did, he offered to drive over and sit with her."

"Well then, Dave's sweet. But so are you," she insisted. and hugged him. "I can't remember ever hearing a more moving speech. You were wonderful. Celia thought so, too."

Bracing his hands at her waist, he pushed back to look at her. "Celia? You were at the hospital?"

Embarrassed by her cowardice to watch the program alone, she wrinkled her nose. "Yeah. I knew I'd go stir-crazy if I stayed here all afternoon, so I went to visit Celia and watch the press conference with her."

"How was she?"

She lifted a shoulder and fussed with the knot of his tie, avoiding his gaze. "About the same, I guess. We played beauty shop. I loaned her one of my wigs and did her makeup for her."

"The red one you wore to the dedication?"

"No. Blond. Her coloring is all wrong for a redhead."

Gil bumped his nose against hers. "And you think I'm sweet? You're the sweet one."

Suzy melted against his chest. "Want to fight about it?"

"No way."

A buzzing sound had them drawing apart again. Suzy frowned as Gil slipped a hand into his jacket. He withdrew his cell phone with an apologetic smile. "Sorry. I had it set to vibrate, instead of ring." He pressed a button and lifted the phone to his ear. "Gil."

He listened a moment, his gaze on Suzy. "I would've called first, but there just wasn't time." He waited, then said patiently, "Yes, Mom, I know it must have come as a surprise to you. But it couldn't be helped." A smile spread across his face. "I'm with her now." Another pause, then, "Sure. We can be there in an hour." Pulling the phone from his ear, he disconnected the call.

Suzy eased back on his lap. "We can be where?"

"At my parents'. They want to meet you."

She leaped to her feet. "Your parents!" she cried. "But I can't meet them now."

Gil stood. "Why not?"

"Because it's late and it would take me hours to get ready, that's why."

"You're fine just as you are."

"But look at me!" she cried, holding out her arms so that he could get a good look at the faded jeans and baggy denim shirt she'd worn to the hospital. "I can't meet your parents dressed like this!"

Chuckling, he slipped his arms around her waist and drew her to him. "My parents will like you no matter what you're wearing."

And he'd been right. His parents had seemed to like her. And Suzy had liked them. They were both as down-to-earth and unassuming as their son. Within minutes of her and Gil's arrival, his parents had put her at ease, their friendliness and warmth quickly dispelling all her uncertainties about meeting them.

"I just hope this meeting goes as well," she murmured to her reflection the following morning, as she checked her appearance one last time in her compact mirror. She plucked at the collar of her oversize cream silk blouse, then smoothed a hand down the side of the black leather skirt she'd selected to wear to the brunch, praying that the outfit was suitable. Though she'd spent more than half her life trying to dress like anyone other than a preacher's kid, today she'd have given almost anything to have something more sedate to wear.

With a resigned sigh she replaced her compact and opened the door.

The woman behind the desk glanced up, then rose,

smiling as she extended a hand in greeting. "You must be Suzy. I'm Mary, Gil's secretary. It's so nice to finally meet you. I've heard so much about you."

Suzy shook her hand. "Thank you...I think."

Mary laughed easily. "It was all nice, I assure you."

Suzy blew a breath up at her bangs. "Whew. That's a relief."

"Gil has some gentlemen in his office. Can I get you a cup of coffee or a soft drink while you wait?"

"Coffee, if you don't mind," Suzy replied, hoping the caffeine would steady her nerves.

Mary hurried for the door. "I'll be just a minute. Make yourself at home," she said, gesturing toward a grouping of chairs.

Too nervous to sit, Suzy prowled the office, stopping before a coffee table to flip through the magazines scattered across its top.

"Dang it," she muttered as some slipped to the floor. She stooped to pick up the periodicals, started to replace them, but froze when her gaze fell on the headline of the newspaper the dropped magazines had exposed: The Governor's Favorite Dish. The words swirled before her eyes, while her stomach churned sickly as she stared at the accompanying photo someone had secretly snapped of her and Gil standing beside her van the night they'd first met.

The sound of voices carried from Gil's office, and she quickly dropped the magazines over the newsprint, covering the hideous headline. Sure that the men with him were there to discuss the newspaper's most recent attack on Gil, she glanced toward the door, straining to hear as it opened.

"I'm warning you, Gil," she overheard a man say, his voice raised in anger. "You're making a big mistake. Whether or not what the press is saying about this woman is true doesn't matter. She'll poison your career. Mark my word. You'll lose every bit of support you've managed to get, because of her."

The blood draining from her face, Suzy took a step back, sickened even more by what she'd overheard.

"Now wait just a damn minute, Henry," she heard Gil say.

The door slammed shut, obviously closed by Gil to block the man's departure, and Suzy couldn't hear any more of the conversation. But she didn't need to hear any more. She whirled for the door to the hallway, desperate to escape before she was seen.

Just as she reached for the knob, the door opened and Mary breezed in, bobbling the cup of steaming coffee when she bumped into Suzy.

"Oh, my goodness," she said in dismay, and darted around Suzy to set the cup on the desk. She snatched a tissue from a container and dabbed at the hot coffee that had splashed onto her sleeve. "I didn't spill any on you, did I?" she asked, glancing Suzy's way in concern.

Suzy shook her head. "No. No, you didn't."

Mary tilted her head, her brows drawing together. "Are you all right? You look so pale."

"Actually," Suzy said, pressing a trembling hand to her forehead. "I do feel rather ill. Would you mind telling Gil that I had to leave? And tell him…tell him that I'm sorry.''

Suzy lay on her bed with a washcloth pressed to her forehead and the drapes drawn to block out the sunlight. She welcomed the dark. Needed it to hide in.

Feeling the tears coming again, she rolled to her side and dragged the washcloth down to cover her mouth, trying to force back the regret. She'd known this would happen. She'd tried to warn Gil that he would be hurt if he insisted upon continuing their relationship.

The telephone rang, but she ignored it, just as she had each time it had rung since she'd returned home from the governor's mansion more than two hours before.

Clutching the cloth to her mouth, she let the tears fall, knowing that she couldn't see or talk to him again. For his own good, she'd end this once and for all.

With meetings scheduled back-to-back all day, Gil could do nothing but dial Suzy's number in between sessions and listen to it ring. He considered sending Mary over to check on her, but decided against it, fearing her presence would make Suzy feel uncomfortable, since she didn't know his secretary. He racked his brain, trying to think of a friend Suzy had mentioned whom he might call, and suddenly remembered her visiting with Erik Thompson's wife at the dedication.

Flipping open his Rolodex, he looked up Erik's number and punched it in. He breathed a sigh of relief when Penny answered after the first ring.

"Hi, Penny. Gil Riley. Listen, I need a favor. Suzy was here earlier, but had to leave unexpectedly because she became ill."

"Oh, dear," Penny said in concern. "What's wrong with her?"

Gil dragged a hand over his already-mussed hair. "I don't know. I've called several times to check on her but only get her answering machine. I'd drive over, but I'm stuck in meetings all day."

"I'll go," Penny offered. "Do you want me to call you and let you know how she's doing?"

Relieved, Gil sank back in his chair. "Would you? I'd sure appreciate it."

"Suzy?"

At the sound of Penny's voice, Suzy groaned and dragged the pillow over her head.

"Suzy! Are you up here?"

Regretting having given Penny a key to her house, Suzy shoved the pillow away, knowing her friend wouldn't leave until she responded. "I'm in my bedroom!" she shouted.

Penny appeared in the doorway. "Are you sick?" she asked hesitantly.

Suzy pulled the pillow across her stomach and hugged it to her. "Yeah. Sorta."

"Gosh. It's dark in here. Mind if I turn on the light?"

Suzy pushed out a hand. "No. Please don't. My head is killing me."

Penny eased closer to the bed. "Can I get you anything?"

"No. I'll be fine."

Pursing her lips at Suzy's stubbornness, Penny headed for the bathroom. "I bet an aspirin would make you feel better."

"Really, Penny. I don't need—" Suzy dropped her head to the mattress in frustration as Penny disappeared beyond the bathroom door.

"Gil called," Penny said from the other room. "He's worried about you."

Suzy set her jaw, determined not to cry. "There's nothing to worry about. I told you, I'm fine."

"Good heavens, Suzy," Penny fussed. "You've got enough toothpaste in here to keep a small town supplied for a year."

"Quit digging through my drawers," Suzy grumped irritably.

"I'm not digging. I'm looking for the aspirin."

"It's in the medicine cabinet on the wall. Right next to my birth control pills." Muttering under her breath, Suzy punched a pillow up beneath her head and settled back to wait, resigned to being coddled.

"Suzy?"

"What?"

"Have you quit taking your birth control pills?"

Suzy pushed up, bracing herself on her hands as

Penny returned from the bathroom. "Of course not. Why?"

Penny reached to switch on the lamp, murmured "sorry" when Suzy threw up a hand to cover her eyes, then sat down on the side of the bed and held open the container. "We've always been on the same cycle, but your dispenser still has pills in it, and I finished mine almost a week ago."

Her blood chilling, Suzy snatched the container from Penny's hand to examine it herself. "Are you sure?"

"I'm positive. I'm very careful about taking my pills. Erik and I want to wait at least another year before we start our family."

Suzy rubbed her temple, trying to remember. "I know I took one this morning. And yesterday, too." She dropped her hand, remembering. "But I didn't take any when I was at the ranch with Gil," she said, lifting her head to look at Penny, her face pale. "I didn't have them with me."

"You only missed taking two?"

Suzy glanced down at the dispenser realizing she should have started her period by now. "No. Three. I didn't take one the following Monday, either."

"Why not?"

Suzy curled her fingers around the container. "Because I forgot," she snapped. "Okay?"

Penny dropped her gaze, and Suzy immediately regretted the sharp words. She tossed the container aside and caught her friend's hand. "I'm sorry, Pen.

I didn't mean to take it out on you. It's just been a really rotten day."

Penny smiled in understanding and squeezed her hand. "Probably made worse because you don't feel well."

It was Suzy's turn to drop her gaze. "I'm not really sick," she mumbled. "I just used that as an excuse to leave the mansion."

Penny's jaw sagged. "You mean you lied to Gil?"

Suzy nodded slowly.

Penny snatched her hand from hers. "You ought to be ashamed of yourself," she scolded. "He's been worried sick about you."

Suzy firmed her lips, knowing she'd done the right thing. "It couldn't be helped."

"Well, of course it could," Penny argued. "You could have just told him the truth if you didn't want to attend the brunch with him."

Suzy shook her head, the tears starting all over again. "No, I couldn't. Not without telling him what I overheard."

Penny leaned closer. "What did you overhear?"

Suzy caught up the edge of the sheet and dabbed at her eyes. "When I got there, there were some men in Gil's office, and I heard one of them shouting. He said that I was poison. That if Gil continued to see me, Gil would lose all his support for the legislation he wants to see passed."

"That's simply not true!" Penny argued. "There's no way you could harm Gil's effectiveness. Not after that press conference he held last night."

"But I already have! Didn't you see the headline in this morning's paper?"

"Well, no. I didn't have time to read the paper."

"'The Governor's Favorite Dish,'" Suzy quoted bitterly. "Big, bold type right on the front page. And the people I was to have brunch with are his *supporters,* his friends, the people who are supposed to be on his side. If even one of them questions Gil's effectiveness because of me, then I've done exactly what that man accused me of doing. I've poisoned his career." Dragging a hand across her wet cheek, she shook her head. "I've got to end this before any real harm is done."

"Oh, Suzy," Penny murmured worriedly. "Talk to Gil first. Tell him what you overheard. There's always the chance that you misinterpreted what the man said, or perhaps even what he was talking about."

"No," Suzy said, shaking her head. "I didn't misinterpret anything. I heard every word clear as a bell."

"Talk to him anyway," Penny urged. "Give him a choice in the decision. After all, you aren't in this alone."

Suzy dropped her gaze to the dispenser of birth control pills again and her stomach took another nauseating turn. "Penny, do you think it's possible to get pregnant if you forget to take a couple of pills?"

Penny's forehead creased in concern. "I don't know. Maybe."

Drawing in a long breath, Suzy slowly forced it out, then glanced up at Penny. "Would you mind going to the drugstore for me and buying one of those home pregnancy kits?''

Though Suzy loved Penny dearly, she sent her friend home after Penny had returned with the pregnancy test. What she had to do was private. Personal. The results a secret that must be guarded more closely than any of the others Suzy had kept through the years. And though Suzy trusted Penny implicitly, she didn't want to burden her friend with yet another secret of hers to protect.

Thus, Suzy was alone when she learned the results of the test. Sitting on the closed toilet seat, she stared at the colored strip through a blur of tears.

I can't be, she told herself, gulping. After missing only a few days' medication? Surely a few measly pills couldn't affect the drug's ability to prevent a pregnancy?

But the evidence was there before her eyes. Whether the fault was placed on three missed pills or Suzy was simply a statistic, one of the minuscule percentage of women who became pregnant while taking birth control pills, the fact was she was going to have a baby.

And Governor Gil Riley was going to be a father.

Groaning, she dropped her forehead to the arm she'd braced along the edge of the sink. And she'd worried that the scandal surrounding her father would ruin Gil's career. Ha! That was nothing compared to the battering Gil's good name would take when news hit the streets that the governor had fathered a baby out of wedlock.

Slowly she raised her head. But they can't find out, she told herself. If anyone learned of this, Gil would be ruined!

She gripped her hands on the edge of the sink and pulled herself shakily to her feet. But no one knows, she reminded herself. No one but me. Lifting her head, she stared at her reflection in the mirror. And no one will ever know, she promised herself.

Penny's phone call, telling Gil that Suzy was fine, that she'd just suffered a small bout with an upset stomach, did little to reassure Gil. Especially when Suzy continued to allow her machine to pick up his phone calls. Frustrated and more than a little worried, he drove to her house once he'd completed his duties later that evening.

When he didn't get an answer to his knock at her front door, he headed around to the back and was surprised to see that her van was missing from the driveway. With his hand lifted to knock on the kitchen door, he heard someone call his name. Turning, he frowned, seeing no one.

"Governor? Is that you?"

He squinted his eyes against the darkness to peer at the dark ivy-draped fence that separated Suzy's drive from the house next door, where he was sure the voice had come. "Yes. Who's there?"

"It's me, Mrs. Woodley, Suzy's neighbor."

Shaking his head at the woman's nosiness, Gil

hopped down from the porch and crossed the drive. "Hello, Mrs. Woodley."

"I saw your press conference on television last night and I was so surprised to discover that you're dating my Suzy. We're very close," she added. "Why, she's just like a daughter to me."

Biting back a smile, Gil nodded, sure that Suzy would deny that relationship. "I'm sure that you are."

"Are you here to see her?" she asked.

"Yes, ma'am. But it doesn't appear that she's home."

"Oh, she isn't," the ever watchful Mrs. Woodley informed him. "She left over an hour ago. Watched her load her van from my bedroom window."

Gil frowned. "Load her van? I wasn't aware that she had an event to cater tonight."

"I don't believe she did. At least, I didn't see her load any trays of food or dishware into her van. Just suitcases."

Gil's frown deepened. "Suitcases?"

"Yes. Several. Must be going on a trip, because she even put the garbage out before she left, and pickup isn't for another two days." There was a short pause, then the woman added, sounding offended, "She usually lets me know when she's going to be away. Always asks me to keep an eye on her place for her. That's what neighbors are for, you know. We look out for each other."

"Yes, I'm sure you do," Gil replied vaguely, then asked, "Mrs. Woodley, could I ask a favor of you?"

"Why, yes, Governor," she replied, perking up. "I'd be honored."

"When Suzy returns, would you call me?" He slipped a card in the slit between two pickets. "The number to my cell phone is on this card."

Suzy sat at her mother's kitchen table, clasping her mother's hand in hers. "I know, Mother," she said. "I'll miss you, too, but it won't be for long. As soon as I get settled, you can come for a visit."

"Oh, I don't know, dear," her mother said uneasily. "I really don't like to travel, you know."

"But Dallas isn't that far. And if you don't want to drive, you could always take the bus."

"We'll see," her mother said vaguely, then tilted her head, tears welling up in her eyes as she looked at Suzy. "Are you sure you're doing the right thing? Shouldn't you talk to Gil about this first?"

Suzy dropped her mother's hand and rose to pace away. "I can't tell him about this, Mother. He would want to get married, and I won't let him ruin his life that way."

"Ruin?" her mother queried. "Marriage is meant to enhance lives, not ruin them."

Suzy whirled, her eyes blazing. "The way your life was enhanced by your marriage to the reverend?" Seeing her mother's stricken face, Suzy immediately regretted the unkind words. She went to her and dropped down on a knee, gathering her mother's hand in hers. "I'm sorry. That was mean and uncalled for."

"No," her mother said quietly. "You spoke the

truth. What was in your heart.'' She clasped Suzy's hand between hers. ''But don't make the mistake of judging all marriages by your father's and mine. Give Gil a chance, Suzy. And give yourself a chance at happiness.''

Eight

Gil didn't bother to call first before heading to Elgin and Suzy's mother's house. He figured if Suzy discovered he was on his way, she would just run again. He knew the trip might well be a waste of his time, but it was the only place left he knew to look for her.

Due to the lateness of the hour, traffic on the highway was light. With each set of headlights that appeared in the opposite lane, he watched the passing vehicle to make sure it wasn't Suzy on her way back to Austin.

As he drove, the same question played over and over through his mind. *Why?* What had happened to make her run this time? Though he racked his brain for an explanation for her sudden disappearance, the only answer he could come up with was that the headline in the morning paper had upset her.

But surely Suzy hadn't expected the media's harassment to end with the press conference? He'd known that some type of retaliation would follow his public address and thought she would, too.

A set of headlights appeared in the opposing lane and Gil narrowed his eyes, watching its fast approach. As the vehicle whisked past, Gil recognized the van as Suzy's. He stomped on the brakes and whipped the steering wheel to the left, spinning his truck around in the opposite direction. He pressed the accelerator to the floorboard and shot his truck across the grass median and onto the highway in pursuit.

Gaining on her, he flashed his headlights, signaling for her to stop. "Come on, Suzy," he muttered under his breath. "Pull over."

A set of headlights appeared behind Gil, seeming to come out of nowhere. He glanced at his rearview mirror and swore when he saw that it was a patrol car behind him. The deck of red lights on the car's roof flashed and a siren bleeped, signaling him to pull over. But Gil wasn't about to give up the chase and take a chance on losing Suzy again. Instead, he sped up and swerved into the fast lane. He pulled up alongside the van and glanced over. Their eyes met for only a brief second, but long enough for Gil to see the desperation, the fear, before she looked away and sped up.

Swearing under his breath, he took another glimpse in the rearview mirror and saw that the patrol car had followed him into the fast lane. In hopes of using the patrol car to block Suzy in, he pressed his foot down on the accelerator and shot past the van, swerving over into the lane in front of it. Slowly he eased on the brakes. With the patrol car on her left and the bar ditch on her right, she had no choice but to match her speed to his. He came to a complete stop, quickly jumped out and ran back to the van, which had stopped directly behind him. He yanked open the door.

"What the hell is wrong with you?" he shouted furiously. "Why didn't you stop when you saw me?"

Her face red with fury, Suzy reached for the door. "Because I don't want to see you. That's why."

Gil slammed a hand against the door, keeping her from shutting it, then moved into the space and grabbed her arm. "What's going on, Suzy? What's wrong?"

"Hold it right there, mister!"

Having forgotten about the highway patrolman, Gil groaned in frustration. "It's all right, officer. I was just trying to stop this lady."

"Please help me, officer," Suzy begged. "This man tried to run me off the road."

Gil slapped a hand against the side of the van in anger. "Damn it, Suzy! What are you trying to do? Get me arrested?"

He heard a pistol cock behind him.

"Put your hands on the side of the van and spread 'em."

"If you'll give me a minute," Gil said in frustration, "I can explain everything." Turning, he reached for his wallet in his hip pocket, intending to offer the patrolman his driver's license. But before he touched a finger to his wallet, a hand clamped down on his shoulder, and he was shoved roughly face-first against the side of the van.

"Now spread 'em," the patrolman ordered. "Are you all right, miss?" he asked Suzy as he jerked one of Gil's hands down and held it behind his back to slap a handcuff around his wrist.

"Yes. I'm fine," she replied, her voice quavering. "But I'd like to go, if that's all right."

"You don't want to press charges?"

"No. I just want to leave."

"Then go on. I'll see that he doesn't cause you any more trouble."

"Suzy!" Gil shouted as the officer clipped the second cuff into place, the sound echoing the van door slamming. The officer pulled him clear of the van and Suzy reversed quickly, then drove away, swinging over onto the shoulder to avoid hitting Gil's truck.

Furious with both Suzy and the patrolman, Gil tried to jerk free from the officer's grip. "The handcuffs aren't necessary," he growled. "I'm Governor Gil Riley."

"Yeah," the officer jeered as he shoved Gil toward the patrol car. "And I'm Bill Clinton. Get in," he ordered as he opened the rear door. "You and me are going for a little ride."

By the time Gil finished explaining that he wasn't trying to run Suzy off the road, but was only trying to stop her, and had provided those at the station with enough identification to prove that he really *was* the governor of Texas, as he'd claimed, Suzy was long gone.

But by that time Gil really didn't much want to see her, anyway. He was afraid if he did get within arm's reach of her, he might be tempted to wring her pretty neck. So instead of resuming his search, he drove back to Austin and to the governor's mansion and crawled wearily into bed.

Six hours later he was sitting at his breakfast table opposite his bodyguard and blowing on his coffee, while scanning the front page of the newspaper.

There were at least three different sidebars directing readers to stories in other sections, where details of the late-night car chase and his subsequent arrest were recorded. But not one of the articles mentioned a word about the charges against Gil being dropped or the patrolman's apology to Gil for the rough treatment he'd received and for not recognizing him right off.

No, instead the reporters had focused on the negative and the sensational, going into lengthy detail about how the governor was caught speeding in the middle of the night while trying to run his girlfriend off the road, following what appeared to be a domestic dispute between the two. They included reports of the highspeed police chase that ensued and painted a dramatic word picture of the patrolman overpowering Gil in order to handcuff him.

After reading all the articles, Gil tossed the paper aside in disgust. "If you take out all the speculation and hearsay," he told Dave angrily, "there wouldn't be enough copy left to fill three lines of print."

"Seldom is," Dave murmured, continuing to frown over the crossword puzzle he was working on.

Gil rose to refill his cup with coffee. "Making me out to be some kind of outlaw," he grumbled irritably. "You'd think they'd have better things to write about than what's going on in my personal life."

"I don't know, Governor. Lately your personal life's gotten pretty interesting."

Gil whipped his head around to light into Dave, but saw his bodyguard's crooked smile and snorted a laugh, his anger dissipating. "Yeah. I guess it has at that."

Dave set aside his puzzle. "A call came in earlier this morning from some lady." He pulled a slip of paper from his shirt pocket. "Gladys Woodley," he verified, then slipped the note back into his pocket. "Said she was Suzy's neighbor and you'd given her this number to call."

"I told her to call my *cell* phone," Gil said in frustration. "Not the mansion line. Did she say that she'd seen Suzy?"

"No. If she had, I would've roused you. But she did mention seeing someone snooping around Suzy's house this morning just before daylight."

Gil frowned as he sat back down at the table opposite Dave. "Did you check it out?"

"Yeah. But whoever was there was gone by the

time we arrived. There wasn't a sign of an attempted break-in. All they took was her garbage."

"Her garbage?"

"Yeah. It's an old trick, used mostly by stalkers and burglars to gain information about the inhabitants of a residence. You'd be surprised what kind of information is revealed in the stuff a person throws out."

Gil frowned in puzzlement. "Suzy never mentioned anything about anyone stalking her."

"If anyone was, she probably was never aware." Dave took a sip of his coffee. "Are you going to try to find her?"

Gil sank back in his chair, scowling. "I wouldn't know where to begin to look. I've already spoken with her mother. If she knows anything, she isn't talking. Same with her friend Penny."

Dave lifted a brow. "You do realize that you have other methods available to you?"

Gil shook his head. "I won't use the power of my office to track her down." His scowl deepened. "Besides, I'd be a fool to try to find her when she's made it more than clear that she doesn't want to see me again. As far as I'm concerned, it's over."

"How long do you plan to stay?"

Suzy lifted a shoulder at her friend Jon's question as she chopped vegetables alongside him in the kitchen of his Dallas-based restaurant. "A couple of months, maybe. I don't know. I just need a place to lay low for a while."

He angled his head to peer at her suspiciously. "Are you sure you aren't wanted by the law?"

A wan smile curved her lips. "No. It's nothing like that."

Shaking his head, Jon resumed his cutting. "The governor," he said, then snorted a laugh. "Imagine you hooked up with the governor of Texas."

"I'm not hooked up with him," Suzy replied irritably, then added in a low voice, "at least, I'm not any longer."

Jon gathered up the lettuce he'd shredded and dumped it into a large bowl. "Well, whatever the reason for your sudden appearance on my doorstep, I'm glad for the extra help. Good cooks are hard to come by these days." He poked an elbow at her ribs. "Besides, being your employer means I get to boss you around."

She waved her knife beneath his nose. "Just try it, big guy," she warned, "and you might find yourself boiling in the pot right along with these carrots."

He stumbled back a step, pretending fright. "You wouldn't dare."

"Try me."

Laughing, he held up his hands. "No way. I've seen how you can handle a knife. When we were taking those cooking classes together, everybody called you slasher. Remember?"

Relieved that she could still smile, in spite of the emotional turmoil her life was currently undergoing, Suzy scraped the cuttings into the disposal, then flipped the switch. "Yeah, I remember." As she watched the cuttings slide down the drain, her smile slowly faded. "Jon?"

"Yeah?"

"I don't want anyone to know I'm here. Okay?"

He moved to stand beside her and slipped an arm around her shoulders. "Whatever you say, Suzy."

"Several radio stations have run unofficial polls, and the results show that the majority of the people still support Gil."

"That's the public," the lieutenant governor reminded the men gathered around the conference table. "He's still taking a beating by the press."

"But it's the public's opinion that counts," another argued.

"Their voices are the ones the congressmen are going to listen to."

"*If* they bother to share their opinions with their congressmen," the lieutenant governor interjected. "But if they keep their opinions to themselves, it's the media who will influence the voting on current legislation."

Gil, who had remained silent throughout the discussion, rose. "Then we need to encourage our fellow Texans to call or write their congressmen. And not with their opinions about me," he added, meeting the gaze of each person in turn. "They need to let their opinions on the issues be known." He turned away from the table, dragging a hand over his hair. "That's what's important here. The issues. Not me or what's going on in my personal life. The focus should be on the laws being written and voted on, not on gossip."

"Laws don't sell papers. Gossip does."

At the muttered statement Gil stopped with his back to the group. He drew in a deep breath, trying to rein in the fury, then turned. "Then we shouldn't have a problem because there isn't anything more to gossip about. Not about me, anyway."

"The word on the street is that the newspaper is going to break some big story about you in tomorrow's paper."

"What story?" Gil demanded angrily. "I haven't seen or talked to Suzy in over a week. Hell!" he said, tossing up his hands. "I don't even know where she is!"

The person who had mentioned the story lifted a shoulder. "I don't know what it's supposed to be about. I'm just telling you what I heard."

Gil glanced at his press agent. "Is there any way we can find out what they're planning to print?"

The man shook his head doubtfully. "I don't know. I can try."

Gil set his jaw. "Then do it. And if it's a lie, by God this time I'm going to drag them through the courts."

"On what basis?"

"Defamation of character."

Jon entered the kitchen and crossed directly to Suzy. He tossed a newspaper on the countertop in front of her. "Have you seen this?"

Frowning, Suzy wiped her hands on her apron, then picked up the paper. In bold print across the top of the page was the headline: GOVERNOR DADDY?

She dropped the paper and turned to Jon, her face drained of color. "How could they know?" she whispered, then said more fiercely, "How could they possibly *know?* I didn't tell anyone, except my mother and she'd never talk to the press."

"Then it's true? You're really pregnant?"

Suzy whirled away, clamping a hand over her mouth as tears rose to choke her, imagining the shock Gil must have experienced when he saw the headline, the hurt and anger that would surely have followed when he realized that she'd kept her pregnancy a secret from him.

Jon touched her elbow. "Suzy? Is it true?"

She dropped her chin to her chest. "Yes," she said miserably.

"Does he know?"

Unable to speak, she shook her head.

"Damn," he swore.

She turned, her eyes flooded with tears. "I couldn't tell him. He would have insisted on getting married, then everyone would know he'd fathered a child out of wedlock and his career would've been ruined."

"Are you sure about that?"

"Well, of course I'm sure!" she cried. "The press had a field day, trying to destroy his image, when they discovered we were just dating." She gestured angrily at the paper. "And look what they've done to him now that it's rumored that I'm pregnant."

"But what they've printed is simply speculation," Jon reminded her, in an obvious attempt to calm her. "They never came right out and said the baby was his. They merely posed a question, suggesting that it is."

Suzy stared, her eyes widening, her mind whirling, an idea taking shape. "That's it," she whispered. "I can say the baby belongs to someone else, that I was already pregnant when I met Gil."

"They're not going to let you off that easy," Jon warned. "They're going to demand the name of the baby's father."

When Suzy remained silent, her gaze on Jon, he backed up a step and held up a hand. "Uh-uh. No way. You're not sticking me with this. Friendship only goes so far."

"Jon, please," she begged. "We don't have to get married or anything, and you don't have to truly be responsible for the baby. You just have to say that it's yours."

"But it's not!"

"I know it's not. And I wouldn't ask you if there was any other way out of this mess."

"There is another way," he reminded her firmly. "You can tell Gil about the baby. He's the one who got you into this mess. Not me."

Gil stared at the headline, after two hours still unable to believe what he was seeing. Suzy was pregnant? And with his child? He shook his head and dropped the paper to the breakfast table. "She can't be," he said to Dave. "She's on the pill. She told me so herself. This is nothing but a smear campaign, based on nothing but a pack of lies."

"Maybe. Maybe not."

"Well, of course it's lies," Gil shouted angrily. "She'd have told me if she were pregnant."

When Dave lifted a brow, Gil slumped back in his chair. "Okay," he said in defeat. "So maybe she wouldn't have told me. But I still don't believe she's pregnant. I specifically asked her if I needed to use protection, and she told me, no, she was on the pill."

A knock sounded at the back door, and Gil yelled impatiently, "The door's open."

His press agent entered. "Morning, Gil. Dave," he said, with a nod to both. He poured himself a cup of coffee and joined them at the table.

"What did you find out?" Gil asked.

"Not much," his press agent admitted regretfully. "No one is willing to reveal their source. But from what information I was able to gather, it seems the story was based on a home pregnancy kit found in Suzy's garbage."

Gil glanced at Dave, anger burning through him as he remembered the morning Mrs. Woodley had called to report someone snooping around Suzy's house. He looked back to his press agent. "Is that legal? Can anyone who wants to dig through your garbage and print a story on what they found there?"

His press agent slid an uneasy glance at Dave, then

looked down at his coffee. "There isn't a law against it that I know of. Once garbage is placed on the street, it's fair game for anyone who wants to rummage through it."

"That's ridiculous!"

"Ridiculous or not," Dave interjected, "it's done all the time. That's why so many folks use paper shredders these days."

Gil forced himself to take a calming breath, trying to find sense in it all. When he failed, he dropped his elbows to the table and his forehead against his palms. "So what do I do now?"

"I'd think the smart thing to do would be to find her," Dave suggested quietly. "Talk to her. Find out if she really is pregnant. Then decide what you want to do from there."

Gil snapped up his head. "If she *is* pregnant," he said through clenched teeth, "then there's nothing to decide. I'm marrying her."

Dave shared a look with the press agent, but both men remained silent.

Gil had suffered through some bad days in his life, but not one of them came close to matching the gut-wrenching day he'd just experienced. The phones in his office at the capitol and at the mansion had rung incessantly, with reporters wanting a comment from Gil about Suzy's purported pregnancy. In order to avoid the media hounds, he'd finally escaped to his ranch, giving credibility and honesty to his secretary's replies that he was out of town and unavailable for comment.

And when he'd arrived at his ranch, he'd made damn sure *this* time he locked the gate behind him. He didn't want to give any overzealous reporter the opportunity to invade his privacy. Not again. Not when he needed time alone. Time to think. Time to come to grips with all that was happening around him. Time to decide what to do.

He rode his horse for the better part of the afternoon, mulling over the possibility that he could very well be an expectant father. But no matter how many times or ways he played the possibility through his mind, it just wouldn't stick. Not that he objected to becoming a father. He'd always wanted children. But, he'd thought he'd first have a wife.

A wife, he thought again, after returning to the house at dusk. With a sigh he dropped down in an easy chair in his den. He'd always planned to have a wife one day. And he'd thought he'd at last found her when he'd met Suzy. Granted, Suzy was nothing like the woman he'd envisioned marrying. He'd always thought he'd marry someone like his mother. A gentle and unassuming woman who would share his love for his ranch and his views on the world and life in general.

Chuckling, he shook his head, then let it drop back against the chair with a sigh. Suzy was anything but gentle, and she was about as unassuming as a three-ring circus. She was full of sass and vinegar and so colorful that a person needed sunglasses to protect their eyes when they so much as looked her way.

Then why do you miss her so much, he asked himself, when she's nothing at all like the woman you had thought you'd choose as your wife. It's because she *was* different, he admitted, smiling a little at the memories and images that filled his mind. He loved the way she went nose-to-nose with him when they disagreed on a topic, the way she thumbed her nose at convention with her crazy hairdos and even crazier way of dressing. He loved her heart, her smile, her laugh. The way she walked. The way she talked. The way she curled up against him when they slept together. Hell, he couldn't think of anything about her he didn't love.

Which made him realize that he couldn't let her go. Not without putting up a fight. He couldn't just sit back and allow her to walk out of his life. Not when he wanted her with him. Beside him. Always. And he wanted their child. The one she carried, but had kept secret from him.

At the thought, he narrowed his eyes, the missing pieces of the confusing puzzle finally slipping into place. He might not know *how* she got pregnant, but he sure as hell knew *why* she hadn't told him about the baby, and he understood, too, why she'd run away. She was trying to protect him, his career and reputation, just as she'd tried to protect him from her sordid past by refusing to see him.

And a woman who chose to sacrifice so much just

to protect a man's reputation did so for only one reason. She did it for love.

Closing his eyes, he relaxed for the first time that day, his mind made up. Tomorrow he was starting his search again.

And when he found her, this time he was proposing.

"Hey, Governor!"

Gil paused on the steps of the capitol and turned to find a young reporter running to catch up with him, followed closely behind by a cameraman with a camcorder before his face. "Yes?"

The reporter pushed a wireless mike at Gil. "Is it true that you're going to be a father?"

"I'd rather not comment on that at the moment." He turned away and continued up the steps.

"I heard she ditched you," the reporter called after him. "Would you like to comment on that?"

Gil stopped at the verbal jab, then turned slowly back around. "Yes. As a matter of fact, I would like to comment on that, though I don't believe she ditched *me*," he added, taking a menacing step down toward the reporter. "I believe she ditched *you* and all those like you. She doesn't particularly care for the media, nor having her life played out on the front page of every newspaper and television screen in the state."

He took another step down the stairs, his eyes narrowed on the reporter. "What's your name?"

"Gary. Gary Whitaker."

"Well, Gary, let me ask you a question. How do you think you would like it if every move you made was recorded for all the world to see or read about? If every time you walked out your door, there was somebody there waiting to flash a camera in your face or stick a microphone down your throat? How would you like it if every time you kissed your wife or girlfriend or had a spat with her, the world saw it on television or read about it in the paper the next day?"

Scowling, the young reporter lowered the microphone. "Kill the camera, Joe. There's no story here."

Gil kept his gaze on the reporter. "No. Keep rolling, Joe," he said to the cameraman. "Your buddy here asked me a question and I gave him an answer. An honest one. But he doesn't seem to want to answer the one I asked him." He narrowed his eyes. "I wonder why?"

The public's response to Suzy's disappearance was surprising...and heartwarming. Billboards and bumper stickers started appearing around Austin and throughout the state with words of encouragement. Though the messages they carried varied, the sentiments were all the same. It seemed the folks in Texas supported Gil's right to a private life and wanted him to bring Suzy home to the governor's mansion.

Gil saw a minimum of ten bumper stickers on the drive to Elgin, all carrying the same message: Go Get Her, Guv! And that's exactly what he planned to do, he told himself as he knocked on the front door of Suzy's mother's house. Though Dave had assured him that it was just a matter of time before he was able to track Suzy down, Gil was tired of waiting. If anyone knew where Suzy was, it would be her mother. Suzy felt too big a responsibility for her mother to leave without telling her how she could be reached, which was why Gil had decided to talk to Ms. Crane again. Only, this time in person.

"Who's there?" a voice called from the other side of the door.

"Gil Riley, ma'am. I wondered if I could talk to you for a moment."

There was a rattle of chain and the door opened a crack. "If you're looking for Suzy, I've already told you she isn't here."

"No, ma'am. I didn't come to see Suzy. I came to see you."

The door opened a little wider, and Gil got his first look at Suzy's mother. The resemblance between mother and daughter was faint, but there, as was the same wariness he'd seen Suzy exhibit so many times.

After hesitating a moment longer, she opened the door and allowed him to enter. She quickly closed it behind him and slipped the security chain into place, then motioned for him to follow her into the living room.

She gestured to the sofa, then sat opposite him in a wing chair. "Why did you want to see me?"

"To talk to you about Suzy, ma'am," he said and pulled off his hat. "I need to see her, Ms. Crane. Talk to her. And I know that you're the only one who can tell me where she is."

She wrung her hands. "She made me promise not to tell anyone. Especially you."

Gil leaned forward, bracing his forearms on his knees and holding his hat between his hands. "I know this is difficult for you, Ms. Crane. And I respect your desire to honor the promise you made to Suzy, but it's really important that I talk to her." He bent his head and stared at his hat as he turned it slowly in his hands. "I didn't know she was pregnant, Ms. Crane. She didn't tell me. But I do know why she's run away. She's trying to protect me. But I don't want her protection. I want her. I love her," he said quietly, then looked up, unashamed of the emotion that choked him. "I love her with all my heart, and I'll love our baby, too."

He watched the tears rush to her eyes, and he slipped off the sofa to drop down on a knee before her, gathering her hand in his. "I swear by all that's good and merciful that I'm not here to bring any more embarrassment or pain to your daughter. All I want is a chance to talk to her. The opportunity to tell her that I love her. That I want to marry her. And that I'll do whatever is necessary to protect her."

She squeezed her fingers around his as tears ran down her cheeks. "My daughter's a very lucky young lady to have as fine a man as you love her."

"No, ma'am," he said, shaking his head. "I'm the lucky one. Suzy's the best thing that's ever happened to me."

She drew in a long breath. "All right. I'll tell you

where she is. But first you must promise me something."

Gil gripped her hand more tightly in his. "Anything."

"Don't accept no for an answer." She laughed softly at his surprised look and pulled her hand from his to blot at her cheeks. "I know my daughter, Governor. She won't give in easily. Especially when she thinks that in doing so she might harm you in some way. She'll fight and kick at you every step of the way."

Smiling for the first time in what felt like weeks, Gil stood and settled his hat over his head. "To tell you the truth, Ms. Crane," he said with a wink, "I'm hoping she does kick up a fuss. I've been hankering for a good fight for over a week."

Nine

"You know where the place is, don't you?"

"Yes, Gil," Dave replied patiently. "I mapped out the route before we left the mansion."

Gil shifted nervously in the seat. "How much further?"

Dave rolled his eyes. "Would you relax? We'll get there when we get there."

Gil dragged off his hat and wiped at the perspiration beading his forehead. "I never should have let you talk me into driving me there. I should have driven myself."

"And picked up a fistful of speeding tickets along the way," Dave muttered. "Come on, Gil. Relax. I'll get you there in plenty of time."

At the mention of time Gil glanced at the clock on

the dash. "I told the press that I'd be there by seven tonight."

"And you will be," Dave assured him. "Just sit back and relax."

"If you tell me to relax one more time, I'm going to—"

There was a loud *pop* and the black sedan veered sharply to the left.

Gil sat up straight. "What was that? What are you doing?" he shouted as Dave slowed and steered the car onto the shoulder.

"A blowout," Dave replied, frowning. "We've got a flat tire."

Gil was out of the car before it completely stopped and was lifting the trunk lid, which Dave had popped.

"I'll change it," Dave said, nudging Gil out of his way. "You don't want to get yourself dirty."

Scowling, Gil grabbed a flashlight from the trunk.

"I don't need any light," Dave told him. "I can see well enough to change the tire."

"I'm not getting the flashlight to hold for you," Gil snapped. "I'm getting it so I can try to flag down a passing car."

Shaking his head, Dave pulled the spare from the trunk and headed for the side of the car. "Whatever you say, boss."

His scowl deepening, Gil switched on the flashlight and stomped to the side of the interstate. As a car approached, he waved the flashlight, swearing when the car kept going. Another vehicle approached, and

Gil stepped out onto the highway, waving the flashlight wildly.

The car slowed, then pulled onto the shoulder. Gil ran for the vehicle as the driver rolled down his window.

"Thank you for stopping, sir," Gil said breathlessly. "We had a blowout, and it's imperative that I get to Dallas before seven. By any chance are you headed that way?"

The gnarled old man driving the car turned to look at his wife in the passenger seat. "Well, yeah," the old man said. "As a matter of fact, me and my wife are going to visit our grandkids there."

The man's wife leaned across the seat to peer up at Gil, and her eyes widened in surprise. "Why, Papa! It's the governor!"

The old man squinted his eyes and gave Gil a closer look. "Well, damned if it ain't," he sputtered, and pushed open the door. He stuck out his hand. "Reed Fisher, Governor. It's a pleasure to meet you."

Gil pumped the man's hand. "A pleasure to meet you, too, Mr. Fisher. Now about that ride…"

"Sure 'nuf," the old man said, and opened the back door. "Climb right on in."

"Dave!" Gil called as he ducked into the back seat of the couple's car. "Come on. I've got us a ride."

Already busy changing the flat, Dave dropped the tire iron and swiped his hands down the seat of his slacks as he hustled toward the car. He climbed in next to Gil just as the old man started up the car again.

"We sure do appreciate this," Gil said as the old man pulled back out onto the highway.

The woman twisted around and offered her hand over the seat. "I'm Mary Ruth," she said, smiling shyly, "but all my friends call me Mimi."

Gil shook her hand. "Pleased to meet you, ma'am."

Dave nodded politely. "Ma'am."

Papa, as Mimi had called her husband, glanced in the rearview mirror at Gil. "Whatcha headed to Dallas for, Governor?"

"Papa," Mimi scolded. "The governor's activities are none of your business."

Gil snorted a laugh. "I wish everyone shared your view, Mimi. Especially the press."

She made a tsking sound with her tongue. "The things they put in the paper these days. Why, in my day, they wouldn't have dared print such derogatory things about a man in your position."

"I appreciate your opinion, Mimi," Gil replied. "It's just a shame more people don't share it." He leaned to peer anxiously at the road ahead. "We're heading for a restaurant on Greenville Avenue, Mr. Fisher. Jon's Place. Have you heard of it?"

"No. Can't say that I have. But give me the address and I'll bet I can find it."

Gil settled back in his seat, nervously rubbing his hands down his thighs as Dave rattled off the address and basic directions to reach the restaurant.

"I think it's a crime the things the press wrote

about that woman you've been seeing," Mimi said. "Suzy was her name, wasn't it?"

Gil nodded. "Yes, ma'am. In fact, I'm on my way right now to see her."

She twisted around in the seat, her eyes rounding. "You're going after her?"

"Yes, ma'am, I am. And I'm not leaving until she agrees to marry me."

Mimi turned back around and reached to pat her husband on the knee. "How romantic," she said, sighing dreamily.

"If you'd like," Gil invited, "you two can hang around and see how things go."

"Oh, we couldn't," Mimi said, shaking her head. "A marriage proposal is a private thing and not meant to be intruded upon by strangers."

Dave dropped back his head and laughed. "Not this one," he said, still chuckling. "The governor's invited the entire press corp to witness *this* proposal."

Jon pushed his way through the swinging door and into the kitchen, carrying a tray loaded with dirty glasses, his face flushed from exertion. "Where in the hell are these people coming from?" he asked breathlessly as he slid the tray onto an empty spot on the counter.

Suzy swiped at the perspiration on her brow as she flipped an order of quesadillas on the grill. "Is that a complaint?"

"Hell, no!" Jon said, grinning. "Business hasn't been this good since opening night."

Suzy shoved a tray loaded with plates of nachos toward him. "If you want to make sure it stays that way, take these to table four. Marcy's swamped and hasn't had time."

"Sure thing," Jon said, and scooped up the tray, holding it above his head as he pushed through the swinging door.

Squinting up at the computer screen of orders, Suzy wiped her hands on her apron as she checked what was up next. "Quesadillas again," she muttered wearily. "Don't these people eat anything but Tex-Mex?"

Pausing a moment to stretch the kinks from her back, she sighed and reached for a stack of tortillas and laid them out on the grill. Just as she scooped up a spatula of grilled strips of onion and green peppers to spread across the tortillas, a shout came from the other side of the door, followed by loud cheers and clapping.

Curious to know what all the commotion was about, Suzy set aside the spatula and crossed to the door to peek through the glass. People stood five deep in front of it, blocking her view. Frustrated, she pushed open the door and slipped into the small dining room, rising to the balls of her feet and straining to see over the people who stood in front of her.

Unable to see anything but the backs of heads, she pushed her way through the crowd, but finally gave up and nudged the man standing beside her. "What's going on?" she asked.

He glanced down. "It's the governor," he shouted

to make himself heard over the din. "Gil Riley just walked in."

Suzy's stomach dropped to her feet, then bounced up to crowd her throat. "The governor?" she repeated sickly. "Here?"

"Yeah, he—"

But Suzy was already turning away. She didn't need to hear more. Gil was here? she thought hysterically. Oh, God! She had to get out of there!

She'd almost made it back to the kitchen's swinging door when a hand closed around her arm.

"Suzy. Wait."

She stopped, squeezing her eyes shut at the sound of the familiar drawl. "Gil, please," she begged, and tried to tug free.

He tightened his grip. "If I could have everyone's attention," he shouted to the crowd.

Voices died in a wave that rolled outward until the entire restaurant was as quiet as a church at prayer time.

"I'm sure most of you came here out of curiosity," he said in a voice that carried to the far corners of the room.

A few mumbled comments and spurts of laughter followed his announcement.

He raised a hand for silence. "And others came knowing what to expect," he added, and smiled at an elderly couple Suzy saw standing by Dave at the front of the crowd.

"The reason I called this press conference," he

continued, "is to set the record straight once and for all."

He dragged a reluctant Suzy forward and wrapped an arm around her shoulders, forcing her to stand at his side. "I know a lot of you have wondered about the mysterious woman in my life."

More mumbled comments and jeers followed. Gil waited until the room was quiet again.

"Well, here she is." He looked down at Suzy and smiled. "Miss Suzy Crane."

"Gil, please," she whispered frantically, trying to duck from beneath his arm. "You don't know what you're doing."

"Yeah, I do." With his gaze on hers, he slipped his arm from around her and turned to face her, catching both of her hands in his before she could escape. "As most of you know," he said to the crowd, "Suzy and I met about a month ago. And this may sound trite, but as far as I'm concerned, it was love at first sight."

"Gil, please!" she begged, near tears.

"Unfortunately," he continued, ignoring her, "any chance of us having a normal relationship was hindered by..." He sent a telling look to the crowd of people watching. "Well, let's just say my position as governor cast a spotlight on our relationship that most couples are spared."

He looked back down at Suzy, and his smile returned, the warmth and encouragement in it reaching into her heart and twisting painfully.

"Gil," she pleaded, desperate to make him listen.

"And I regret that," he said, his eyes softening in apology as he gazed down at her. "Not for myself. But for Suzy. No one deserves the beating she's taken from the press because of her association with me. And no woman should be deprived the romance normally associated with falling in love, just because the man she's involved with is the state governor. Isn't that right, Mimi?" he asked.

"You're darn right it is!" the elderly lady standing by Dave replied indignantly.

Gil went on. "There's not much I can do about what's happened in the past, but I want everyone in this room to know how much this lady standing in front of me means to me." He paused a moment and gave Suzy's hands a reassuring squeeze. "Even if it means giving up the office of governor to get all of you to leave her alone, to keep her name out of the headlines, then that's what I'm prepared to do."

Suzy's gasp was like an explosion in the silent room. "Gil!" she cried, trying to jerk her hands free. "No! You can't! I won't let you!"

He tossed back his head and laughed. "Did you hear that?" he shouted to the crowd. "She says she won't let me quit." As he gazed down at her, the laughter slowly faded from his eyes. "But I will, Suzy," he said quietly. "If that's what it takes to keep from losing you, I'd walk away from the governor's mansion and never look back."

"Gil..."

"I love you, Suzy," he said firmly. "But I won't see you hurt anymore. And I won't sacrifice what we have together for a public office. If it comes to a choice, I want you to know I'll always choose you every time."

"Hey, governor!" someone shouted from the far side of the room. "Can we quote you on that?"

"You're damn right you can!" Gil yelled.

"What about the rumor that she's pregnant?" someone else called. "Can you verify that for us?"

His gaze turning tender as he continued to look down at Suzy, Gil swept a strand of damp hair from her cheek. "Are you?" he asked softly.

Choked by tears, Suzy could only nod.

A smile slowly spread across his face. "Yes," he reported for all to hear. "She's definitely pregnant. And for the record," he added proudly, "the baby's mine."

"Does this mean you're getting married?" a female voice asked.

Mimi turned to look at the woman in exasperation. "For heaven's sake! Give the man time!" She turned back around and pushed a hand at Gil, urging him to continue. "Go on, honey," she said kindly. "Say what you came here to say."

Gil inhaled deeply. "Suzy," he said, releasing the breath with her name. "Will you—"

"Wait!" Mimi cried, and rushed forward. She quickly untied the apron from around Suzy's waist and lifted it over her head. "A woman receiving a proposal wants to look her best," she fussed gently as she straightened Suzy's collar and fluffed her hair.

Satisfied, she stepped back and smiled. "Now we're ready, Governor."

Gil bit back a smile. "Are you sure?"

Blushing, Mimi fisted the apron at her waist. "Positive."

Taking Suzy's hands again, Gil sank down to a knee, his gaze on hers. "I know this probably isn't the way you'd choose to hear what I have to say. But I think it's important for everyone here, as well as those who will read or hear about this later, to understand how I truly feel about you. From the day we first met, you captured my heart, my soul. But what I felt for you then was nothing compared to what I feel for you now."

He paused and swallowed hard, suddenly choked by emotion. "I love you, Suzy," he whispered, giving her hands a squeeze. "I love you with all my heart and will until the day I die. And I will love the baby we've made together and will protect it with my life, just as I promise to protect you."

He paused again, his face somber, his eyes filled with hope. "Suzy Crane, will you honor me by agreeing to become my wife?"

Her lips trembling uncontrollably, Suzy sank to her knees before him. "Yes," she whispered and reached to cup his face. "Yes," she said again, smiling through her tears as she drew his face to hers.

Cheers erupted around them as their lips met, and bits of shredded napkin were thrown in the air to rain down over them as they hugged, laughing.

Drawing away, Gil stood, pulling Suzy to her feet,

as well. With his gaze on hers, he drew her into his arms again. "I love you," he whispered.

Her fingers trembling, Suzy gathered his face between her hands and looked deeply into his eyes. "And I love you."

He kissed her again, more passionately this time, while holding her tightly against his chest, their hearts beating as one.

"Hey!" someone shouted. "Are we invited to the wedding?"

"You're damn right you are," Gil replied, leaning back to beam a smile at his bride-to-be. "The whole damn state is going to be invited to this wedding, aren't they, darlin'?"

Suzy arched a brow. "On one condition," she replied, then turned to peer at the crowd of reporters gathered. "They have to bring the beer."

Gil tossed back his head and laughed. "That's my Suzy!"

* * * * *

THE BARONS OF TEXAS: JILL

**by
Fayrene Preston**

SILHOUETTE DESIRE
presents

Fayrene Preston's

enticing trilogy

The Barons of Texas

Meet the Baron sisters—Tess, Jill and Kit.
Inheriting the family fortune is easy.
But what about falling in love?

June 2002
THE BARONS OF TEXAS: TESS
(*in* Her Ideal Man)

July 2002
THE BARONS OF TEXAS: JILL
(*in* His Kind of Woman)

August 2002
THE BARONS OF TEXAS: KIT
(*in* The Millionaire's First Love)

FAYRENE PRESTON

published her first book in 1981 and has been publishing steadily ever since. Fayrene lives in north Texas and is the mother of two grown sons. She claims her greatest achievement in life is turning out two wonderful human beings. She is also proud to announce the arrival of her first grandchild: a beautiful baby girl. Now she has even more to be thankful for.

One

Jill Baron came to an abrupt halt. Her backyard was spinning around her. Slowly she took a deep breath and waited, knowing, hoping, logic would soon reassert itself. She'd owned her North Dallas home for the past ten years, and not once had its grounds ever moved, much less spun.

In fact, not one acre of Texas's vast land had ever moved. Sandstorms could whip large amounts of West Texas sandy topsoil through the air. Tornados could lift entire houses, trees and cars. But the ground always stayed still. She took comfort in the thought, and soon her backyard came to a stop.

There…there. Everything was going to be just fine.

"Can I do anything for you before I leave?"

Jill flinched. She'd thought she was alone. She turned and made an effort to smile at her executive assistant. "Not a thing, Molly."

"Are you sure? You're looking pale."

"Everyone looks pale at night." She valued Molly for her quiet efficiency and organizational ability, but Molly occasionally showed the regrettable tendency to try to mother her. She hadn't had a mother since she was three years old, and she certainly didn't need or want one now.

"You never look pale, Jill. Listen, I can run upstairs and bring down your medicine."

"No." She briefly closed her eyes. "I'm sorry. I didn't mean to be so abrupt, but you know how I feel about that stuff. Anyway, I'm fine, and you've worked hard today. The party went extremely well. Thank you for your part in that. Now go home and get some sleep."

"If you're sure?" Molly still looked concerned.

"I am."

"Then I'll see you in the morning."

"Good night." Jill sipped again from the champagne bottle she carried, then stared down into the pool. Blue filters over its lights had created a lovely pale-blue oasis of breeze-rippled water with lotus-blossom-shaped candles floating on its surface.

Her eyes narrowed. Bright. The flames were too bright. She poured champagne onto one of the candles, dousing its flame. Resuming her walk along the edge of the pool, she continued pouring until every candle flame was out, then drank more champagne.

She wasn't yet ready to go into the house. This was her favorite time of any party she gave. The last of her guests had gone. Both the band and the caterers had finished packing up and were also gone. She liked reclaiming her home and its grounds. She liked the return of the quiet and the order. But more than that,

GET A FREE BOOK and a FREE MYSTERY GIFT WHEN YOU PLAY THE...

Lucky 7 SLOT MACHINE GAME!

Just scratch off the silver box with a coin. Then check below to see the gifts you get!

YES! I have scratched off the silver box. Please send me the FREE book and mystery gift for which I qualify. I understand I am under no obligation to purchase any books, as explained on the back of this card. I am over 18 years of age.

D2GI

Mrs/Miss/Ms/Mr   Initials

BLOCK CAPITALS PLEASE

Surname

Address

Postcode

7 7 7	Worth **ONE FREE BOOK** plus a **BONUS** Mystery Gift!		
🍒🍒🍒	Worth **TWO FREE BOOKS!**		
♣♣♣	Worth **ONE FREE BOOK!**		
🔔🔔🍒	**TRY AGAIN!**		

Visit us online at www.millsandboon.co.uk

Offer valid in the U.K. only and is not available to current Reader Service subscribers to this series. Overseas and Eire please write for details. We reserve the right to refuse an application and applicants must be aged 18 years or over. Offer expires 31st December 2002. Terms and prices subject to change without notice. As a result of this application you may receive further offers from carefully selected companies. If you do not wish to share in this opportunity, please write to the Data Manager at the address shown overleaf. Only one application per household.

Silhouette® is a registered trademark used under license.

The Reader Service™ — Here's how it works:

Accepting the free book places you under no obligation to buy anything. You may keep the book and gift and return the despatch note marked 'cancel'. If we do not hear from you, about a month later we'll send you 2 brand new books and invoice you just £4.99* each. That's the complete price - there is no extra charge for postage and packing. You may cancel at any time, otherwise every month we'll send you 2 more books, which you may either purchase or return to us - the choice is yours.

*Terms and prices subject to change without notice.

THE READER SERVICE™
FREE BOOK OFFER
FREEPOST CN81
CROYDON
CR9 3WZ

NO STAMP NEEDED!

NO STAMP NECESSARY IF POSTED IN THE U.K. OR N.I.

she liked the feeling of accomplishment she felt after a really successful party.

The pool moved. The ground beneath her shifted. She stopped and frowned down at her bare feet, which peeked out from beneath the hem of her cream-colored designer gown. The ground wasn't moving. Neither was she. *Damn.*

Perhaps she'd had more champagne than she had realized, but just as fast as the thought occurred, she dismissed the idea. She'd never been drunk in her life, plus she rarely drank at her parties until the last guest had left. She didn't like to give up control of anything, much less her mental faculties. She waited, and after several moments her patience was rewarded when everything stilled once again.

With a mental shrug, she took another sip of champagne. It was going to be okay.

The party had been extremely productive. She had been able to bring Holland Mathis to the point that one more visit with him would have him signing on the dotted line for those three buildings in the southeast corner of downtown Dallas she'd been trying to get for so long. She'd even been able to get Tyler Forster interested in renovating the buildings into residential condominiums. All in all, things had gone very well.

Her business was booming. She should feel more than satisfied at all she was accomplishing. And she was.

Except...

The lit pool had an odd aura around it, she noticed, as if the blue lights had risen into the air to form a shimmering, transparent cloud. Shimmering, transparent cloud? That made *no* sense at all.

Mind over matter, she told herself firmly. She refused to give in to this. She couldn't, *wouldn't,* let it happen again. She turned her back to the pool and strolled to a grassy area, where a border of red geraniums backed by white spring bells bloomed. The grass felt soft and cool to her bare feet. Yes, this was much better.

Sipping at the champagne, she determinedly returned to her original train of thought, which was the feeling of fulfillment at all she was accomplishing. Her achievements were a source of great gratification to her.

Yet...there was something missing.

All her life, she'd set goals and met them. This was the year that, according to her father's will, if she was able to meet a certain financial criterion set by him, she would inherit one-sixth of the family company. But she'd met that goal several years ago, and her business was going better than it ever had. So what could possibly be missing?

She came to a dead stop. *Des.* Of course. *Des!*

To date, winning her stepcousin's agreement to marriage was the only goal she had not been able to attain.

"What's the matter? Couldn't find a glass?"

Startled, Jill whirled around, in the process almost losing her balance. *"Colin."*

Colin Wynne smiled lazily and reached for the champagne. "If you're going to drink from the bottle, this is the way you should do it." He tilted his head back and downed the remaining champagne in a matter of seconds.

"I don't need lessons in drinking champagne." She snatched the bottle back from him.

"No, you don't, which is why it's so interesting to see you drinking straight from the bottle. I've never seen you do that before. Come to think of it, I've never seen you barefoot before, either. Pale pink toenails—not a very strong statement, Jill."

He was talking uncharacteristically loudly, she thought. It was almost as if she was hearing his words in Sensurround sound. "I wasn't trying to make a statement."

"That's good, because you didn't." He shrugged in a way that clearly indicated he couldn't be held accountable for her bad taste, goading her as he so frequently did, pushing her buttons until she lashed back.

"There are a great many things you haven't seen me do before, but that doesn't mean any of them are interesting or, for that matter, that you'll ever see me do them."

"Ah, but that's where you're wrong."

"Wrong?" She pressed her fingers to a spot above her right temple. He was confusing her. Of all her acquaintances, why did it have to be *Colin* who had returned? They moved in the same charity and social circle, but lately that circle seemed to be getting smaller and smaller, until every time she turned around, Colin was there. Tonight, though, she had only herself to blame, since she had included him on her guest list.

"Everything you do interests me, Jill. Where are your shoes?"

He still wasn't making any sense. And now that he mentioned it, where *were* her shoes, and why did he care? "What are you doing here? I thought I saw you leave."

A memory flashed through her head of Colin escorting an attractive young woman around the side of the house toward the front and the driveway. She remembered thinking that the woman's red hair had clashed violently with the unfortunate orange dress she'd chosen to wear. "You *did* leave. You left with Corine."

"I drove her home, which is exactly three blocks from here, as you know, then returned to wait out front until all the guests had left."

She frowned. "For heaven's sake, why?"

"Why did I take Corine home? Because the people she'd come with weren't ready to leave, and she was."

"I meant, why did you come back here?"

"To check on you."

"To check…?" Stunned, she barely managed to keep her footing when the ground starting whirling around her again. She closed her eyes, willing the ground to be still. This was *not* happening. It couldn't be. She would not allow it, most *especially* in front of Colin. When the ground stabilized beneath her, she opened her eyes and saw a thoughtfulness and concern in his regard that completely unnerved her.

But then, *he* unnerved her. On some level, and in some shape, form or fashion, he always had. As usual, he looked annoyingly handsome and self-confident, with his golden skin that constantly looked as if he had just returned from a vacation in some terribly exotic, sunny locale, and his golden-brown hair that never seemed combed. Every time she looked at him, she had to fight an incomprehensible impulse to finger-comb his hair into tidiness.

And then there was that dimple in his left cheek.

Even a half smile from him could bring it into play. She had seen grown, stone-cold-sober women become totally mesmerized by it, to the point that they would forget what they'd been saying or even where they were.

As for his eyes, they were brown with golden streaks that radiated outward to create a star formation. Those eyes... She'd seen him flirt outrageously, until the woman caught in his sights was pink with delight and quiveringly ready for whatever he had in mind. It was absolutely disgusting.

But the very worst was the way he treated her. No one teased her. No one except Colin, that was. Plus, often in the middle of a party or a meeting, she would turn to find him watching her with laughter in his gaze, as if he knew a joke she didn't. On other occasions, she would get the strangest feeling that he knew *exactly* what she was thinking and why.

But now his gaze was solemn and unwavering as he looked at her. She tried to remember what she'd been about to say and couldn't. "What did you just say?"

"That I came back to check on you."

"That's right. I knew that." She took a deep breath. "What I meant to ask is *why* you came back to see..." once again, she touched her forehead "...I mean, to *check* on me?"

"Toward the end of the party, I sensed something was wrong with you, or bothering you. I thought I'd come back to see if there was something I could do to help."

She let the champagne bottle slip to the grass, not trusting herself to bend down in case the ground chose that particular moment to move again. It was like she was tipsy, except she knew she wasn't. Maybe it was simply that her blood sugar was a little low. She should have eaten more at the party. "You could have saved yourself the trouble, Colin. Nothing was or is wrong."

"No?"

"No, of course not."

When she'd first met Colin a couple of years ago at a charity function, he had shown definite interest in her, but when she hadn't returned the interest, he'd immediately backed off. Since then, she only saw him in groups. They had mutual friends and business associates, and their shared circles were made up of people just like them—high-energy, high-achieving men and women of approximately the same age.

She knew he watched her, though she couldn't understand why. But even stranger, she often found herself watching him. He could actually be quite funny, charming and interesting at times. But most often, he disconcerted or annoyed her. Like now.

She had no idea how he'd known there was something wrong when even *she* hadn't. And she had no idea what to do with him now that he was there. She frowned. No, that was wrong. She *did* know. She had to get rid of him as soon as possible.

"Look, Colin, it was very kind of you to return to check on me, but I assure you, it wasn't necessary. In fact, I was just about to go, uh…" She glanced toward her house, but couldn't think of the word, so she simply pointed. Oh, no. She silently groaned. Words were deserting her—definitely a bad sign.

Planting one careful foot in front of the other, she started walking toward the house. He fell into step beside her, and before she knew it, his warm hand slipped beneath her elbow as if to steady her. The last thing she wanted was his help or for him to guess what was wrong.

Up ahead, the path forked. Left led to the house, which wasn't that far now. She was convinced she could make it with no problem. Right led around the side of the house to the front, where Colin's car was no doubt parked. That was the path he needed to take.

"You're going inside to do what? Work?"

She started to tell him it was none of his business what she was about to do. But if she did, he was bound to make one of his barbed remarks that would leave her no choice but to answer, and she really wasn't up to it. "It's been a long day. I'll probably just go to bed."

"Pity."

Startled, she glanced around. "Excuse me?"

"It's a pity that such a beautiful woman as you is about to go to bed alone."

She stumbled. His hand on her elbow tightened to steady her. Damn the man. He never did or said what she expected. And she wanted his hand *off* her elbow.

"Unless, of course, you've got Des trapped up there in your bedroom and I don't know it."

There. He'd done it again, gotten to her with one of his barbed remarks. She jerked away from him, freeing herself from his grasp, and glared at him. "You know...you know nothing about Des."

"Ah, that's where you're wrong. I know a great deal about Des. He's become a very good friend of mine. I also know he's dead wrong for you."

"You..." She couldn't think of a single thing to say. Plus, she realized, she could no longer see

Colin's entire face. There was a blank spot covering part of it. Her field of vision was narrowing.

She couldn't deny it any longer. She was in trouble. What was more, in only a few minutes, it was going to get worse.

"Go home, Colin. *Now. Good night.*" She hurried her pace to try to get away from him, but her legs didn't seem to work right, and she miscalculated a step. This time she would have fallen if he hadn't caught her.

"Something *is* wrong," he said grimly, the loud volume of his voice beating against her in a way that was beyond excruciating. "What is it?"

She gritted her teeth. All she had to do was make it to her bedroom. "Leave me *alone*. I—"

He swept her into his arms and headed toward the back terrace. She couldn't protest anymore. Piercing pain had struck one-half of her head. She closed her eyes and tried to relax against him, but he was walking too fast. The movement felt violent. Nausea threatened. When she felt him step over the threshold into her house, she managed to open her eyes a slit.

"Just put me down here," she whispered.

He didn't answer. "Is your bedroom up or down?"

"Please—"

"Never mind." Apparently guessing, he took the stairs to the second story two at a time.

She moaned. "Please…slow down."

"What in the hell is wrong with you?" he muttered, but he did as she said. "I'm calling 911 as soon as I get you on your bed."

"No. Pharmacy…in the drawer."

"Pharmacy? You want me to call the pharmacy?"

"No. I mean…medicine."

"There's medicine in the drawer? Is that what you're saying?"

She whimpered. "Don't yell."

"Honey, you've never heard me talk as softly as I am right now. You've also never known me to be as worried as I am at this exact moment."

Worried. He was worried about her. She didn't want that, but she couldn't think of a thing to say to get him to go away.

With her eyes still closed, she sensed when they passed through the double doors of her bedroom. There, with a gentleness she wouldn't have thought him capable of, he laid her on the bed and adjusted one of the pillows behind her head. Without further discussion, he switched on her bedside lamp and opened the drawer of the nightstand. He cursed beneath his breath.

She knew what he'd seen, but she no longer had any control over the situation. Tears were stinging at the back of her eyes. The light was piercing her skull. She blindly reached out for a pillow and pulled it over her eyes.

She heard him stride into her bathroom, heard water running; then, after several moments, the mattress shifted with his weight as he sat down beside her.

"Jill, honey? Can you open your eyes? You need to look at me for a second."

It was the last thing she wanted to do. The light was going to be intolerable. She dragged the pillow off her face and slowly opened her eyes. With each hand, Colin held up six pill bottles by their tops.

"Which do you need?"

She pointed to one.

"How many?"

She held up one finger.

He lifted her head and slid his arm behind her shoulders to brace her. She took the pill with a gulp of water from the glass he offered.

She settled back onto the pillow, her eyes once again closed. "The light…" The lamp was turned off before she could finish the sentence. The only other light came from a low-wattage lamp in her bathroom. She tended to leave that one on all the time, which was good, because once he left, it would be safer for her if she had some light, in case she decided she needed more medication or had to go to the bathroom. "Thank you. You can leave now. I'll be fine." If the pain didn't let up soon, she was going to have to try something else.

"I'm glad you're going to be fine, but in the meantime, I think I should call your doctor."

Even with pain pounding in her head, she could appreciate the texture of his voice—low-pitched and husky with concern. "No."

"Jill, I'm not blind. You're in severe pain. Your doctor should know."

"He knows."

She heard him exhale a long breath. "Okay, if I see that you're feeling better within the next thirty minutes, I'll hold off calling him for now. But I *am* staying with you."

"No." She would never be able to relax with him there.

"Shh. Don't try to argue with me, because you won't win. Besides, it's clearly too much of an effort for you."

He was right about that. Then, though any movement was going to be hard, she managed to roll her head slightly on the pillow and tried to reach the hairpins that had her hair bound so tightly into its French twist. Her movement brought a wave of nausea with it, and she faltered.

He gently brushed her hand aside and did it himself. When all the pins were out, he slowly, tenderly combed his fingers through her hair until it was loose and her scalp didn't feel quite as tight. Then he took her hand in his and softly stroked her forearm. She wouldn't have thought it possible, but surprisingly, his touch soothed. Normally she didn't like to be touched.

She tried to calculate the consequences of Colin's having seen her at her most vulnerable, but no thoughts could form when there was so much pain, pain that was exhausting her as she tried to fight it. So she lay very still, waiting, praying for the medicine to kick in.

"What about your dress?" she heard him ask. "Would you be more comfortable in something else?"

Yes, she would, but she simply wasn't up to changing. "Not now."

"Let me know when you think you can move without so much pain."

She attempted to blank her mind, but she was too aware of the pain, too aware of the man stroking her arm.

Colin carefully watched her, trying to think of what else he could do for her. He had recognized a couple of the names on the prescription bottles. It was medicine used for migraine headaches. Several people he knew had them. How long, he wondered, had Jill been suffering from them?

From what he'd heard about migraines, she was a prime candidate for them—type A personality, a perfectionist through and through who worked extremely hard.

Tonight had been a perfect example. She hadn't enjoyed the party. She had *worked* the party. And he knew her well enough to know that his invitation, along with many others, had been extended to make up the numbers she needed. There had really been only two or three people she had wanted to talk to, though she was a professional at camouflaging her intent.

His eyes traveled down her body. For the party, she had worn a high-necked, narrow column of ivory silk crepe that discreetly skimmed her body, leaving only her arms bare. It was a dress in perfect taste, yet on her, it had a subtle sexiness to it that was enough to bring a man—hell, *him*—to the point where he was almost ready to beg to see more. But he knew that was no way to get to Jill, so he had forced himself to stay away from her and merely watch.

From the first moment he'd met her, something about her had gotten to him. She was a classically, breathtakingly beautiful woman, with her sleek dark hair and lovely bourbon-colored eyes. They had both been attending a glittering affair in a gilded ballroom with tall candles, the room filled with women draped in jewels and shimmering gowns. But to him, Jill had stood out among the peacocks. She'd worn no jewels, only the unadorned elegance of a slim, strapless, red velvet gown. He could still remember how her skin had glowed in the candlelight.

Right off the bat, she'd rebuffed him in a manner that had been almost automatic. He'd been amused. Rebuffing men was obviously instinctive with her, and because of it, he'd been challenged.

At first his attraction had been simple and basic— a burning, hungry, primal need that made him want to grab her, take her to the nearest place where they could be alone and have sex with her until they were both too spent and tired to do anything but go to sleep.

He had watched her for the rest of that evening, and as he did, there had been a moment when she had turned away from someone she'd been talking with. In that instant, he'd seen something that had connected with him on his deepest, most elemental level. In that moment, he had recognized a depth in her that held much more than what she allowed the world to see. Still, he wasn't certain what it was about her that he had connected with so strongly. Only later, after other encounters, had he figured it out.

Loss and need.

He had seen scars of loss in her, wounds not entirely healed and hurts remembered as if they had happened yesterday. He had recognized that in her because he had some of the same things in him, maybe not as deep, maybe not as hurtful, but he definitely knew what loss and need were all about. Their experiences might have been different, but the pain was the same.

The knowledge made him realize that the wait for her to turn and look at him as a desirable man whom she wanted in her life would be well worth the patience that would be required. The knowledge also made him more determined than ever to have her, because he knew that, deep inside, where all the holes and hurt were, they could help each other.

It hadn't taken him long to learn she was interested in only one man. Des Baron. Once he'd figured out the whys and wherefores, he had known she and Des wouldn't work out. The bone-deep certainty had come from knowing that *he* was the only man she should ever be with, and that sooner or later he was going to make her his. What he hadn't known was how long it would take him. Luckily, he had plenty of patience.

He had made it his business to study her, learn her moods—what made her happy, what made her unhappy. It hadn't been easy. Jill, by her own design, had built a formidable barrier around herself. Only recently had he begun to see cracks in her barrier—small cracks, true, but for Jill, even a tiny splinter fracture was extraordinary.

Maybe the ongoing problem of the migraines had been the cause of the cracks. Or perhaps she was simply running out of challenges, something he knew, because he had made it a priority to know every move she made, business, as well as personal. And because of it, he could almost guarantee he knew what was coming next. It was what he'd been waiting for.

But tonight, as the party had continued, he'd noticed that her eyes had taken on a bruised look, something someone who knew her only on a social or a business level wouldn't have noticed. But he had, and it was the reason he had returned.

"How are you doing?" he asked, his voice barely above a whisper. "Do you feel like putting on something else now?"

A shudder racked her body. "I'm cold."

Before she could say anything more, he was up and

walking into her closet. He dismissed the rows of perfectly hung business suits, dresses, blouses and skirts, and zeroed in on a full-length beige knit nightgown with long sleeves and a matching robe. His hand closed over the knit. It was a cashmere blend. Perfect. Someone in pain should be encased in softness.

Beside her again, he saw that her eyes were open. He tossed the matching robe on the end of the bed. "Is this okay?" He held up the gown.

She gave an ever-so-slight nod, then closed her eyes once more. "I can do it."

It made sense that, under any circumstances, she would be adamantly opposed to having him help her change her clothes, but tonight her formidable determination to control all things involving herself was vastly diminished, and as weak as she appeared, she wouldn't be able to change her clothes without help.

He had to divert her attention, and he had the perfect topic. "I know you can," he murmured casually, "but as long as I'm here, I might as well make myself useful."

With the greatest of care, he raised her to a sitting position. He had pitched his voice so low he wasn't certain she could hear him, but there was one statement he knew would probably raise her from the dead. "Besides, there's something I need to tell you—well, really it's a confession, and it's this. I know you'll agree with me when I say how seldom I'm wrong." She made a faint sound of disgust. He smiled. She could hear him. Good. "Well, as it turns out, I was wrong tonight. You don't have Des up here, after all."

"Des didn't...come."

"He never comes to your parties, does he?"

"Some."

"Anyone would think he didn't like you." He quickly slid the zipper down to below her waist, then slipped the dress off her arms.

"He likes..."

The lined dress fell to her waist. He paused, and his throat went dry when he saw the cream-colored, sheer lacy bra she was wearing. He brought her forward to lean against him so that he could reach around her and undo the bra. Perfume rose from her skin as the bra fell away to reveal rose-colored areolas and tight pointed nipples. He felt himself harden, and his mouth began to water.

He tossed the bra toward the closet and forced himself to continue. "I'm guessing that you've decided now is the time to pull out all the stops and go after him, am I right?" He slipped the sleeveless knit gown over her head. "Raise your arms for me."

"No." There was a lack of comprehension in her bruised eyes, but he sensed she was trying hard to focus on what he was saying. "Des likes me."

"Yes, he does—as a member of his family. Lift your arms, honey, so I can put on the gown." Slowly she did. "But I feel I should tell you that you don't have a chance in hell of getting him into bed, much less to the altar."

"No. I do. I mean, why...why would you think I don't?"

He forced himself to concentrate on getting her arms through the openings of the gown's sleeves and not looking at her breasts. Still, the back of his hand brushed the top of one of them, causing his breath to catch in his throat. He almost groaned. Her breasts were exactly as he had imagined them to be—high, round and firm, large enough to fill his hands, but not large enough to make a man's neck whip around when she walked by. Just as he liked, wanted.

"Well, first of all," he said, the huskiness in his voice revealing the effect she was having on him, "as I said before, he considers you family, and I can't see you changing his mind on that. After all, you're not exactly a femme fatale, now are you?"

"I am…"

He pulled the gown down over her breasts, thankful that he had finished that part of undressing her. It had to be the most difficult part. At least, he hoped it would be. He didn't know how much temptation he could stand. "You are what?"

"A femme…"

"Fatale?" he supplied when she couldn't seem to come up with the last word.

"Yes." She looked down at the gown that covered her to her waist as if she'd didn't have a clue how it had gotten there.

"Lie back down." He cradled her head in his palm and eased her back to the pillow and bed. "As for you being a femme fatale, I would really like to agree with you, but I'm afraid I can't." An out-and-out lie, but now was not the time to profess how easily she could make him want her. Even a gesture as simple as lifting a canape to her mouth could have him fighting to resist vaulting the table and kissing her until all her barriers were down and she didn't care where she was or who was watching.

He stood, bent over her and eased the rest of the ivory sheath over her hips, down her legs and off. For a minute he just stared. She was wearing a tiny scrap of silk and lace that matched her bra.

"I'm going to have Des eating out of my..."

"Hand?" Once again he supplied the word she couldn't seem to come up with, but his voice was rough with the desire that was rising in him, too fast, too uncontrolled. He had to be careful. As out of it as she was, she still might begin to notice.

"I need him."

He cleared his throat. "The problem is, you say you need him, but you don't. It's a matter of what you *want*—you *want* the fifty percent of Baron International Des will inherit from your uncle William when William dies, so that you can screw your sisters to the wall with your majority holding." He forced himself to toss the panties toward the bra and pull the gown down as much as he could.

"Yes. No." She pressed her hand to a spot above her right temple. "When we marry, I'll gain his fifty percent of...our, uh...business. Company."

"That's what I just said."

She remained silent, obviously trying to figure out the conversation.

"Are you that anxious for your uncle William to die?"

Her eyes flew open, then quickly closed again. "No. I love him."

"Sometimes I wonder if you even know how to love," he muttered. "No one would think so if they heard your plan."

"What?"

"Nothing. Sit up again." As before, he helped her up. She was like a limp doll, her body working only because of his strength. He pulled the top covers from beneath her and slid her pillow back into position as he slowly returned her head to its softness. He couldn't tell whether she was feeling less pain or not. "Besides, strictly speaking, *you* won't gain the fifty percent, Des will, and who knows what he'll want to do with it."

"Once we're married..."

"*If* you marry him, you mean. But for argument's sake, let's say you do get him to marry you. Do you honestly think he's going to be so overwhelmed by your feminine charms that he'll just hand over his percentage?"

"Yes, he—"

"Think again, honey. Besides, do you really think you're the only woman who wants Des? And not for his future percentage of Baron International, either."

"Who?"

Now it was a fairly easy task to pull her gown over her hips down to her ankles, straighten it, then draw the covers from beneath her legs, up and over her.

"Is that better? Do you feel warmer now?"

She gave a small sigh, and he hoped the sigh meant she felt at least a bit more comfortable.

After a moment, she frowned. "Des will..." Once again she pressed her hand to the same spot she had before, the spot above her right temple. "He's never shown interest..."

"You're right. He's never shown any interest in Baron International, but I wouldn't bet against him once he inherits his father's portion. In case you don't know it, Des is a very astute businessman. How are you feeling now?"

"I..." She stopped, and he had the feeling she was having to evaluate the pain, which meant he'd been somewhat successful in preoccupying her.

"It's still bad."

He checked his watch. "It's been fifteen minutes since I gave you your medication. Should you be feeling less pain by now?"

"I will."

"You mean you'll feel better soon?"

She didn't respond. Looking down at her beautiful pale face, he felt more helpless than he could ever remember. "I'm going to call your doctor. Where's the number?"

She moaned and made an attempt to move that was quickly ended. "Sniffer."

"What?"

She lifted a shaky hand and pointed to the nightstand. "Sniffer."

He jerked the drawer open, causing pill bottles to roll every which way. "Sniffer?" Then he saw it. An inhaler. He held it up. "Is this what you want?"

She stretched out her hand for it, and he gave it to her. With his help, she struggled up to one elbow, then looked at him. "This will...put me out and I'll...be fine."

"Okay."

"Will you...go?"

"As soon as I know you're okay, I'll go."

One puff from the inhaler and she fell back onto the pillow.

He watched her for several minutes. She lay very still, though it seemed to him that she was starting to breathe easier. She had no way of knowing it, but he had zero intention of leaving her alone tonight in this big house. Anything could happen, and she wouldn't be able to help herself. "Jill?"

She didn't answer. He slid off the bed. Immediately her eyes flew open.

"Do you have to…go just yet?"

"No."

"Just a…little longer."

He could barely believe she was actually asking him to stay. For her to ask, she must be in a kind of hell he could only imagine. "Of course I'll stay, for as long as you want me to."

Her eyes closed again. "Only a…little…" Her words trailed off.

He shrugged out of his jacket, slid his tie from around his neck, rolled up his sleeves and slipped off his shoes. He eased himself down on the other side of the bed. Taking a couple of pillows, he arranged them to his satisfaction, then settled back.

She moaned, and in her drugged sleep, she edged closer to him. She must still be cold. Slowly he drew her against him, though he was on top of the covers and she was beneath them. He put his arm around her and rested her head on his chest.

For so long he'd wanted to hold her, but not like this. All he could think of was how to get her more comfortable. Again she moaned. What could he do?

Two

Something disturbed her. A scent invaded her senses. Something was happening that she didn't want to happen. Unwillingly, Jill felt herself being drawn upward through layers of blissful sleep to wakefulness, but she resisted moving or opening her eyes. Instinct told her something was wrong. She was warm and comfortable, but she felt...fragile. *Extremely* fragile.

Then she remembered. She'd had a migraine last night. It was gone, but as always, her head retained the memory of the pain. She softly sighed. She hadn't had a migraine in two months and had convinced herself that she was over them. *Damn.* To make it worse, this one had been a killer, one of the worst she'd had.

What had happened? And what was it that she was smelling? And feeling?

Trying to piece together the previous night's events, she grasped at remnants of the pictures that were floating in and out of her consciousness. The party—it had gone well. Holland Mathis and Tyler Forster were to the point of agreeing to what she wanted, which had been the main purpose of the party. Yes, she remembered. And she had even been able to lay the groundwork for future projects with others.

Champagne. Blue filtered lights. Golden brown eyes. Hair that always seemed to need combing.

Colin.

Now she remembered. He had returned, showing up in her backyard after everyone had left. He had said he'd returned because he had sensed something was wrong. That had been really strange.

Sometimes Colin could be the bane of her existence. No one could get to her the way he could. When she tried to ignore him, he refused to let her. And when she tried to cut him dead by turning a cold shoulder, he would just laugh at her.

A year ago he had offered to fly her and quite a few of their friends down to Corpus Christie in his latest toy, a new plane. The occasion had been her sister Tess's birthday party, but he'd left without her. The reason? She was fifteen minutes late, and he had refused to wait. She had been furious.

Yet other times, she would find herself attracted to him. That is, until she could manage to regain control of her senses and sternly remind herself why she couldn't be attracted to Colin. *Des* was the man she planned to marry—if she could just get him to cooperate.

Still…she owed Colin. As much as she hated even to consider the idea, she definitely owed him. When the pain had hit, he had been there for her.

She liked to think she could have taken care of herself, but truthfully, she would never know, because he had stepped in and helped her. She was going to have to come up with some appropriate way to thank him. Perhaps a plant for his office.

She inwardly groaned. How should she know what was appropriate? Maybe she would just wait until she went in to work and discuss the matter with Molly. For now, her thinking was still too fuzzy.

Slowly, she opened her eyes and saw sunlight flooding her bedroom. She gave another inward groan. Normally, as soon as the sun slanted its first rays into her bedroom, she hopped out of bed, eager to attack the day. But she didn't feel all that well just yet. She felt enervated, weak, and the urge to stay in bed was strong.

However, she had tried hard never to allow herself to use the migraines as an excuse to slack off, and she wasn't going to now. When she was at work, she tried to be more aware of the signs of an oncoming migraine. There, if necessary, she would even give herself a shot that would stop the headache dead in its tracks and allow her to continue her business day. But since she had been alone last night, she'd been reluctant to rely on medication and had tried to fight the pain off by willing it away. So much for her will.

She turned her head to glance at her bedside clock. Seven-thirty. Usually she was in her office by seven. If she got up now, she could be in by eight-thirty, nine at the latest. Experimentally, she pushed herself up in bed.

"Feeling better?"

Every muscle in her body froze. *Colin.* She twisted around and gasped.

He was lying on his back, his arm behind his head, the covers at his waist giving her a breathtaking vision of his bare chest. Golden-brown hairs curled over its width and downward to disappear beneath the covers. Dear Lord, was he naked? She closed her eyes, then quickly opened them again. "What are you doing here?"

He shifted, and the bed dipped as he angled his body toward her, came up on his elbow and propped his head up with his hand just inches from her. His face was so close she could see the fine golden-brown stubble on his jaw and the gold streaks in his eyes.

"You don't remember?"

"I..." A memory floated to the forefront of her brain. She'd been reluctant for him to leave, though she couldn't actually recall asking him to stay. But that memory brought others. The pain had been so bad she'd felt a vital, essential need to hold on to him, as if his strength could keep the pain from sweeping her away. But...

Her brow creased as she prodded her memory further. "I remember you walked around the bed and got on top of the covers." And once he was on the bed beside her, his warmth had drawn her toward him. Without really knowing what she was doing, she'd cuddled against his upper body, doing her best to soak up the heat and strength of him. But she was sure the covers had been between them.

And now she recognized the scent that had invaded her sleep. The covers and the air around her were filled with the scent of spices and musk. It was the bold, sexual scent that was uniquely Colin's and was probably on the sheets where he'd slept. "I didn't expect you to stay all night. And I didn't expect you to...uh...undress.''

He pushed himself up in bed to a sitting position. The covers fell away enough that she could see the black elastic waistband of his briefs. She breathed a quiet sigh of relief. At least he wasn't totally naked.

"The truth is, I never had any intention of leaving you alone. If you hadn't said something, I had planned to wait outside the door until I thought you were asleep, then come back in."

She blinked. "Why?"

"I couldn't leave you alone. You were too sick, too out of it, and there are a hundred other reasons why you shouldn't have been left alone. If you'd gotten worse, or had a reaction to the medication, or if you'd needed something, I wanted to be here. Hell, what if the house had caught on fire? You would have been defenseless. No, Jill, I couldn't leave you alone."

She had never seen his eyes as soft as they were now. She caught her bottom lip between her teeth. A moment later, she realized what she was doing. Chewing on her bottom lip was a bad trait left over from a stressful childhood. "And, uh, what went into the decision that moved you from on top of the bed, fully dressed, to under the covers and undressed?"

He grinned. "Even after the medicine hit you and you went out like a light, you couldn't seem to get comfortable. I decided you still might be cold, and I was right. As soon as I undressed and got beneath the covers, I pulled you against me. Almost immediately you relaxed."

There was nothing she could say. None of what she'd done had been conscious, and therefore she couldn't explain her actions. The medication always made her feel odd, as if she might float away. She had a vague recollection of his arm around her, of being pulled against him, of at last feeling secure and, strangely, anchored to something strong.

"How long have you been awake?"

"Since the sun came up."

"Why didn't you wake me?" For the first time irritation shaded her tone.

He responded by smiling, slowly, and she found herself caught up in watching the movement of his lips, their fullness, their sensual shape. And then there was his dimple. She stared at it, vaguely fascinated.

"Manners."

"Excuse me?"

"I didn't wake you up because it wouldn't have been polite."

"Why on earth not?"

"You were all tangled up with me."

The air went out of her lungs as the feeling came back to her of her leg between his and her arm laid across his middle. Her face grew hot. She would swear she never blushed, but now she couldn't be sure, because his gaze had suddenly narrowed on her face.

"Besides, you were sleeping so well I hated to wake you."

"But when I did wake up, you...I mean, *I* was...over *here*."

He shrugged. "I'd been lying in one position all night. My muscles had started to cramp, and I needed to stretch out. I disentangled us, though I tried hard not to wake you. Sorry."

She nodded, though she had no idea why. She was

just grateful that she hadn't awakened in his arms. That would have been incredibly awkward and excruciatingly embarrassing.

"How are you feeling?" He threw back the covers and slipped off the bed. His solid black briefs fit him as if they'd been cut just for him, and he seemed as comfortable in front of her as if he paraded around her bedroom every day, nearly naked. To him it was obviously not a big deal, but then, he must have dressed and undressed many times before in other women's bedrooms.

She barely had time to absorb that strangely disturbing thought when, with his back to her, he bent over to retrieve his trousers, offering her a view of his muscled back that tapered down to a narrow waist, then continued on to the tight roundness of his buttocks. Her throat went dry. She'd known him for more than two years, yet she'd never once thought to wonder how he would look with no clothes. Now she wouldn't have to. The close fit of his briefs left very little to the imagination.

"Jill?"

"What?"

"You never answered my question. Are you feeling better?"

In what seemed like slow motion, he drew on his trousers one leg at a time, so that she could see the arresting play of his muscles beneath his skin. In the sunlight, the hair on his legs was more golden than brown and gilded his tan. When his pants were settled around his waist, she heard the swift, efficient zip of his trousers.

She felt a pang of regret. It was such a foreign feeling to her that it left her shaken and more than a little bemused. It was only when she realized that Colin was looking at her with an amused expression on his face that she realized she hadn't answered him.

"Okay. I feel okay."

"Just okay?"

"I'm fine."

"Is the pain *completely* gone?"

"All but the memory."

His eyes narrowed on her. "What's wrong, Jill?" His words were soft and filled with concern, the concern she remembered from last night.

"Nothing. It's just...I'm sorry you felt you had to stay all night. You couldn't have been comfortable." Not the way she'd clung to him. "Were you even able to sleep?"

"Yes. After you calmed and I was sure you were sleeping well, I went to sleep."

She forced a short laugh. "I guess you're accustomed to sleeping with women."

With a glance at her that she couldn't interpret, he reached for his shirt. "How long have you suffered from these migraines?"

She stared at his bare chest. "Not long."

He shrugged into the shirt. "Wrong answer. I got a glance at the dates on those prescription bottles. A few of them date back nearly a year."

She couldn't get her mind past the fact that they had slept in the same bed. She'd never slept in the same bed with *anyone,* and that included her sisters. Even more disturbing, there wasn't anything platonic about the way she and Colin had slept together. As he had said, she'd only really been able to fall into a truly restful sleep when she'd been tangled up with him. Even though sex hadn't been involved, to her way of thinking, their night together had been incredibly intimate.

To Colin, it probably wasn't that unusual. Not that she was branding him as a womanizer. From her observation, he was as likely to show up at a function without a date as he was to show up with one. Even then, he never seemed serious about any of his dates. She should know. More than once she'd been trapped by one or the other of her female acquaintances as the woman alternately salivated over him and moaned over his lack of interest.

"The migraines aren't anything to be ashamed of, Jill." He tucked his shirt into his trousers. "What has your doctor said about them? I mean, does he know what causes them?"

She slowly shook her head. "I'm perfectly healthy, if that's what you mean. I've been through numerous tests."

His expression darkened. "If all your doctor can do is write out prescriptions for you, you should see another doctor."

"I have, and he said and did the same thing." She already felt too exposed, too vulnerable to him. She didn't want him to know any more than he already did. "But I'm getting better. The last headache I had was two months ago." She pushed the covers off her, then stopped. Since she'd awakened, she'd been so focused on Colin, absorbing the fact that they had slept together and watching him as he had dressed, that she hadn't given much thought to what she was wearing. Now she realized she was wearing only a nightgown.

"Before that, how often had you been having the headaches?"

"Never mind that. How did I get this gown on?"

"I put it on you."

"Which means you took off my clothes."

He gave her one of his lazy grins, fascinating dimple included. "Don't worry. I didn't take advantage of you."

"It never crossed my mind that you did."

The fact that he'd seen her nearly naked was enough to make her want to hide under the covers until he left. Even worse, if she had slid her leg between his, it meant that her gown could have ridden up, which brought on another thought. She shifted her bottom ever so slightly.

She began to chew on her lip. She had never been as embarrassed about anything as she was about this. From now on, whenever their eyes met, they would both know that he'd practically seen her naked. The only thing she could think to do now was to try to avoid him as much as possible in the days to come. Hopefully she would soon be able to regain her composure around him. Hopefully.

"Have you ever had to use that inhalant before? It seemed pretty potent stuff."

"No." Her doctor had warned her to be standing by her bed when she used it, because it would probably knock her out. Now she knew he had been right. But he hadn't warned her what she would do if there happened to be a man in her bed. She barely stifled a groan.

"That means that last night's headache was one of your worst. I think you should call your doctor today and tell him about it."

It took a tremendous effort, but somehow she pulled herself together. "Look, I really appreciate your being here for me last night. The headache *was* a bad one. But I'm late.'' She glanced again at the clock and saw that it was already eight. She was surprised Molly hadn't called her, but since she'd known about the oncoming headache last night, she'd probably decided not to bother her. "I'm *very* late, and I need to get up and get dressed."

She slid off the bed and stood. "Before you go, though, I'd like to ask a favor."

Damn. She really hated to be beholden to anyone, especially someone who now knew more about her—and had *experienced* more of her—than even her doctors. Irrationally, she wanted to get back into bed and pull the covers over her head. But that wasn't the way she had been taught to handle things. Instead, she looked at him and saw that his gaze was fixed on her breasts. She didn't even have to glance down to know that her nipples had tightened. She folded her arms across herself.

"Colin?" She waited until his gaze was once again level with hers, and her knees went weak at the heat she saw in his eyes. She cleared her throat. "I said I'd like to ask a favor of you."

"I heard you. Ask away."

"I'd appreciate it if you would keep the information regarding my problem to yourself."

"Problem? You mean the fact that you suffer from migraines?"

"That's what I mean."

He slung his tie around his neck. "What's the matter, Jill? Are you afraid someone might actually think you've got a chink in your armor?"

As he had so many times before, he was baiting

her. But this time, she wasn't going to bite. "Will you keep the information to yourself?"

"You know, migraines shouldn't be looked at as some sort of failure on your part, or a weakness. Besides, you're not the only one who has migraines. Quite a few of our acquaintances also have them."

"How do you know?"

He shrugged. "I listen."

She took a deep breath, disgusted with herself at how easily she let him divert her. *"Will you?"*

"Of course I won't tell anyone."

"And, uh...the rest?" Once again, she caught her bottom lip between her teeth.

He lifted his jacket off a chair and, holding it with two fingers, slung it over his shoulder. "What happened between us will stay between us."

She exhaled. He hadn't made her say the words. "Thank you."

His golden-brown eyes on her, he slowly strolled toward her. Stopping in front of her, he murmured, "You're welcome. I'm just grateful you're not still in pain." Then he slowly lowered his head and pressed a kiss to her forehead. "Take it easy on yourself today." His mouth descended to her lips, where it hovered. "Take your time getting to the office."

The warmth of his breath whispered over her lips. She held her own breath as a quiver shivered through her. Was he going to kiss her?

He touched her face in a light caress. "Eat something before you leave, and drive slowly to work." He lifted his head and gazed down into her eyes. Then he smiled. "See you in a few hours." He swiveled and headed for the door.

His hand was on the doorknob before she came to

her senses. "Wait. What do you mean, you'll see me in a few hours?"

"Have you forgotten? I have an appointment with you at two." He walked out and quietly shut the door behind him.

Stunned, she sat down on the bed.

A few hours? That was all the time she was going to have to get over what had happened? She exhaled a shaky breath. Well, okay, then. Even though she had been counting on not seeing him for a while, she would have to find some way to face him this afternoon. She had never before let herself walk away from something just because it was difficult, and she wouldn't now.

If she hadn't exactly asked him to spend the night with her, she *had* asked him to stay with her a little while longer. She didn't know why she had felt she needed him, nor did she know why she had slowly slid toward him to seek his warmth. And more.

All she really knew was that she had felt strange and lost until Colin had drawn her against him and held her through the night.

Three

"Good afternoon, Colin." Jill eyed him cautiously across the gleaming, neatly organized expanse of her mahogany desk.

"Is it?" She was trying very hard to present her usual composed and imperturbable persona, Colin reflected, but she was trying too hard. With a satisfied smile to himself, he dropped into one of the chairs in front of her desk. After last night, no matter what she said or did, he knew she would never again be able to reconstruct the barrier she had tried so hard to keep between the two of them.

"Is it what?"

"Is it a good afternoon? Are you feeling better than you did this morning?"

"Yes, I'm just fine."

"No sign of another headache?"

"No." Her jaw clenched.

He hid another smile. She was *really* regretting his part in helping her last night. Unfortunately for her, it had happened, and though she was going to try her best to get them back to the casual acquaintanceship with which she had been so comfortable these past couple of years, he had no plans to let her.

"Now that we've covered that subject," she said tersely, "let's please drop it."

"Sure, whatever you want." He took in her outfit. She'd chosen a tailored, pin-striped navy suit paired with a cream silk blouse, buttoned at her neck. A plain gold watch at her wrist was her only jewelry. The look was unusually severe, even for her. And her hair was back up in that damnable French twist she seemed so fond of, though not as tight as it had been last night. He would bet money her head was still tender from the pain she'd suffered. "I won't ask you again unless I see you looking like you did last night."

She stared at him for several moments, emotions chasing across her face too fast for him to decipher; then she broke eye contact, opened the folder in front of her and quickly scanned its contents. "Why did you even bother to schedule this meeting, Colin? I could have told you over the phone what I'm going to tell you now. I have no intention of selling you the property that's adjacent to yours."

"Why?"

She folded her hands together and rested them on the desk. "Let's not play games. You know every one of the reasons I want to keep that piece of land. Even alone, it's going to provide a big payoff once it's developed. But I have another, very strong reason for keeping the property. You flat out stole your property away from me. And *that,* Colin, is my last reason for not selling to you. It's a matter of principle.''

''Interesting. I never knew you held grudges.'' He leaned back in the chair and rested one ankle on the knee of his other leg. He was going to enjoy this. ''Besides, *stole* is a pretty strong word. I did nothing illegal or, I might add, immoral.''

''That last is debatable.'' She got up and paced to the window, which offered a panoramic view of downtown Dallas, but she didn't even give herself time to register the view before she turned back to him. ''I don't know how you did it, but somehow you got wind of the fact that I was going after both of those properties. I think they got your check ten minutes before I arrived with mine.''

His shrug and expression clearly indicated, *So what?* True, he did his best to keep up with what was going on in her life, but it had been sheer luck that he'd learned of her interest in the two adjoining properties mere hours after she had made her bid. Since there were no other bids higher than hers, she had assumed hers would be accepted. Moving quickly, he had called in several favors and promised more. In the end, he had topped her bid and bought one of the properties out from under her, with the hope that she would still go ahead and buy the other.

Both parcels of land were gold mines, considering their location near the proposed new sports arena. With the right development, both of their properties would help revitalize the entire area north of the arena. If she decided not to sell to him, which he was counting on, or if she didn't buy into what his real purpose was in being there today, he wouldn't have lost anything. As she had said, just one of the properties was enough to bring in, to say the least, a very nice-sized income.

What he couldn't have foreseen was the serendipitous timing of this appointment. It had given him a chance to see her just hours after she had awoken to find him in her bed, which meant that no matter what she said or did to prove the contrary, she was still off balance with him.

"Tell me something." She strolled to her taupe leather chair and rested her hands on its high back. "Why didn't you simply buy both properties? You could have so easily. Unless...unless you couldn't come up with the money for both of them at that time. Was that it?"

He knew that not having enough money was the only reason she would be able to understand, but just to needle her a little, he chose not to completely satisfy her curiosity. "That was partly it. I bought the property outright, without offering it to other investors. As to my other reasons..." He shrugged again.

Her brow creased in puzzlement, but before she could ask another question, he spoke. "Did you even consider my offer?"

"I consider all offers that cross my desk."

"It was a good, solid offer, Jill."

"I know."

"What if I increase it?"

She shook her head. "Save yourself the time."

It was the response he'd counted on, but if he hadn't tried to buy her out, she would have wondered why. If she'd taken him up on his offer, he would have lost the chance to work closely with her, which had been the whole idea behind his purchase in the first place.

After knowing and studying her and her family for about a year, he had figured out two ways he could go about making her his. What he hadn't known was when he could put his plans into action. Buying the property had been part of his first plan. Then last night, heaven had parted its clouds and a gift had fallen into his lap. As a result, he was almost certain his second plan was about to start. Content, he waited for what he knew would come next.

She leveled a steady gaze on him. "Have you reviewed *my* offer for *your* land?"

"I've reviewed it, yes."

She fidgeted with her slim gold watch band. *"Well?"*

With a regretful expression, he spread out his hands. "I'm inclined to hang on to my land."

"I see." Once again she stared at him. When she was on top of her game, she was as good as he was at masking feelings. Today, though, he could tell she was thinking about last night. Abruptly, she reached around the chair and closed the folder. "Then we're at a stalemate. There's no sense in continuing to talk about offers and counteroffers. This meeting is over."

"Not quite."

"If I'm not willing to sell and neither are you, then I don't see what else we can talk about."

"What about working together?"

Her brow crinkled. "You mean develop our properties together?"

He nodded. If she agreed, it would give him more time with her to work on his main goal, which was to change her mind about her plan to marry Des Baron. If he couldn't, the worst thing that could happen was that he would still make millions. Plus, he now had his second plan in place.

She shook her head. "I never take on a partner in any project I'm involved with. You should know that."

"I do. But I also know that, as far as I can see, that practice is not grounded in practicality." She started to say something, but he hurried on. "I know, I know. It was what your father taught you and your sisters. But think about it, Jill. With that many acres, plus a shared vision of what we want, we would be a force to be reckoned with. Besides offices and retail stores, we could add entertainment facilities and housing. And you know as well as I do that if we work in unison on the design, configuration and spacing of green belts, the city will smile benevolently on us and grant us any permit we ask for."

"I don't do things that way, Colin." She rounded the chair and sat down again.

"I think the problem is more that you don't know *how* to work with anyone else." He slowly smiled. "Come on, Jill. You're already one of the largest land barons in Texas, plus you own enormous amounts of property around the globe. It's not as if your reputation would be ruined if, just this once, you joined up with someone else. In case you haven't noticed, very few people work alone anymore. Besides, just think of the fun we'd have."

"Fun?" For several moments her gaze fastened on his smile, his lips, his dimple. Then she seemed to catch herself. "My sister Tess sold out to another oil company in her last venture and in the process lost millions. That's not going to happen to me."

"It wouldn't if we formed an alliance. In fact, it

would put us in a position to make more than we would if we worked separately. Besides, you and I both know that Tess didn't *sell out*. She made a great deal. And anyway, that was an entirely different situation from this one." His voice softened. "She made that deal for love. That wouldn't be the case with us, would it?"

She frowned. "No, of course not."

"Well, then?"

"No, Colin."

"You know what? I think that 'no' of yours is automatic, as so many things are with you."

"What do you mean?"

"All I'm asking is that you not dismiss my idea out of hand. Think about it." He pushed himself up from the chair, leaned forward and placed the bound folder on her desk in front of her. "This holds a few ideas I've sketched out. Study them with an open mind, and I think you'll see the benefits of working together—an *open mind* being the key. Whether you want to, though, is an entirely different matter." He reached out and lightly stroked his fingers down her cheek. She flinched. "Take care," he murmured with a smile, then straightened and headed for the door. He walked as slowly as he could. The last thing he wanted to do was draw her suspicions. He had his hand on the doorknob when she stopped him.

"Wait. There is, uh, one more thing I'd like to talk with you about."

He exhaled a pent-up breath, then turned with a feigned look of surprise on his face. "Oh, yeah? What's that?"

As he moved back toward her, a dozen thoughts went through her mind. Unfortunately, they were all about him. He was dressed casually in a shirt, slacks and a sport jacket, which made him look wonderful. The problem was, she now knew what he looked like beneath his clothes, and try as she might, she couldn't wipe away the memories.

She remembered exactly how his muscles had rippled across his back as he'd dressed and the way those black briefs had fit him so well that she could picture the shape of his buttocks. Then there was the warm, safe way she'd felt when she'd awoken in his arms. His scent, his feel...

She wiped a hand across her brow and was surprised to find she wasn't sweating. She had to be crazy to do what she was about to do. Bringing up *anything* about last night was dangerous, but in this case...

Instead of sitting, he stood to the side of the chair and slipped his hand into his slacks pocket. It was a casual stance, but in his case, it was almost a stance of power. "What is it?"

She cleared her throat. "I've been remembering more about last night, and I, uh, remember you talking about Des."

"That's right."

Nodding her head, she fiddled with the corner edge of the folder he'd given her. "As I recall, you seemed to have very definite opinions about what he likes and doesn't like."

"As I said last night, we've become very good friends."

She glanced down at the folder. "I would never ask you to betray a confidence of course, but I was just wondering...has he ever said anything about me?"

"Only in the most general of terms."

"What do you mean?"

"He sometimes refers to you and your sisters as 'the girls.'"

"As if we were one entity?" Equal parts surprise and offense filled her voice. She and her sisters had never been one entity, never been so close to one another that they were like one. Their father had seen to that.

"I don't know how much you remember about our conversation, but I did tell you that he considers you family."

Lord, the task of getting Des to the altar was going to be even harder than she had anticipated. She wiped her fingers across her forehead, realized she was repeating something she had just done, then straightened and leveled her best businesslike, unblinking gaze on him. "You also said that you felt he was dead wrong for me. That was an outrageous statement to make, Colin."

"Maybe, but it is also true."

"You can't know that for sure. No one can."

"Maybe not, but I can have an opinion based on a certain amount of knowledge."

"I see." She rose from her chair and paced to the window, then back to the desk. "And that knowledge, I assume, is partly based on your belief that I'm not a femme fatale." She hated even saying the words. She'd always prided herself on the fact that she had never used her womanly wiles to get where she was today. Now she had to wonder if she even had any womanly wiles.

"You've pretty much remembered our entire conversation."

"Yeah, it's just other parts of the night that I'm having a little trouble with." She paused, picked up a pen and tapped it against her hand. "I also remember your statement that you think I've decided that now is the time to go after him."

He smiled. "I'm right, aren't I?"

She couldn't help it. Her expression turned perplexed. "How could you possibly come to that conclusion? You don't know me that well."

"I know you better than you think, so don't even bother telling me I'm wrong on that. Let's focus on the other thing I said—that you're not a femme fatale. Are you telling me I'm wrong?"

She chewed on her bottom lip, then stopped herself. But the tapping of the pen became faster. "I've never thought about it." Until now, she added to herself.

"And now that you have…?"

Now that she had, she had to admit that he was right, though she wasn't going to give him the satisfaction of telling him so. "Up to now, I haven't focused on that particular aspect of, uh…"

"Being a woman?" he supplied helpfully.

She shrugged. "I've always been a quick study. How hard can it be?" She eyed him, something, perhaps an idea, tickling at the back of her mind. "You didn't answer my question."

"That's because I can't." He smiled. "I've never been a woman."

She almost laughed at the thought. He was one of the most masculine men she'd ever known. Why hadn't she noticed it before? As soon as the question formed in her mind, the answer followed: she wore blinders that kept her from seeing anything but business. If she hadn't been born with them—and she wasn't entirely certain that she hadn't been—then her father had strapped them on her shortly thereafter. "But you're certainly around a lot of women. I mean, you seem to...*attract* women."

"What's your point?"

"I don't know." Her answer was an honest one, but she kept prodding at her mind, trying to figure it out. Whenever she was uncertain about a decision she needed to make, she usually made a list of what she knew for a fact, so that was what she did now. "You seem to know a lot about Des. And you certainly know a lot about women."

"Where did you get that second idea?"

She drew her brows together, annoyed that he'd interrupted her fragile train of thought. "I've talked to quite a few of your castoffs."

"I don't cast off women."

"They seem to think you do."

"Think about what you just said, Jill." His tone was surprisingly gentle, but his expression was uncompromising. "That can't be true."

She threw the gold pen on the desk. "Okay, okay—they're usually just disappointed that you don't get serious about them and normally don't ask them out again beyond the first or second date."

"I don't lead women on, Jill."

She sighed, sorry she had even brought up the subject. "Look, what you do with women is your business, okay?"

He stared at her with an expression that clearly said he wasn't going to let her get away with anything.

"Don't look at me like that. You *know* women only

have to look at you to start drooling over you. And if you happen to smile at them and they see that damned dimple of yours, they're suddenly planning their wedding."

"Once again, I think you're exaggerating."

She folded her arms across her chest. "No, actually, I'm right on that one. You seem to only want to be friends with most of them, and from what they say, you make a great friend. But that doesn't keep them from being extremely disappointed, or hoping that one day you'll look at them in a more romantic way. At any rate, why are we talking about *your* relationships with women when we started out talking about *Des* and what he thinks about me?"

"I believe you brought up the subject of my, as you put it, relationships with women."

"I did?" She frowned. It was what she privately termed the day-after-a-migraine syndrome. She often had trouble keeping her mind on a subject. And after last night with Colin... *Damn.*

"What's bothering you, Jill?"

She attempted to erase all thought from her mind and tried again. "Des. Des..." The idea that had been tickling at the back of her mind suddenly came to the front, fully formed.

He shook his head. "Sorry, but you don't have a chance with him."

"So you say." She eyed him warily. "Can I trust you?"

He seemed to relax, and with a smile, he sat down on the corner of her desk. "You slept in my arms last night. If you can't trust me, who *can* you trust?"

She almost groaned. "Will you please just *forget* about that?"

He chuckled. "You're kidding, right?"

Everything in her was tensed as she walked around the desk and stopped in front of him. Even though he was sitting and she was standing, their eyes were almost even. "I'm simply trying to find out if I can confide in you without you running off to Des and telling him everything I say to you."

"I would never betray you."

She got the impression his words had a deeper meaning, but perhaps it was her imagination. But there was another problem that had nothing to do with her imagination. She was standing so close to him that she could smell him, could smell the scent she had awoken to just hours before. As unobtrusively as possible, she moved a couple of feet away.

But it didn't do her any good. Last night was indelibly etched in her brain, which was odd, since half of it had been spent in severe pain and the other half in sleep. When she had time, she needed to figure that one out.

"Okay, then, see what you think about this idea. You know Des. You know women. Would you consider teaching me how to attract Des and become a—" she swallowed against a hard lump in her throat and prayed he wouldn't laugh at her "—femme fatale?"

She paced farther away from him, then turned and came back to him, unsure what she would see on his face. But to her surprise, he was eyeing her thoughtfully.

"Say I did. What would be in it for me?"

The idea was so new she hadn't considered that part, but it made sense that he would want some form of compensation. "I don't know. What would you want? Money?"

"I've got plenty of money."

"Then what?"

"Something that wouldn't cost you a dime."

"And that would be?"

"Your agreement that we work together in developing our land."

She hadn't even seen it coming. "Damn you, Colin. You know—"

"I *do* know," he said, cutting her off. "Family custom. So you're going to have to decide which is more important to you—the teachings of a father who is long dead or getting Des."

With a sound of anger, she whirled away and began pacing the conference area of her office. Comfortable chairs surrounded a long meeting table. Couches flanked a fireplace. A refreshment center was in a corner. But she barely noticed any of it. It seemed her brain would only hold Colin, and to think clearly, she had to get away from him, away from his smell that was still in her sheets at home, away from his smile that kept diverting her.

The funny thing was that she wasn't a pacer. The new habit seemed to have started since last night. Damn, she had done it again. Even the two words— last night—had the power to bring memories flooding back. As firmly as she could, she pushed those thoughts aside and tried to train her mind on the problem at hand.

Thinking rationally and adding up everything she knew to be true, she could come to no other conclusion. Colin would be an enormous help to her in her effort to gain not only Des's attention but, more importantly, his agreement to marriage.

What was more, without even looking at his ideas, she knew he was right. If they developed their properties together, they stood to make more money. It made sense. Everything he had said made sense. She would make millions *and* gain the skills to achieve her greatest goal.

So why did she feel there was something she hadn't thought of in this bargain to which she was about to agree? But even if there was, the positives far outweighed any possible negatives. With Des's wedding band on her finger, she would at last control Baron International, something she had wanted for as long as she could remember.

She stopped and looked across the office at Colin. "Okay, it's a deal."

He slowly smiled. "Good decision."

"When do we start?"

"On you, or on our two pieces of land?"

Impatiently she closed the distance between them. "I'll look over your ideas and come up with some of my own. Then we can make another appointment to discuss the land. But for now, I'd like our focus to be on turning me into whatever you think I need to be in order to attract Des."

He came off the desk. "Great. Would tonight be too soon to start?"

She hesitated. Why? she wondered. He was only trying to set into motion what she'd just told him she wanted. "No, tonight would be fine."

"Then I'll be at your house at eight."

"Why?"

"We're going out to dinner, but before we do, I

need to go through your closet and pick out what you should wear."

"For heaven's sake, why? I go out to dinner at least four times a week."

"Maybe, but your dinners are always about one of two things—business or one of the charity committees you work on."

She thought about it and decided that, once again, he was right. "Okay, so how will this be different?"

"Tonight is going to be a *date*." His brown eyes held a golden-colored twinkle that for some reason made her feel warm *and* uneasy inside. "Tell me something, Jill. Can you even remember the last time you went out with a man that had nothing to do with work or charity?"

She tried to recall such an occasion and couldn't. "No, but how hard can a date be?"

"That's what we'll find out tonight. Okay?"

She nodded, once again feeling as though there was something more to this deal than she was seeing. But how could that be? She'd agreed to what Colin wanted, and in turn, he was going to teach her what she needed to know. Quid pro quo. So why was she concerned?

Apparently he read her mind. "Don't worry, Jill. I'll do my best to make sure that, in the end, you get exactly what you want."

Four

"I was right." Colin exited her vast walk-in closet. "You don't have anything appropriate to wear for tonight."

Tapping her foot, Jill stood in the middle of her bedroom, dressed in an ivory silk bathrobe, beneath which she wore neutral-colored bra and panties. Her hair and makeup were already done. She was just waiting for Colin to find something for her to wear of which he approved, and her patience was almost gone. "First of all, what do you mean, you were right?"

"I didn't think I'd find anything for you to wear tonight."

"And how could you possibly know that?" Her irritable tone matched her mood.

"I see you often enough to know what type of clothes you wear. Plus, I was in your closet last night, looking for something warm to put on you, and even though I was in and out pretty fast, I didn't remember seeing anything that would be appropriate for our purposes."

She inwardly sighed. *Last night*. The more she tried to forget what had happened between the two of them the night before, the more she was reminded. "Somewhere in that closet there *has* to be something appropriate for our purposes, whatever that means."

He grinned, and suddenly she remembered how easily that same grin could make a woman melt at his feet.

"Why, Jill, I can't believe you've forgotten. Something that will be appropriate for our purposes means something that will attract Des's attention."

She blinked. Heaven help her, she *had* forgotten. Ever since this morning, when she had awoken with Colin in bed beside her and discovered he'd held her all night long, she had been focused almost totally on him. That had to stop. "There must be something in there," she said, gesturing toward her closet. "The contents would stock a clothing store."

"I agree with that. And by the way, I'm not knocking your taste. It's impeccable."

She threw out her arms. "Then what is it?"

"There's no color in your wardrobe. You always wear neutrals. Men like color. Plus, you dress in a very tailored style, which is fine. But every once in a while men enjoy something less tailored, something that shifts and flows and, at the same time, fits closer to your body and perhaps shows a little more than you like to show."

She crossed her arms and sent him a suspicious look. "Shows a little more *what?*"

"Flesh, honey. Flesh. I've never seen you look anything less than ladylike, even though I have to admit that sometimes you come up with something that strikes me as discreetly sexy. For our purposes, however, that's not good enough."

Honey? She'd thought she had remembered everything from the night before, but now she recalled that he had called her "honey" several times. She couldn't decide whether she was in the middle of her worst nightmare, or if she was merely taking advantage of a gift from the gods. She was trying to convince herself it was the latter.

After Colin had left her office this afternoon, she had gone over every phrase of their conversation, turning his offer to help her attract Des inside out and upside down, and had still come to the same conclusion. He represented her best chance to get Des. But there was only so much she could let him get away with. "For your information, I've never suffered from a lack of men who've been interested in me."

His brows rose. "Have any of those men been Des?"

Damn. He had her there. She chewed on her bottom lip.

"Exactly my point. We'll go shopping tomorrow, but for tonight, I bought something for you to wear." He disappeared into the hall, then reappeared with a glossy honey-colored dress box tied with a matching satin ribbon. She recognized the name on the box. It was from a very exclusive dress shop that carried only the best. She was relieved. At least the dress wouldn't be a piece of trashy lingerie labeled as outerwear.

He handed her the box. "Go try it on. I'm pretty sure it'll fit. There are shoes in there, too."

She wasn't even going to ask how he had known what dress and shoe size she wore. He was entirely too experienced with women for her peace of mind. She took the box from him and went into her gold-and-cream bathroom. With the door closed behind her, she stared at herself in the mirror, bewildered over her last thought. Why should she care how much experience Colin had with women? She shouldn't. She *didn't*.

With that firmly settled in her mind, she untied the bow, pulled off the lid, parted the honey-hued tissue paper and lifted out a handful of material. It was a deep hot pink and created out of some sort of silky blend. When she put it on over her head, it floated down around her, light as gossamer.

She stood at the full-length mirror, assessing herself, turning this way and that, all the while wondering why she felt so uncomfortable in the dress. There was nothing lewd or vulgar about it, and its designer was world-famous. Deservedly so.

The dress was almost a piece of art, ingeniously constructed so that it took nearly all its shape from her body. Clinging to her in an uninhibited manner, the material crisscrossed her breasts in free-form pleats to a plunging V neckline, then curved inward at her waist. From there, the light-as-air material followed the line of her hips to fall without restraint and end at midcalf. The back had the same plunging V.

The weightless material of the dress, combined with its cut, left her feeling as if she wasn't wearing anything at all.

"How does it look?" Colin called.

"I'm not sure," she muttered. "I'll be out in a minute," she said, more loudly. Or not, she thought.

She couldn't find a single fault with the dress, not the design, the fit or the fabric. But she felt...*exposed.*

She returned to the box and the shoes, which turned out to be the same color as the dress, with three-inch heels that were held to her feet with nothing but straps. Taking a few experimental steps, she found that the shoes felt surprisingly stable *and,* drat it, just her size. As for the size of the dress, it adhered to her body so well it was as if it had been made just for her.

She pulled the honey tissue paper from the box and gave it a good shake, hoping a cover-up of some sort might appear. Unfortunately, only a small pink purse fell out. She scooped it up and gave one last look at her image in the mirror; then, with dread and a strange, expectant flutter in her stomach, she returned to the bedroom.

Colin glanced up, saw her and froze. The expression on his face made her heart stop. *Pure, naked lust.* In all the time she'd known him, she had never seen him look at a woman the way he was looking at her now.

Excitement slammed into her; then her heart thudded. Between her legs, full-blown heat appeared and, embarrassingly, she began to moisten.

It all happened within a matter of seconds; then his naked desire disappeared as if it had never been. But her body still felt its impact, and she was left to try to cope.

"Turn around," he said hoarsely.

Without argument, she did. It was as if he was a puppet master, pulling her strings, and she had no other recourse but to let him control her movements, because she still couldn't manage to get command of her feelings.

"Beautiful." The word came out on a breath.

"Did the..." She chewed on her bottom lip for longer than she would ordinarily have allowed herself. Then she straightened. "Did the dress come with any undergarments?"

"No." Slowly, methodically, his gaze touched her from the top of her head to the tip of her toes. "You need to take off the bra you have on. It shows both in the front and the back."

"I know, and I'm sure I have another bra I can wear with it."

"And now that I think about it, those panties need to go, too. Their line shows through the material."

"I'll find replacements." She tossed the small pink purse onto the bed, managing to land it near the navy one she'd carried to work today, then hurried into her closet.

When Colin walked into the brightly lit closet, she was sorting through a large, shallow drawer filled with bras.

"That dress was never meant for a bra. Besides, you don't need to wear one. You have beautiful breasts."

Her face flushed hot. Her head snapped around. "How do you—" *Last night.* "Never mind. I'll find something. Just get out."

"Okay, but remember—you can't wear anything that will show or ruin the line of the dress."

"How very style-conscious of you."

"That's what I'm here for."

"Get out, Colin."

He tilted his head and looked at her. "Why is your jaw tensed?"

She gave a hollow laugh. "You're kidding, right?" She straightened. "It's this...this dress. It may be designed to attract a man, but I might as well be wearing nothing. And if I *don't* wear a bra or panties, I really *will* be wearing nothing."

"And wearing them would make you feel better?"

"Yes."

Ruefully, he shook his head. "We've got much more work to do than I originally thought."

"If you think for one minute that I'll ever go out of this house without wearing—"

He held up his hand. "Never mind. We'll get to that part later."

"Later?" She almost sputtered.

His gaze lowered and his voice thickened. "As for now, panties with a different line are okay, but don't put on a bra. In fact..." He reached behind her, unsnapped the bra, and before she knew what was happening, he had somehow managed to slide the bra straps down her arms, then with one last tug at the bra's front, it was off and tossed over his shoulder. "There," he murmured, his voice thick and filled with satisfaction. "The bodice looks amazing, clinging to your breasts the way it does."

She fell weakly against the drawer, closing it. "That's quite a party trick. No wonder you're such a hit with women."

He stretched a hand toward her, reaching as close to her as he could without actually touching her, and when he spoke, his hand moved around her breasts, demonstrating his words. "Your breasts are perfect—high...firm...just large enough..."

Heat filled her lungs. She felt as if she was suffocating. "Will you please just get the hell out of here?"

He dropped his hand to his side. "Keep your eye on the prize, honey. This is only the first lesson. I know you're finding it hard, but when you get Des, it'll all be worth it." He paused, his eyes suddenly piercing. "Won't it?"

"*Leave.* And don't call me *honey!*"

He chuckled. "Sure. Anything you say."

As soon as he left, she banged her forehead against a cabinet door several times. If this was only the first lesson, she didn't know if she would survive the rest. This one was definitely baptism by fire.

Yet if she did survive, the rest would be a piece of cake. Plus, Colin had said *when* you get Des. Not *if*. That meant he felt he could teach her how to land Des. If she did, it would all be worth it. Wouldn't it? She frowned to herself. Where had that doubt come from? Of *course* it would all be worth it.

She took a deep breath, slipped on a different pair of panties and positioned herself in front of the closet mirror. Automatically she brushed her hand down the dress, straightening it, then eyed herself critically. Colin had been right again. The dress *did* look better without a bra. Though it wasn't obvious that she wasn't wearing anything beneath it, her breasts filled the bodice perfectly.

She went still. Colin knew the shape and size of her breasts. Last night, the pain and medication had made her responses slow, and she hadn't been able to think straight, yet she hadn't been unconscious. He had undressed her, but he hadn't caressed her. If he had, she would have remembered.

Her breasts began to ache as she thought of his hands closing around her, measuring, weighing. His hands were large, his fingers long. How would they feel around her? She groaned at her wayward thoughts.

"Everything all right?" Colin asked.

"Oh, just peachy keen."

"Peachy, huh?"

She heard the amusement in his voice. Shaking her head at herself, she turned off the closet lights and closed the door behind her.

"You look...remarkable." His arms were crossed over his chest, his expression objective, but she couldn't miss the heat in his eyes.

"Thank you...I think."

He chuckled. "Sorry you're finding this so rough."

She mentally chastised herself. She didn't completely understand why, but she had obviously overreacted to Colin's efforts to help her. "Not rough. Just...different." After the hard, regimented way her father had brought her up, wearing a different type of dress than she was accustomed to and without a bra couldn't even compare.

"Then I hope you won't mind me telling you that the color of your toenails is not right."

"What's wrong with them? They're pink."

"They're too pale."

She jerked up the navy purse and transferred what she would need for the evening to the smaller pink purse. "Be strong, Colin. You'll get over it."

"I'm sure you're right, but there's one more thing I need to do before you're completely ready."

"I can't imagine what it could be. You've seen to every single detail."

He stepped toward her. Instinctively she took a step backward.

He gently smiled. "What are you afraid of, Jill?"

Good question. Was she afraid she was going to enjoy herself? Or learn to like being around him too much? Impossible. "I'm not afraid of anything."

"Good, then stand still for just a minute." He reached out and pulled the hairpins from her head, letting them drop to the cream-colored carpet.

"What on earth are you—"

"Your hair," he muttered. "It's way too severe. *As usual.*" When every last pin was gone, he pushed his fingers through her hair and combed until the dark tresses fell loose and full to her shoulder blades. "Much better. Let's go."

"Oh, uh, wait. I need one more thing." She darted into the closet and reappeared with an ivory, finely crocheted shawl wrapped around her. "The night air might be a little cool." Her expression dared him to tell her differently.

He slowly smiled. "Of course. Let's go."

A sudden thought occurred to her. "Wait. You haven't told me where we're going yet."

"Midnight Blues. It's a brand-new blues club down in Deep Ellum."

"Blues—okay. Then there's one more thing. Please, *please,* tell me we won't run into anyone we know there."

"We won't run into anyone we know there."

Her eyes narrowed suspiciously on him. "Are you sure?"

Amusement glinted in his eyes. "I have to admit, I don't know where all our friends and acquaintances are spending this evening, but the club is new, and most people haven't caught on to it yet." The amusement vanished as his gaze darkened and heated. "Besides, what's the worst thing that can happen? That they see you looking like an incredibly desirable woman?" He put his hands on her shoulders, and when she started to pull away, his hold tightened. "Relax, Jill," he said, his voice soft. "You look more beautiful than I've ever seen you look."

"Don't *touch* that door handle."

Confused, she glanced around at Colin. "Why?"

He strolled up with that almost irresistible lazy smile of his, all signs of heat gone from his eyes. "Because, Jill, a woman always waits for her date to open the car door for her."

An objection formed in her mouth, but she swallowed it. Politely, she stood aside while he opened the door for her; then she slid in. He tucked the excess of her skirt inside the car, then shut it.

As he circled the car, settled his long frame inside and drove out of her driveway toward downtown, she reflected that she was beginning to understand how the women he dated felt. When he concentrated all his attention on a woman, as he had on her for the past hour or so, he was incredibly sexy.

He glanced at her. "Allowing me to open the door for you wasn't so hard, was it?"

"Of course not. But since most women are as able as a man to open a door, it's a silly custom." She held up her hand in a pacifying gesture. "But if that little gesture helps to build up a man's ego, then I'll do it—though, as I said before, it's silly."

He chuckled. "You sound as if you're suffering."

"Sorry. It's just that you're asking me to turn one

hundred and eighty degrees on how I think and dress, which must mean that a man, or rather Des, values a woman's looks over a woman's brain. It's rather disheartening."

"Maybe at first a man is drawn to a woman because of the way she looks. But to keep him beside her without anything else going for her but her looks is a whole different story."

"Really?" She'd never thought about it before.

He nodded. "So what I'm trying to do is *soften* you, Jill, and to teach you to accept attention from a man, any man you want—Des, if it turns out he's your heart's desire."

Des? Heart's desire? What a funny way of putting it, she reflected. Not only funny, but wrong, all wrong. "And you're going to teach me how to attract a man, right? I mean, Des."

He nodded. "And keep his attention once it's on you. Let's face it, you're a formidable woman who lets all men know, right off the bat, that you're not interested in them—unless, of course, they have something you want for your business."

"Am I really that bad?"

He smiled gently. "Pretty much."

She mulled over what he had said. "Did you mean it when you said I looked like a very desirable woman?"

He glanced over at her. "Honey, believe me, that was an understatement."

A thrill shot through her. She should remind him not to call her honey, but at the moment it was beyond her. She *felt* desirable, she realized with a start, and it had nothing to do with the dress. Surprisingly, it had everything to do with Colin. She wondered if he knew it, then decided he did. It was all part and parcel of the little indoctrination program he was putting her through.

She picked at the hot-pink silk of her skirt in the same way she would pick at lint. "How did you know how this dress would look on me? It probably didn't look like much on a hanger. And not only that, how did you know it would fit me so perfectly? You even found matching shoes that fit."

He shrugged, taking a corner. "Just lucky, I guess."

"Oh, come on. Luck had nothing to do with it. You must have a lot of experience in buying clothes for women."

"Actually, no, but I'm a quick study. And don't forget, I did have the advantage of spending last night with you in bed."

She closed her eyes. She'd walked right into that one. But he needn't worry. If she lived to be a hundred, she doubted she would ever forget, in her fog of pain and medication, that she had slept the night through in his arms. "I'll pay you back for the dress and shoes of course. Every nickel."

"Whatever you like. By the way, did you have a chance to look over my ideas for our two properties?"

There it was. The reminder of the reason he was doing all this, and she supposed she should be relieved. She chewed on her bottom lip. If there was one thing in the world she understood, it was business. So why, then, did she have butterflies in the pit of her stomach and heat crawling through her veins? It was almost as if she was a teenager on her first date.

And why did she have the feeling that learning to

be a femme fatale with Colin as her teacher just might be the hardest thing she had ever tried to do?

From the moment she'd hit puberty, she had known that she was beautiful. She only had to watch the reaction of the boys at her school, and even some men, as she walked into a room or passed by them on the street.

Only her father appeared unmoved by her beauty. In fact, if anything, he seemed to keep her at more of a distance and treat her with slightly more coolness than he did her sisters, although it was so subtle she doubted anyone else saw it. Sometimes she was even able to talk herself into believing it was just her imagination. After all, why would he be harder on her than he was on Kit and Tess? It didn't make sense. But then he would slight her again, and she would know she was right.

Her father never kept any pictures of her mother out, nor did he allow anyone to talk about her in his presence. But once their uncle William had pulled out an old photograph of a breathtakingly lovely young woman and had told her and her sisters that the woman was their mother. Studying the picture, she had realized that she'd been born with her mother's classical beauty. She'd also realized that perhaps the resemblance to her mother might explain her father's attitude toward her. She had always had the impression that her father had never forgiven his wife for having the automobile accident that had killed her.

Nevertheless, since he was the only man whose approval she wanted, she had learned early to disregard her beauty. And like any child seeking love from a parent, she would work all that much harder to please him with her brains and hard work. To her knowledge, she had never succeeded.

He had been dead for many years now. And she had fulfilled the condition of his will, which stated that unless she and her sisters earned *his* idea of a fortune, they would lose their portions of the company. Yet, his powerful, domineering presence remained, and she still lived her life the way he had taught her. It was not only the way she had learned to survive, it was the only way she knew to live.

In order not to be hurt, she had become completely self-contained, emotionally isolating herself from people as much as possible. She didn't even like to be physically touched. No wonder that even the idea of these upcoming lessons in learning to beguile a man was making her nervous.

"Jill?" Colin snapped his fingers in front of her face.

"What?"

"We're here."

"Oh." She glanced around and saw that they were in a parking lot. *"Oh."* She automatically reached for the door handle.

"Uh-uh."

Damn. She waited impatiently for Colin to walk around to her side of the car, open the door and extend his hand toward her. She took it, allowing him to help her out, but not happily. "Tell me something. Does a man's ego really rise or fall on whether or not his date allows him to open the door for her?"

He smiled down at her. "A man's ego is a fragile thing, Jill."

"I don't believe that for a minute. I'd bet money that yours isn't. And I'm sure Des's isn't."

He put his hand on her back and guided her across the parking lot. "Let me put it this way. A man who truly likes and respects a woman enjoys doing things for her, such as opening doors. And usually it makes the woman in question feel honored that the man thinks enough of her to go out of his way to do things for her."

That idea had never even occurred to her, and reflecting on it, she couldn't think of a thing to say.

When they reached the sidewalk, he took her hand. She barely managed to stop herself from pulling away. She couldn't remember ever holding a man's hand before. Odd, she supposed. Most couples held hands, but then, she had never been part of a couple.

Deep Ellum was so named because it consisted of the blocks literally at the end of Elm Street, lying in the shadows of downtown Dallas and stopping at the gates of Fair Park. In its heyday, during the twenties and thirties, Deep Ellum became famous for its many blues clubs. All the greats had come there to play. Since that time, the street and the area had gone through many reincarnations, but always it had remained an alternative to the norm.

Today the term had grown to incorporate 170 acres of previously run-down, deserted warehouses three blocks east of downtown Dallas. But now the warehouses were being turned into high-priced lofts for people who wanted to enjoy a different way of living, and the waiting list was long.

But the main strip remained Elm, and its present-day clubs were the birthplace for many new cutting-edge bands and the home for trendsetting styles. Some of the old shops that had been there for fifty years or more still remained, but other shops now held art galleries, fashion-forward jewelry and clothing boutiques, restaurants, coffee houses and more.

With a firm grasp on her hand, Colin maneuvered them through a mixed crowd, where people seemed to be chatting and laughing with one another, oblivious to the fact that they were blocking pedestrian traffic.

It was hard for her to find one person who didn't have tattoos, or rings in either their noses, eyebrows, tongues or belly buttons, or a combination thereof. Their hairdos ran from bald to spiked, and the hair colors rainbowed from scarlet and orange to blue and gold. But finally she also saw more normal-looking people, even older couples coming out of restaurants or coffee houses.

At one point Colin looked at her and laughed. "Fun, huh?"

"Do you come down here a lot?"

"Maybe not a lot, but whenever there's something interesting going on, and there usually is, I try to come down. Don't you own quite a few of the old warehouses down here that are being converted?"

She nodded. "I bought up as many as were available, but I've never come down here at night."

"Maybe after this you'll want to."

He angled them toward a black doorway. As soon as he opened the door, music sailed out. She hesitated only because the interior of the club was so dark, but Colin kept her hand in his and ushered her into the club.

Inside, Colin stopped to talk with a big, burly man who had walked over to meet them as if he was an old friend of Colin's. While the two men talked, her eyes gradually began to adjust so that she could see the stage.

A young, white, skinny guy played the guitar. An older black man sat on a straight-back chair slightly to the right and behind him, playing another. There were also a drummer, a saxophonist and a pianist, but they might as well not have been there, as far as the two guitarists were concerned. They were each taking different parts of the song, trading licks as if they could read each other's minds, making their guitars talk to each other in a language that everyone there seemed to understand at some level. She was no expert, but even *she* knew she was hearing something transcendent.

She felt the shawl being whisked off her shoulders; then Colin led her toward the back of the room. She glanced at him just long enough to see that he had her shawl over his arm, then returned to inspecting the club.

Blue neon made random pathways of light across the ceiling and walls. The neon revealed large, stark, black-and-white photos of blues legends, all holding their beloved guitars. She recognized the names— Robert Johnson, Muddy Waters, Howlin' Wolf and other masters. Other pictures showed Billie Holiday and Bessie Smith.

Interspersed among the portraits were other black-and-white pictures of old black men, sitting in rocking chairs on their run-down front porches, playing their guitars. The pictures plainly said that the men might not have glass for their windows, but their souls were full, fed by their guitars and the music they made. Other pictures showed black people walking up and down rows of cotton, stooped over, picking and filling their burlap bags. Under all these pictures were brass plaques that simply said The Birth of the Blues.

Colin's hand extended past her and pointed to an empty booth of midnight-blue leather. She slid in, and Colin slipped in beside her. Her nerves jumped at his closeness.

The music was loud, but a long way from earsplitting. Nevertheless, he put his mouth close to her ear. "Move over a few more inches and give me some room."

She gestured to the other side of the booth. "What about sitting over there?"

He shook his head and gave the waitress a smile as she walked up to them. Jill had no choice but to move closer to the wall, though it did no good, because he simply followed her until his side was against hers.

The blond waitress, who had an ample bosom and a pin on her white blouse that spelled out Maggie, gave Colin her entire attention. But Jill did manage to get in her order of white wine. Colin ordered beer.

As Maggie sashayed off, leaving menus, Colin slid his arm behind her along the top of the booth's leather back. "What do you think of the place?" he asked, leaning toward her, his mouth once again close to her ear, his breath warm on her skin.

She swallowed a feeling of panic. He had her pinned against the wall and the back of the booth. He was too close, too male, too overwhelming, and though he was no longer actually touching her, he was. In every way she could think of. Somehow she managed a smile. "Great music."

His smile held such genuine pleasure it almost took her breath away. "I'm so glad you like it. I love it."

"Those two—" she nodded toward the two guitarists "—are something special."

"What?"

Even though she didn't understand why he couldn't hear her, she positioned her lips close to his ear. "The two guitarists are really special."

He turned his head to reply so fast that he caught her off guard, and his lips brushed hers before she had a chance to turn her head. She literally jumped about half an inch. He placed his left hand on her forearm and slowly rubbed his palm back and forth over it. "You've got to learn not to flinch every time a man touches you."

She looked down at his hand on her arm and nodded. He was right. It would never do to jerk away from Des. But then, this was Colin. "Normally I do much better."

He nodded in agreement. "You do—as long as you don't perceive the person to be a threat to you in some way."

It was an odd thing for him to say, and probably true, though she had never bothered to analyze why she did things. But Colin was fast changing that and, in the process, making her feel extremely vulnerable.

She did her best to edge away from him, failed, and decided to look around at the other patrons. As soon as he had told her they were going to a club in Deep Ellum, she had been certain she would feel out of place in the dress he had bought her. But, to her surprise, she didn't.

The people there spanned all ages and wore all manner of dress. There were those who wore clothing even dressier than she and Colin wore, as if they might have just come from the Morton H. Myerson

Hall, where they had attended a symphony, or perhaps the Music Hall, where they might have attended an opera or a musical.

She thought she even caught a glimpse of a few of the Dallas Cowboys, including the quarterback, at a back table. Normally she would expect them to be mobbed, but here, everyone was leaving everyone else alone. They were there for the music and the company. And Colin had even been right about something else. She didn't think she knew a single person there. Her spirits lightened.

Maybe she could relax, after all, and enjoy herself.

"You need to be looking at me."

She started. "Excuse me?"

"It's a basic rule, Jill. Your attention should be on the man you are with."

"Oh. Well, it's just that the club is so interesting."

"And during conversations, you should hang on his every word, as if he's the most fascinating person you've ever met."

She slowly exhaled. Just as she had decided she might be able to relax and actually enjoy herself, Colin had to remind her that they were there as part of her lessons. She was beginning to hate the word *lesson*. "Look, you can *tell* me things like that—after all, that's the bargain we struck. But do I actually have to *do* the things you say?"

His half smile gave her a peek at his dimple. "You absolutely do. Otherwise, how are you going to learn? I mean, if you don't practice these things with me, you might do them wrong when you're with Des."

He was right, she supposed. Damn it.

Five

The band was on a break, and Billie Holiday's voice filled the club with her heartbreak as she sang "I Don't Stand a Ghost of a Chance with You," a song about her unrequited love for a man.

She didn't understand that kind of love, Jill reflected. How could a woman continue to love a man if he didn't love her? It didn't make sense, and it certainly wouldn't be productive.

She and Colin had finished dinner, though she hadn't eaten much. The fare was basically Cajun, and the few bites she'd taken from her plate had been very good. But she was having problems relaxing. Everything about Colin was overwhelmingly compelling. He was the most intensely virile man she had ever known.

Why hadn't she seen it before now? With her next

breath, she answered her own question. Because she hadn't *allowed* herself to. And now she knew why.

Instinct had led her to keep Colin at arm's length, and in retrospect, it had been a wise decision. She completely understood now why her female acquaintances tried so hard to get, then keep, his attention on them, and why they would become so distraught when inevitably, politely, he slipped away from them.

She was after another man, but that still didn't make her immune to Colin. Not by a long shot. Why? she wondered. She'd had men come after her before—powerful, attractive, important men—yet she'd had no trouble handling them. If it would gain her something, she would play them along until they had served their purpose, then she would walk away.

So why couldn't she be that objective with Colin?

Intellectually, she knew she had his full attention because of a business deal they had made, but emotionally, she could feel herself coming dangerously close to being completely caught up in him. How could that be?

She touched her forehead. She needed to regain control of herself and remember why she was with him in the first place.

She felt his hand touch her shoulder. "Are you getting a headache?"

He looked so concerned that, before she knew it, she had rushed to reassure him. "No, not at all."

"Are you sure? The music isn't too loud for you?"

"No, really, I'm fine."

Now another Billie Holiday song, one that made even less sense to her, was coming over the speakers. "Don't Explain" was about a woman who loved her man so completely that she didn't care what he did, including cheating on her. In her joy and in her pain, the woman would still continue to be his.

She had a vague idea about what love between a man and a woman would require. She wasn't kidding herself. She didn't think she and Des would ever have the kind of marriage her sister Tess and her husband, Nick, had. For one thing, she didn't even begin to understand that kind of marriage. The two of them together seemed so complete, such a whole. Every time she saw her sister, Tess practically glowed with happiness. But as for herself, she wasn't certain it would be worth it to give up so much of herself to another person.

However, as soon as Des agreed to marry her, she would be willing to do her part. If they each went into the marriage with open eyes and minds, they would get along just fine. But she didn't think she could ever love a man to such an extent that nothing else would matter.

"What are you thinking about?"

She was becoming accustomed to Colin's soft, husky voice, so instead of starting, as she might have at the beginning of the evening, she merely turned her head and looked at him. "The lyrics of the song."

"Powerful, aren't they?"

"Yes, and delivered with a wealth of emotion few of today's artists can match."

"Ah, but you have to know the blues to sing them. Plus, there was and will always be only one Lady Day. Unfortunately, she knew all about the blues."

She stared at him, thinking about what he'd said. Her upbringing had been rough, but she'd survived, just as her sisters had, though each in her own way. She probably wasn't as well adjusted as some people were, but she had never allowed herself the luxury of self-pity and had always succeeded in what she set out to do. So she had no self-reference for the blues, but of one thing she was absolutely certain: she would never love a man in the way Billie Holiday sang about.

She believed in learning what you could from the past, then pushing forward to accomplish your goals for the future. Which was why she was here tonight, she reminded herself. She took a sip of her wine.

She felt a finger beneath her chin turning her head to face him. "What kind of blues are those lyrics conjuring up for you?"

"None," she answered quickly, perhaps too quickly.

"No?"

"No." She shook her head in emphasis, freeing herself from his touch.

"Have you ever loved someone that much?"

How in the world did he read her mind like he did? It was not only disconcerting, it was annoying. "Have you?" she asked, deciding to throw the potentially explosive question back at him.

He slowly smiled, his eyes fixed so firmly on her that she had to consciously stop herself from squirming. "Maybe."

It was the last thing in the world she had expected him to say. But now that she thought about it, his answer might explain a question none of her women acquaintances had been able to answer. If he had been deeply in love with a woman before he had come into their group, and something had happened to ruin that love, it would explain why he walked away from a woman every time he sensed she was getting serious.

Maybe his heartbreak still hurt too much. Funny, she reflected, but he was the last man on earth she would imagine allowing a woman to break his heart.

"Who?" she asked, curious, but also on some vague level disturbed.

"Why do you want to know?"

"Because you're a hard man to figure out."

"And do you want to figure me out?"

She shrugged, uncertain what to say. "Some of the women you've dated would like to."

"That wasn't what I asked."

The truth was, now that she'd spent some time with him, she *would* like to know what made him tick. And the thing she would like to know most was what kind of woman would it take to win his heart?

Amusement glittered in Colin's eyes as he reached out and stroked his fingers through her hair. "*You* haven't answered *my* question. Is that because you don't know or don't want to say?"

"I'm not sure." It was the most honest answer she could give him, and he seemed to understand.

His smile broadened. "Let's dance."

"Dance?" She glanced toward the dance floor and saw that it was full of couples completely absorbed in each other, swaying and moving to the music. She took a sip of her wine. "Why?" Her mind was still on the mystery woman in Colin's past.

"Because it would be fun, or isn't that a good enough reason?"

"This is business. We're not on a date, Colin." A sudden realization hit her. She just assumed the woman was in his past, but what if she was still around? She frowned, troubled in a way she couldn't understand.

"No, we're not, but you need to learn how to dance the way Des would expect you to."

That got her attention. "What do you mean?"

He took her hand. "Come on. I'll show you."

Before she could protest, he had her hand and was drawing her across the seat of the booth to her feet. Maybe she *should* have claimed a headache, she realized belatedly.

"I don't need lessons in dancing, Colin. I know how."

He swung her into his arms. "I suppose you do, after a fashion. But you only dance with a man as long as he doesn't hold you close."

"So?" Without the stage lights, the club was darker, more intimate, making it seem as if each couple on the dance floor had their own world where no one else could enter.

"So what's the point of dancing at arm's length?"

"For one thing, it's more civilized. For instance, if you can look at your partner, you can actually carry on a conversation with him."

With that enigmatic half smile of his, he slowly shook his head. "You know what I think?"

"No." But at that moment, she would have given a lot to know.

"I think it's a very good thing for you that I came along."

She couldn't help it—she laughed. "There's certainly nothing wrong with your ego, is there?"

"No, but there's something wrong with the way you're dancing." He pulled her tightly against him. "*This* is the way you dance with a man." He pressed his mouth to her ear. "And if you want to have a conversation with him, *this* is the way to do it."

Each word he spoke feathered warm air against her hair and into the sensitive shell of her ear. Tingles raced down her spine. Instinctively she tried to pull away, but he was quicker; anticipating what she would do, he simply tightened his hold on her. "Trust me, Jill. Des will expect you to be this close to him, or closer, especially if you expect him to marry you."

She was certain he was right, and to his credit, it wasn't something she would have thought about if he hadn't brought it to her attention, but at the moment, Des was the farthest thing from her mind. Colin, with his musky, woodsy, all-male smell, was guiding her to a place, both mentally and physically, where she was quite sure she shouldn't go. But she seemed to have no choice.

A slow song by an artist she didn't recognize played over the sound system, saturating the club with music and lyrics that wailed about painful wants and deep, complex love.

Colin pulled her arms around his neck, then slipped one of his hands beneath the V at the back of the waistline of her dress to settle on her bare skin; with the palm of his other hand against her buttocks, he pulled her pelvis into his. Feelings so hot they stole her breath from her lungs washed through her. She closed her eyes as she attempted to withstand the onslaught of pure longing that was flowing through her like molten lava.

"Relax," he breathed into her ear. "You're safe. You're with me, and we're in the middle of a public place, surrounded by people."

He didn't understand, she thought helplessly. For that matter, neither did she. But for the first time in her life, she was afraid of her own feelings.

And the music...it was low and sexy, with a beat that throbbed and slipped into your bloodstream until you were part of the song and it was part of you. The singer's voice was raw and ravaged, but still, he held nothing back. With the music and the lyrics, he was opening himself up in such a way that the listener could almost hear his heart bleed.

She'd never experienced anything remotely like it. The song, Colin—both were conjuring up feelings from deep within her she'd never known she had. She tried her best to summon up her normal, protective coating of reserve, but it was no use. The music decreed that their movements be as slow and hotly sensual as the song, and Colin was obeying, dancing them both deeper and deeper into the song and each other.

He held her firmly against his strong body, her breasts pressed against his chest with only thin fabric separating skin from skin. His hand caressed her bare back. Lower, she could feel his hard arousal. Her blood thickened; her legs weakened. She might have fallen if he hadn't been holding her to him as if they were one.

And for this space of time, they were. Her body and everything that made up who she was had melted into him, and there wasn't a thing she could do about it. She didn't even have to think in order to follow his dance steps. It was automatic. As they swayed together, her pelvis moved in the exact direction his did, swinging right, left, then erotically circling.

Heat swirled in and around her, and she tightened her arms around his neck and threaded her fingers up into his hair. Want was building in her, and she didn't have a clue how to stop it, assuage it. His arousal was growing, but he made no effort to pull away. As for her, she was incapable. She didn't even want to. His size and shape were now indelibly imprinted onto her skin and into her brain. She had seen him in his tight-fitting briefs. Now she didn't even have to imagine what was beneath them. Some part of her brain was telling her that this couldn't continue, while another screamed that it had to.

Then he thrust his leg between hers and pulled her onto his muscular thigh. Pleasure, unimaginable pleasure, shocked through her, but he gave her no chance to recuperate. Taking her with him, he began to snake sinuously downward, then undulate back up. Blindly she emulated his every twist, breathless at the constant feel of her panties rubbing against his thigh.

Again and again, they did the same thing, and all the while, the heat and pleasure that had taken her over climbed ever higher. On a dance floor, surrounded by couples, they were making love. Heavy, throbbing heat ached between her legs. Need and desire held her in a grip so strong she might never escape. She didn't think she could take any more. Something had to happen. Something, someone, had to help her. And not surprisingly, Colin seemed to know exactly what she was feeling.

At the same time that she went limp against him, he stopped and straightened. And as the music and dancers continued around them, he simply held her trembling body against his own. With one hand holding her upright at her waist, he used the other to rub up and down her back, soothing her.

Minutes later, hours later, he pulled slightly away from her, though his arm still firmly held her at the waist. He raised a hand to her jaw and tilted her face up to his. "Maybe that's enough for now."

She couldn't speak. She couldn't even look at him. Somehow she found the strength to wrench herself from his arms and make her way back to their booth. There she dropped onto the cushioned midnight-blue leather and reached for her wine. Her hands were trembling so badly that some of it sloshed out of the glass. Nevertheless, she drank the rest of it straight down.

"Coffee might help more."

She looked across the table and realized Colin had taken a seat there. Thank heavens he hadn't resumed his previous seat beside her. She wouldn't have been able to stand his closeness. Even now, with the table separating them, she thought she could still feel his heat. Or maybe it was her own.

His hands were folded together on the table. He looked perfectly composed, but his chest was rising and falling faster than usual. He hadn't been unaffected. The fact gave her a portion of satisfaction, but not much.

"I'd rather just leave."

He stared at her for a long moment, and she prayed that, just this once, he wouldn't be able to see what was going on inside her. Because if he could, he would see that a heated desire was rampaging through her body, and that out on the dance floor, she had come to realize that he and only he could assuage her desire. But finally he nodded, and she let out a long shaky breath of relief.

"Fine. Just let me pay our bill."

Within minutes she had her shawl around her and he was ushering her out of the club. Outside, she stopped, needing to orient herself. The streetlights seemed extraordinarily bright after the blue neon lights of the club. And the scene on the sidewalks was, if anything, more crowded than it had been when they had entered hours before.

Hours? Had it only been hours? She took a deep breath of the fresh air. It seemed as if she had lived a lifetime in the club. She felt Colin's hand at her back and stepped away from it.

"The car's not far away," he murmured, gesturing in the direction of the parking lot.

She was drained, with no energy left, yet she managed to put one foot in front of the other, and soon Colin was opening the car door for her. She slid into the seat, then watched numbly as he bent to move the overflow of her skirt into the car so that it wouldn't get caught when he shut the door.

Neither of them spoke on the drive home. Jill used the time to regain her strength, her sanity and her composure, a feat not easily accomplished. But by the time they reached her home, she had been able to come to at least one conclusion.

He pulled the car into her circular drive, braked and turned off the ignition. Silence and the beat of her heart were all Jill could hear. She looked down at her interlocked hands, knowing what she had to say, but waiting, though she wasn't quite sure for what. Colin unbuckled his seat belt, then angled his body toward her. Without even turning her head, she could feel his assessing gaze on her, waiting....

She didn't have the nerves left for a waiting game, so she said what she had to. "I think I've had enough lessons."

"I disagree. We have at least another two or three full days' worth. Possibly four."

Her head jerked around. *"Days?"*

He nodded. "Originally I had planned to stretch the lessons out over a couple of weeks, but after tonight, I've decided that we should accelerate our schedule."

After tonight. That said it all. Out on the dance floor, in his arms, she'd come undone. He'd entered into what he thought was a business agreement, and the first time he had taken her into his arms, she had melted into him. Quite obviously, he wanted their lessons to be over.

"You're going to have to clear your appointments for the next few days."

"Clear my..." The words clogged her throat. "Look, I have no idea what you have in mind, but I think tonight was enough."

"What's bothering you, Jill?" He leaned closer to her. "What's really, down deep, bothering you? That you don't understand what happened between us tonight?"

Once again he had read her mind, so why bother denying what he already knew? "That's one thing," she said slowly.

"Which is exactly *why* you need more lessons. You're not accustomed to a man's touch, *or* dancing closely, *or* anything remotely sexual. And if you know Des at all, you know that he is going to want his wife to respond to him, both in and out of bed. Just in case you didn't know it, that's what happens when two people fall in love."

She cleared her throat. "I know, but I also know Des may not ever love me."

"And you're willing to settle for that? A loveless marriage?"

"Of course." Her answer was automatic, one she'd had in her mind for a long time. "But I would be willing to, uh, respond to him. I mean, I know sex is part of any marriage, but I also know...or rather, *think,* that maybe in our case, we could also have a marriage that is more about business than—"

His roar of laughter interrupted her. "If that's what you truly think, then, honey, you need my lessons more than even I thought. How could you know so little about the man you think you want to spend the rest of your life with? Des is not only going to want love and sex and babies, he's going to want much more than that."

Her brows drew together. What was left? "Like what?"

"Like a companion and a friend, for one."

"That's two." *Babies.* She hadn't even considered that. And *love.* Would Des really want love? She had thought he would understand a marriage arranged for the convenience of a business; plus, he had to know how happy it would make Uncle William if he married one of his nieces. But now Colin was saying that wasn't enough.

Suddenly she felt the beginnings of a migraine. She had to get into the house without Colin realizing that she had a headache coming on. The last thing she needed was a repeat of last night.

As for tonight... She couldn't allow her mind to follow that thought. Abruptly she opened the car door, slid out and slammed it shut.

"Wait." Colin quickly got out of the car and was

by her side just as she was inserting her key into her front-door lock.

"I'll think over what you've said and call you in the morning." She turned the key and pushed the door open.

With his hand, he turned her face up to his. Alarmingly, her first instinct was to lean into his hand for the comfort of his warm caress. *Lord, when had she become such a slow learner?* She jerked away, stepped into her house and started to close the door. Colin's well-placed foot stopped her.

"I know tonight upset you, Jill, and I also know why. But all it proves is that you really haven't thought through this plan of yours. You don't have the slightest idea how to go about getting and keeping Des."

"I'll do whatever I have to." Again an automatic response, but this time it tripped her up.

"Good. Then I'll pick you up here at nine in the morning. Be ready."

Panic hit. "Wait. I haven't even decided whether I'm going to continue with these lessons."

He stepped over the threshold and ran his thumb over her bottom lip. "But you will. You will." Then suddenly he slipped his hands along her cheeks and lowered his mouth to hers. His tongue thrust into her mouth, and heat exploded inside her. Once again, he had easily taken possession of her feelings. She wanted to cry at her lack of control, but she also wanted to learn more about what it felt like to kiss him.

His lips were full and firm, his taste heady, like the finest wine, and the inside of his mouth was moist and warm. He kissed with a surety that spoke of experience as his tongue delved deeper and deeper, engaging hers in an intimate, sexual dance of heat and desire. She closed her hands over his wrists to steady herself.

When he finally raised his head, he whispered, "Another lesson. At the very *least*, Des will expect a kiss at the end of your first date. After that..." His shrug explained perfectly.

The headache was becoming stronger, and she wasn't going to make last night's mistake in thinking she could fight it with only her will. She had to get upstairs as soon as possible and take something for it. She had never known why they came, but the aftermath of tonight had certainly left her stressed. "I'll call you in the morning," she repeated.

"I'll *see* you then," he murmured, and with another soft kiss he was gone.

She closed the door and leaned back against it for support. No man had ever kissed her the way Colin just had. No man had ever held her, touched her, treated her, the way he had tonight. And because of it, she somehow knew she would never be the same.

Six

Jill awoke tired, but with no headache hangover. Taking the medicine at the first sign of the migraine last night, then going to bed, had been the best thing she could have done for herself. She just hated being so dependent on medicine, or admitting that there was an aspect of her life over which she had no control. But by catching the headache early, she had ensured she hadn't had to take any of the heavy-duty medicine she'd had to resort to the night before, when Colin had spent the night with her.

With a groan, she reached for a spare pillow and pressed it over her face. Even as she did it, she knew she wasn't accomplishing anything. Besides, it wasn't like her to try to hide from anything or anyone. Not for a very long time.

But Colin…

With another groan, she threw the pillow across the

room. It was time to start her day. She sat up and pushed the hair from her eyes. Why was she so tired? Then she remembered and collapsed back on the bed. Erotic, disturbing dreams of Colin had filled her night.

That settled the matter. She needed to get out of their business agreement. She hated like blazes to admit it, even to herself, but she couldn't handle another evening like the one they had shared at Midnight Blues.

She reached for another pillow but couldn't find one, so she settled for covering her face with her hands. What was wrong with her? She couldn't hide. She had learned that lesson well when she had been small.

Back then she would crawl into her closet and shut the door, thinking that if her father couldn't find her, she could escape the ordeal of their nightly dinners. It was her secret. As far as she knew, even Tess and Kit didn't know.

The only person who did was the woman who was their housekeeper at the time. She had always known where to find her. The woman wasn't unkind, but even she had been intimidated by her father, so she would straighten Jill's clothes and shoo her downstairs.

There, sitting as straight as they could make their little bodies, she and her sisters would be grilled about their day by their father. In turn, they each would have to tell him what they had learned that day in school and recount their participation in any scholastic or physical competitions. If they couldn't report a win, or the top grade in their class, they would feel the iciness of his disapproval, which was formidable. Invariably she left the table with her stomach in knots.

Later she would lie in bed, hungry, trying to think of ways she could do better the next day.

As soon as she and her sisters were old enough, he saw that they were involved in individual sports, such as tennis or golf, and he would stage competitions among the three of them, pitting them against one another. To this day, she refused to play any kind of sport. She had buried her competitive nature in her business pursuits.

In fact, until Tess married a year and a half ago, Tess, Kit and she would fight tooth and nail to be the one who, at the end of Baron International's fiscal year, had made the most money for the company. But since Tess's marriage, Tess was so blissed out she no longer even tried. Her withdrawal made the competition a lot less fun. As for Kit, who knew what was up with her these days?

No. Hiding never worked. Besides, she wasn't afraid of Colin. She would simply tell him there would be no more lessons, and he would have no choice but to accept her decision.

With a sigh, Jill forced herself to get up. It was past time to start her day.

She had taken exactly three steps when she hesitated and something made her look back at the bed. Her mouth fell open. She'd never seen her sheets in such a tangle. In fact, the whole bed was a mess. The contents of her erotic dreams came rushing back to her, and her face warmed. Hurriedly she made the bed.

"May I see my appointment list, please?"
"You bet." With brisk efficiency, her assistant laid

a brown leather folder in front of her. "This is your day."

Jill opened the folder. Her first appointment wasn't for another hour, but once they started, they were scheduled back to back. At least she had an hour to return calls, review reports and check on several projects she had under way. "Thanks, Molly.

"Do you have something else for me? Because if not, I'm still working on the Barstow report."

"That's fine." As Molly left the office, Jill lifted a cup and sipped at the decaffeinated coffee Molly always freshly brewed for her. There were mornings when she would have killed for a good strong cup of regular coffee, but because of her headaches, the doctor had banned them.

"Good morning."

She almost choked on the coffee. *"Colin."*

He bypassed the chairs and settled himself on a corner of the desk. "Great morning, isn't it?"

Molly immediately reappeared in the doorway. "Mr. Wynne? Did you have an appointment?"

It was Molly's polite way of letting the intruder know he wasn't scheduled. Jill was much less polite. "What in the hell are you doing here?"

Colin flashed Molly a grin. "Does she swear like that very often? Never mind. Before you offer, I'd love a cup of coffee, thank you. Oh, and make mine black and fully leaded."

Molly looked at Jill. With a sigh, she nodded. Molly disappeared, but left the door open.

Colin's sudden appearance had instantly caused her composure to disintegrate, but Jill managed to quickly pull herself together. She sat back in her chair, folded her arms beneath her breasts and gave him a hard look. "Would you like me to repeat the question?"

"Thanks, but no thanks. I heard the first time."

"And the answer is?"

"Fact of the matter is, we *did* have an appointment this morning. Remember? I said I'd see you at nine." He glanced at the gold watch on his wrist. "It is now fifteen minutes after nine. Sorry I'm a little late, but I dropped by your house first. I was sure I had said I would pick you up there. My fault, I'm sure. I must have said here." The gold streaks in his brown eyes suddenly became more pronounced, more mesmerizing. "But then, I was a little preoccupied with the evening we had just spent together."

She sat very still, willing herself not to blush. "You shouldn't be here, Colin. I distinctly remember saying that I'd *call* you this morning."

He gave a nonchalant nod toward the sun currently flooding in through her office's floor-to-ceiling windows, which offered a spectacular view of downtown Dallas. "Well, I don't know about you, but *that* is what I call morning."

Molly returned, carrying his coffee. He took it from her with a smile. "Thanks. Listen, Molly, please correct me if I'm wrong, but it's morning, right?"

"Right." Puzzled, she glanced at Jill, her brows raised in question. When Jill didn't respond, she asked, "Anything else?"

Jill shook her head in resignation. "No, that's it for now."

Molly left and this time closed the door behind her.

"I had planned to call you, Colin, but it's been a busy morning." A well-placed little white lie from time to time never hurt anything, and in this case it would help.

"And I said I would *see* you, but no matter. I'm flexible." He reached into his jacket pocket, pulled out a thin cell phone and held it out to her. "Want to call me?"

"You know, I never realized before just how impossible you are." She pushed away from the desk and stood. He was looking only moderately spectacular this morning, she reflected with annoyance, along with appearing completely rested.

The lightweight sport jacket he wore perfectly complemented his chocolate-brown slacks and tan shirt, unbuttoned at his throat. And as usual, the sun had managed to turn his golden-brown hair to a dark honey. As for his eyes, since she had spotted the intensity of their gold streaks a minute ago, she was trying very hard not to look into them. She was too afraid she would see something that would remind her of last night.

Last night. That made two nights in a row she needed to forget.

She turned her head away from him. The Dallas skyline had always been a soothing sight to her, but for some reason it just wasn't working at the moment. Maybe because she could only see Colin in her mind's eye. "I did what I said I'd do. I thought over the idea of continuing the lessons, and I've decided to stop."

"No guts, huh?"

An irritating response delivered in a soft, almost tender manner. How was she supposed to react to that combination?

Barely contained anger seemed to be the winner.

She looked at him over her shoulder. "It's got nothing to do with guts. I made my decision based on business considerations. First of all, there's no way I can clear my appointments for the next few days."

"What's the matter? Afraid Dallas will fall down without your constant vigilance?"

"And secondly," she said, returning her gaze to the skyline, "I've decided I don't need any more lessons. I told you I'm a quick study, and I am. You've given me more than enough to go on."

"Honey, you're still at the starting gate."

She whirled around. "*Don't* call me honey. And what do you mean, the starting gate? After last night—" She stopped herself. Any mention of anything that concerned what had happened at the club could prove dangerous.

"After last night, what?"

Damn. She'd made the mistake of looking into his eyes, and she'd seen heat flare in them at the mention of last night. She managed to shrug. "It was fun and quite informative, but I can take it from here." Surely there were books she could read on the subject. She would have Molly search the Internet bookstores. "Naturally I won't renege on our business agreement. We'll develop our land jointly." She would assign one of her top people to it, but there was no way she was going to personally work with Colin.

"How extremely ethical of you, but I'm not letting you out of the other half of our deal. I feel a moral obligation to continue, plus—"

"Moral obligation? Give me a break. And while you're at it, consider yourself released."

"*Plus* last night you told me you'd do anything to get Des. I've never known you to exaggerate. Therefore, I'm taking you at your word. Now—" he shot back his cuff and glanced at his watch "—it's nearly nine-thirty. We're already running late." He slipped off the desk. "Let's go."

She must have missed something. "Go? Go where?"

"I've made some appointments for you. Have you cleared your calendar for the next few days as I told you to?"

"No, of course not."

Before she knew it, he was around the desk, her hand was in his, and he was leading her out of her office. He opened her office door and breezed through Molly's smaller office to the door that led to the reception area. "Hi, Molly. Please cancel Ms. Baron's appointments for the next few days. Great coffee, by the way. Thanks a lot." He opened her office door. "Bye, Molly."

Molly stared after him with a stupefied expression on her face. "Jill?"

"I, uh…"

He briefly paused and gazed down at her. "Just do it, Jill. Please. I promise you, what's going to happen today is not going to be near as hard on you as last night. In fact, if you allow yourself to, you'll enjoy it."

"Say the word, Jill, and I'll call the police."

Great, just great. Molly was in full-fledged protective mode. It was the last thing she wanted. She could take care of herself. She would either cope with whatever Colin had planned for today, or she would walk away and call for a cab back to the office. "It's okay, Molly. I'm fine."

She saw Colin flash her assistant a smile that had

brought more than one woman to her knees, but he hadn't come up against Molly's maternal leanings. And apparently he realized the same thing.

"I promise you she's in no danger, nor will she be," he said to Molly. "Have a great day."

"Wait. My purse—it's back in my office."

"That's okay. You're not going to need it."

Now she was curious and, heaven help her, more than a little intrigued. After this was all over, she should probably seriously consider some sort of mental-health care.

"Are you comfortable, Ms. Baron?"

The low, soothing voice of Helen, her assigned masseuse, irritated her. "As comfortable as I can be, half-naked, lying facedown on a massage table with a stranger's hands on me."

"I gather you've never had a massage before."

"That's correct." She'd never had time, nor did she now. What was more, she couldn't believe she had allowed Colin to drag her to this day-of-beauty salon.

"I'm not hurting you, am I?"

"No." In truth, the experience so far wasn't altogether unpleasant. The room was dimly lit. Soft, lilting music played somewhere. But she didn't have time for this indulgence. Plus, she couldn't figure out what having a massage had to do with getting Des.

"You're very, very tense. I can feel it in your muscles. So just try to relax and let me do my job."

She lifted her head off the table and looked hopefully back over her shoulder. "You wouldn't happen to have a cell phone in here, would you?"

"No, Ms. Baron." Helen gently pushed her back

down. "Conducting business at the same time I'm giving you a massage would be counterproductive. Besides, even the busiest of people find that an occasional day here at Jacqui's is beneficial. But you have to give yourself a chance. So, please, just try to relax and let me see if I can get these knots out of your shoulders."

She yawned as Helen rubbed more warm oil into her back. Despite her protestations to the contrary last night, Colin probably felt he couldn't count on her to fulfill her side of their business agreement unless he fulfilled his. Fortunately, that was an easy fix. As soon as she returned to the office, she would put her lawyers to work on drawing up the agreement. Then Colin would *have* to believe her.

Where was he, anyway? The last time she'd seen him, he had been in the main salon, waving her goodbye, as the very beautiful Jacqui, the spa owner, had escorted her into the massage room with a graciousness that was an art unto itself. She sighed. If she only had her cell phone, she could...

"Ms. Baron? Ms. Baron?"
"Yes?" She forced open her eyes. "What is it?"
"The massage is over."
"It is?" Disappointment tinged her voice.

As the massage had continued, she remembered going into a kind of twilight rest, where she felt as if she were drifting on a cloud. Every once in a while she would become aware of Helen's heavenly touch as the woman worked her fingers up and down her body, murmuring occasionally about knots. And she'd been conscious enough to turn over when Helen had asked her. But after that, she'd sunk back into her cloud. And now she couldn't feel a bone in her body.

"Sit up slowly," Helen cautioned. "You may feel somewhat dizzy at first, but it will pass in a moment."

She sat up just fine, but immediately wanted to lie down again for another hour of massage. She couldn't remember the last time she had felt this relaxed. But Helen was carefully urging her off the table, even going so far as to kneel down and guide her feet into a pair of peach terry-cloth slippers—peach and green being the spa's colors. The slippers matched the robe she put on a moment later.

Helen straightened and beamed at her. "Do you feel better?"

"Yes, thank you very much. You're truly gifted."

With a pleased nod, Helen led her out of the room. "Follow me. Your facial is next."

"Do you know where Mr. Wynne is?" He had assured her that he would not leave the premises. At the time, her theory had been that he had brought her there and he could damn well stay as long as she did. He'd laughed and agreed.

"No, I'm sorry, I don't."

"Here we are." Helen pushed open another door in a hall that seemed lined with endless doors, and Jill entered another dimly lit room to see three green-smocked women waiting for her. There was also the most comfortable-looking lounge chair she had ever seen. "Ladies, she's all yours."

Helen left, quietly closing the door behind her.

A woman with beautiful silver hair came forward. "My name's Mary, Ms. Baron. I'll be doing your facial." She turned and introduced the other two ladies, Cordelia and Alyssa.

"Hello," she said politely, and received a duet of hellos in return.

"While I'm doing your facial," Mary said, "Cordelia will be giving you a manicure and Alyssa will be doing your pedicure."

"How efficient," Jill said with true approval.

"Some of our clients like to linger all day, while others would rather not," Mary explained. "Mr. Wynne said you fell into the latter category."

"He did, did he?" Colin knew her entirely too well. "Do you happen to know where he is?"

"I believe he's in one of our private salons with Jacqui."

Private salon? "Do you know what they're doing?"

"No, I'm afraid I don't."

Why should she care what Colin was doing? With the beautiful Jacqui? She didn't, she told herself. She really didn't.

"If you would please sit down, we'll make you as comfortable as possible and begin."

She complied, sank into another cloud and nearly groaned with delight. She had no idea who made this chair, but she was going to find out and order a dozen, she thought, as once again she drifted off into the twilight.

"Are you ready to wake up?"

Jill heard the question through cotton layers of sleep. The voice was soft, filled with amusement and very, very masculine. The voice was *Colin's*. Jill instantly awoke.

He was sitting beside the cloud chair, holding her

hand and smiling over at her. "I gather the morning has been a relaxing experience for you?"

"It's been okay," she said cautiously. After all, she'd come here under protest, so she didn't want him to be too pleased with himself. "I didn't sleep all that well last night, so I took the opportunity for a catnap."

"Good. I'm glad you were able to get some rest. Are you ready for lunch?"

If there was one thing she was dead certain of, it was that she was too relaxed to get dressed and go out to one of the trendy restaurants where the movers and shakers lunched. "No."

His brows arched skeptically. "Don't you want to get your money's worth? It's included in the package price."

"Oh, I hadn't realized."

"Well, now that you have, come on." He gave a light tug on her hand. "After lunch, you've got only one or two more things to do, and then we're out of here."

She was so relaxed she wasn't certain she could have made it out of the chair without his help. When she was finally on her feet, she suddenly remembered that she was naked beneath the terry robe. She adjusted it and tightened the belt. She hadn't been conscious of her relative nakedness until he had shown up.

He looked down at her and stroked her hair away from her face. "I don't think I've ever seen you this relaxed."

She gave a light chuckle. "I'm sure no one has. They not only relax your muscles here, I think they also relax your bones."

He slid his hands along the sides of her face and tilted it up to his. "Relaxed looks good on you," he said softly, huskily, the glints of gold in his brown eyes holding her gaze until she felt in danger of falling into them.

When he lowered his mouth to hers and lightly brushed his lips back and forth over the full softness of hers, it was almost as if she'd been waiting for it. Suddenly nerve endings sprang to life, carrying tingling warmth to all parts of her body. And the thought fluttered through her mind that he wasn't being fair. She was too relaxed to put up any defense against him. Not that she could remember that a defense had helped her last night when they had danced.

He slowly parted his mouth, and she parted hers in response. Heaven help her, she knew what was coming next, and she wanted it. His tongue delved deeply into her mouth, not with the force he had used last night, but with a leisurely gentleness that had her almost incoherent. Heat bloomed between her legs. Surroundings were forgotten. She could only concentrate on what he was making her feel.

His hand slid inside her robe to cup one bare breast, and his thumb stroked her nipple until a soft moan escaped her. As soon as it did, he pulled away.

Her next breath came hard. Her body had been left aching and hurting. She gazed up at him, confused and unsure. What was he doing to her?

He exhaled a long, shaky breath. His face seemed etched in torment, but his next words erased that idea.

He gestured vaguely. "That's what Des would have done." He took her hand and practically dragged her toward the door. "Come on."

Dazed, she followed him out of the room and down

the hall toward yet another door. "Jacqui has set our lunch up in here so we can have some privacy."

Privacy. Oh, yeah, right, she reflected with numbed sarcasm. That was exactly what they needed.

He opened the door to a brightly lit room awash in greens and peaches. The colors had been translated onto sumptuous fabrics that upholstered the chairs and couches. In one corner, where a green ficus grew tall and lush, there was a table set for two, with their plates and glasses already filled.

She headed for it and the champagne she saw. Without looking at Colin, she chose a chair and lifted the flute to her lips. When she'd emptied it, she looked for the bottle.

A second before she could grab it out of the silver bucket, he got it and refilled her glass. "It might be better if you ate something before you have any more."

The suggestion, though gently made, was received with all the humor of an enraged rhino. Still, she did finally look at her plate. There were large portions of chicken, spinach and fruit salad, along with two small muffins.

With every one of her senses now alive, she realized two things: she was hungry, and she desperately needed to block Colin from her mind.

She picked up the sterling-silver fork and proceeded to attack the food. It was satisfying and delicious.

Her mind was blessedly blank, and amazingly, the relaxation she had gained this morning was still with her. By the time she was finished eating, even her heartbeat had returned to normal and the heat had receded. But she remembered the kiss, the touch—oh, *how* she remembered.

She looked at Colin and saw that he was staring at her. She glanced at his full plate. He must have been watching her the entire time; he hadn't taken so much as one bite of his food. Her gaze returned to him. He was reclining in his chair, his elbow propped on its arm, his face bracketed by his thumb and forefinger.

Carefully she laid her napkin over the arm of her chair. "You said something about one or two more things I had to do?"

He nodded.

"What?"

"A hairstyling and makeup lesson."

"I don't need makeup lessons, but I'll agree to the hairstyling."

"Good." His expression was absolutely enigmatic.

What was he thinking? Did he remember, as she did, how she'd reacted to his kiss? Did he know how his simple touch on her breast had nearly leveled her? Did he know that she felt different from the person she had been the night of her party? And that the difference had started when she awoke the next morning to find that she had slept the night through all tangled up with him?

"And do you have anything planned after the hairstyling?"

He hadn't once shifted position, nor had he dropped his gaze from her. She had the feeling that this was one time when he couldn't figure out what she was thinking. That made two of them.

She looked down at her folded hands and absently noted the clear polish they had applied to her nails as she had slept. It was what she always wore. Her toenails were another matter, though. They had painted them a hot pink. Colin had finally gotten a color on her toenails that made a strong statement.

"We're driving to the airport, where we'll board my plane and fly to the American Virgin Islands."

He paused, obviously expecting her to say something, to object, but instinct told her to remain silent. There could be danger in speaking before she figured out what was bothering her. Besides, she knew there was more to come.

"A friend of mine owns a private island down there that he's agreed to lend us for a few days."

Once again he paused, but she continued to remain quiet. As motionless as she held herself, though, her mind was racing. A private island meant they would be alone, with the possible exception of a staff. Colin and she would basically be alone. For a few days, he had said. Her heart gave a hard thud.

After a moment Colin straightened in his chair. "One of the reasons we're going down there is to give me the opportunity to teach you how to snorkel. Des loves to snorkel." He fidgeted with the edge of his plate, then pushed it away and looked back at her. "So, as I said, we're driving straight from here to the airport. As a matter of fact, our luggage is already in my car. I packed my bags this morning, and while you were busy with your massage and so on, I had Neiman's send over a selection of things you'll need, beachwear and the like, along with suitcases. Jacqui helped me pack the bags and assured me there was everything in them that you'll need. I also called Molly, who drove to your home, collected your medicine, along with a few other things she said you'd want, plus your purse, then brought them over.

They're all packed in a separate case, where you can get to them easily if needed."

He had thought of everything, and he had taken it on himself to arrange everything behind her back. She knew he expected her to get angry, to tell him in no uncertain terms that she wasn't going anywhere else with him, nor would she let him hijack her aboard his plane. She should. She also knew that, to Colin, she probably appeared eerily calm. She was.

But things were shifting and turning inside her as surely as if they were something tangible she could see on an X ray. She could *feel* them. It was as if she was having her own private, internal earthquake, and it felt every bit as violent as the shifting of tectonic plates. She just wasn't sure yet what the changes were and why they were occurring.

"I promised Molly that you'd call her from the plane so that the two of you can go over anything you need to."

If she stayed in town, she would throw herself back into her work with her usual intensity, and her questions would be shoved into the back of her mind. She would make sure of that.

Instinctively, though, she knew her questions were too important to go unanswered. Besides, why shouldn't she take a few days off? She'd been working her whole life, starting when she was three years old, when she had begun to work so hard to please a father who could not be pleased.

"Jill?"

She lifted her gaze to him. He looked worried, wary. He wanted an answer. She would give him one. "Fine."

Seven

Jill stretched slowly awake. Sunshine and a mild breeze glided through a large open door, filling the room with light, the scent of tropical flowers and the soothing sound of the sea's relentless movement. At the door, flowing, sheer, cream-colored curtains blew inward in a slow, undulating motion. It was the same material that was draped over the tall posters of the bed.

The sounds, the scents were all so completely different from what she was used to that for a few minutes she simply lay there, trying to orient herself.

When they had arrived on the island last night, Colin had shown her to this room and set her new pieces of luggage on two matching teak chests at the foot of her large bed. Two smaller bags had gone into the bathroom. He'd also said that when she was ready, there would be a late dinner served on the terrace, but she'd been too tired. Instead, she had showered, rifled through the luggage until she had found a pink silk chemise, crawled into bed and gone straight to sleep.

In retrospect, she supposed the inner turmoil she had endured the past few days had left her exhausted. Even on the trip here, she and Colin had exchanged very few words. She'd taken him at his word and called Molly, issuing instructions as to how to rearrange the rest of her week. Then, instead of going to sit with Colin in the cockpit, she had taken a nice long nap. Even so, she had still arrived on the island feeling exhausted.

She slid out of bed and padded over to the doorway that led out onto a wide stone terrace. Last night, she remembered, Colin had driven them up a hill from the landing strip that he had told her was on the other side of the island from the house. He had said the strip had been carefully constructed so that, no matter where you were on the island, it couldn't be seen, except from the air.

Last night she had been too tired to try to get her bearings. Now, though, she saw that the house did indeed sit on a hill.

She didn't even have to step out onto the terrace to see the deep-green vegetation that carpeted the hill all the way down to a shimmering white beach and the multihued blue sea beyond. Flowers so brightly colored they didn't seem real made enormous bouquets amidst the trees and bushes. She could even see white wicker lounge chairs with several matching small tables placed slightly to the left of her doorway, so that they would be convenient but wouldn't block the view.

She had made a good decision to come here, she

thought. The island was an entirely different world, with a different kind of beauty than what she was used to. If any place could get her out of her normal routine where she lived, slept and ate business, it would be this island. The tranquil beauty would allow her a perfect environment to try to process all that had happened to her in the past few days. Yes, she had definitely made a good decision.

And since she was going to be here for a couple of days, she might as well get dressed and venture out to see what or who she could find.

Colin had said the purpose of the trip was to teach her to snorkel, so she rummaged in the suitcases and found six different two-piece bathing suits with matching cover-ups in an array of colors. She eyed a dark-pink two-piece with a critical eye. Skimpy. Decidedly skimpy. But the other suits didn't look much larger.

With a sigh, she took the bikini and its cover-up into the bathroom and put it on.

Viewing herself in a floor-length mirror, she frowned. The bottom half of the suit started inches below her navel and its legs were cut high. The top was little more than two bra cups held together by string. At the same time, nothing vital was exposed, and it wasn't *completely* outrageous. She twisted around to get another view, and the conclusion she reached surprised her. She looked pretty good in the suit.

She smiled at herself. The very fact that she was here, with two scraps of fabric serving as a swimsuit, was yet another clue that she was changing. What she didn't know, and what she was here to figure out, was whether or not she liked the changes.

Plus, she had never been on a tropical island before, and swimsuits did seem to be called for. She took one more glance at herself in the mirror. How stupid of her. Why did she feel she had to defend herself *to* herself?

The cover-up was a lovely soft drift of pink-flowered material. She slipped it under one arm and tied it at the top of the opposite shoulder. There, she thought with another smile at herself—nothing showed but a shoulder and her arms.

Last night she'd delved into one of the smaller bathroom bags only long enough to find a new toothbrush and a tube of toothpaste. Now she took a longer look in each bag and found the touch of the beauteous Jacqui in the variety of facial creams, cleansers and makeup, all bearing the Jacqui's logo. According to several of her female acquaintances, Jacqui's products were excellent, so okay, she would use them.

She didn't have to look in the other bag. She knew it bore Molly's touch and contained all her medications. Hopefully she wouldn't have to use any of them.

She washed her face, brushed her teeth and slathered one of the creams on her face and neck. Then she turned to the task of her hair and found there wasn't much to do.

The hairstylist who had cut her hair yesterday had layered it. The cut had lightened its weight and revealed the wayward natural curl she had fought all her life to tame. The stylist had also shortened her hair to brush her shoulders and added wispy bangs. As a result, all she had to do was run her fingers through it, wet or dry, and it looked the same as when the stylist had sent her on her way yesterday.

She briefly shook her head at her reflection in the mirror. The haircut was one change she definitely hadn't gotten used to yet. Returning to her bedroom, she donned a pair of sandals she found in one of the suitcases and headed for the terrace.

But after only a few steps, she stopped. Colin was standing at the other end of the terrace, staring out at the turquoise sea, one hand braced against a post, the other hand holding a cup of coffee.

And he was wearing nothing but a pair of dark blue, tight, low-cut swim briefs.

Very brief. Very tight.

She flushed and swallowed with a suddenly dry throat. Seeing him in profile as she was, the bulk of his sex was obvious.

She was riveted by the sight, and her heart began to pound as if it were about to burst out of her chest. But why? She had already felt his size and shape when they had danced. In his arms, on the dance floor, encircled by other couples, she had nearly come apart at the feel of him pressed against her lower body. She still could remember how she had ached for him.

She couldn't allow that to happen here. She wouldn't.

Besides, as she had just told herself, they were on an island where bathing suits were called for. She might as well get accustomed to the sight of his hard body, his sex....

Unbidden, heat flowed into her veins, until her whole body felt feverish.

She barely managed to stop herself from retreating to her bedroom. This was *not* a good way for her to start off her visit here on the island. She had stopped hiding in her bedroom closet a long time ago, and she had no intention of starting now, however metaphorical it would be in this situation.

Slowly she walked toward him, but she forced her gaze away from him and scanned the rest of the terrace. Behind Colin was an outdoor living area, complete with comfortable-looking couches and chairs covered with fabrics that faithfully duplicated the tropical colors around them. There was even a fireplace, and overhead, a ceiling fan turned, as did several others along the terrace.

His gaze was so fixed on the sea, he didn't see her as she approached, which was just as well. No matter how hard she tried, she could no longer avoid looking at him. Closer now, she saw water droplets drying on his muscled body and golden-brown hair.

"Good morning," she said. Hopefully conversation would get her mind off his body.

He turned with an uncomplicated smile of welcome. "Good morning."

His smile warmed her in a way that had nothing to do with sex. Thank *goodness*. "Is it? Morning, I mean? Time-wise, I'm thrown. All I know is that I fell into bed last night, slept the sleep of the dead, and when I awoke, the sun was already up."

"That's pretty much all you need to know. Time really isn't important here in the islands." His gaze skimmed her attire. "You look lovely."

"Thank you," she said, then instinctively tried to deflect his attention away from her. "This island is dazzling."

"I'm glad you like it." His smile told her he knew what she was doing.

Damn it. He was back to reading her mind. "Have you already been for a swim?"

He nodded. "The water was great. You're going to love it."

She glanced toward the sea. "That remains to be seen."

"Right." He reached for a blue-printed T-shirt that matched the blue of his swimsuit, slipped it over his head and down over his chest. Water quickly stained it in the places where he wasn't yet dry, such as his chest, where she'd just seen water droplets glistening. She closed her eyes, as if the act would banish the sight from her mind. It didn't work.

"First things first," he said briskly. "Since you missed dinner last night, I bet you're hungry."

"You'd win that bet," she said, glancing around and seeing a long rectangular table off to the side of the living area. It was set for two.

He took her hand. "Come with me."

It seemed that was all she had been doing for the past three days.

She settled into the chair he held out for her; then he took a chair at a right angle to her. There were several covered dishes already on the table, along with a large fruit centerpiece.

As if on cue, a caramel-colored young beauty with close-cropped black hair glided into view, carrying a white carafe. "Coffee, ma'am?"

"Yes, thank you. Oh, I need decaffeinated, please. Is that a problem?"

"Not at all. That's what this is."

"Jill, this is Liana. Liana, this is my friend Jill."

"Hello," Jill said and received a warm smile in return.

"Welcome to Serenity," Liana said as she poured Jill's coffee.

"Serenity?"

Liana moved to a sideboard, exchanged carafes, then strolled around the table to replenish Colin's cup. "It is the name of our island."

"Liana and her family are caretakers of the island," Colin inserted.

"How nice," Jill said, looking back and forth between the two of them. "I can already see that the island was well named."

Liana and Colin exchanged smiles, and something clutched at Jill's heart. Their smiles were filled with intimate familiarity. Were they involved? Was Liana the woman with whom he had fallen in love? And if so, how had she broken his heart? Obviously they still felt warmly toward each other.

Liana directed her lovely black-eyed gaze on her. "Was there something special you'd like to eat this morning, Ms. Baron?"

"I'm not sure," she said, staring at the island beauty, reflecting that Colin had a way of drawing beautiful women to him. Yesterday it had been Jacqui. Today it was Liana. She gave a soft sigh. What did it matter, anyway? "I am hungry, though."

"Just name your first choice," Colin said. "If we don't have it, you can go on to choice number two."

"All right, then. How about French toast with—" she glanced at the fruit bowl "—kiwi fruit, and crisp bacon on the side?"

"We can do that, ma'am."

"Wonderful." She stared at Liana's warm smile and decided she couldn't blame her if she was in love with Colin. It sometimes seemed as if half the women she knew were. "And please, call me Jill."

"Thank you, Jill. Colin?"

"What she's having sounds good."

"Mama and I will get right on it." Liana turned and disappeared through a doorway.

Just then a gust of wind blew through the covered terrace and ruffled Jill's hair. Instinctively she lifted her face to the breeze.

"You look as if you belong here," Colin murmured.

Slightly embarrassed to be caught in what had been an unguarded moment, she turned the comment back on him. "So do you. You must come here often."

"Why do you say that?"

"Because you and Liana seem to know each other well."

He nodded, eyeing her thoughtfully. "Well, to answer your question, I do come here often—or rather, as often as I can manage. And yes, Liana and I know each other very well."

"How well?" As soon as she said it, she wished for the words back.

Suddenly Colin's eyes began to twinkle. "What have you got going on in that beautiful head of yours? Do you think Liana and I are lovers?"

The sight of gold lights dancing in Colin's eyes was something to behold. She felt a quickening low in her belly. It could mean she was just hungry, but she seriously doubted it. "Are you?"

He shook his head. "No, Jill. I've known Liana and her family for ten years, ever since I started coming here. We're good friends, and that's it. Plus, I don't think her husband would approve." He tilted his head and gazed thoughtfully at her. "Okay?"

She shrugged as if it didn't matter one way or the other. "Sure." She reached for a glass pitcher of orange juice and poured herself some. "So you've been coming here for ten years?"

"Yes."

"The person who owns this island must be a very *good* friend."

"He is."

"*You* own this island, don't you?"

He smiled. "Along with Des."

"I didn't realize you two were so close."

"I told you right from the beginning that we were good friends."

She chewed on her bottom lip. She supposed Colin had done her a great favor by bringing her to an island Des owned half interest in. So why did she feel a sudden panic?

"Why didn't you tell me who owned the island?"

"Because I was afraid if you knew it was partly mine, you might feel trapped in some way."

That was *it*. Her panic had nothing to do with Des and everything to do with Colin. He had her in a place from which she couldn't escape—escape from *him*.

"If at any time you decide you want to leave, just tell me."

She nodded. Once again he had read her mind, which by now she had come to consider almost normal. Maybe it was because he had told her they could leave any time she wanted, but all of a sudden she didn't feel trapped anymore. And strangely, anticipation bubbled through her like champagne. The question was, *what* was she anticipating?

"Are you and Des planning on developing the island?"

"It's as developed as it's likely to get. We love it just as it is, though someday we may build another residence for those times when we both might like to bring our families here at the same time."

She had been about to point out the money they could make if they did decide to develop it, but the thought of Colin with a family constricted her throat to the point that she doubted she could even make a sound.

Colin with a wife and children.

Troubled by the idea, she frowned. But after all, she reasoned, just because he hadn't yet married and started a family, that didn't mean he wouldn't in the future. And the fact that he had even brought up the possibility of building another residence meant that marriage and a family were something he hoped to have.

"While your breakfast settles, I thought I might take you on a mini tour of the island. Or, if you'd rather, we can go straight into the swimming pool."

The hand holding her orange juice halted halfway between the table and her lips. "Swimming pool? There's a swimming pool on the island?"

He nodded. "Within walking distance, though you can't see it until you get there."

"Isn't a pool redundant here?"

He chuckled. "I think so, but Des and I decided to go ahead and put one in. Apparently there are some people who want to be able to see what's under them when they swim at night—therefore, the pool."

"I bet you're not one of those people."

"You're right. The ocean is wonderful at night."

She found herself tangled up in the depths of his eyes. Lord, it was no wonder women fell for him left, right and center. "You mean you're going to teach me how to snorkel in a pool? Colin, *I* have a swimming pool in my own backyard. For that matter, so do you. We could have just stayed home."

"I want to go over the basics in the pool first, so I know you'll be able to handle it out there." He nodded in the direction of the sea. "Once you've got it down, then we'll head for the reef I've got picked out for you."

"Oh." She sipped at her orange juice, then decided to go back to the coffee. "I suppose that's a good idea. But tell me something. From what little I know about snorkeling, it looks relatively easy."

"Once you learn the basics, it is."

"Okay, so I don't see you—or Des, for that matter—being content to merely swim along on the surface of the water. If you two do anything, it would be scuba diving."

His dimple appeared. "You're right, but there are two reasons I decided to bring you down here and teach you how to snorkel. First, you can learn it much faster than you can learn to scuba. And after your first snorkeling trip, it will whet your appetite for scuba diving." He paused and eyed her speculatively. "And if you do convince Des to marry you, that would be something he could teach you."

Once again his answer made sense. But what *didn't* make sense was that she hated the answer.

"By the way, can you swim?"

She couldn't help but laugh. "Do you honestly think I would consider snorkeling if I couldn't?"

"Okay, but how *well* do you swim?"

She thought over his question. "I used to be pretty good, but I haven't been swimming since I was in high school. My father made sure my sisters and I could swim."

"Considering there's an enormous lake at the edge of the Double B, I can see why. He wouldn't have wanted any of you to fall in and accidentally drown."

"I doubt if he would have blinked an eye if one of us had drowned."

"You can't mean that."

"I guarantee you, the day after the funeral, he would be back to business as usual."

"People grieve in different ways, Jill."

"It's not important." She waved the issue aside. "But the reason he made sure we could swim was so that we could race against each other. It was all part of his teaching us to be competitive. It was also the reason he taught us to play golf, tennis, baseball, horseshoes and any other sport he could come up with. It's the reason I stopped swimming as soon as possible, and as a result, truthfully, I'm not sure how far I can swim now."

He stared at her for several moments as if he was contemplating saying something—no doubt something about her father—but then he seemed to change his mind.

"You won't have to worry. You'll be wearing a belt that will keep you buoyant, and a vest if you still don't feel secure, plus the saltwater helps. However, I would never take out someone who didn't know how to swim at all."

"Then why didn't you ask me before now?"

He smiled. "Because if you couldn't swim, I figured I'd just teach you."

"Teach me to swim, huh? As easy as that. You know, you missed your calling. You should have been a teacher."

"You think?"

She nodded. "I'm sure teaching history and mathematics couldn't be that much different from teaching a woman how to accept a man's touch, or teaching her how to dance close to a man, or even teaching her snorkeling. Just another lesson in a long line of them, right?"

He smiled. "Right." He looked up. "Ah, here's our breakfast. Thank you, Liana."

Jill untied the pink wrap and draped it over a lounge chair by the pool. Colin let out a long wolf whistle. "I've got to say that I have excellent taste."

She shrugged, self-conscious. Colin was standing with his hands on his hips, staring at her with open appreciation.

"I did one hell of a job picking out that suit, but then, you've got a great body to show it off."

Annoyingly, unnervingly, his compliment sent heat to every part of her body. "Oh, quit congratulating yourself and let's get on with it."

"Come here."

Irritated more by the way he was making her feel than his words, she pointed to the underwater steps she was standing by. "This is where we go in."

"Not yet. Come here."

The huskiness she heard in his voice caused her irritation to melt away. And just so she didn't do the same, she stiffened her spine and quickly walked to him. She didn't want him to have a chance to study her body too closely, nor did she want the opportunity to do the same to him. As it was, she was having an extremely difficult time keeping her eyes *above* the line where his swim briefs ended.

When she reached him, he grasped her shoulders and turned her around.

"What...?" Suddenly she felt his hands smooth over her back, spreading lotion.

"No one should go anywhere on this island without having sunscreen on, but especially you, with your fair skin."

She tried to reach around to get the bottle. "Okay, but I can put it on myself."

"Not on your back, you can't. This suit exposes too much skin."

"And whose fault is that?"

"The designer's, I suppose."

She rolled her eyes in exasperation, but since he couldn't see her face, the effort was lost on him. Thank heavens, because in the next moment, her exasperation turned to pleasure.

As he rubbed the lotion onto her shoulders, he gave her a light massage. Then he continued slowly downward in a very thorough and sensuous manner. His long fingers didn't miss an inch of her, even slipping beneath the string that held the bikini top around her, slowly sliding toward the sides of her breasts, coming breathtakingly close to the fullness, lingering there, caressing, stroking.

The air blocked up in her lungs. She couldn't breathe. If he reached just a little farther...just a little farther...his fingertips would brush her nipples.

She closed her eyes and felt herself sway. She wanted to ask him to stop but couldn't find the words.

She wanted to walk away, but her legs would not obey.

Now he was below her bra line, to her waist, still caressing here, massaging there. When he reached the line of the suit's bottom, his fingers dipped beneath its edge, not far, but just enough to make her hold her breath.

Then he was on his knees, rubbing oil into her upper thighs, delving beneath the high cut of the suit's legs, then around to the sides of her buttocks.

She reached out for the support of a lounge chair. "I—I can do the rest," she said, though her voice was only a whisper.

Without answering, he simply continued down her legs to her calves and ankles. Then he was in front of her, and she hadn't even seen him move.

She couldn't see. She could only feel his hands stroking lotion on her ankles, her shins, her knees and up. He was using both hands, one on each leg, and the concentration he was giving to the task had to be the same as the concentration Leonardo da Vinci must have brought to the task of painting the *Mona Lisa*.

She cleared her throat. "I really think—"

At the tops of her thighs, his fingers slipped beneath the suit, deep enough to feel the tightly curling hair there.

She gasped.

He stopped, froze, but he didn't move his fingers. His breathing was ragged. He stared at the place where her thighs joined.

Suddenly he stood, took several steps and dived cleanly into the pool. And as his body arced against the blue sky into the crystalline water, she caught a glimpse of his hard, full arousal straining against the material of his swimsuit.

Eight

She faked a headache. As soon as Colin surfaced in the pool, Jill claimed that a sudden, excruciating pain had struck one-half of her head. And all the time she was doing it, she called herself ten different kinds of coward.

But she didn't care. There was no way she could get into the pool with Colin now, be close to him and bear having his hands on her again—not after he had just stroked and rubbed most of her body in an intimate sensual manner that had left her knees weak and her limbs shaking.

What was more, the sight of him as he dived into the water had been proof positive that he had also been affected, though she knew it was in a different way than she.

She understood that men didn't need to feel all the things women did to get sexually excited. All it took for them was the most minor stimuli, which made it all the worse for her. What he could make her feel with a mere twinkle of his eyes meant nothing to him. As for her...she would think about it later.

She grabbed the cover-up, wrapped and tied it around her, then started back up the path to the house. He quickly caught up with her, lifted her into his arms and carried her the last half of the way.

There was no way she could protest. After all, he had helped her through the real thing and was concerned. As soon as she had told him she had a headache, he had surged out of the pool and headed after her. He hadn't even bothered to dry off.

Instinctively, it seemed, she rested her head on his shoulder and wound her arms around his neck. His skin was still wet and slick. She tried not to feel anything, but her effort was doomed. Just the contact of her skin against his was enough to bring back the heat and the memory of his fingers inside her bikini bottom.

Blessedly, Colin walked fast, and soon he was gently laying her on the bed. "What medication do you want?" he whispered.

She closed her eyes. She didn't want to see his concern for her. She didn't want to see the masculine bulge in his swim briefs. Though his arousal had disappeared, no doubt due to his anxiety over her, just the outline of his sex through the spandex was enough to make her mouth water. "Don't bother with it. I'll get up in a minute."

"Just tell me, Jill."

This was going to be tricky. She needed to get rid of him as fast as possible, but based on how he had acted the other night when her pain had been very real, he wasn't going to leave until he was satisfied he had done everything for her that he could. "Bring me the bag."

He did, along with a glass of water. He helped her sit up and opened the bag for her. She picked one of the milder prescriptions, opened the cap and shook one into her hand. "Would you please get me a washcloth for my eyes? A cool, wet one?"

He frowned down at her. "Take the pill first."

She had no recourse. She put the pill into her mouth, surreptitiously maneuvered it under her tongue and took a swallow of water. Satisfied, he returned to the bathroom. She had just enough time to replace the pill in its container before he reappeared with the cloth.

"Thank you."

She lay back amidst the pillows and covered her eyes with the cloth.

"What else can I do? Do you want me to close the shutters to make it darker in here?"

"No, I want to feel the breeze. The cloth will keep the light from my eyes." It suddenly hit her that she was talking in complete sentences, even communicating with the proper words. She was lousy at deception, she reflected ruefully, or at least she was when it came to Colin. She hoped he hadn't noticed, but just in case, she slurred her next words. "Leave. I'll sleep."

She felt him sit down on the bed beside her and take her hand. "Are you sure? Last time..."

"Last time I didn't catch—" she took a breath, reminding herself to slow down and slur the words "—the headache in time. This won't be as bad." She gently pulled her hand from his. "All I need is to sleep it off."

"Listen, Jill. There's a clear button on the phone, here on the table to your immediate left. It's within easy reach for you. If you need something, *anything,* all you have to do is push it, okay?"

"Yes...but I won't have to."

She waited, but he didn't move. For a while she thought he was going to stay, as he had the other night. The fact that his concern was genuine made her feel horrible. And strange. Other than Molly, there was no one who worried about her. Yet Colin obviously did. Why? she wondered, and received no answer.

She forced her mind back to the problem at hand—getting rid of him. Little by little she managed to relax and to check her breathing until it was even and slow. Finally he eased off the bed and quietly left by the terrace door.

And at last she was alone, but any coherent line of thought continued to elude her, so, falling into an old habit, she went over the few things she knew for a fact.

She had agreed to come to the island because she had felt it would give her the opportunity to figure out what the changes she was feeling were and why they were happening. She also knew that, so far, she hadn't had the time or the opportunity. Colin had been all-pervasive in both her waking and sleeping hours.

She had the time now, though. Yet the harder she tried, the more confused she became. Her thoughts were too scrambled, too tangled up with sensations and emotions that, in one way or another, all had to do with Colin.

Des, she told herself sternly. *Des. Des.*

She repeated the name over and over in her head, trying to get herself back on track to her original goal.

Three days ago, she had agreed to cancel all her appointments for the next few days. She had even taken the unprecedented step of agreeing to a partnership with Colin to develop their adjoining parcels of land. And she was putting herself through an emotional and physical ringer by taking these lessons from him.

But her problem was, she kept forgetting why she had agreed to Colin's plan in the first place. Everything she had done in the past few days had supposedly been to help her win Des's attention as a woman and not as a stepcousin to whom he had never been particularly close, anyway. Yet all she could think about was Colin.

She took a deep breath. Her brain obviously needed oxygen, although heaven knew, the island had a surplus of fresh air.

She supposed it was inevitable that she hadn't been able to think clearly. If these lessons had taught her nothing else, it was why her female acquaintances lost their heads and hearts to Colin. He was a virile, deeply sexual, wildly attractive man.

And the lessons he was giving her provided a full dose of all those elements. To get her accustomed to a man's touch, he'd had to stroke and caress her. To teach her how to dance with a man, he'd had to demonstrate. She understood. Some things simply couldn't be told. They had to be shown.

But as a result, her mind and body were reacting to Colin, when she was sure that was the last thing he wanted. From his viewpoint, she was sure he saw himself as merely a substitute for Des.

And the changes she felt inside her? Maybe it was as simple as the fact that Colin's lessons were working—that in some indecipherable way they were making her softer, more open to loving a man.

Des. Of course she had meant that Colin's lessons were making her more open to loving *Des.*

She barely managed to stifle a groan. The answers she had come up with all made perfect sense, yet for some unfathomable reason, she couldn't accept them.

The afternoon wore on. Hard as it was to believe that she might still be sleep deprived, she actually managed to doze on and off. But even with the cloth over her eyes, she was always aware when Colin came to check on her. He would stand at the end of the bed, watch her for a few minutes, then leave again.

By five o'clock, she was bored. Her faked headache had accomplished what she had hoped. It had enabled her to regain her equilibrium and put what was happening to her into a context. If she couldn't accept the explanation one hundred percent, at least it made sense. Sort of.

Plus, if she tried to analyze what was going on with her any more than she already had, she would get a *real* headache. She wasn't used to inactivity, and there was a paradise right outside her door.

She got up and went in search of Colin. She now felt strong enough for that snorkeling lesson.

On the terrace, just outside the open doors of the house's enormous main room, their dinner had been served on a round table. Surrounded by freshly picked red hibiscus, a candle burned in the center of the table. Soft, romantic music floated in the air around them. Small white lights in cleverly placed, hollowed-out spaces of the terrace had come alive. Exotic night-blooming flowers perfumed the gentle breeze. A full moon laid a shimmering silver path across the now dark sea.

Jill had never been given to flights of fancy, but she could truly say that tonight had an almost magical quality about it.

To top it off, Colin sat across from her, looking like every woman's dream of a man, dressed with casual elegance in an open-necked, light-green silk shirt and tailored tan slacks.

They had finished their dinner, and Liana had cleared the table. When she had inquired if there was anything else they would like, Jill had decided on a glass of champagne, instead of dessert, and Colin had ordered a cognac.

After Liana had served them their drinks, she said good-night. Colin had told Jill that Liana and her family lived in a compound of homes built on a private section of the island that offered them their own beach.

Which meant that she and Colin were now completely alone.

Jill sat back and took another sip of her champagne, aware that she was experiencing yet another new feeling—contentment. It wouldn't last of course, but while it did, she planned to savor it. "You know, if you and Des could somehow bottle up nights like this one and sell them, you could each make a fortune. Or perhaps I should say *another* fortune."

Colin's dimple appeared as he gave her a lazy

smile. "I know what you mean. Nights like this are just one of the many reasons I've come to love this island so much."

"I can see why. I've always loved dawn, not only because of the colors of sunrise, but because the sight of it offers the promise of a fresh new day. But with nights like this, I could change my mind."

"Ah, but you haven't yet seen one of our dawns."

She nodded. "I plan to do that very thing in the morning. I'm looking forward to our snorkeling trip."

"I'm really glad. There's unbelievable beauty beneath the sea. The place I've chosen for your first snorkeling trip tomorrow is extraordinary. The reef has grown up to around fifteen to twenty feet below the surface in that area, and you'll easily be able to see it all."

Anticipation rippled through her at the idea. "How are we going to get there?"

"By boat."

"I can't wait."

He grinned wryly. "Even though you haven't yet entirely mastered the art of clearing the snorkel tube?"

She shook her head. "I still don't understand how you expected me to do that. When the tube fills with water, what good is blowing three times in quick succession?"

"That's how you clear out the water."

"Uh-uh. Not if the water comes in at the exact same time you've breathed out and your lungs are empty."

He laughed. "That's why I wanted you to practice in the pool today. At least now you're familiar with what to expect once we're in the sea tomorrow."

She grinned. "It's just a shame that you don't have a glass-bottom boat."

He tilted his head, looking at her with an amused expression. "Oh, come on. You're not going to let a little water in your snorkel scare you off, are you?"

"No way."

"That's my girl. All you need is a little more experience and it will start to come naturally. You'll see."

Her pulse quickened. He'd called her his girl. Naturally it was just one of those casual phrases that people throw out on occasion. She wasn't even sure he knew he had said it. But she did.

Yet more changes in her. Four days ago, if someone had told her she would actually be looking forward to a snorkeling trip, she would have told them they were crazy. And if a man had called her his girl, she would have verbally cut him off at the knees. But now... "I'm not overly concerned. If the snorkel fills with water, or if I forget to breathe through my mouth, instead of through my nose, I'll simply lift my head out of the water."

"And I'll be right there beside you in case you get into any serious trouble."

She nodded.

This afternoon, in the pool, he had given her his instructions without once unnecessarily touching her. She had solved the problem of having him apply sunscreen to her by borrowing one of his T-shirts to cover her. Then she had been able to easily apply the sunscreen to the rest of her body.

And if her heart had given an occasional thud at what she had perceived to be a heated look in his eyes or an expression of desire on his face, it was simply because her body hadn't caught up with her mind's new rational line of thought.

"Have I told you how beautiful you look tonight?"

Her heart gave another thud. At this rate, she reflected ruefully, she might want to consider having a thorough cardiological exam when she returned home.

"Thank you."

She had chosen a long, cool sundress made of silk-lined voile in blues and greens. It had been the colors that had made her reach for it earlier this evening, plus its modest neckline, along with a skirt that consisted of separate pieces that tended to drift outward when she walked. Small straps spanned her shoulders, then crisscrossed her back to about three inches above her waist.

Since the bodice was lined, she hadn't felt the need to wear a bra, which made the dress even more comfortable. Yet one more sign of change in her. Their "date" at the Midnight Blues Club had been the first time she had ever gone outside her home without a bra. Then, she remembered, she had felt naked. Tonight she hadn't thought twice about it.

Everything was happening so fast it was no wonder she was having trouble catching her breath and thinking straight.

"Has anyone ever told you that you have a wonderful instinct for women's clothing?"

His eyes began to twinkle, and a funny fluttering started in her stomach.

"No, and coming from you, that's quite a compliment. As I've said before, you have impeccable taste."

She gazed down at her champagne flute, picked it

up and put it back down again an inch from where it had been. "Have you ever invited another woman down here before?"

"No."

"Have you ever done anything similar with another woman—similar, I mean, to the lessons you're giving me?"

"No."

Those two answers drew a smile from her. "Not even trying to get a woman to wear a softer look?"

He laughed. "And don't forget the part about showing more skin."

"Believe me, I couldn't."

He shook his head. "I don't think you can say anything I've bought you would fall into the risqué category." He paused, considering. "Sexy, maybe, but not risqué."

She had never thought of herself as sexy until Colin had come along and given her his undivided attention. With his lessons, with the clothes he had chosen for her, but most particularly in the way he looked at her and treated her, he had made her feel aware of being a woman in every sense of the word.

It sounded like such a simple and natural way to think, but not in her case. She had never before thought of herself as a woman with her own individual sexuality, much less with the ability to feel at least partially comfortable with it. It was as if Colin had removed an obstacle and given her a completely new outlook.

She took a sip of champagne. "You know, in retrospect, I realize I've probably made these lessons difficult for you. For one thing, I was more set in my ways than I thought. And I also realize now that you were right about my approach to men. It was extremely...businesslike."

He chuckled. "You must be feeling very mellow tonight to admit to all that."

She laughed. "I must be. I think it's a combination of the night and the champagne."

"Then I'll simply have to order up more nights like this one, along with cases and cases of champagne."

His statement had sounded as if he, *personally,* had liked the results of the combination, and heat quickened through her body. *Stop it,* she ordered herself. More than likely he had meant he would order the combination on Des's behalf.

His expression turned serious. "I'm just thankful you caught that headache in time. I wasn't sure whether or not you'd even be able to have dinner tonight."

She hated the knowledge of her deception, but she refused to let herself break eye contact.

He tilted his head in that thoughtful way of his to which she was becoming accustomed. "You know, I don't think I've ever seen you as relaxed as you are right now, or even heard you laugh as you did a minute ago. No matter what comes out of this trip, it will have been worth it to have seen you this way."

"No matter what comes out of this trip? You mean if I don't get Des?"

He shrugged off her question. "There's just one thing missing." He plucked one of the red hibiscus blossoms from the centerpiece, leaned across the table and slipped it behind her ear. Sitting back in his chair, he studied her. "Perfect," he whispered.

Warmth shimmered throughout her. She had to

clear her throat before she spoke again. "You know something else I've just realized about you?"

"I can't even begin to imagine."

"You're a very patient man."

He gazed at her for a moment with an expression so enigmatic she didn't even try to decipher it. Finally he said, "I suppose I am."

"And there's something else I've realized. I don't know that much about you. I mean, you and I have traveled in more or less the same group for two years now, yet I don't know even the most basic facts about you."

A slow smile appeared on his face. "That's very good, Jill."

"What is?"

"You've just arrived at another very important lesson, and all on your own, too."

"What are you talking about?"

"The lesson we haven't gotten to yet. The lesson that teaches you the need to show interest in the man you are trying to attract."

"I'm not just *showing* interest in you, Colin," she said with real annoyance. "I really *am* interested."

"Even better. So, okay, what would you like to know? I'm pretty much an open book."

In the blink of an eye, her annoyance vanished. She grinned teasingly. "Oh, yeah? I'm not sure I believe that about you."

"Try me."

His soft, husky voice drifted over to her on a wave of the music and sent warmth skimming down her spine. "Well, okay—as I said, basic stuff. For instance, where were you two years ago before we met?

No, wait—let's start even farther back than that. Where are you from?"

"A small town in East Texas you've probably never heard of."

"You may be right, though I do own land in East Texas."

"I know, but in a different part."

She had gotten past the stage of being surprised that he knew more about her that she did about him. "Do your parents still live there?"

"I wish they did, but no. My mother died when I was twenty-nine. My dad died just a few years ago."

She needed to respond, but since grief over the loss of a parent was foreign to her, she had to fall back on a cliché. "I'm sorry. Do you have any other family still there?"

"An aunt and three cousins."

"And are you close to them?"

He nodded. "We make it a point to get together every so often."

It was funny, but she had never thought of Colin as having a family, roots or ties. Perhaps it was the way he had seemed to appear out of nowhere two years ago. And to hear that he was still close to his remaining family also vaguely surprised her.

Her father had never fostered closeness between her and her sisters—just the opposite, in fact. Since Tess had married, she was making an effort to change that. So far, though, Jill had managed to avoid most of Tess's family gatherings. As for the ever elusive Kit, Tess was going to have to catch her first.

"Tell me more about your parents. What did they do?"

"My mom was a homemaker. She took care of my

dad and me, grew her own vegetables and canned them. And once she even won a blue ribbon at the state fair for her peach pie."

Her eyes widened. "You've *got* to be making that up."

He burst out laughing. "Why do you say that?"

"Because *no one* has a mother like that."

"Sorry, but I did. She was wonderful. I still miss her."

Colin was a sophisticated, urbane man, yet he was telling her that he had been raised in a small town by a mother he had obviously adored and fed food she had grown herself. It didn't seem real, but then, most people would probably say the same about her own upbringing.

"What did your father do?"

"He owned a general store. He wasn't setting the world on fire with it, mind you, but the income was sufficient for the three of us, and that was all that mattered to him."

"Oh, I get it now. You grew up in Mayberry, right? Your aunt's name is Bea, and Andy Griffiths was the sheriff, with a deputy named Barney and a son named Opie."

He chuckled. "Sorry to disappoint you, but no. My parents were good, simple people who raised me with a great deal of love and taught me, by example, the difference between right and wrong. It was a marvelous life for a little boy, but as I grew older, I also learned that life can be difficult, too."

"What happened?"

"When I was ten years old, my father lost everything."

"You mean his store?"

"His store, our home and most of our belongings. He even had to sell our good car and buy a junker that ran only half the time. And it all happened because Dad trusted the man who kept the books and paid the bills for the store, along with our personal bills. Unfortunately, that trust was grossly misplaced."

"But why did your dad trust this man so much? Surely there were signs, something that should have clued him in early on?"

"There probably were, but you see, Dad's education had stopped in the eighth grade because he had to drop out of school. His father had died, and he had to go to work to help his mother. Believe it or not, it's a common enough story when you live in the country deep in East Texas. At any rate, by the time Dad realized something was wrong, it was too late. The man had bled Dad and the store dry, and Dad had no savings to fall back on."

She sat forward. "But the man was caught, right?"

"Yeah, but by that time he had already spent the money. He was put in prison, but justice didn't do Mom and Dad any good. The people to whom Dad owed money went to court to force Dad to liquidate."

"It must have been awful for your parents."

He nodded. "It was. Yet in one way, it was good."

"How can you say that?"

"Because by watching how my parents handled their problems, I was taught invaluable life lessons, things I probably would never have learned in any other way."

"I'm not sure I understand. How did they handle them?"

"With great pride and dignity. We rented one of

the smallest, shabbiest houses in town, but my parents never showed any sign of being ashamed of their reduced state. And because they didn't, I didn't, either. In fact, I never once saw anything to be ashamed of. They hadn't changed. They were still the same loving people who provided me with the same stable upbringing they always had."

"But how? I mean, how did they cope? How did they put food on the table and buy all the things they needed, not to mention things a growing boy needs?"

"Mom planted a new vegetable garden, but she planted three times as much as she had before, so that she could sell the extra to the neighbors. And she started buying my clothes from the town's thrift shop. At any one time I probably had only two pairs of jeans and three shirts that fit, but Mom made sure they were clean and neatly ironed. She also took in other people's ironing.

"As I became more and more aware of what was going on, I became even prouder of my parents. If anything, the love they gave me grew stronger, as did their love for each other. Many nights after I went to bed, I could hear my mom waiting up for my dad to come home so that she could serve him a hot meal. And I saw her rub his shoulders and back at night when he'd done so much physical labor his whole body would be screaming with pain.

"But through it all, Dad very calmly, and with great perseverance, went about working to get his store back. He worked two jobs, sometimes three, but he never complained, and he never once wavered in his determination. Eventually his patience and hard work won, and he was able to buy back his store."

Completely fascinated, Jill had been hanging on his every word. "That's an *incredible* story, Colin."

"My parents were incredible people."

"Obviously. I would have liked to meet them."

"Why?"

"Because they made you the man you are today."

He stared at her, his eyes dark. Then, slowly, a smile formed on his face. "Careful. You're very close to giving me a compliment."

She grinned. "You don't need a compliment from me. I've never known a more confident person, and now I know where that confidence comes from. You watched your parents handle the worst and successfully come out on the other side, and that taught you that you could do the same."

"Yes, except losing material things is not the worst thing that can happen to you. Losing someone you love is."

"Of course." His answer momentarily flustered her, because she hadn't expected it. As quickly as she could, she went on, "Now I also know why you're such a patient man. Like your father, you're willing to wait and work for what you want."

"So now you know everything there is to know about me."

Not even close, she thought. She might have learned certain things about his background, but it was very clear to her that he kept a great many things on the inside, just as she did. "I have another question. How did you get from the boy who had two pairs of jeans to the man you are today, a self-made man with enough money to buy anything he wants?"

"With dignity and pride, I hope. As soon as I was old enough, I got a job, but no matter how tired my dad became, he wouldn't let me work so many hours that I neglected my schoolwork. He didn't want me to ever find myself in the position he had. He told me to let him take care of Mom and me and of getting back the store. My job was to concentrate on school. That concentration earned me a scholarship. I don't think I ever saw Mom or Dad prouder than they were the day they saw me graduate from college, not even when Dad got back his store or I began to make really big money."

"I can imagine." And she could, just from the tone of his voice. "So what did you do after graduation? Go to Dallas?"

"Yeah. For the first eight years or so, I lived there full-time. I set quietly to work and began making contacts. Soon one deal followed another and, not so inconsequentially, my first million was followed by more."

"Eight years is a fairly short time to make that much money. You make it sound so easy, but I know it couldn't have been."

"No, but don't forget, I learned early on all about hard work and patience. And by the way, I also met Des my first year in Dallas." He paused. "I'll always be grateful for those eight years."

"Why?"

"Because everything I was able to accomplish during those years gave me the opportunity to shower my parents with things they had never had before—a luxury car, a really nice home, furniture, vacations." He shook his head. "They'd never even been on a vacation before, and they still wouldn't have gone unless I hadn't packed them up and taken them."

She chuckled. "Much like you did me, you mean?"

He smiled softly. "Yeah. In fact, as soon as the first part of the main house here on Serenity was built, I got to bring them here. They loved it. I was also able to arrange their finances so that Dad never had to work another day in his life if he didn't want to, though he did. I also had the opportunity to tell them how proud I was of them and to thank them for all they had done for me." He paused. "That's really the thing I'll always be *most* grateful for."

A lump formed in her throat. She had no reference for understanding his gratitude to have been able to do those things for his parents.

"But then my mother died unexpectedly. Naturally Dad was devastated, so I returned home and began to run my business out of the back of his store with computers, modems and faxes. Whenever I sensed Dad was doing okay, I'd make overnight trips to Dallas. But by then his health wasn't good, and there was no way I was going to leave him alone for long. He refused to stop working, so to ease some of his burden, I helped him in the store and tried to make it look as if I wasn't doing much."

The memory drew another smile from him. "And while I was at it, I continued to use the money I had made up until then to make more. But when Dad's health began to seriously fail, I became his main caretaker."

"But why? You had the money to hire someone to take care of him."

He looked at her. "Taking care of him wasn't a chore or an obligation for me. It was something I felt privileged to do, though I used my money to make him as comfortable as I possibly could in other ways." He reached for his cognac and took a sip. "And that's the long version of why I only appeared on the social scene a couple of years ago. Before then, I had other priorities."

She sat there for a moment, attempting to absorb all that he had told her. "You know, you may have had the patience, plus everything else you learned from your dad, to help you accomplish what you have, but you also have a rare brilliance."

He shook his head. "Not brilliance."

"No, it's true. Since I became aware of you, I've seen evidence of your work. And you were smart enough to go into exactly the right business. As a venture capitalist, you used other people's money to make money of your own."

"But no client of mine ever lost a cent."

She smiled. "Don't I know it. In some circles, your name is whispered with reverence."

"Funny. That's how I've heard your name mentioned, too."

She laughed. "Oh, sure you have."

"You should do that more often."

"What?"

"Laugh." He stood, reached for her hand and pulled her to her feet. "That's enough of the past. For now, let's concentrate on the present."

"How?"

"By dancing."

Nine

Like the night, their dance felt magic to Jill.

Colin moved them slowly around the terrace in a way that was as romantic as the music that filled the air. He held her lightly, one hand at her waist, the other hand holding hers out to the side.

The dance was as different from the way they had danced at the blues club as sunlight was to moonlight. Their first dance had been rawly sexual and darkly dangerous. This was more like a dream, soft and sensual.

At times they simply swayed together; at other times they did a slow, graceful waltz. But always, always, their bodies were in tune. She didn't even have to think to follow him. It was as natural as breathing, as sweet as the flower-scented night, as inevitable as the tides.

She wasn't even aware of her feet touching the

ground. She was floating, the lightweight panels of her skirt drifting outward like undulating ribbons of silk. She was intoxicated, not on champagne, but on the night, the music and most of all Colin, yet she felt no alarm.

Her gaze was locked with his, because there was nothing else she wanted to see. And when his steps became even slower and he drew her even closer, she decided there was nowhere else she would rather be than held tightly in his arms. Her body recognized his, softened and melted into his.

She drew her hand from his, slid it around his neck and up into his hair. His hands joined at her back, and his fingers delved beneath the dress's straps to her bare skin.

The heat started gradually, winding its way through her veins. Her nipples hardened against the silk fabric; her breasts began to ache and swell. She had experienced the same things many times over the past few days, but this time she had no urge to try to censure her feelings. Then the heat reached the spot between her legs and flared. She would have fallen if he hadn't been holding her so firmly.

The solid ridge of his arousal pushed against her lower body. Physically Colin wanted her, but intellectually, emotionally, she was sure he didn't. After all, to him they had made a business bargain, a bargain, moreover, that involved one of his best friends.

But it didn't matter to her, not tonight, not at this moment. Since the beginning, there had been a sexual tension between the two of them that couldn't be denied. Every time he had touched her, he had made her entire body pulsate with desire for him. His kisses had left her decimated to the point that nerves and needs had continuously warred inside her.

And it had all left her confused, her thoughts and feelings twisted and tangled to the point that she hadn't known what was happening to her or what it all meant. She still didn't. But now, suddenly, she was tired of trying to figure it out. Most of all, however, she was tired of fighting her feelings.

Just this once, she wanted to make love with Colin. And she wanted to do it now, on this magic night, while the trade winds blew over them.

She pulled herself out of his arms and looked up at him. In his eyes she could see the same heat that she felt inside her. She had seen that same heat before. She had also witnessed his control and the way he could pull himself back from the precipice without taking that one tiny step too far that would have them both falling over the edge and into full-scale passion.

So this time, before he had time to think of all the reasons they should rein in their feelings and say good-night, she grasped his hand and wordlessly began to draw him toward her door.

With each step she took, she expected him to pull her to a halt, but miraculously it didn't happen. She wondered what he was thinking, feeling, but she wouldn't let herself look back at him. She didn't want to chance seeing doubt or wariness or any other negative emotion. Not tonight, when she knew so clearly what she wanted. She continued to her room, through the doors and to the side of her bed.

Liana or her mother had already turned down the covers and turned on the nightstand lamp. A small bowl of freshly cut hibiscus that matched the one in her hair sat beneath it. The lamp's pale golden light lit a portion of the bed. The only other light came from the spill of moonlight through the open doors.

It was more than enough. If she had been blind, she would still have been able to sense Colin if he had been anywhere in the room. His presence disturbed the molecules of the otherwise peaceful atmosphere, threatening to set it on fire; his body heat reached out and wrapped around her; his musky male scent invaded her every pore.

She released his hand, and still without looking at him, she reached behind her back to unzip her dress.

His hand closed over hers and the zipper tab. "Look at me, Jill."

She didn't want to. She didn't want to see his calm visage or hear his rational words.

"*Look* at me," he said, this time his voice hoarse with emotion.

She exhaled a trembling breath. Reluctantly she turned and gazed up at him. His eyes were darker than she had ever seen them, and his face was tight, the muscles in his neck rigid. "Are you sure?"

She could hardly believe it. He wasn't telling her he didn't want to make love to her. Instead, he was thinking of her, leaving the decision up to her without trying to influence her more than he already had.

"Oh, yes." Her eyes moistened with emotion; her words sounded barely above a whisper. "I'm very sure."

He didn't ask another question or give her a chance to say another word. Before she knew it, he had unzipped her dress and pulled it down her body. She stepped out of it, and at the same time her trembling fingers attempted to unbutton his shirt. He pushed her hand aside and quickly did the job.

"Get in bed."

His intensity and desire were suddenly coming at her in pounding waves, and it dawned on her just how much control he had actually been exerting the past few days.

She kicked off her shoes and did as he said. Once on the bed, she used her feet to push the covers down to the end, then lifted her hips and slipped off her panties.

Colin came down to her, naked and with every muscle in his body hard. He eased himself on top of her, opening her legs with his, then positioning himself.

Her heart hammered with excitement and anticipation, so hard it felt as if her ribs might break. Somewhere in the back of her mind, she knew there were bound to be consequences for stealing these moments out of time with Colin and for taking what she wanted, what they *both* wanted. But she had never felt like this before and probably never would again. And for this one time, this one night, if there was a piper to pay, she gladly would.

"Colin." It was a whisper. It was a scream. She wasn't certain which, because above all it was a demand.

His mouth crushed hers, and his tongue thrust deep. She wrapped her arms around his neck, then slid her palms down his back, relishing the feel of the rippling muscles beneath his bare skin that, before now, she had only seen. He closed a hand over her breast and roughly kneaded her flesh, taking her beyond reason and into the realm of heat, haze and animalistic urges and cravings.

She moved restlessly beneath him, her hands covering every inch of him she could reach. She had never been to this place before, where she had absolutely no control over her body, nor did she want any. The kisses and touches had taken her close. The dancing at the blues club, along with the application of the sunscreen, had brought her even closer. But none of them had brought her to the point where she was now.

To be kissed without restraint and touched in a wild urgency of need was incredible, amazing, wonderful. But she wanted more. She wanted Colin inside her so badly and with such violence that if someone had happened to walk in the door and tried to interrupt them, she would have been beyond caring.

And she wasn't afraid. If she had learned nothing else on this island, she had learned that letting herself go was okay and that, no matter what happened, Colin would keep her safe.

She made a sound of frustration and arched against him, convinced she would shatter if she couldn't have him soon. She turned her head, tearing her mouth from his, but she didn't have time to say anything.

"I should go slower," he muttered harshly. "I've wanted this so..."

He entered her with one violent push and buried his thick, long length completely inside her. She caught her breath as sharp, exquisite pleasure jolted through her. Then again. And again. And again.

And then she didn't have time to consciously breathe anymore. He began to slam into her, time after time, and with such ferocity that the bed shook and her body was jarred. But she met his every thrust with her own, lifting her hips to take him more deeply into her. She felt possessed, like a wild woman who couldn't get enough of him.

She was on fire. Her blood was boiling. Her nerve endings were being scraped with a hot, soothing, stimulating, liquid ecstasy. He entwined his hands with hers and pressed them back on either side of her head. She looked up at him and saw that his eyes were almost black, his expression pure male aggression.

She had never known she would love the powerful, sexual mastery of a man. She had never even known such rapture could exist between a man and a woman. She wasn't even sure what was coming next, but she could feel her body readying.

Unbearable, sweet, hot pressure was building inside her. She tightened her grip on his hands and, with tears streaming down her face, bucked beneath him. He bent his head and drove his tongue deeply and roughly into her mouth, taking her there in the exact same fast, exhilarating, jackhammer rhythm he was using to drive into her.

Suddenly overpowering sensations gripped her. She arched her upper back off the bed and came apart, climaxing with a loud cry as she was carried away on waves of pleasure so large, so intense and so incredible, she could only go with them. Seconds later, Colin's entire body stiffened and he followed her as a deep, hoarse growl came up out of his being, carrying the sound of her name with it.

He had blown it.

Colin cradled Jill against him with her head resting on his shoulder. Tenderly he brushed tendrils of damp, dark hair away from her face. Her eyes were closed, and she was as still and limp as a rag doll.

As for himself, his heartbeat had yet to return to normal.

What was he going to do now?

The plan had been to get her away from her everyday life and pressures, so that here on the island, with its slower way of living, she would have very little to focus on but him. In this environment, he had hoped she would relax and get to know him as a person, rather than as someone to banter with at parties or, conversely, ignore.

Well, she had certainly gotten to know him, he thought grimly. The problem was, things had happened out of order.

His first objective, actually his *only* objective, had been to make her fall in love with him.

He had never thought it would happen over these few days. But he had thought, hoped—God he'd *prayed*—it would give him, at the very least, a niche in her life and, at most, a solid foundation on which the two of them could build a deep and lasting relationship.

He loved her. He had known it since the day he had figured out why he had initially been so attracted to her. She didn't know it, but her scars and his were the same. And her wants and his were also the same.

She had never had a family, not in the real sense of the word, and though she might not consciously consider that a loss, the scars had been there that night for him to see, to recognize, to feel. And he had seen something else, too. Deep down, in a part of her soul that she had done her best to seal off long ago, when she had lost her mother and her father had taken over her raising, she wanted one.

He, on the other hand, had had a family—no one could have had a better one—but he had lost them. And ever since, he had wanted a new one, one of his own making. But until that night, when for an instant something had opened up inside her that had allowed him to see into her soul, he hadn't known with whom he wanted to make that family.

But because of what had just happened between them, they both could be doomed never to have one, at least, not the kind they both wanted. He was convinced they could only have that with each other. For once in his life, though, he hadn't been patient. During the past few days, despite his best intentions, he had rushed and overwhelmed her.

She moved against him; her hand slipped onto his chest, and he felt his loins stir. Closing his eyes, he gritted his teeth. He could take her again, right now, but making love to her a second time would only compound his error—or much worse, since he doubted he would be able to stop at twice.

He had purposely set out to make the night a romantic one, including the dance. But as the dance had continued, he had instinctively drawn her closer. When it came to her, he had so little willpower it scared him to death.

And when she had pulled away, taken his hand and drawn him into her bedroom, his brain had started to shut down. Saying no to her would have been a near impossibility. He didn't even know where he had gotten the strength to ask if that was what she really wanted. But when she had said yes, it would have taken the end of the world to stop him from taking her.

Still, he had been too rough, too quick. Their first time should have been different, yet looking back on it, he didn't know how it could have been. Quite simply, he had been starved for her.

How was he going to turn things back around when he still wanted her so badly he was in danger of exploding?

She moved, rubbing her cheek on his shoulder, and one leg found its way over his.

"Jill?" he murmured, despite himself, kissing the top of her head.

"Mmm?" Her foot flexed and rubbed against his shin. Her hand slid through the curls of his chest hair over to his nipple.

He groaned and put his hand over hers to still it. "Are you all right?"

"Uh-huh."

Beneath his hand, her fingers slid back and forth over his nipple. This time he firmly clasped her hand and rolled over on top of her. Her hair lay in a tousled mass around her head; her lips were red and swollen, her lids half-closed, her eyes drowsy with sensual lethargy.

"I better warn you," he said, his teeth gritted, his control held by a slender thread, "you keep that up and I'll be so deep inside you again, so fast and so hard, you won't know what hit you."

She slid her hand up the side of his face and parted her legs. "I'll know."

Without another word he drew his buttocks back and once again drove into her, hard, fast and without mercy. A powerful, white-hot passion held him in its grip. Sanity had been stripped from him. Beneath him, willing and hot, she writhed and strained. He slammed into her time and again, taking them both higher and higher, then clung to her as he soared with her to a pinnacle of ecstasy he had never known before.

After that, he knew there was no way he could stop. He might have only this one night with her to last the rest of his life, and he planned to make the most of it. Actually, there was nothing else he could do. He was like an addict who had gotten a taste of a drug and now couldn't do without it.

The next time he pulled her to him and entered her, he extended the lovemaking as long as he could bear. By now, he knew just how sensitive she was and that, at times, he only had to touch her in a certain way to make her climax.

Gently, slowly, he stroked in and out of her pulsating velvet flesh. At the same time, he stroked his hand up and down her side, stopping occasionally to tweak her nipple and lightly massage her breast. Soon she was trembling and clawing at his back for completion. Then he slowly withdrew from her and rested his hard sex on her lower abdomen.

It was torture for him, but it was the sweetest kind, watching her face react to everything he did. He spent a lot of time nibbling at her nipple, pulling it into his mouth, then scraping his tongue back and forth across it until she softly cried and said his name over and over. Then he switched to the other.

In the next moment Jill did something he hadn't even considered. She took control, reached for him, shifted, and just like that he was inside her again. She arched and writhed against him, high and hard. He lost his control, his mind, pounding into her until seconds later he felt the tight squeezing of her inner contractions. And as she bowed her upper back off the bed, he heard the soft, wild cry he had come to love. Then he exploded into her and everything faded to black.

The dawn was everything she had expected it to be, Jill reflected, standing in the doorway of her bedroom, watching the blues and roses shift across the sky, the dark waters of the sea gradually lighten to purple and indigo. Just for a moment she allowed herself the luxury of lifting her face to the morning trade winds. They wound their way through her hair, wet from a shower, and moved over her freshly moisturized skin.

She threw a quick glance over her shoulder at Colin. He was still sleeping. Under any other circumstances, she probably would be, too. This morning, however, she had too much on her mind.

She had known what she was doing last night when she had taken his hand. Every bit of what had followed had been her fault. She had told herself that she wanted to make love to Colin just once, and she had. She should have been satisfied with that once, but she hadn't been. She had been greedy, hungry, and had practically made him continue.

Granted, it hadn't taken much encouragement, but then, he was a man, and as she had noted before, if a woman shows herself to be willing, a man doesn't need any more motivation. But to give Colin his due, up to that point, he had shown remarkable restraint, considering the job he had set out to do.

No, it was her fault. She didn't regret it, but she

also couldn't be more embarrassed about it. If there was a way she could get off this island by herself before he awoke, she probably would. As it was, she didn't know how she was going to meet his eyes.

And the ultimate irony? She had come to the island to give herself time to figure out all the changes that were happening inside her. At one point yesterday, she thought she had figured it out. But after last night, she was more confused than she had been when she arrived.

Making love to Colin had shaken her world apart, and she wasn't certain it could ever be put back together again—at least, not in the way it had been.

"What are you doing up so early?"

Her heart gave a hard thud at the sound of his sleepy voice. Would there ever come a day when her heart wouldn't react in that way to him? Would there ever come a night when she could look across a crowded room without wanting him?

"You were right," she said, without turning to look at him.

"About what?" He sounded irritated, grumpy, not fully awake yet.

"The dawn. It's spectacular."

She heard his heavy exhalation of breath, then movement, as if he was rearranging pillows.

"What are you doing up, Jill? You can't have gotten enough rest. And why the hell are you dressed?"

After her shower, she had slipped on the pair of slacks and plain white T-shirt she had worn on the flight here. "I think it's time I left. You can stay if you like, and I'll hire a charter from one of the bigger islands."

Behind her, he swore, then more movement. Her

blood started racing as she realized he was getting out of bed.

"Jill…"

He was coming toward her. She stepped out onto the terrace and glanced in the direction of the other end. "The table is already made up, and there's a carafe of coffee out. I think I'll go have a cup while you dress."

"Jill, come back. We need to talk."

She turned and looked at him. He was standing in the doorway, a sheet wrapped around his waist. His hair was a complete mess, more so than usual, and his face sported a night's growth of beard. His eyes were even red and blurry. Yet she didn't think she had ever seen him look as devastatingly handsome as he did right then. "I don't think so." Quickly she walked away.

Showered, shaved and dressed, Colin joined Jill on the terrace. Without looking at him, she broke apart a croissant. "Liana and her mother are wonderful. They didn't really expect us to be up this early, but they had these ready just the same."

"I don't want you to leave, Jill."

Carefully she spread guava jelly on the croissant. "I know I haven't had my final snorkeling lesson, but after my lesson in the pool, I'm sure I could manage in the sea if I decide I'd like to do more of it."

"I couldn't care less about the snorkeling. Let's talk about the real reason you want to leave—what happened last night."

"Last night has nothing to do with why I want to leave." She had never known she could be such a good liar. She had never known her heart could hurt this much without breaking. "And there's really nothing more that we need to talk about. You've done a great job with all the lessons, but—"

His head jerked back as if she'd hit him. "If you think for one minute last night was about those damn lessons, you're dead wrong."

"It doesn't matter."

"It happens to matter a *hell* of a lot."

"Then, no, Colin, I don't believe last night was about the lessons. It was just about two people on a beautiful island, surrounded by a beautiful night, who had been in close proximity to each other for several days. Something was bound to happen and it did. But now it's over and I need to get back to Texas."

Silence stretched between them. Jill could feel his gaze on her, almost hear him thinking. She just wished she knew *what* he was thinking.

She had known it was going to be difficult to get him to forget last night, especially since she herself would like nothing more than to go back to bed with him right now and not get up for another week. But she couldn't betray what she was feeling by even so much as a flicker of an eyelash. She needed to get away from him, and she was running out of ammunition.

"Okay," he finally said. "We can leave today if you want, but not before we talk."

"Do you happen to know where Des is today?"

Colin froze. Color leeched from his face. His gaze filled with black rage. His chair scraped back and he stood. "He's at the Double B visiting his father. We'll leave in thirty minutes. Be ready."

Ten

Using one foot, Jill slowly pushed herself back and forth in the swing that hung in the gazebo. A soft breeze filtered to her through a screen of junipers. Somewhere she heard a bird call. In a distant meadow, cattle grazed.

She was in the backyard of the Uvalde farm where her sister Tess and brother-in-law, Nick, were spending their summer. In fact, no matter what the season, they would hop on a plane and come here every chance they got.

And after three days here, Jill had to admit, the place did have a certain charm. It also had a peace and warmth about it that she had badly needed.

Not too far away, Tess bent to cut yet another iris from her garden to go into her already full basket of flowers. When she straightened, she looked over at Jill. "I'm going to put these in the house and bring us out some iced tea," she called. "Does that sound good to you?"

"Great," Jill called back.

Three days ago, acting on an instinct she still didn't entirely understand, she had contacted her sister from Colin's plane and asked if she could come and stay with them for a short while. Tess's yes had been full of enthusiasm. And now, seeing how happy Tess was that she was there, Jill felt guilty for all the times she had rebuffed her.

Her mind returned to Colin and their flight back to Dallas. He had broken his silence only once, by calling her on the intercom to ask if she wanted him to arrange a charter for her to take her to the Double B. She had declined, saying that she had already called Molly and asked her to make the arrangements. What she hadn't told him was that she had no intention of flying to the family ranch to see Des.

Hearing the screen door slam, she glanced up to see Tess, dressed in shorts and a brief top, strolling toward her with an iced tea in each hand. When she reached her, she handed her one, then sat down beside her.

"I like your farm, Tess."

"Thank you. Nick and I both love it. Strictly speaking, though, it belongs to Nick's family—well, actually his grandmother—but Nick and I are the only two who actually want to make it our second home. Nick's sister and her family know they are always welcome, and we try to have as many gatherings as we can. As a matter of fact, since Nick's grandfather died, his grandmother Alma usually comes and stays for a few days when we're here, and it makes us all so happy. During the winter, we fly in for as many three-day weekends as we can."

Jill nodded. "Like I said, nice. Good tea, too, by the way."

"The mint came from the garden."

Jill chuckled. "It's been hard for me to accept that you actually *like* to garden. I mean, you never have before. It was something we were never exposed to."

Tess nodded pensively. "I know, but the difference is, this is a real home, something I'd never known. Before I married Nick, I had my place in Dallas, but it wasn't a home, not really. I was always traveling or working." She shook her head at the memory of her past. "Now Nick and I also have our Austin home. I still work and travel, though I try to limit the latter as much as possible. And Nick has his own work. But no matter which home we're at, it's filled with love and the memories we're making with every moment we spend together. I've learned *that's* what makes a home. And—" she grinned "—we're hoping very soon now to start turning a room in all three homes into a nursery."

"Nursery?" Jill asked, shocked. "Is this an announcement?"

"I *wish,* but no, not yet. Soon, though. I can feel it'll be soon."

"That's wonderful," Jill murmured sincerely. "I'm very happy for you and Nick."

"Okay," Tess said, her tone suddenly brisk and businesslike, "that's enough about me. It's time to tell me what's going on with you. When you arrived here, you looked pale as a ghost—in fact, almost sick. Since then, you haven't said much except for superficial conversation, but I'm relieved to say that you do look a little better."

"I'm sorry. I know I haven't been very good company."

"I'm not complaining. I just want to know what happened to bring you here now, at this particular time, when you've turned down countless other invitations. And while you're explaining, I also want to know what you're running from."

Jill studied her sister. Tess's blond hair was pulled back into a ponytail and tied with a wrinkled ribbon that couldn't quite manage to hold the myriad escaped tendrils. Her face positively glowed. "You know what? I've never seen you look more beautiful or happier. Love obviously suits you."

Surprise crossed Tess's face. "You're calling *me* beautiful, when you're the acknowledged beauty in the family? Now I know the answer to my questions—you're obviously sick."

Jill's lips curved in wry amusement. "It's true, you know. You've always been beautiful, but now..." She let her words trail off, and her gaze drifted away from her sister toward the garden. "Instinct brought me here. As for what I'm running from...I guess I have to say Colin."

Tess frowned. "Colin? Colin Wynne?"

Jill nodded, then proceeded to fill her sister in on the bargain she and Colin had struck—and its outcome. She finished with, "So once again I'm confused. When I arrived here, I knew only one thing for sure. I'm in *lust* with Colin."

Her sister choked on a gulp of iced tea.

With a glance at her to make sure she was all right, Jill continued, "But since I've been here, I've watched you and Nick. Tess—" she turned to face her sister "—there have been times when you and Nick have been sitting across the room from each other, and one of you will smile at the other, and I can actually *feel* the love you have for each other. Actually, that's very likely what brought me here in the first place—an instinct that you and Nick have the real thing. I wanted to learn about it."

"Our love?"

Jill nodded again. "To start with, the love I've seen between you two has simply confirmed a decision I made before I left the island. I don't want to marry Des. He doesn't love me and I certainly don't love him. When I decided to try to learn how to go about getting him, I was convinced that we could have a marriage that would work for both of us on some level, even though I doubted we would actually love each other. I now know just how wrong I was."

"Deciding you didn't want to marry Des must have been the equivalent of an intellectual earthquake for you," Tess said, impressed, "but I've got to say, I'm very glad you came to that conclusion before it was too late. Which brings us back to Colin."

"Colin." Jill shook her head. "I'm pretty sure he hates me now."

"Why?"

"Because he wanted me to stay on the island and talk about our night together. But I knew I couldn't do that without revealing what I felt for him, so I gave him the impression that as soon as we landed in Dallas, I was going to the ranch to use all the lessons he'd taught me to catch Des."

"But why should that upset him? It's the reason he

gave you the lessons in the first place. That doesn't make sense."

"I know." She gnawed on her bottom lip for a moment. "The only thing I can think of is that maybe he believes I'm going to renege on our bargain. I won't, though."

Tess fished out a mint leaf from her tea and nibbled thoughtfully on it. "There *is* another possibility."

"What?"

"He loves you."

Jill shook her head. "There's no way. When we parted at the Dallas-Fort Worth airport, he was ice-cold with anger."

"Do you care?"

"Yeah, I do. Tess, he's a *remarkable* man. On the island, I learned about his background, and it made me feel so humble."

"Why?"

"Because he's accomplished so much, yet started out with so little." She paused. "He also made me feel incredibly sad that I never knew the kind of parental love he had."

"I understand, because for a little bit, I felt the same way about Nick."

"You did?"

Tess nodded. "And you know what conclusion I reached? You, Kit and I are the only people in the world who really know that our so-called privileged life was actually a nightmare. And we each had to learn in our own way how to survive, how to make it through our childhood to become functioning adults. Our father even robbed us of each other's comfort. Nick and Colin may not have had the material things that we had, or the money we inherited to start out like we did, but they had something a lot better. They were able to grow up knowing that, no matter what they did, they were loved unconditionally. If you look at it like that, they started out way ahead of us."

"I guess that's true," Jill said slowly, trying to assimilate what her sister had just said.

"Oh, it definitely is. So don't ever feel humble again, Jill. We've *more* than earned our inheritance, plus we've each taken our portions of the company and skyrocketed them to a success and prosperity our father never even dreamed of."

"You're *right*."

Tess grinned. "Of course I am. So let's get back to Colin."

Jill sighed. "As I told you, I have a bad case of lust for him."

Tess's grin broadened. "Let me give you a little sisterly advice. Great sex is nothing to be sneezed at."

Jill tentatively returned her sister's grin. "I learned that. But, Tess, this is what I want to know. How do you tell the difference between love and lust? I mean, you must have faced the same thing with Nick. How did you decide it was more than lust, that in fact it was true love?"

Tess leaned over and set her glass on the gazebo floor beside the swing, then straightened and reached for Jill's hand. Jill was so startled she nearly jerked her hand away, but Tess merely tightened her hold.

"Listen to me, Jill. You, Kit and I were never taught anything about love, because our father never showed us any. So when it came to figuring out if I loved Nick or not, I didn't have a clue. But in my case, I had some help. Uncle William flat out told me

I loved Nick. And believe me, when I realized he was right, no one was more surprised than I was."

Jill's brows drew together. "So as soon as Uncle William told you that you loved Nick, you instantly knew he was right?"

Tess nodded. "Because as soon as he said it, I started getting these flashbacks of things that had happened during the relatively short time I had known Nick. And I finally understood that it wasn't anything big that had happened between us that should have clued me in to the fact that I loved him, but a series of little things."

"Such as?" Jill leaned toward her, paying close attention.

Tess smiled softly as she remembered. "There was the way that with just a smile he could make me go weak at the knees. The way I practically melted into him when we danced on the night of my birthday."

Jill gasped, but Tess went on, "The easy way he could make me want him. The way I had turned down Des's offer to come rescue me when Nick kidnapped me and brought me here. It all added up. I just hadn't connected love with the way I felt about him, because I didn't know how it felt to love a man—or anyone, for that matter."

Jill stared at her, her eyes wide with shock. "Tess, everything you just said—I can apply every *one* of those things to what has happened between Colin and me, right down to and including how he makes me feel."

"Plus the fact that you are no longer interested in marrying Des."

Jill sat back. "Oh, my God, Tess. *I'm in love with Colin.*"

Tess laughed with pure delight. "Then we've got to get you back to Dallas as soon as possible. And at our very next board meeting, we simply have to address buying our own corporate jets. We spend a fortune on charters."

Tears of happiness spilled down Jill's face, and for the first time in their entire lives, the two sisters hugged.

Jill deliberately arrived late at the charity function. She handed her invitation to the attendant at the door of the large ballroom, then nervously slipped to the side and along the wall, until she had a good view of the front portion of the room. As she had hoped, dinner was over and people were busy milling about, visiting or dancing, but she couldn't see Colin.

The overhead lights were off. Most of the room's illumination came from the glowing flames of the six-inch candles clustered in the center of each round table. In addition, a ceiling had been formed from strings of cleverly intertwined, tiny white lights backed by a cobalt-blue fabric, so that it looked as if thousands of night stars sparkled overhead.

She chewed on her bottom lip, thankful for the coverage provided by the room's atmospheric lighting, along with the preoccupied people. She didn't want to be noticed just yet. As a matter of fact, if she could have had her way, no one would see her but Colin. But she had determined that meeting him for the first time in five days at this event would be the best way to convince him that she loved him. The thought that she might be wrong tightened the myriad knots already present in her stomach.

Molly had doubled-checked the RSVP list, and unless Colin had changed his mind between the time he had accepted and now, he should be here. Gnawing on her bottom lip, she slowly made her way farther down the wall toward the back of the room.

The dress she had chosen for her task tonight was far more daring than anything he had chosen for her, though she had purchased it from the same store where he had gotten the hot-pink dress she had worn to the blues club.

This dress was made of a remarkable liquid-silver fabric that appeared to have been poured over her body. Its cowl neckline dipped dangerously to just above her nipples. In the back, the line of the cowl continued down past her waist and stopped right above the dimples of her bottom. To help her move, the skirt was slit up one side. The dress took its shape entirely from her body, and there was no way the dress could accommodate any underwear, though heaven knows she had tried.

She doubted she would have even had the nerve to wear the dress out of the house if it hadn't been for the matching shawl, lined with an icy aqua silk. Currently it was draped to cover her breasts, with one long end tossed over her shoulder to fall down the middle of her very bare back.

Suddenly she saw Colin, and her heart began its now all-too-familiar thudding. He was as devastatingly good-looking and charismatic as ever in a black tuxedo, one hand slipped with casual elegance into his trouser pocket, the other holding a drink.

He was facing her, with three women arranged in a semicircle in front of him, and he was laughing at something one of them had said. But she could tell his laughter was only a facade. She wouldn't have been able to realize that before their time on the island, but she could now.

Watching him, she turned hot, then cold, then hot again. Lord, could she do this? Her palms were clammy. Her heart was pounding so hard she was sure the fast rhythmic movement was visible through her skin. And if even one more physical symptom struck her, she reflected with a mixture of amusement and terror, she would probably have to seek medical help.

But she wouldn't allow herself to take the easy way out and confront him later in a more casual environment. She drew a deep breath and called on every ounce of courage she could muster. She had a formidable job ahead of her.

With a small prayer, she unwrapped the shawl from around her, turning it into a mere accessory, instead of a cover-up, by draping it over her forearms and letting it fall down the back to beneath her hips.

She started toward him and knew the moment he saw her.

He stiffened, and his smile vanished. Curious, the three women turned to see what or who had caught his attention, and as she neared, it was their greetings that helped alleviate his conspicuous wall of silence.

"Jill, we were wondering if you were going to make it tonight."

"You look wonderful. The new way you're wearing your hair is very becoming."

"My *word,* that dress is gorgeous, though not your usual style at all. What's happened? You must have gotten a complete makeover somewhere."

Still as stone, Colin trained his icy stare on her.

She could now completely understand and empathize with Billie Holiday's lament of unrequited love.

Refusing to be intimidated, she stared right back at him. "Actually, yes, I did—with Colin's help."

"*Really?*" As if choreographed, all three women looked from her to Colin and then back to her.

She nodded. "Even to the point of buying me clothes. He thought I was dressing too primly and decided I needed to wear more revealing clothes."

"*Softer.*" The one word sounded as if it were strangling him. "And I never bought you *that* dress."

One of the women looked at Colin. "Do you mind me asking why you were, uh, making over Jill?"

He didn't answer, continuing to glare at her, so *she* answered. "It was a business bargain we made, wasn't it, Colin? And as most business deals are, this one is private. However, I will tell you that part of the deal involved lessons."

Ravenous curiosity now etched the faces of the three women.

"Lessons?" one of them ventured.

Jill nodded. "Actually, the lessons could best be summed up with the phrase, *how to torture Jill.*"

With a soft curse, Colin grabbed her hand. "Will you ladies please excuse us?"

With open mouths, the three women nodded in unison.

Tightly gripping her hand, Colin strode toward the rear of the room and the exit, but that didn't fit into her plans. Not yet. Besides, now that the three women were out of the picture, his control had slipped enough for her to see he was practically foaming at the mouth with anger. It would be safer for her to stay within sight of people.

She wrenched her hand from his and stubbornly

halted. He had no choice but to stop and look back at her.

"I'd like to dance," she said.

"What gave you the impression I *care* what you'd like to do?"

He made a grab for her hand again, but she slipped away to an empty space at the back edge of the dance floor, bordering an area close to a wall that held only tall plants and offered a certain degree of privacy. When she turned around, he was there, and she offered up a grateful prayer that he had followed her.

"What in hell is holding that dress up?" he asked, his voice as sharp as razor blades, his eyes as dark as midnight.

With a smile, she moved into his body and slid her arms around his neck. "Willpower," she whispered into his ear.

He yanked her arms from his neck and pushed her away. "I don't know what kind of game you're playing, unless you've got some demented idea of trying to make Des jealous, but it isn't going to work. He's not here."

She shrugged, and the action lifted one breast until the top edge of her nipple's rose-colored areola appeared. His gaze followed the movement, and she saw him swallow hard. "I didn't expect him to be."

His hands clenched into fists at his sides. "Where have you been for the last five days? I know you weren't at the Double B, because I called Des."

"Really? Why were you looking for me?"

"Because..." He stopped and briefly closed his eyes. He must have suddenly realized how he appeared—tensed, almost white with fury, as if he was about to strike her.

He roughly pulled her to him, though not close enough that her body was touching his. "Because," he said in a lower voice, "I called Des to tell him to expect you."

"How thoughtful, but not at all necessary."

A vein throbbed at his temple. "And then I called to make sure you'd arrived safely."

She shrugged again. "I never said I was going to the ranch."

"The hell you didn't. You told me you'd called Molly to arrange a charter for you."

"That's right. To Uvalde. I decided to spend a few days visiting Tess and Nick."

"You...?" His teeth clamped together.

"It's a good band, isn't it?" They were playing a blend of oldies and newer songs, and at the moment a romantic ballad that Elvis had once recorded, "And I Love You So." She doubted Colin was even hearing it. She reached up, slid her arms around his neck and began to dance, moving against him to the song, though he remained still.

"What are you doing?"

She pressed her body closer to him and whispered into his ear, "If I remember correctly, Lesson Number Three. Dance very close to your partner, so that if you want to carry on a conversation, you can press your mouth to his ear." She waited a beat and received no response. "Am I doing it right?"

A growl rumbled up from his chest, and he slid his hand down her spine, encountering nothing but perfumed skin. He yanked one of her arms from around his neck, so that he could hold her hand out from their body. "It's more conventional for *two* people to participate in a dance."

"More fun, too."

His face tightened until he looked like a violent storm cloud about to burst. "Okay, I'm only going to ask you once more, Jill. What are you doing? And do *not* say dancing or attending a party. You know exactly what I mean, so tell me."

Once again she put her mouth to his ear. "I'm putting into practice what you taught me. Lesson Number One was dressing in a softer style and showing more flesh. I believe I accomplished that tonight, don't you?"

Almost involuntarily, it seemed, his hand slipped past her waist down to the edge of her gown, then, just for a moment, he allowed his fingers to dip beneath the fabric to caress one round buttock. He jerked his hand back as if he'd touched fire.

"Damn it to *hell*, Jill. You're not wearing any underwear."

"The outline of any kind of undergarment would have shown through and ruined the line of the dress. You taught me that, remember?"

He uttered a low, violent string of oaths.

If he was suffering, so was she, Jill reflected ruefully. Being in his arms again, inhaling his musky scent, feeling his hands on her—it brought back all the needs and desires she had felt for him that last night on the island. Even now, heat was crawling through her veins and gathering between her legs. But there was no way she could stop now. "Lesson Number Two was allowing your date to help you in and out of the car, which obviously isn't applicable for tonight. And..."

"Never mind."

The band switched to "Layla," one of the most

passionate love songs in the history of rock and roll, playing a bluesy version that was close to the same tempo as the song they had danced to in the club. In every way, the song couldn't have been more appropriate.

The dress and her lack of panties prohibited her from spreading her legs and straddling his as she had done that night, though Lord knew she was burning to. But the famous melody and words, combined with the heavy, sensual beat, compelled her to move her pelvis back and forth against his.

He gripped her shoulders, attempting to hold her away from him. "Don't *do* that."

"Why?" she asked, continuing. She needed the contact. She needed to feel the familiar hard ridge of his sex against her. She needed something to stop the nearly unbearable hot achiness building inside her. "It's what we did at the blues club."

"That was different."

"How?"

"Damn you, Jill." He tightened his grip on her and pushed her away. *"Stop it."*

She glanced around, but everyone was engaged in other activities, and no one seemed overly curious about the two of them, though heaven knew how they could miss what was going on. She could no longer control her breathing. She wasn't sure she would be able to control herself at all if she didn't get some relief from the way she was feeling. But she forced herself to remember why she was doing this in the first place.

"What's the matter, Colin? You can dish it out, but you can't take it?"

He shook his head as if trying to clear his mind.

Abruptly he wrapped his fingers around her wrist, dislodging the shawl from that arm, and pulled her out the exit door and down the hall. The end of her silver-and-aqua shawl trailed on the floor after them.

He shoved her into a deserted service corridor and up against a wall, pinning her there by holding each of her wrists on either side of her head. "Why are you practicing the lessons I gave you on *me* when it's *Des* you want?" His voice was raw; his hands on her wrists were trembling.

She wrested her wrists free, planted her hands flat against his chest and pushed him a step away to give herself some breathing room. "*First* of all, I don't want Des. Not anymore. And *secondly,* I wanted to find out if what you taught me would be good enough to make a man forget a woman he's been in love with for a long while."

"You wanted...?" He looked thunderstruck.

"Well, *is* it, Colin? Can I, using your lessons, cure you of her? Can I make you forget her?"

His brows drew together. *"Who?"*

She lifted her chin. "The woman you're in love with. The woman who broke your heart. The woman who doesn't return your love. The woman you told me about at the blues club," she prompted, wondering why he wasn't getting what she was saying. "You asked me if I had ever loved a man the way Billie Holiday was singing about, so I asked you the same thing."

"Right," he said, slowly nodding, obviously remembering now. "And I said *maybe*. I said *maybe,* Jill. I didn't say *yes.*"

"But it made so much sense. I mean, I've watched women throw themselves at you for the past two years, yet you've remained politely but firmly unattached. When you said 'maybe,' I decided the reason was because you were already in love with a woman, and that she had either broken your heart by turning you down—which, by the way, I can't imagine—or that she was nearby, but for some reason she wasn't in love with you."

"You got all of that out of my *maybe?* And then for some reason decided to see if you could make me fall out of love with her?"

She nodded, watching him carefully. He still seemed astounded, yet his anger was fading.

"Why, Jill? As an experiment? Just to see if the lessons really worked? Or for the kick of it?"

"No," she said slowly, knowing she was about to leap off a cliff with no assurances about where she would land. The old Jill would never have even contemplated such a leap. The new Jill, with her heart bursting with love, did it. "Because I realized when I was at Tess's that I have totally and completely fallen quite madly in love with you."

For several long moments, it didn't seem as if he breathed. Finally he drew a deep breath and slowly exhaled it. Golden lights began to glitter in his eyes. "Okay, well, here's the answer to your question. You can't cure me of my love for the woman I've been in love with for the last two years. No one can." With his hand he tilted her face back up to him and smiled tenderly down at her. "Because it's *you,* Jill. I'm totally and completely in love with *you—quite madly,* as a matter of fact."

She looked at him in disbelief. Her heart gave the expectant thud, then soared. Colin brought his mouth down on hers, kissing her with the same ferocity with which he had kissed her on the island, and as his tongue drove deeply into her mouth, his hands moved up and down her spine, then dipped beneath the low back of the dress to cup and grip her firm, round bottom. Clinging to him, she became lost—in time, in place, but most of all in him.

Colin drove them to her home as fast as was possible. Inside, on the bed, he pushed the dress off her shoulders and down to her waist, and she lifted her hips to pull it the rest of the way off. Impatiently and with shaking hands, he undressed. Then she was straddling him, sliding downward until he was completely sheathed inside her body. An exquisite pleasure immediately flooded through her, engulfing her, making her shudder, making her moan.

She felt free at last. She no longer had to censor what she felt. She never would again. Loving Colin had given her the freedom of feelings at long last released.

They made love slowly, exquisitely, and completely, their love for each other spilling over into their actions. Every second, every sound, every sensation, was savored. Every caress and every touch was cherished. Until finally, they climaxed together and the world crashed around them.

Later, as she lay beside him, he ran his hand over her still-trembling body. "I've been half out of my mind with worry about you. Molly wouldn't tell me where you were."

"That was my fault, not hers. I needed the time to try to figure out some things."

"Next time you need time like that, *tell* me, okay?"

"Okay, although it won't happen again. Everything is finally crystal clear to me."

"Thank God." He reached for her hand and kissed it. "So when did you decide to give up on trying to get Des?"

"Almost as soon as you started those damn lessons. I couldn't keep my mind on Des. In fact, after that first night at the blues club— No, it started even sooner than that. It started the morning I woke up and discovered I had slept the night through in your arms. I couldn't get that intimacy out of my mind, or your scent, or the way you looked in those briefs. Then you proceeded to send one shock after another at me." She lightly laughed. "There were times when, if you had said 'Des,' I would have said 'Des who?'"

"Lord, I wish I had known. It would have saved me a lot of agony."

"And if *I* had known, it would have saved me the same torture. But you gave me no sign—" she paused and thought "—other than what I thought was normal for a man in close proximity with a woman."

He groaned, and she lightly hit him. "You have to understand, I didn't know a lot about men other than in business. I also didn't know about love." She gave an embarrassed little shrug. "The way I was raised—"

Two fingers quickly covered her lips. "You don't have to tell me. I know. Des, remember? He said your dad kept you girls on such a regimented schedule that you rarely saw him or his father, which might have given you at least a glimpse of kindness and love." His lips curved. "Except he did mention something about William's housekeeper sneaking you a cake on your birthday."

"Yeah, that was pretty much it."

"That was cruelty, plain and simple. From what I've heard, your father was a monster."

She sighed, then rolled over until her head was resting on his shoulder, her hand lying lightly on his chest and her leg thrown over his. "No more. That's all in the past. From this moment forward, we can make the future what we want it to be."

A shudder wracked his body, and he pressed a kiss to her forehead. "One thing. What about your ambition to gain control of the company?"

She fell silent for several moments, and when she at last spoke, her voice was soft. "You have to understand—for so long, my part of the company was all I had. And because of the competitive way we were raised, it was natural for me to want control. But it's simply not important to me anymore, not in any way. And you know, during the last couple of days, when I thought about it, I realized that my sisters and I have never disagreed on anything major concerning the company, anyway. For all our competitiveness, our bottom line has always been what's best for the company." She shifted so that she could look up at him. "Thanks to you, I have so much more now. I've learned what true happiness really is. It's all about loving and being loved."

He bent his head and gently kissed her. "You can't even imagine how happy I am at this moment."

"Yes, I can, because I feel the very same way."

He smiled down at her, then let his head fall back to the pillow. "So tell me about this future of ours. Do you have any specifics in mind regarding what you want?

"Yes," she said slowly, thoughtfully. "I want to

love you and be loved in return, every single moment of the rest of our lives. I want to make our houses into real homes, homes that will not only make us feel comfortable and safe, but be a sanctuary, a retreat from the rest of the world. And I want babies—lots of happy babies who will be so loved they'll never have to think that they have to prove themselves to us."

His hand moved caressingly over her arm. "Anything else?"

"Yes. There'll be a garden in every one of our homes where irises from Tess's garden will grow and our children will play."

"Anything else?"

"I want you to take me to East Texas so that I can see where you grew up and meet your family."

"Anything else?" Amusement was creeping into his voice.

She looked up at him. "I'll want to continue to work of course. But I won't eat, sleep and drink it as I have in the past. For that, I'll have you."

His smile broadened, and he tightened his hold on her waist. "Anything else?"

She lightly laughed. "That's all I can think of for now."

"What? Nothing else? Are you sure? In my opinion, you've forgotten one very important thing."

Her brow creased as she tried to figure out what it could be. "What?"

"Doesn't marriage figure into your wishes anywhere?"

She sat straight up. "Oh, my goodness, *yes*." She looked back at him. "*Yes*. But—"

He pulled her back down to him. "No buts."

She struggled to breathe, because suddenly he was holding her so tightly, but she managed a grin. "I guess I sort of took that for granted. But now that I think about it, I guess I should ask if that's what you want, too."

He gave a loud shout of laughter. "Honey, I've waited for you for over two years. The whole point of working with you on the land development deal in the first place was to give us an excuse to be together. And the whole point of the lessons was to get you to fall in love with me. You're *never* going to get away from me now."

He had called her honey. Contentment flooded through her, and with a secret smile, she snuggled against him. "Just think of all the fun we have ahead of us, teaching each other new lessons."

He rolled over on top of her and slipped into her. "Let's start with a lesson about trying to learn to get enough of each other."

She closed her eyes and gasped with pleasure as he pushed deeper and deeper into her, until he couldn't go any farther. "I'm positive that's one lesson we'll be trying to learn for the rest of our lives."

* * * * *

Look for THE BARONS OF TEXAS: KIT, coming in August 2002 in a volume called **The Millionaire's First Love**.

SILHOUETTE DESIRE

AVAILABLE FROM 19TH JULY 2002

THE MILLIONAIRE'S FIRST LOVE

THE MILLIONAIRE COMES HOME Mary Lynn Baxter
When Denton Hardesty returned to his home town he never intended to stay. But the unexpected sight of former flame Grace Simmons made him yearn to turn his first love into his forever love!

THE BARONS OF TEXAS: KIT Fayrene Preston
For Des, burying his true feelings for his delectable step-cousin Kit had never been easy. But now Kit needed his legal genius to keep her freedom, so they had to be together…in more ways than one!

SEDUCED BY THE SHEIKH

SLEEPING WITH THE SULTAN Alexandra Sellers
The Sultans
In the midst of a power struggle for his family's stolen throne Sheikh Ashraf had to be sure that Dana Morningstar was an ally. To control the vixen, he would keep her close as a lover and conquer all doubt.

HIDE-AND-SHEIKH Gail Dayton
When Sheikh Rashid whisked Ellen Sheffield to his hideaway he hadn't expected to favour winning her heart over seduction. Now all he had to do was prove passion was not all he had on his mind…

HER PERSONAL PROTECTOR

ROCKY AND THE SENATOR'S DAUGHTER
Dixie Browning
Rocky Waters only went to warn Sarah, the senator's daughter, of impending scandal. But found himself determined to win over this sensual widow who aroused his protective instincts—and so much more…

NIGHT WIND'S WOMAN Sheri WhiteFeather
Something in single mum-to-be Kelly Baxter called to Shane Night Wind. As he helped deliver her baby he finally saw that his heart could be whole—if only he could find the courage to claim Kelly as his own.

AVAILABLE FROM 19TH JULY 2002

SILHOUETTE®

Sensation™

Passionate, dramatic, thrilling romances

HARD TO HANDLE Kylie Brant
A HERO IN HER EYES Marie Ferrarella
TAYLOR'S TEMPTATION Suzanne Brockmann
BORN OF PASSION Carla Cassidy
COPS AND...LOVERS? Linda Castillo
DANGEROUS ATTRACTION Susan Vaughan

Special Edition™

Vivid, satisfying romances full of family, life and love

THE NOT-SO-SECRET BABY Diana Whitney
BACHELOR COP FINALLY CAUGHT? Gina Wilkins
WHEN I DREAM OF YOU Laurie Paige
DADDY TO BE DETERMINED Muriel Jensen
FROM THIS DAY FORWARD Christie Ridgway
HOME AT LAST Laurie Campbell

Superromance™

Enjoy the drama, explore the emotions, experience the relationship

THE WRONG BROTHER Bonnie K Winn
THE COMMANDER Kay David
BIRTHRIGHT Judith Arnold
THE FAMILY WAY Rebecca Winters

Intrigue™

Danger, deception and suspense

THE MAN FROM TEXAS Rebecca York
THE HIDDEN YEARS Susan Kearney
SPECIAL ASSIGNMENT: BABY Debra Webb
COLORADO'S FINEST Sheryl Lynn

MARIE FERRARELLA BEVERLY BARTON LINDSAY McKENNA

DANGEROUS TO LOVE

3 SENSATIONAL, SEXY ROMANCES!

On sale 21st June 2002

THE STANISLASKI *Sisters*
NORA ROBERTS

From the bestselling author of the Stanislaski Brothers, Nora Roberts brings you the spirited, sexy Stanislaksi Sisters.

Bestselling author of Night Tales

Available from 19th July 2002

Available at most branches of WH Smith, Tesco, Martins, Borders, Eason, Sainsbury's and most good paperback bookshops.

SILHOUETTE® SENSATION™

presents a thrilling new continuity series:

First-Born Sons

Bound by the legacy of their fathers, these first-born sons were born to be heroes!

July: **BORN A HERO**
by Paula Detmer Riggs

August: **BORN OF PASSION**
by Carla Cassidy

September: **BORN TO PROTECT**
by Virginia Kantra

October: **BORN BRAVE**
by Ruth Wind

November: **BORN IN SECRET**
by Kylie Brant

December: **BORN ROYAL**
by Alexandra Sellers

SILHOUETTE® SENSATION™
proudly presents

a sensually addictive trilogy,
only from
Kylie Brant

Charmed and Dangerous

With their quick wits and killer smiles,
these men are irresistible.

HARD TO HANDLE
August 2002

HARD TO RESIST
September 2002

HARD TO TAME
October 2002

SILHOUETTE® SENSATION™

brings more...much more from

Suzanne Brockmann

TALL, DARK AND DANGEROUS

These men are who you call to get you out of a tight spot—or into one!

TAYLOR'S TEMPTATION
August 2002

WILD, WILD WES
March 2003

SILHOUETTE® SPECIAL EDITION™

is proud to present the all-new, exciting trilogy from

GINA WILKINS

HOT OFF THE PRESS

This small town's reporters are about to be shaken...by love!

THE STRANGER IN ROOM 205
July 2002

BACHELOR COP FINALLY CAUGHT?
August 2002

DATELINE MATRIMONY
September 2002

SILHOUETTE SUPERROMANCE

Welcomes you to

RIVERBEND

Riverbend... the kind of place where everyone knows your name—and your business. Riverbend... home of a group of small-town sons and daughters who've been friends since school.

They're all grown up now. Living their lives and learning that you can get through anything as long as you have your friends.

Five wonderful stories:

August 2002	**BIRTHRIGHT**	by Judith Arnold
September 2002	**THAT SUMMER THING**	by Pamela Bauer
October 2002	**HOMECOMING**	by Laura Abbot
November 2002	**LAST-MINUTE MARRIAGE**	by Marisa Carroll
December 2002	**A CHRISTMAS LEGACY**	by Kathryn Shay

SILHOUETTE INTRIGUE

presents

two stories from popular author
Sheryl Lynn
set in

McClintock Country

High up in the Rocky Mountains is a place where the wind blows fast and fierce, where trust is precious and where everyone has a secret.

TO PROTECT THEIR CHILD

July 2002

COLORADO'S FINEST

(a LAWMAN LOVERS story)
August 2002

SILHOUETTE® INTRIGUE™

proudly presents its new Confidential series with four sexy, rugged agents in

MONTANA CONFIDENTIAL

Men bound by love, loyalty and the law—these specialised government operatives have vowed to keep their missions and identities confidential...

SOMEONE TO PROTECT HER
Patricia Rosemoor
July 2002

SPECIAL ASSIGNMENT: BABY
Debra Webb
August 2002

LICENSED TO MARRY
Charlotte Douglas
September 2002

SECRET AGENT HEIRESS
Julie Miller
October 2002

▼™ SILHOUETTE® SUPERROMANCE™

is proud to present

The Guardians

An action-packed
new trilogy by

Kay David

This time the good guys wear black. Join this highly skilled police SWAT team as they serve and protect Florida's Emerald Coast.

THE NEGOTIATOR
(July 2002)

THE COMMANDER
(August 2002)

THE LISTENER
(September 2002)

1 FREE
book and a surprise gift!

We would like to take this opportunity to thank you for reading this Silhouette® book by offering you the chance to take ANOTHER specially selected title from the Desire™ series absolutely FREE! We're also making this offer to introduce you to the benefits of the Reader Service™—

- ★ FREE home delivery
- ★ FREE gifts and competitions
- ★ FREE monthly Newsletter
- ★ Exclusive Reader Service discount
- ★ Books available before they're in the shops

Accepting this FREE book and gift places you under no obligation to buy, you may cancel at any time, even after receiving your free shipment. Simply complete your details below and return the entire page to the address below. *You don't even need a stamp!*

YES! Please send me 1 free Desire book and a surprise gift. I understand that unless you hear from me, I will receive 2 superb new titles every month for just £4.99 each, postage and packing free. I am under no obligation to purchase any books and may cancel my subscription at any time. The free book and gift will be mine to keep in any case.

D2ZEA

Ms/Mrs/Miss/Mr ....Initials........................
BLOCK CAPITALS PLEASE

Surname ....

Address ....

....

....Postcode..................

Send this whole page to:
UK: FREEPOST CN81, Croydon, CR9 3WZ
EIRE: PO Box 4546, Kilcock, County Kildare (stamp required)

Offer valid in UK and Eire only and not available to current Reader Service subscribers to this series. We reserve the right to refuse an application and applicants must be aged 18 years or over. Only one application per household. Terms and prices subject to change without notice. Offer expires 31st October 2002. As a result of this application, you may receive offers from other carefully selected companies. If you would prefer not to share in this opportunity please write to The Data Manager at the address above.

Silhouette® is a registered trademark used under licence.
Desire™ is being used as a trademark.